The Heartless One

USA Today bestselling author Emma Hamm grew up in a small town surrounded by trees and animals. She writes strong, confident, powerful women who aren't afraid to grow and make mistakes. Her books will always be a little bit feminist, and are geared towards empowering both men and women to be comfortable in their own skin.

Also by Emma Hamm

Gravesinger

The Deathless One
The Heartless One

THE HEARTLESS ONE

EMMA HAMM

CANELO

First published in the United States in 2026 by Gallery Books, an imprint of Simon & Schuster, LLC

This edition published in the United Kingdom in 2026 by

Canelo, an imprint of
Canelo Digital Publishing Limited,
20 Vauxhall Bridge Road,
London SW1V 2SA
United Kingdom

A Penguin Random House Company
The authorised representative in the EEA is Dorling Kindersley Verlag GmbH. Arnulfstr. 124, 80636 Munich, Germany

Copyright © Emma Hamm 2026

The moral right of Emma Hamm to be identified as the creator of this work has been asserted in accordance with the Copyright, Designs and Patents Act, 1988.
All rights reserved. No part of this publication may be reproduced or transmitted in any form or by any means, electronic or mechanical, including photocopy, recording, or any information storage and retrieval system, without permission in writing from the publisher.
No part of this book may be used or reproduced in any manner for the purpose of training artificial intelligence technologies or systems. In accordance with Article 4(3) of the DSM Directive 2019/790, Canelo expressly reserves this work from the text and data mining exception.

A CIP catalogue record for this book is available from the British Library.

ISBN 9 781 83598 374 4

This book is a work of fiction. Names, characters, businesses, organizations, places and events are either the product of the author's imagination or are used fictitiously. Any resemblance to actual persons, living or dead, events or locales is entirely coincidental.

Printed and bound in Great Britain by Clays Ltd, Elcograf S.p.A.

Look for more great books at
www.canelo.co | www.dk.com

For my mother, who loved me no matter how strange I became

1

Dappled sunlight was just as Elric remembered.

The crystalline patterns of golden rays broke through emerald leaves and scattered across his features. Sparks seared his vision when he stared at them for too long, but that was just part of the beauty. A little pain was worth every sacrifice to be *alive*.

Lying in the grass, he felt every blade that brushed his skin. He could smell the greenery that grew around him and hear the wind blowing through the leaves. Oak stars rustled in harmony with the rhythmic twitters of birdsong. The brush of the wind over his bare chest cooled the sweat from his skin. And the sapphire sky above him was dotted with fluffy clouds that drifted over his head. Boats on the sea of the sky, they gently rocked forward as he watched.

Fingers carded through his hair, sliding between the thick strands that were longer than the last time he'd taken this form. There were changes in this body, but not as many as the last time. He'd been different in every reincarnation. But this time, he wanted to look like he had in his last form. It was the one humans were more likely to recognize, after all.

And maybe it was because this form was the one she had seen. This body was the one she had looked upon as a statue, and it had made her blush. Some part of him wanted to make her feel that same way. Or perhaps to see that blush for himself and not just an inanimate object.

His head rested in Jessamine's lap. She'd been leaning back on one hand, staring up at the clouds with him as they just enjoyed each other's silent company. They'd beaten Callum only a few days ago, and everything had been a tangled mess of preparing for their next step, trying to get him used to this new body, and finding Sybil. He had less time with her to himself than he'd wished.

The trail had led them to Fortuna Beaumont, a noblewoman of the Pleasure District and close confidante of both Callum's and Leon's. Unfortunately, that had taken up far too much of their time. He wanted more of everything with her.

Jessamine's fingers worked through a tangle that had started at the end of the strands before sighing. "Is it everything you remembered?"

He knew what she was asking. Life. Living. Was breathing in the crisp air everything he had dreamt it to be?

Of course it was. It was everything that he had missed, and far more than that. This life surged through him in pulses of magic and power. He wanted to consume it. To devour every part of living for the moment when he wouldn't be here anymore.

And yet, there was another part of him that feared losing all this. If he was too close to this life, if he enjoyed it too much, then he would only suffer more when he returned to that realm of darkness.

Her fingers slipped down from his hair to his temples and gently lifted his face. Elric was forced to look up into those dark eyes that saw too much. But gods, what a view.

Jessamine truly was a nightmarish witch. After their fight with Callum, she'd embraced everything it was to be a gravesinger. Not only was she deeply connected to him, but she'd resurrected him. She'd done all that a gravesinger needed to do, and now she shared in his glutted power. Her wild, dark hair billowed around her face like smoke. His mark around her neck fairly glowed, as though he'd locked a silver collar around her throat. It was a sure sign that she was as bound to him as he was to her. His gravesinger.

A tiny spark of unbidden magic trailed through her fingers, zinging along his skin as she traced the outline of his jaw. "I can tell what you're thinking," she murmured. "This is not a fleeting moment. This is yours. I have gifted it to you, and I will not take it back."

"I know," he whispered, pressing a kiss to her inner wrist and lingering there for a few moments. He filled his lungs with her grave scent before adding, "But it will take a while to believe, gravesinger."

"How you break my heart, dear one." As though compelled, she leaned down and pressed a kiss to his lips.

They lingered there together, connected only by a soft, plush touch. But it was everything he needed to fill all the stores of magic in him again. He breathed her in. All that power, just simmering under her skin, built there by a connection that was only growing stronger by the day.

She was more than just a witch, and she had to know that. She was *his* witch.

When she drew back for a breath, he drank in the dazed expression on her face. He'd seen so many women in the throes of passion or witches who tried to pretend they were. He knew what a liar looked like, and he'd learned to read humans in his many centuries of life.

Jessamine was as truthful as they came. Her blown-out pupils and that drunken smile as she stared down at him were genuine.

What was he supposed to do with her? Other than wrap his hand around the back of her neck and draw her down for another kiss?

Her exhale became his inhale. They became linked through breath as he explored the depths of her mouth. He could taste the passion in her kiss. He could feel it as magic sparked between them, another electric zap that made every muscle in his body tense.

Of all the experiences in life, this was what he had missed the most. In that shadow realm, he'd never been able to taste her. He'd never been able to clearly hear the little sighs that caught in the back of her throat as he touched her. He hadn't felt how soft her hair was, or seen how vivid her eyes were as he drew back. They were more than just brown. They were dark, haunting orbs he wanted to drown in.

What a beauty he had captured. What a stunning gravesinger to draw into his life. Perhaps there was still a lingering presence of the gods in this world, because certainly he was not the one to have wished her into being.

She drew back, her fingers lingering on his jaw. "What are you thinking?"

"Merely about your beauty."

"I am hardly the princess I once was," she replied with a soft laugh. "You should have seen me in the castle."

"A prim and proper princess meandering about the halls? You must have been waiting for something exciting to happen every day. No, I choose to see you as you are now." His fingers tangled in the hair at the back of her neck, arching her head away so he could press his lips to the swanlike stretch of her throat. "I like to see you wild and undone, princess."

That sigh. That soft, lingering sigh she always gave when he kissed her made him feel like a god again.

He reveled in this freedom, this knowledge that he was alive and well and that nothing was going to change that. Even if he had to scrape on his hands and knees to stay this way, he would. He would beg if she needed him to.

Something scratched at the back of his mind. Fingernails trailed down the entirety of his body. He could feel them dragging down his neck, his shoulders, his back. Such a touch should be impossible. Unless…

He sat straight up, nearly cracking their heads together as he realized what it meant.

"Elric?" she asked, shoving her hair out of her face. She stared at him with those big eyes, and for a moment, he was shocked she hadn't felt it, too.

But how could she? Jessamine was a gravesinger, but she had not tied herself to his coven beyond the simple bonds of friendship. She couldn't sense the presence of another witch unless they were near. She couldn't know how it felt like a ghost had ripped its talons along his entire soul.

"Elric?" she asked again, this time sounding far more concerned than the first time. "What is it?"

"Another witch," he murmured. "Someone is worshipping me."

Fear rippled through his body at the knowledge that another witch had tried to connect with him. His guts twisted, his stomach rolling with nerves, but even those feelings were a marvelous experience. He knew he should be elated at the thought of another witch, but more people in the coven meant more voices who may wish to sacrifice him. A coven of witches was powerful, sometimes too powerful.

The wells of his magic were deep and old, but that did not mean they were endless. Witches who sacrificed in his name gave energy to him. The more people who sacrificed in his name, the stronger he would become. Already he could feel what this newcomer was doing.

This was a determined witch. He stretched out his magic, feeling his way through their world to the woman who sacrificed to him. She had gone off into some field and taken a man's prized cow. The beast had been the best performer for milk, better than any other in the herd, which made it far more special. Someone had given the animal attention and reverence, so its death meant far more in the grand scheme of magic.

"What is she doing, Elric?" Jessamine asked.

"She's sacrificing a cow to me," he muttered, his vision almost gone as he focused on the sensation of what the witch was doing.

"You can feel that?" She reached out to hold his hand as though to help ground him.

"She wants something. They all do."

But what?

The old words spilled from the stranger's tongue, and he knew in that moment it wasn't a woman playing at witchcraft. This wasn't someone who had stumbled upon a spell book and thought she would try it out. This woman had been taught.

The sacrificial spell had to be spoken in the ancient tongue. Anyone reading those words would have stumbled on them or pronounced them wrong. But this recitation was nearly perfect. She built a strong spell, one that flowed throughout the realms of the living and the dead to find him.

Whispered words glided through his mind as the witch called out to him for help. "God of the dead, the Deathless One himself, I ask you to cast pity upon a poor worshipper who has long forgotten the old ways. I beg for your forgiveness in my lack of worship for too many years. I have nearly lost the dearest person to me, and I pray that you might fight on my behalf to tear away the darkness that follows her. I beg of you to fight death so that I might have more time with her."

"She wishes for me to stop someone from dying," he muttered. "A simple request. I will ignore it."

"Ignore it?" Jessamine's hand tightened on his arm. "Elric, this is the first time someone has worshipped you in centuries!"

"Sybil worships me."

Speaking of the witch, he could already see her sprinting toward them from the house. She had her tattered skirts up above her knees as she ran, her hair nearly tumbling out of the knot at the top of her head.

He watched Sybil struggle to get to their side, remaining seated even when Jessamine stood. His gravesinger cast an unimpressed glance in his direction.

"You're going to make her run all the way out here?" Jessamine asked.

"Yes."

"We could meet her at least halfway."

"She is the one who chose to run to my side, Jessamine."

"That doesn't mean you have to sit there like an ass," she hissed. "Clearly something is wrong."

He reached out and wrapped a hand around her ankle, pinning her in place when she might have started toward the other woman. "Jessamine, I am a god. I do not rush to anyone's side but yours. Ease your tone, gravesinger."

Soon enough, Jessamine would need to come to terms with what it meant to be paired with a god. Their power put them above others, simply because of what they could do. A single word from her, and he would raze the entire world to nothing but brimstone and ash. She was no longer a normal woman.

But then again, she never had been. He wondered how her mother had taught her that being a princess was not the same as being a woman. Perhaps he would need to seek out that particular memory within her soul and learn how to handle this wild woman.

Sybil finally reached them, panting, her eyes wild as she stared at him. "Did you feel it?" she asked, sounding frantic. "Tell me you felt it as well."

"I felt it."

Jessamine looked between the two of them. "You can both feel it when someone is making a sacrifice?"

"It's more than that," he replied, leaning back on his palms and tilting his head to the sun. "A witch sacrificing to me makes ripples throughout the entire coven. She dedicates her magic to me, and therefore the sisterhood, when she does so. Which means not only can I feel it, but so can the rest of the coven. In this case, Sybil."

"Another witch is sacrificing to you, Deathless One," Sybil interrupted.

He could hear the reverence with which she said the words. But they only made him feel an icy tendril of fear, the ghost that walked with him through every step of his life. Witches always wanted to build their family. They wanted more women and more witches and a larger coven. They wanted a bigger house and more power, magic that streamed through them all until they had more than they could use in a lifetime.

They wanted all of that and more. Because witches always *wanted*.

They devoured the world, and even then, it wasn't enough. Power was addictive, but so was the knowledge that they could protect themselves. He'd always known where their desire came from, just as he knew he was the only one who could satiate it.

Soon enough, they would pick apart his bones and suck them clean for one last drop of magic.

"Elric?" Jessamine said, and he was drawn back into the present. The two women stared at him as though he was supposed to answer a question he hadn't heard them ask.

Pushing aside the anxiety, he focused on them instead of the churning memories inside of him. "What did you say?"

"Are we going to help her?" Sybil asked, presumably again.

He stared at his gravesinger, knowing what her answer would be. Jessamine had been through so much, but there was still a girl inside of her who wanted a family. She desperately needed connection, and he'd be lying if he said that didn't sting.

For him, she was enough. He could end the world now and spend the rest of his immortal life with just her, and that would be a life he was pleased with.

But his Jessamine needed more than just that. So he was bound to provide it.

Sighing, he stood and savored the ache of his knees and the bite of a small pebble digging into the back of his thigh. Life wasn't all about pleasure, and he would forever savor the slight sting of pain while he could still feel it.

The silhouette of their manor mocked him, an empty tomb that once had been filled with laughing witches and spells that had affected the entire kingdom. Now only the ghosts of those women wandered through those halls. His only solace was that those women were tethered to the muck and the mire of the same realm where they had imprisoned him.

"Come," he said gruffly as he started toward the manor. "I will not speak of this where just anyone can hear our words."

He could feel the looping of chains around his shoulders, digging into his flesh as the woman finished her sacrifice and the cow's blood spilled in a field far from here. He was bound to witches. Elric had spent centuries serving them, feeding upon their sacrifices so they could gorge themselves on his magic. It felt like he was taking another step toward that same dangerous future.

Living in the same cycle he'd never been able to break.

2

Jessamine was practically vibrating by the time they made it back to the manor. No one spoke. The few times she tried to ask a question, both Elric and Sybil cast her a glance that said she needed to shut her mouth. But she didn't understand why they weren't speaking.

There was no one here. No one had come to the manor since she'd been here, nor for years before that. The last raid by the crown had made everyone quite certain there were no witches lingering in this house, thanks to Sybil. Surely no one would overhear them.

But no one said a word until they were inside. She trailed along behind them toward the kitchen, which was odd on its own. Elric preferred meeting in the tombs, or in the room with all of his siblings' statues. He rarely met with them in the kitchen because that was where Sybil was at her strongest. Knowing that he was leading them there? Surely that wasn't a good sign. He never gave Sybil the upper hand.

Which could only mean this was a conversation that she would not like.

Both she and Sybil filed past their god, each of them taking a seat at the island. Elric stayed by the door, leaning against the frame with his arms crossed over his chest. He wouldn't even make eye contact with her; instead, he stared at the floor. Sybil burst up from her seat and started pulling herbs down from where they hung on the ceiling, muttering to herself as she started cooking.

Opening her mouth to say something, Jessamine paused as Nyx bolted into the room. Her familiar had clearly been hunting. There were cobwebs hanging from the kitten's whiskers. She didn't slow her wild careening run, somehow making the leap onto the table and skidding to a stop on the counter.

Once there, the tiny black cat merely cleaned her paws and started removing the cobwebs. As though they couldn't start talking until the familiar was with them.

Shaking her head, Jessamine focused on the witch, who was currently piling a plate high with vegetables and herbs.

"You only cook when you're nervous," Jessamine said. "Another witch is a good thing, isn't it?"

"In a way," Sybil muttered. "Another witch could mean many things. Perhaps she is one of our coven that I missed from the old days. That would probably not be a good thing, considering some of the other witches in the coven were more bloodthirsty than others."

"They were all bloodthirsty," Elric interjected. Jessamine noticed his hands were clenched into fists against his ribs. "That is the least of our worries. I remember them all, Sybil. This is not one of the originals."

"Ah, well." Sybil set a cutting board down hard on the island. The sharp crack made Jessamine jump. "Might I suggest that with the Deathless One back in his physical form, more magic has been released into this world? Those who have a proclivity to magic may be feeling that power for the first time."

"She knew the old words," he said, the words almost sounding… sad. "She said them correctly. Someone trained her."

"Then it is a witch we do not know who has decided to worship you after all this time." Sybil appeared troubled. Her brows drew down in concentration as she placed a wrinkled green pepper and a mushy onion on the cutting board. "I don't know if that's a good thing or a bad thing."

Jessamine was having a hard time following. "I'd imagine it's good? You two were so adamant that I should accept who I was as a gravesinger, so I find it hard to believe you're uninterested in this new person."

Neither of them spoke.

Jessamine looked between them. They were either hiding something from her or they were both thinking the same thing. Elric was still looking at the floor, a frown on his face and those scarred brows creating furrows between his eyes. Sybil stared at her cooking, chopping the vegetables a little too hard. The knife in her hand left gouges in the cutting board, and the blade flashed unnaturally fast.

Neither of them spoke, clearly waiting for the other to say something. And here she was, in the dark, like she always seemed to be.

She leaned forward and braced her elbows on the kitchen island. "All right. Which one of you is going to explain this to me?"

Sybil flinched before cutting the green pepper so hard that the knife stuck in the cutting board. She sighed before leaving the knife where it was. "We wanted you to accept who you were as a gravesinger because you were the only person who could bring him back to life. A resurrection is done by a gravesinger and a gravesinger alone."

"Yes, you've made it ever so clear that I am not the same as a regular witch." A distinction that still stung a bit. "I don't see how you're fine with a gravesinger, but not a witch."

Elric's foot shifted on the floor, and both women froze to look over at him. His shoulders had lifted in discomfort, just slightly. Enough that Jessamine noticed how uneasy he was.

His voice was raspy and low as he replied. "Another coven member makes the coven stronger, that much is certain. But another witch brings about her own wants and desires. Needs we cannot control. Sacrifice makes me stronger and feeds into my power, but if I accept it, I must make another witch powerful in return."

"And that is bad because?"

"Because a witch can ask for anything in return. A witch is unpredictable. We do not know this woman or what she will want. We only know that she worships me now, and that comes with its own chains."

Looking at him, she finally understood where his fear came from.

More witches meant more people who might want to hurt him. Another witch could bring up the idea of sacrificing him again, depending on what she wanted or what the kingdom needed. Witches were selfish at the best of times. But then, who wasn't when they lived in a kingdom that was crumbling at their feet?

Sybil's honeyed voice broke through the silence. "Witches are stronger together. A coven is the most powerful group of women that has ever existed. We live and breathe for each other. Our magic comes from the Deathless One, yes. He gifts it to us as you have seen him gift it to me. He would need to bind himself in the same way to this new woman. He can give and take the magic that she has, and in return, the sacrifices we make in his name give him more power."

Another woman. Another mind. She understood that things could be complicated, depending on who this woman was. But a particular phrase Sybil had said stuck with her above all else.

"Witches are stronger together," Jessamine repeated. She reached for Nyx, dragging the cat into her lap so she had something soft to pet. "That's what this all boils down to. It doesn't matter what we think or want or fear. We are stronger together, and in times like these, I think we need to look toward strength."

There was a flare of pride in Sybil's eyes, and perhaps something a little greedy as well. Because the words that slipped out of the witch's mouth were, "If we want to look toward power, gravesinger, then sacrifice is the only option."

In a flash, Elric disappeared.

Not to the realm where he had once hidden, but somewhere else in the manor, most likely. He was no longer in the doorway, and Jessamine felt the absence of his presence so deeply. Even Nyx grumbled in her lap, the discontented sound of a cat who wanted to leave.

Sybil cursed. "I shouldn't have said it like that. I should have known he would—"

"It's all right," Jessamine interrupted. "I'll get him."

"Jessamine." Sybil grabbed her arm, forcing her to remain where she was. "You're right, you know. We need to build a coven if we're going to continue to support you. I know he believes a god can mold this world into his own image, but it will be easier for people to see you as a queen if you do not have a god king at your side."

The words echoed in her mind as she nodded and slipped out of the kitchen to find him. First, she looked in the room where the statues of his family still stood. But he wasn't lurking in their shadows, as he so often was. Nor was he in the great room with the chandelier still broken in the center of the floor. She'd almost given up on finding him before she passed by the door to her bedroom and noticed that the curtain had been shifted.

Carefully moving it aside, she saw he was sitting on her bed. Back rounded, head in his hands, he looked like someone had left an old jacket there in a forgotten heap.

"Elric," she murmured, stopping in front of him.

"Don't," he replied in that raspy tone. "I know what I have to do."

"You don't have to do anything."

"You heard what she said. A sacrifice is the next reasonable step." He removed his hands from his face, looking up at her with dark rings around his eyes and the weight of the world on his shoulders.

She'd never seen him look so tired. Not sad or worried or plagued with fear. Just bone-deep tired.

Dragging her thumbs along the dark circles beneath his gaze, she stepped between his legs as he looped his arms around her hips. "Why are you sad?"

"They will beg you to sacrifice me soon enough. And one day you will see the reason in it. You will regret your vow to me, but a vow to a god cannot be broken." His hands spasmed against her back. "You will die trying to protect me, and there is no way to stop the future that barrels toward us. The coven is just the first step toward that end."

"The coven will be what we make it," she insisted. "You will be the god we serve and you will not have to die."

"It is a pleasant dream."

"A dream we will sew into the fabric of reality." Jessamine tugged him forward, pressing their foreheads together as she breathed him in. "We need her, Elric. I need to take this throne back the right way. And I need to find Fortuna so we know what Leon is planning, and how he destroyed an entire royal family in one day. I saw her in Callum's mind. She worked with him, just like Callum did. I am not prepared to fight Leon yet, but I damn well will get answers out of her. We cannot remake this kingdom without giving the people of Inverholm a reason to trust me before we do it."

Please, she thought. *Please believe me.*

Because in the end, this was all his choice. Elric was the last living god, and the one most humans feared. He was the blackened shape that took on the form of their nightmares. And yet, without him, she and Sybil were nothing. Just a duo of witches who had no real power.

He sighed, and the breath played across her collarbone. "Get your scrying bowl, gravesinger."

"Why?"

"I want to see this witch who sacrifices such a great deal to me. I want to know who she is, and where she is."

"Can't you just go to her?" Jessamine leaned back to look into his eyes. "You always just appeared to me."

"Because I wanted to." His gaze moved over every one of her features, and she could see when he looked at them. Reveled in the darkness of her eyes, lingered along the slightly downturned edges of her lips, and basked in the savagery of the scar across her throat. "I do not wish to appear to this witch so easily. The worship of a god should never be simple, Jessamine Harmsworth. It should be a labor of belief."

He released his hold on her hips so she could fetch her scrying bowl. The behemoth made of silver was hard to move, especially when she filled it with water, so she made certain it was in the perfect spot before she began the spell.

Elric approached behind her, his hands on her hips as he guided her words. The spell fell from her lips with ease, even as the heat between them built. As always, the tension of their magic summoned her baser needs.

She could feel the breath in his lungs feathering down her shoulders and across her collarbone. His hands clenched at her sides, the grip almost too tight and yet inspiring so many memories.

They'd only had one night of passion after they'd defeated Callum. One night that she dreamt of every single moment that she could. A flash of a memory burned behind her eyes as she closed them, tilting her head back against his shoulder and breathing in his scent. She knew how strong those hands were. She knew now what it was like to feel him gripping her thighs as he plunged inside of her.

She knew the taste of his passion, and she wanted more than just a lingering sip.

"Focus, gravesinger," he murmured in her ear as she arched against him. "Focus on what you seek."

What she sought was him. The taste of him, the magic of him, the power that surged through her body with every thrust.

"Bend to my will." His voice echoed in her mind, like he was part of her. Like he was already inside of her. "Open your eyes and find the witch who worships me."

It was her. Jessamine worshipped him even though she was terrified to admit it.

But no, that wasn't who they were looking for. Jessamine opened her eyes and stared into the still water that reflected their image back at her. Then the reflection of her own face warped, shifted, and suddenly she was looking through a mirror at another woman. A pale, sickly looking creature with sunken eyes and mousy brown hair that stuck up in every direction. Curls, a riot of them around her face as she looked into the water with equal amounts of horror and intrigue.

"Who are you?" the woman asked, but her voice was warped, as though she was underwater.

"I am no one and everyone." The words spilled from Jessamine's tongue as though another person had grasped her jaw and puppeted her mouth. "I am the one you seek and the one who was summoned. I seek you, witch, to reward your bravery."

"Deathless One?" the woman breathed, but she had to know that who she saw in the mirror was just Jessamine. Not…

But then she could see it as well. The dark shadow behind the witch was the same one that Jessamine felt pressed against her spine. Elric was here with her, but he was also with the other witch.

"We are coming for you," Jessamine said, her voice strangely warped. "Where are you?"

An image appeared in her mind. A place she recognized, although had not been in many years. The connection in the scrying bowl severed until all she saw was their own reflection in the water.

"Where are we going, Jessamine?" Elric rested his chin on her shoulder, his arms snaking around her waist.

"The Pleasure District," she replied. "The gods have looked kindly on us, Deathless One. That is where we needed to go to find Fortuna."

"Indeed, it seems luck is on our side." But the kiss he pressed to her shoulder felt bitter. As if it wasn't luck at all, but a wheel turning that neither of them could stop.

3

Elric wasn't certain he wanted to leave the manor again. The last time they'd left, he'd found himself having to save Jessamine's life. Again. And he grew tired of saving her from death itself. The Pleasure District had its dangers, but his memories of the place were old.

Long ago, he had visited the Pleasure District many times with his brothers, the women there ready and waiting to service a god. They'd always disappointed him, though. While there were plenty of powdered and perfumed women to tempt him, none of them had power.

He'd always sought women with some form of magic. He liked to feel their energy in his veins when he kissed them. He enjoyed the sparks that literally flew when they both indulged in each other. Perhaps that had always been his downfall.

As he stood before the crumbling statues of his family, he stared into what had once been his brother's visage. The God King was known throughout the realm as the supreme warrior, worshipped by soldiers. He gifted people the ability to fight through any pain, endure more than any other in this realm, and still continue forward in the name of their god.

"What would you do?" he murmured, even though he knew his brother could not respond.

The answer had always been simple when it came to the God King. When something scared him, his brother simply killed it. He'd remove it from the world and then he didn't have to fear it anymore. But that had turned him into a creature who existed solely on destruction and terror.

All these people thought they were being guided by benevolent and wise creatures. Instead, the gods had brought their own people to ruin, and suffered for it in turn.

"It is odd to see a god in this room," Sybil's voice echoed.

"Why is that?"

"It's hard to imagine that a god worships." She walked into the room with her hands tucked behind her back, her eyes on the floor and not on him.

"Is it worship if I'm speaking to family?" He contemplated the statue in front of him before sighing. "I suppose some might say it is. That's what you do, after all. You walk into this room and you speak to us."

"That is my understanding of worship, yes. We beg for answers or help, and a god sometimes answers. Sometimes they don't."

"I remember a time when we were all together. When the gods walked the earth and I had no questions or difficulties. I was still young, compared to the others. They were my guides. More than just family, they made certain I didn't lose my mind to the pressure and the responsibility of the coven of witches who followed me."

"Do you have all of your memories back, then?"

Most of them. Some were still hazy; perhaps they always would be. He remembered being created. Born out of a witch's blade and so much raw magic that it had splintered him into the creature he was now.

Elric feared what that meant. Touching the memory proved futile as it hovered just out of his reach. His origin was still not something he could see clearly. But he knew with certainty that at some point, each of the gods had been made.

They stood for a while in silence, both of them surveying the monolith of a god who had once lived. This depiction of his brother had him in full armor. There was a helm on his head with only a small cross to see out of, and the black gems that formed his eyes still gleamed in that hidden space. Eyes that saw straight into a person's soul and could sear their flesh from bone.

He heard Sybil's sharp swallow before she spoke. "I forget that you had a relatively small following, compared to the other gods. You had a coven of witches, but they had…"

"Thousands," he filled in for her. "Thousands of followers who prayed to them every single day. So often I thanked my luck and the magic of the realm that I did not have as many. There is no way to exist without disappointing all who need you. I know it plagued him."

"You rarely disappointed us, if it makes you feel better."

It didn't.

Because not disappointing them had required sacrificing so much of himself. He'd let them carve into his flesh time and time again in their pursuit of power and seen only the rare handful who even felt a modicum of guilt for it.

Then Jessamine walked into his life, and she had a different mindset. There was no pain with her. No sacrificing. She needed his power, true. But she had refused to use him the way others had.

His voice was low, the question barely audible. "If I hadn't let them scorch my bones with curses or shape their runes with my organs, would they ever have made me a god?"

Sybil's tiny intake of breath was all he needed to hear. Elric knew the truth. They had seen him as a weapon then, and nothing had changed in the many years since. They hadn't seen a being with thoughts or feelings when they had stolen his magic. All they saw was a tool.

And once he had performed his job, they threw him to the side.

"We loved you," Sybil finally said. "We worshipped the ground you walked on. And when you were alive, we treated you with the honor you deserved."

He looked into those tormented eyes that knew the words she said were a lie. He took one step toward Sybil, his most faithful follower, and pressed her hand to his chest, where his magic tangled through her fingers.

"Do you feel this?" he asked.

"I have always been able to feel your power."

"And you know the wound I give you all so that I may gift you power more easily?"

Without hesitation, Sybil shifted the fabric away from the fissure that ran down her chest. The one that now writhed with dark shadows, stuffed full with power. "Always."

He touched the ragged chasm that would never heal and breathed out a long sigh. "This is my mark. A symbol of the same wound I once bore. A centuries-old scar that will never heal, so I will never forget the pain your kind inflicted upon me so that I could become a god."

He remembered those days. Not his life as a man, because those memories were long gone. But he remembered being made. The pain, the torment, the months of serving as a sacrifice and losing every piece of himself, all of it culminating in godly power that had consumed him. They unmade him, so that he could be reborn.

She stared up at him, eyes wide with unsaid words. She shook beneath his touch, and he had to wonder if it was with fear. But then she bit her lip and whispered, "I'm sorry."

"For what?"

"For everything we did to you."

He shook his head and dropped his hand from her chest. "It is in the past, Sybil. You were not even part of my last sacrifice."

"I could have said something."

"And done what?" He spat the words, harsh but with the ring of truth. "What were you going to do? You who were the weakest among them. A witch who barely even took the magic so that no one would notice her? You were nothing but a child in those days."

"I was forty years old."

"And I was hundreds of years old!" He turned his back to her, unable to look at her. "I could have stopped them at any point. I was the one with the power. *I* was the god."

The silence between them was deafening. He'd berated himself over this countless times, and still the wound festered. He could have stopped them, but he didn't. Instead, he allowed himself to hate them, letting the feeling brew more and more until it consumed him. He'd been weak back then, a god begging for power and worship. To deny them what they asked would have weakened him. It would have left him vulnerable to his siblings.

Elric had created his own doom back then. And now, he was walking right into it again.

"What did your siblings say at the time?" Sybil's words trembled, as though she feared what he would tell her.

She should. Their advice had not been kind. But his siblings were known to be cruel. He had been the god with the bleeding heart.

"They told me to destroy the coven and start anew. There will always be witches, and they will always need a patron. Burn the coven to the ground. Savor their screams. Take back my power and create a new coven to worship me as the god I was."

"Perhaps this is your opportunity to do just that."

Was it? The mere thought tangled his guts into a mess of knots.

He'd seen these women and the tattered rags of their pride. He'd watched them sell their bodies, their time, their very souls so they could live in a world where people looked down upon them for something they were born with. Helping them had never been a choice. It was just a question of how far he was willing to go.

"Why are you here?" he asked, tucking his hands behind his back and taking another step away from her. "I assume you need something for preparations?"

"I came to ask if I could stay here."

"No."

"Deathless One, I have helped you both before, but I do believe—"

"No."

"Elric," she breathed, using his true name for a rare moment. "I am afraid. This is the home of the coven, and if we leave it…"

"Then someone else might take it? Indeed. Someone else may come to this crumbling ruin and see that it still has use. There will be no more witches here, Sybil. We will not bring another coven back to this cursed place. We move forward and we move on."

Her shoulders tensed with every word, but she did not argue, merely ducked her head in a sharp nod before leaving the room.

Elric feared he had been too hard on her. He knew the depths of her anxiety in leaving the place that had been her home for centuries. She'd been here, alone, and these walls had given her comfort. She'd lived with the ghosts of the past for too long, though.

If she stayed, those ghosts would consume her soul.

He turned his attention back to the statues behind him, but he did not see their stony expressions. Instead, he focused on the new tether that had wriggled its way into his soul. Like the witches, he had a well of power from which he drew.

All the actions he'd taken of late had drained that well significantly. But he hadn't used any power in many centuries. There was still plenty left to share with a witch who had gifted him so handsomely.

Accepting a sacrifice took time. He had to allow the magic to gather in this realm, and even then, the spell needed to rot the surrounding ground. Wherever a witch had made a sacrifice, there was a black mark on the world, which made it even more surprising that the witch had sacrificed a cow right in the middle of a field. Anyone who saw that black stain would know instantly what had happened.

Taking a deep breath, he followed the magic and felt his form disintegrate and then re-form. One moment he was in the manor, and the next, he stood in a field of wheat among knee-high yellow fronds. Wind waved the stalks of gold in a subtle breeze. Crows wheeled overhead, their caws grating at his ears even as he saw what they feasted upon.

The bloated body of the cow lay in a circle of flattened wheat, fallen where it had been killed while grazing. Its long tongue lolled out of its mouth, where even maggots and flies refused to land.

The black stain of the sacrifice leached into the ground, spreading around the beast and pulsing with power. It waited for him, and who was he to deny such a gift?

Elric bent, feeling his form warp and distend with power as he crouched beside the reeking body to accept the witch's sacrifice. Black ooze cracked out of the cow's splitting skin and rolled toward him in strings of inky goo that latched on to his wrists and body. The dark magic consumed him, clinging to him like a cape that billowed from his shoulders and boiled in waves of movement.

A faint sound reached his ears, one that made little sense for an empty field with a dead cow and crows above his head—but the soft gasp was expected from someone spying on a feasting god.

He looked up, feeling the magic already writhing underneath his flesh. Tiny fissures of black ink had reached up his face and were already pooling in the sockets of his eyes.

A farmer stood there with his mouth hanging open and his face white as parchment. He was a stout man, born ready for a life of hardship. His hands were worn with calluses. His clothing was simple and well-used. Leathery skin had long been burned by the sun's touch, but it was the man's eyes that gave away who he was.

There were laugh lines all around his face, the deep grooves of a man who knew what happiness was, and that was the only reason Elric allowed him to live. If he had revealed even a hint of violence or greed, Elric would have killed him instantly.

Instead, he gifted this man with the sight of a god.

He stood, feeling power stretching around him. The great cloak of ink spread from his shoulders like raven wings.

His frame grew taller than he normally was. Wider, longer, stretching until the very sky seemed filled with night.

The man began to pray, whispered words of shaking fear that claimed he would be a good man if the gods would protect him.

"There are no gods," Elric said, his voice deep and booming in the field. "None but me."

The farmer fell to his knees, vowing to be a good man for the rest of his life. He would not allow any to sway him. If there were gods, then he would worship them until the very last moment of his life. Spare him.

Family.

Farm.

Love.

The same words everyone spat as they claimed value in their lives not worth saving. There were a hundred men just like him. A hundred men more who were gone and forgotten. And still a hundred more yet to be born. This man was just a drop in the ocean of humanity, and losing him would in the long run affect nothing.

But Elric was not the same god he once had been. Now he had a voice in his head whispering that people had value. That even after they had killed him so many times, there were still people worth fighting for in this kingdom. And that voice, that soft feminine voice, calmed his rage.

So he stood there, allowing the man to drink his fill of a feasting god. He enjoyed the fear coursing through the man's veins, let it linger in the air, and then drew it deep into his lungs.

"Tell all what you have seen here today," he intoned, spreading a warning before he left for the manor. "For I am the Deathless One, and I have returned."

4

Jessamine hadn't thought travel to the Pleasure District would be so easy. They had a few run-ins with the infected, but less than expected. Perhaps that was because there were so many guards on the road. All of the men wore Leon's dark navy colors with hard expressions and orders to make sure that nothing happened.

She wasn't certain why. Sybil thought they were a sign that Leon was on the move. No one wanted the king to run into the infected on the streets. Elric thought the same. Regardless of the reason, every time they mentioned his name, Jessamine felt like she was going to come out of her own skin. She couldn't think about her murderer's plan. Not yet. Fortuna still stood between her and him. There was still time for her to build up the bravery to face him.

The closer they got to the Pleasure District, the more guards they saw. Jessamine kept her hood pulled close around her, making certain that her face wasn't easily seen. Nyx rode upon her shoulder underneath her cloak, giving her the look of a hunchback. Few people would recognize her, but that didn't mean it wasn't a risk. Some former palace servant might have survived Leon's coup, and notice that her face looked an awful lot like the princess's.

It took them two days of walking. They'd taken the longer path, avoiding the Factory District entirely. They were too easily recognized there after their battle with Callum. Which meant they had to walk along the coast with all the other folks denied easy passage through any of the districts.

At first, she assumed the others that continued to gather with them were travelers who would wander off eventually. But they quickly created a caravan. Groups of people were safer from the infected, others mused. Together, they would stay safe.

Jessamine felt anything but with so many strangers surrounding them.

She'd slept with one eye open and Nyx keeping watch on top of her. No one wished to anger the yellow-eyed demon who crouched over her heart.

The first night was when she heard rumblings of a god having returned. She had set her bedroll down beside Elric's and Sybil's; the latter began preparing dinner over the fire Elric started.

"Did you hear what that farmer was claiming?" a passerby mentioned, their voice carrying over the fires. "The gods are coming back."

"That's a myth. The gods are all dead and you know it." His companion had a bristly silver beard, and he scratched at it as though it had bugs.

"Not according to him! He said the god looked right at him, some black beast with strings of viscera hanging off his form. He looked right into the man's soul and told him, 'The Deathless One has returned.'"

Everyone was quiet, listening in on the conversation without even attempting to hide their eavesdropping. Clearly, the storyteller liked the attention, though. He kept going, adding embellishments that simply couldn't be true. The Deathless One had fangs like a bat, and wings like a raven. He'd eaten the cow in two bites. First the head, and then the rest of it.

Jessamine sat down in the sand across from Elric, plopped Nyx into her lap so her familiar could also give him a judgmental stare, and raised her brow.

He mirrored her expression with a raised brow of his own. The god was quite pleased with himself.

"You said you visited the sacrifice and that was it. What did you do?" she murmured, making sure not to be overheard. But no one was paying attention to their odd trio, not when the man was now talking about how the god had summoned the crows to attack the farmer.

"I accepted the sacrifice." Elric shrugged. "I can't control if someone was there while I did it."

"You could have looked around!" she scolded.

"Next time, perhaps I will heed your advice." He took the bowl Sybil offered him and grinned.

His smug expression didn't budge for the rest of the night or the next day. He was still grinning even as the Pleasure District came into view. The damned man was far too pleased with himself.

The caravan they traveled with was far more subdued after the conversation about the gods. Perhaps they were all wondering if they should start sacrificing and worshipping again. They would have rioted if they knew they were traveling with one of those very gods.

The golden buildings and gleaming towers overtook the horizon, however, and Jessamine forgot all about the previous evening. This area of her kingdom was blindingly beautiful, a stark contrast to the corners where Jessamine had been dwelling these past months.

They'd once called it the Pleasure District because it was home to those who sold their bodies for pleasure. But over many years of flourishing business, it had grown into so much more. Now it was a feast for the senses, a destination for those who wished to dine on fine foods, or who sought the finest clothing or the rarest of jewels. Every building gleamed, dripping with gold and silver and gemstones that sparkled in the sunlight.

Even from afar, she could see how the district gates were made of plated gold. There were figures sculpted into it. Men and women, nude and in repose, beckoning all those who sought to indulge their senses. All were welcome here—if they could afford it.

There were blue-coated guards at the front gate as well, asking people for paperwork to enter. The buttons on their jackets were made of gold, and their clothing was so perfectly pressed she swore she could smell the starch. But it was the swords at their sides that made her far more uncomfortable.

"Papers?" she muttered, looking to Elric and Sybil for direction. "No one's ever needed papers to get into the Pleasure District."

"Papers proving we've been invited, I'd guess," Sybil muttered, lingering at the back of the crowd. "Considering all of the king's men surrounding the place, I'd guess this means the Pleasure District has rather important visitors. They don't want just anyone walking in. We'll have to try again later."

"No, we won't," Elric muttered.

The last thing she wanted was for a god to get involved and cause a scene. Everyone was already talking about him, and he'd made it very clear that he couldn't handle himself in public.

"Elric!" she hissed, grabbing his arm and trying to yank him back to her side. "Don't you dare."

The glare he cast upon her would have made anyone else freeze in their place. But Jessamine knew he wouldn't hurt her, no matter how much he wanted to in the moment.

"Do you want to get inside or not?" he snarled. "We have a witch to find, and I was under the impression you wanted to get your throne back sooner rather than later."

"What's another few days when I've already been waiting for months?" Jessamine tried to stop him again. She clung to the fabric of his shirt, but he would not let her stop him.

Elric shook her off like she was a gnat. He stalked through the crowd, pausing to speak to one of the guards. She'd never been very talented at lipreading, but she could see the guard's face go bright red.

She tugged her hood a little further over her face, making sure no one could see what was beneath the shadows. "What do you think he's doing?" she asked Sybil.

"Getting us in trouble."

"That's what I'm afraid of. Those guards don't look very forgiving."

"They aren't." Sybil looked through the crowd, likely trying to find them an exit for when the guards attacked. "If we go through the back alley there, it should loop around to the beach. I don't think they'll try to chase us much farther than that."

"I'll follow you."

But then she saw Elric grinning and waving them over like a lunatic. She didn't want to go to him, but everyone was staring. By the time she and Sybil had made it to the front of the crowd, the guard was chuckling at something Elric said.

The intimidating man then looked her up and down before asking, "You the ladies he's traveling with?"

"Yes, sir." She tried to keep her head down, but he was peering right into the shadows as though he had to see her face.

"That's good. He seems a right good man. You keep track of him in this district, you hear me? It's easy for a man to get taken for a fool in this place. Keep an eye on his wallet."

What in the fuckery was going on here?

She nodded, sharing a glance with Sybil that confirmed the witch also thought the guard had lost his mind before they were waved into the district beyond. They got a mere two steps out of hearing range before she slapped Elric's shoulder three times and then shook him hard.

"What was that?" she hissed. "You could have gotten us caught! Do you know what those men would do if they recognized me? Those are Leon's guards, you absolute bumbling buffoon!"

"I twisted his mind, Jessamine, calm down. He thought I was a good friend from when he was a lad. His mind was easy to break, and his memories were so simplistic it was child's play to get him to let us in." Elric cracked his knuckles, and that stupid grin was right back on his face. "Now, do you think the

Pleasure District has changed much in two hundred years? I'm curious to find out."

She was going to hit him. She was going to clock him right in that chiseled jaw. All the risks he had taken were going to end her life, she was certain of it.

Sybil's hand pressed against her lower back, steering her away from the god she wanted to murder and instead forcing her to look at the dark witch. "We're fine," she said. "Jessamine, everything worked out in the right way. We're in the district."

"No thanks to him."

"All thanks to him," Sybil corrected. "You are a gravesinger, my dear, but you are not a god. Do not test the man who gives us power."

She could see Elric behind Sybil's shoulder, that shit-eating grin only spreading wider. And then, like the absolute child he was, he raised a hand and flipped her off.

"Sybil," she said, making sure her tone was reasonable and mature. "I need you to look away while I punch the man behind you in the throat. When he has finished writhing on the ground in agony, I will treat him like a god... *if* he behaves like one."

Sybil sighed and stepped away from the two of them. Pinching the bridge of her nose, she shook her head. "I wash my hands of you both. I have a great-grand-cousin two or three times removed here that I would like to check on. She's not a witch, don't worry about that. But it would be nice to see her and her little ones."

"You're not coming to find the witch with us?"

Sybil shook her head with a soft smile. "I think meeting a god and a gravesinger will be more than enough of a surprise for her. Nyx, are you coming with me?"

The familiar gave a little chirp and hopped from Jessamine's shoulder to Sybil's. And with that, the witch and familiar disappeared into the crowd.

Jessamine had mere moments to get her bearings before she was struck by the realization that she felt at home here. These weren't the dank and dirty streets of the Water District. No one surrounding her was covered in smoke or dust from the factories. Everyone was in silk and satin. The latest fashions whirled in colorful streaks all around her. Vendors offered gems that put her royal jewels to shame. These were the people she used to see every day as she fulfilled her duties in the palace—and everyone was looking at her like she didn't belong.

Jessamine felt every streak of grime that covered her skin. She could sense how tangled her hair was, and how awful it must appear, like billowing smog that followed a dirty cretin who had wandered into their home.

Even the buildings seemed to lean away from her, as though the very walls were afraid she would put her grimy hands on them. What would happen if she leaned against one? Would she leave behind a smear of filth?

Looking down at her feet was easier than seeing the expressions of all these clean and glorious people. But even the streets were perfect, as if dirt was afraid to mar this place. Closing her eyes, she focused on her other senses.

The Pleasure District smelled like rosewater and lemons. It wasn't a strong enough smell to make her head ache. It was light and airy and oh so perfect in every single way.

She'd been to the Pleasure District when she turned sixteen as a gift from her mother. The experience was supposed to be her first adventure as a woman. She'd walked these streets and not a single person had looked at her with anything other than adoration and perhaps the slightest amount of jealousy.

Even now, she could remember the slide of her silk skirts against her legs. She'd worn a pretty lavender dress that day, with sleeves that hung off her shoulders and a bodice that hugged her waist so perfectly it almost gave her curves. Her hair had been twisted up on her head in immaculate braids, and one of the makeup sellers had complimented her on her fine complexion.

Now, she was little more than a worm beneath their feet.

Elric's arm coiled around her shoulders and tugged her against his side. "Come on, gravesinger."

She tried to build confidence around herself. "To find the witch?"

"You are better than every person here. They do not know that magic runs in your veins. They do not know that we are mere steps away from starting a coven of witches who will make them quake under their thin sheets. And they do not know that you have a god at your beck and call." He leaned down to press a kiss to her temple, lingering against her skin. "They do not know the danger they put themselves in for looking at you as though you are anything less than a goddess."

Heart racing, she followed him through the streets of gold and silver. More and more people gawked, but that was all right. Eventually, they crossed into a more residential area where there were less judgmental stares and more people moving about their day.

"Do you know where we're going?" she asked, her voice catching in her throat.

"I can find a witch anywhere she hides from me," he replied.

At last they stopped in front of a house. Or a sort of house. In truth, it looked more like a birdcage. Great pillars stretched up and over the structure that was inside the cage itself. Even a small ornament at the top made it look like some giant could pick it up and move the whole thing. A very pretty front garden filled her senses with the strong scent of peonies.

"Here?" she asked, peering through the giant cage at the tiny cottage within. Beautiful, as everything in the Pleasure District was. But entirely unexpected.

"Here," Elric repeated. "This is where our witch lives."

5

The house was not one any witch of his previous coven would have deigned to live in. Those witches were dark and dangerous. They cast blood magic and sex spells. Regular people knew angering a witch resulted in boils, lunacy, and famine. That was the coven of the old days. A coven to fear.

But this house? This was ridiculous. There were bright pink and yellow flowers in front, and they weren't even poisonous. As he nudged the front gate open and strode into the garden toward the *birdhouse* that contained the tiny cottage, he paused.

"What's the matter?" Jessamine asked as she paused with him.

He was staring at the flowers. He couldn't stop staring at them, because they were the most ridiculous thing he had ever seen.

Jessamine leaned to look, and the little "oo" in her throat made him want to turn right around. Fuck the witch and her sacrifice.

"Nasturtium! Have you tasted these before? We used to put them in salads at the palace; they're quite delightful." She plucked one, lifting it in her hand so she could spin the pretty yellow flower between her fingers before popping it in her mouth. "I wonder if this is where we ordered them from? I know they came from the Pleasure District, but I never paid much attention to the food orders."

"This is the home of a witch," he rumbled. "Herbs and plants for spells are understandable. Raising poisonous plants in your garden is an impressive feat for most witches. Not... edible flowers."

Jessamine gave him a rather saucy look before swallowing. He could smell the peppery tang on her breath and, somehow, it only made him more disappointed.

"Elric, there are new witches now. We don't all have to murder people."

He watched her sashay toward the birdcage, and all he could think was that he'd already lost control over whatever coven he might build in this new century.

"Of course you have to murder people," he muttered, following her through the beautifully made metallic doors and down the cobblestone path that led to the quaint little cottage. "You're using my magic. Black magic that I have gifted to all of you. It's death magic, Jessamine."

"Maybe you can do things you don't know about, too." She lifted her hand and tapped her knuckles on the front door of the stone cottage.

It was something out of a storybook. This home was made of stone and rounded walls, and there was vivid ivy growing all over it. The door itself was a glossy brown, and the central knocker on the door was in the shape of a bright gold bee.

Was he hallucinating? Was this part of having a physical body? Perhaps something was wrong with this form and his mind had fractured. Or he'd conjured this moment in his sleep, and he was about to wake up at any moment.

"Coming!" a bright voice sang out from somewhere inside the cottage, and he swore he heard the trill of birdsong.

Nightmare. Definitely a nightmare.

The door eased open to reveal the strangest little being on the other side. She was so small that he almost mistook her for a child. But with that curly mop of hair on her head, she was unmistakably the same woman they had previously seen in the scrying mirror. He just hadn't realized she would only come up to the center of his chest.

She wore the most ridiculous dress. With hip caps and massive bell sleeves at her shoulders, she looked like a cupcake. A decorated cupcake with chocolate frosting on top.

"You can't be her," he muttered, certain that his expression had crumpled into one of complete disgust.

This new witch gave him an odd look before turning her attention to Jessamine. "Are you here to pick up the new budgerigar? It's quite an unusual color, and I am very proud of its lineage."

He watched Jessamine's nose scrunch. "A... budgerigar?" she asked.

"The parakeet?" The woman looked at the two of them, clearly becoming more confused by the minute. "Or are you here for some other reason?"

He noted that her voice deepened on the second question. There was a warning in that tone.

So, there was a backbone in this woman, even if she was fragile in appearance. *This* was the witch he had expected to see. He was far more inclined to help her if there was a bit of evil inside her, after all.

"May we come in?" he asked.

Her hand tightened on the door. "I'm afraid not. I don't know who either of you are, and I don't have a habit of letting strangers into my... private abode."

He allowed some of his power to seep out of his skin. He could feel it crackling in the air around them, raw magic that was so tempting to any witch. Her pupils blew out the moment she felt it, and then he leaned down so he could look her directly in the eye. "You're the one who summoned me, witch. No one denies a god entry."

There went all the blood in her face. Just gone. Leaking out of her flesh to make space for the fear that sent her heart thundering in her chest. He could almost hear it, the rabbitlike thumps of a creature who knew they were standing before a predator. And he would like nothing more than to clamp his jaws around something soft and fragile.

Jessamine's hand pressed against his back, and the two of them entered the house before they made even more of a scene. The witch before them stumbled back as she tried not to touch him.

The room beyond was pretty and quaint. There was a small hearth in the corner, more plants growing on every surface that could hold them. She had a strange metal contraption hanging from the ceiling where she'd attached her copper pots and pans. A cozy chair in the corner had been patched with multicolored fabric, but it seemed a stylistic choice, as there were no worn bits and all the patches were rich and colorful.

And then there were the birds.

Some of them were massive, with long orange beaks. One for every color of the rainbow. Their feathers glimmered like sapphires, emeralds, rubies, and pearls. Others he could have grasped in one hand, they were so small. And there were easily a hundred of them, if not more.

He ducked as one of them flew too close; the witch made a sound of worry, as though he would kill the little beast. Frowning, he looked up and saw they were surrounded by multiple levels of birds on roosts above their head.

"Birds?" he muttered, sidestepping another one that dove out of the air and seemed to make a beeline for his head.

"Birds," Jessamine replied, but there was wonder in her voice. "You're Lady Elissa Burnham, aren't you?"

The witch sagged against her door and seemed incapable of response.

"You know her?" he asked.

"Everyone knows *of* her. She's a very exclusive bird breeder. Nearly all the nobility I have met have one of her parrots. They're prized possessions, and surprisingly long-lived for creatures like this." Jessamine's dark eyes widened as she looked back at the woman. "Are you all right?"

He turned to find that the bird witch had slid down the door until her bottom reached the ground. Under the weight of his gaze, she rolled onto her knees and pressed her face against the floorboards, prostrating herself before him.

Oh, this disappointing witch was going to be the death of him. "Elissa, what seems to be the problem?"

"Glorious Deathless One," she cried out, her voice shaking with emotion. "Most powerful of your siblings and giver of magic. You honor me with your presence, and I humbly offer my mind, body, and soul in your service if you but grant me one wish."

Jessamine met his unimpressed stare, and he shrugged while rolling his eyes. "Witch, I have accepted your sacrifice. You may ask anything of me."

Her only response was to mutter continued supplications and prayers as though she hadn't summoned the god she was looking for.

Another bird dove toward him, and he ducked yet again. Before he could even think about the words, he muttered, "If one of these birds shits on me, I'm going to kill them all."

That seemed to do it. The witch on the floor froze, and then looked up at him with big, sad eyes. "Please don't do that."

"I will have little choice."

"I beg of you, god of my mother, have mercy."

"God of your mother..." he repeated, before crouching in front of her. With his arm braced on his leg, he tilted his head to the side and really looked at her. "Your mother was one of my coven?"

"Well, my great-great-grandmother, who passed on much of her power throughout the lines of women in my family. She was your devout follower until the day she died. She believed you were not dead, not like the others. And that someday, you would come back to save us all." Elissa looked a little uncomfortable. "My mother gave me the remains of her power, but I am not a true witch. I have no coven. And I... bottled it."

"So that's how you knew the words," he muttered, drumming his fingers on his knee before he stood. "Your great-great... maybe another great... grandmother. Who was she?"

"Gloria Burnham."

"Burnham," he muttered, trying to place a face to the name. "She was a hedge witch, wasn't she?"

"Green magic, yes. That was her speciality."

"Poisons."

"Sometimes. But in the later generations, my family just enjoyed growing whatever plants would thrive under their touch. There was very little magic left." Elissa cleared her throat. "And what little my mother had preserved, she wished to give to me. She said someday I would feel magic in the realm again, and that was the time to make a sacrifice to you. That in my hour of greatest need, I should always trust that you never really left us."

And there it was. That burning sensation in his chest that whispered he owed this woman something. Because she believed in him. She needed help so badly that she was willing to make a deal with the most dangerous god in this kingdom, and because of that, she deserved to be heard.

She was alone. Without him, all witches were alone.

Pity made him weak. But then again, it always had.

Growling low in his throat, he held his hand out for her to take. "Rise, witch. You have pleased me with your sacrifice."

Her big eyes rounded even more. She took his hand like it was a snake that could bite her, but Jessamine smiled at the touch.

"I will show you the greatest part of my soul," Elissa said as she dropped his hand and guided them into a back room. "I cannot lose her."

He steeled himself for an equally odd woman who was likely going to disappoint him yet again. Witches should not have weak consorts, and yet, how was he to know what these new witches wasted time on?

But when he walked into the room, there was no one here. Just a bird. Lying on a table.

Under a blanket.

Fucking hell.

"A bird?" he hissed. "You summoned a god to save a bird?"

"Not just any bird," Elissa said. "She's the love of my life."

Silence. That was all he could manage. Because now that he was really looking, he could see the remnants of a spell gone awry. There were loops of dark magic chained around the creature, but they were all broken. Wrong. A spell cast by a novice who had no idea what she was doing.

"What did you do to this poor woman?" he muttered, striding around the table to get a look at the spell from every angle.

"I tried to make it so she could talk to them," Elissa whispered. "Sarah always loved them so much. And I thought, with a bit of my mother's magic, I could give her a gift that would make her ever so happy."

"You turned her into a bird?"

"I didn't think that was what I was doing at the time!"

Jessamine paused at his side, tangling their fingers together so she could look as well. Gently, she pointed out a portion of the spell that looked like it had rotted into the bird's flesh. "That doesn't look good."

"That's because it's not," he replied. "Magic like this cannot be undone. It's beyond fixing. The spell is embedded into the creature. You've turned her for good."

Elissa gasped and pressed her hands to her mouth. "But you're a god! You can do anything."

He stared her down, hoping that all of his fury was shown in his features. She was shaking in fear, but he was shaking with rage. "Magic is not for the unpracticed. Magic has a price, and sometimes it is permanent. Even a god cannot unravel it. Do you wish for me to kill her? I can do that. I can prevent her from dying, too, if you wish to have her by your side for the rest of your life. But I cannot undo what you have done."

"Elric," Jessamine whispered.

He'd been harsh, but witchcraft was not for a novice. Especially not a spell like this.

"Oh dear," Elissa said, her shaking hands still pressed against her mouth. "What have I done?"

"Nothing good," he muttered, but then jolted when Jessamine stomped her foot hard on top of his. Hissing out a pained breath, he sighed at her pointed glare. "The two of you should leave. I will see what I can do. There is no bringing her back to her previous form, but I might be able to conjure some… staying spell that will give her the lifespan of a normal mortal."

"Thank you," Jessamine whispered. She squeezed his hand, and he knew he'd done something right, even if it was just to satisfy the needs of a witch who wasn't even a witch.

Watching the two women walk out of the room, all he could think was that he'd gotten himself in bigger trouble than he'd thought. Because here he was, expecting a powerful new coven member, and all he'd gotten was a parrot on a table.

Sighing, he looked down at the bird, which was lying eerily like a human in a coma. "All right, you," he muttered. "Let's see what magic we can muster."

6

Jessamine guided the new witch into the kitchen and sat her down at the table that was covered with a patchwork quilt. Elissa was shaking like a leaf, her entire body in a state of shock.

Leaving Elissa to her thoughts, Jessamine set about making her a cup of tea. Shockingly, she hadn't been pooped on yet. She was more of a lady than Elric was a gentleman, so she had yet to mention it. But while she was tossing the leaves into the teapot and waiting for the kettle to shriek, she noticed one of the birds did poop. In a flash, the refuse was caught by magic and whisked away out the kitchen window.

She'd never seen magic so readily used, especially not in a district so close to the castle.

The Pleasure District got away with a lot more than the rest of the kingdom. After all, if magic was used to entertain, then surely it wasn't all that dangerous. As long as it amused the rich and the powerful, it wasn't scary.

"Here we are," she said. The kettle whistled, she poured the boiling water, and collected two matching teacups with bees painted on the sides. She set everything in front of Elissa, who still looked like she'd seen a ghost, and then attempted to get the woman out of her own feelings.

"This is a lovely tablecloth." Jessamine fingered the hand-stitched edges.

"My mother made it."

"Such precise stitches."

"Better than me." Elissa's hands were still shaking as she lifted the cup to her mouth and took a rather loud, unladylike sip. "She would never have made a mistake like this."

"All witches make mistakes. It's hard not to when you're given so much power but have no one to teach you how to wield it." Or at least, that's what she assumed.

"Are you a witch?"

Should Jessamine lie? It seemed wrong to do so when they'd only just met and Jessamine needed this woman to help them. A contact in the Pleasure District, especially one with Elissa's connections, would only aid their cause.

"Not really," she replied. "I'm a gravesinger."

Oh, it was the wrong thing to say. Elissa froze again, staring at her with wide eyes as the blood yet again drained from her features. Either the woman was very expressive, or she was going to have a terrible headache with all these terror responses.

"A gravesinger?" Elissa repeated. "Like... *the* gravesinger?"

"Well, from what I understand, there used to be more of us."

"You're the one who raised him?"

"Resurrected," she couldn't help but correct. "But yes."

"Oh." The rattling teacup was set down on its dish, and Elissa then planted her hand on the table. "I think I need to lie down."

Jessamine leapt up and grabbed Elissa by the shoulders. She was already weaving where she stood, and if she wasn't careful, she was going to pass out on her own kitchen floor. "Why don't you sit down and put your head between your legs for a second? Catch your breath, have another sip of tea, and then we'll talk some more. I promise, nothing bad is going to happen to you."

A knock on the door made Elissa nearly slide out of her chair before it burst open and Sybil strode through. She wore a new scarf around her head, a rather pretty crimson color with black butterflies hand-painted on it. Her coiled hair was now swept back to show her gleaming skin, Nyx riding on her shoulders like a warrior going into battle. "I stole this from my cousin, and then your god summoned me."

"In the back."

"Good enough." Sybil didn't even acknowledge the other woman in the room, walking through the house like she owned the place before disappearing into the back room.

Elissa made a soft sound in the back of her throat. "Who was that? And was that a cat?"

"Sybil, another coven member. And yes, a cat. My familiar. She'll behave herself." Jessamine knelt between the other woman's legs, holding on to her hands as though she could give Elissa some point of grounding. "Listen, from my understanding, when you sacrificed to the Deathless One, you willingly became part of his coven. You worship him, do you not?"

Still far too pale, Elissa's gaze met hers with frantic intensity. She whispered, "I didn't think he was really alive."

"None of us did. But that's quite all right, don't you think? He's going to help you. And now you're part of something so much larger. A coven. Isn't that what your mother always wanted?" Perhaps it was a bit manipulative, but Jessamine knew how to convince someone to accept their mistakes.

Her mother had been impossibly good at that. She'd seen the queen tell people right to their face that they'd chosen to make a mistake because they would learn from it. And they had been happy to believe her. A good leader knew how to ease someone's mind, even if that meant twisting it a bit.

"Is having a coven a good thing?" Elissa asked.

Jessamine could see how important the answer was to the other woman. Elissa wanted to believe that a coven would give her something she didn't currently have. They could be friends, teach her magic, give her power and security beyond what she could even imagine. All the things girls dreamt of.

She squeezed her hands, resolving to help this young woman no matter what the cost. "It's a very good thing. I think you're going to like us quite a bit."

The door to the back room banged open so hard that the birds above their heads all burst into flight.

Jessamine shouted over her shoulder, still on her knees, "Would you stop doing that? Open the door like a gentleman. Don't slam it open like a bull!"

The shadowy figure in the doorway shot her a glare. Elric was practically bloated with magic. Deep streaks of black marked his cheeks where he'd touched his face while casting the spell, and she could see it writhing underneath his skin like eels in a bucket.

His black gaze turned to Elissa. "Kill one of your birds."

"E-excuse me?" she stammered.

"Kill one of your birds, or your beloved ends up dying like a common animal."

"Well, she does appear to be a macaw, so... that's a long life." Elissa swallowed hard, and then wilted beneath his unimpressed stare. "Does it matter which bird?"

"Magic always comes with a price. You cast the spell, and you sacrificed magic of your own. Now there needs to be intent to save. Kill the bird that matches that value of the spell. Do you understand me?"

Elissa nodded and slowly stood. She took a while looking up at the birds before she finally reached out her hand for one. A delicate creature landed on her outstretched hand. It was beautiful, with long tail feathers that almost reached the floor. A riot of cool tones, greens, blues, and delicate whites.

Without another word, she went out the door and made her way into the garden. Jessamine could only see her silhouette from this far away, but she knew Elissa was petting the bird and talking to it.

"Is this really necessary?" Jessamine asked, feeling her own heart break just a little. "She loves these birds."

"She loves the woman she turned into a bird, too." He crossed his arms over his chest.

"You aren't doing this just to punish her? She must feel bad enough already."

"If I didn't need the sacrifice to do this, I wouldn't take it. My magic comes from death, Jessamine. I have never pretended otherwise."

She turned her gaze away from the woman in the garden and looked at him. He was otherworldly when he cast spells. He stood taller, stronger, more confident in moments like this. Clearly not a man, but a god.

He was everything she had always wanted to have with her as a child. A protector, someone who wasn't afraid to do terrible things to make sure that she stayed safe. And yet, in this moment, she feared that wasn't the right choice.

He stared back at her, and she knew he was sending her a message. She needed to believe him, to know that magic never came easily. It was the cost of being a witch, something she might never understand. She was connected to him as a gravesinger, but not in the same way the rest of the women were. He *was* their sacrifice. A feast of magic if they fattened him up first, like a prize pig.

Elric's throat bobbed in a swallow, sympathy in his gaze. "It is done. I will return for her in a moment. I need to help Sybil weave the spell before I can come and talk with her."

"I'll be here."

She waited by herself for a while, standing when Elissa came back inside. The witch's hands were shaking, but she returned as a different woman. Stronger. More steely in her expression. "Will that suffice?"

"He's already weaving the spell. He'll be back in a moment." Jessamine took the other woman by the elbow and guided her into a chair. "Sit. Drink your tea. It'll all be over soon."

"I didn't think witchcraft would be like this."

"Neither did I," she replied with a soft smile. "I was dead when he found me. He tricked me into coming back and then used Sybil to guide me into his service, I suppose."

"Do you regret it?"

Now, that was something she could answer honestly. Without hesitation, Jessamine replied, "Not a single bit. I am who I am because of what they did. I trust them both with my life, and I've seen with my own eyes that they would do anything to protect me."

"But you are the gravesinger. That is your purpose. They protect you so that you can protect him."

"No." Jessamine shook her head. "We all protect each other."

The door creaked open, much more respectfully this time, and Elric exited the back room. He paused for a moment, staring at the two of them. Anyone else might think his glare was one of hatred. Jessamine knew him better than that, though. She could see the discomfort in that gaze, and how he was trying to school himself into dealing with a witch softly. He was used to powerful witches with dark magic at their fingertips who wanted to break the world. He didn't know how to talk to someone as fragile as Elissa.

"She'll live," he finally said. "I can't turn her back. That part is beyond any of us. But her life is now bound to yours."

"Thank you," Elissa whispered. "It was naïve of me to ask you for more than that. Or to even expect it."

"Magic should not be cast without knowing what you are doing."

Jessamine was certain he was about to launch into a lecture on Elissa's foolishness. But he didn't.

Instead, he looked down at her with a much softer expression. He held out his hand for her to take, and when she did, he helped her stand until she straightened as tall as she could before him. "You sacrificed to me," he said. "More than once, now. Your intentions are pure of heart, and I will admit that is a breath of fresh air compared to the witches who summoned me in the past. If you wish to continue worshipping me, then I will gladly be your patron."

"Is this a fool's bargain?" Elissa asked, her eyes dancing between Jessamine and Elric. "I do not trust you, god or not."

"You don't have to trust me. But deep inside, you hunger for power. I can sense it, just as you know it to be true. You cast the spell upon your beloved, and something in you felt pride, even though you failed. If you wish for more magic like that, more power that only you can control, I will give it to you."

With an audible gulp, Elissa said, "Why are you here? It can't just be because I summoned you."

Jessamine shared a look with Elric and then nodded.

"We seek a woman here," he replied, his voice deepening with rage. "A woman who has taken much from us. We seek a throne and a bloody kingdom that will purge the streets of all that plague it. If you join this coven, you agree not only to worship me, but to acknowledge that the man who now sits on that throne is not your king."

"I supported the real royal family," Elissa replied, and truth rang clear in her words. "But they're all dead."

"Just like the gods are all dead?"

Jessamine stood, letting Elissa give her a once-over. She knew she didn't look like she used to. Jessamine the princess had been a beautiful, delicate girl clothed in spiderweb silk and pretty baubles. Jessamine the gravesinger was a scarred creature with vengeance in her gaze and a heart that beat only for death. But still, she was the same woman underneath it all.

Elissa's voice shook as she asked, "Who are you?"

"My name is Lady Jessamine Harmsworth."

"My lady," Elissa gasped. "But you're dead."

"I was."

And that was all she had to say. At the question in Elissa's gaze, she nodded toward Elric. "It is a testament to his power, Elissa. He is a real god."

She saw the shift. There was no longer so much fear in Elissa's gaze, but instead, awe. "And who are you here to find?"

"Fortuna Beaumont. We believe she is consort to the king, or something along those lines. His favorite entertainer. She was part of the coup that killed both my mother and me. I wish to find her and repay the same kindness." She grinned, and she knew it was a feral expression. "My hope is that you will help us."

"I am not an assassin, I'm..." Elissa shook her head. "I sell birds."

Elric placed his hand on her chest, right over her ribs, down the center, where her power would be. "Do you wish to be more than that?"

The reverence in Elissa's eyes gave Jessamine all the answer she needed. Elric could be very convincing when he wished to be.

It only took a few moments before Elissa broke. "I didn't think it was ever possible to be more."

"With me—with this coven—you can be whatever you want."

All it took was a single nod. The barest movement of her head, as though she was still frightened of what it meant if she agreed to do this. And she should be. Elissa should be terrified to become a witch, a figure hated by most people in this kingdom, but it was what she had been born to be.

Elric reached his hand into Elissa's flesh and cracked it open. Shadows slithered from his grip, filling the empty well that would soon be Elissa's to command. The void grew, and Jessamine felt it expanding inside her as well.

Deep within her breast, she felt her soul crow in pleasure at another witch finally coming into her power. There were more of them. More women who would know what it was like to be endless and terrifying.

She watched as her god made a new monster and rejoiced, knowing the world trembled in fear.

7

Elissa was rather quiet after all that. Elric knew what he'd asked her to do wasn't easy. Let alone the sudden power that now flowed through her veins or the fact that she had a wide-open crack down the center of her chest. Such changes were a lot to get used to.

He hated that he even worried about her. He shouldn't care what a witch was feeling or thinking. He was their god. She had asked him to do something, and now she had to live with the consequences.

And yet, he worried when she took them behind the cottage, where there were a few outbuildings. Like tiny cottages, they must serve as guest quarters for anyone the witch allowed to stay. Three miniature versions of her cottage, and she didn't even explain what they were. She just stood there, staring blankly at her feet for a few moments before she seemed to shake herself out of a daze.

"You can stay here," she said, her voice a little rough. "My mother made these before she died. They are perfectly protected."

"Where are you going to stay?" Jessamine asked.

"I'll stay with Sarah. I want to be there when she wakes up so she can... Well, so she doesn't feel so alone."

"Right."

They all watched the new witch turn toward her home before pausing. "Each room should be tailored to what you need. There are few spells remaining around this house, ever since the crown started making it known that magic wasn't welcome here. But that one is still very much alive and well."

And with that, she disappeared back into the main house.

Sybil quickly entered the cottage at the very end, leaving the middle one for Elric and Jessamine in the next. He stood there, a bit unsure of where to go until he looked over at Jessamine's soft smile.

She looked right at him and said, "Good night, Elric."

She always called him by his name. Not Deathless One, no honorary title or even referring to him as a god. To her, he was just Elric.

And that made up his mind. After everything they had done today, he didn't want to be alone. And if he was reading her expression correctly, neither did she.

The door to his own cottage forgotten, he followed her to the farthest cottage. Jessamine hadn't closed the door behind her, as though she knew he would follow her like a moth to a flame. And why wouldn't he? When there was so much comfort in each other, there was no way he was going to let her wander too far from his side.

The room within had indeed changed to reflect Jessamine's desires. He recognized the soft creature comforts from her memories. A four-poster feather bed with a blanket of the lightest blue filled most of the space, and a warm fire already crackled in the hearth made of pristine white stone. And then there was the mirror. A massive, well-over-seven-foot-tall mirror took up a good portion of the back wall right beside a warm wooden vanity.

She sat down at the vanity, already pulling her hair over her shoulder. She looked so prim and proper sitting there like that. All he wanted was to run his fingers through those strands and muss it all over again.

He much preferred his little hellion. The witch who had come to life under his touch and burned with need just as she burned with power was far more intriguing than the princess who expected him to bend a knee to her desires. But, he supposed, he did quite like the princess as well.

She opened the drawer, a curious expression on her face as she drew out a silver-handled brush. "Would you mind?"

He was a god. He had brought kingdoms to the ground and forced kings to bow on their hands and knees before him. Elric had seen countless people die, begging him to save them, and he had not done a single thing to help.

But if this woman asked him to brush her hair, then he would damn well brush her hair.

He lulled her into relaxation as he brought the brush through the very ends first, making sure that he didn't tug too hard on any of the knots that were there from days of travel. But he watched her in the mirror, keeping his gaze on the beauty of her expression as she tilted her head back into him. Her eyes drifted shut, that long neck with its silver scar bared to his rapturous gaze. She made a little hum in the back of her throat, and everything in him tensed.

What was it about this woman? She barely even had to exist, and he was hard as stone. He wanted her every moment of the day. From the first morning look, when she teased him with those long lashes, to the end of the day, when she was bone tired and yet still trusted him to take care of her.

Elric had never experienced this heady emotion in his many lifetimes. Everything about her was a siren song he didn't know how to escape.

"You look beautiful," he murmured, leaning down to press his lips to her neck. "Absolutely delicious, princess."

"Delicious?"

"I would like nothing more than to feast upon you."

He looked into the mirror to see her smiling. She lifted her hand, reaching up to place those delicate fingers on the back of his head. Together, they were a picture of wanton desire. Her cheeks burnished with a red stain, the deep hollows of her collarbone calling out for him to taste.

Dragging his hand down her raised arm, he held her gaze as his fingers met the buttons that dotted down the front of her bodice. The red on her cheeks became more pronounced as he popped one button, then the next, dancing down the entire line until her bodice sagged open. He slowly slid his hand underneath the fabric.

They both sighed at the first touch of skin on skin. He hadn't seen her in such a long time. They'd been busy, yes, but he would have taken her every single day, multiple times, if she'd let him.

Keeping his gaze on hers in the mirror, he flicked his thumb over her nipple, circling the peak until it became hard enough to see through the thin fabric.

"I want to touch you," he murmured against her throat. "I want to hear those little noises you make when you're so close to shattering. I want to feel you come wrapped around me like a fist."

"Then kiss me, Elric."

She'd already tilted her face toward him. All he had to do was seal his lips over hers and his restraint immediately snapped. His grip on her tightened. He wrapped his free hand around her neck, holding her in place so she had to endure the fervor of his need as he claimed and devoured her lips. His hand slid down her stomach, feeling the muscles tense there as he pushed her bodice down to the skirts around her waist.

"All of it," he growled against her mouth. "Take all of it off."

He wasn't sure who stood first, only that they did. He ripped his shirt over his head, tossing his pants down as quickly as he could until they were standing naked before each other. Bare as they were the first time.

This was different. They weren't drowning in the adrenaline of a successful battle. They weren't in a magical cave where they were wild and free to be themselves.

They were here, together, in a bedroom with soft firelight that turned her skin from pale to pristine marble. Her dark hair had been brushed into a waterfall that fell over her shoulders, the dark locks glistening like oil poured over water. She was beyond stunning. She was beauty incarnate, and he had never seen a creature such as this. The shadows between her ribs called to him. The dusty pink of her nipples made his mouth water, and the dark thatch of hair that hid her from his sight made him want to throw her to the ground and claim her with animalistic need.

"Elric," she whispered, perhaps growing a little uncomfortable with his staring. "Would you like me to get onto the bed?"

"No," he growled, his voice barely recognizable. "No, I want you to come over here, turn that ass to me, and hold on to the bedpost."

"The post?"

But she did as he said. She walked over to him and turned, her hands wrapping around the post. The mirror gave him the perfect angle to watch her. He could see everything from where he stood. Her pretty face and the bright red flush traveling down to her chest. And all he had to do was glance down to admire the round peach of her ass and the delicate arch of her spine.

She met his gaze in the mirror and held on to the post without him having to remind her. It made her back arch so perfectly, with a little shadow in the dip, and he had to plant his hand there. He had to put his palm right in that hollow she'd created.

He said nothing. He just kept his gaze locked with hers as he slowly sank to his knees behind her. Pressing her down, giving him the best view in the world as she leaned just right.

The visuals were the first thing he had to give up, but he was graced instead with her taste. He buried himself in her, licking through her folds as her flavor exploded on his tongue. She was salty and earthy and everything a woman should be.

Her moan echoed in his ears. The perfect sound. The only sound that he wanted to hear as the faintest creak from the bedpost warned him that her grip had tightened.

Elric worked her as though he were a dying man. He needed her to know that he adored her. That of all the witches he would meet, she was forever the one that he wanted. The only one who made him feel like a person, and so he poured those feelings into her flesh.

Every lick, every suck, every lingering stroke of his tongue was made to make her addicted to him. He didn't give her a break. Not when her legs started to shake, nor when her knees buckled. He just wrapped his arm around her hips and held her there until she shrieked his name.

He could feel her pulsing, just as he said he'd wanted to. Clenching around his tongue, but that wasn't even enough. So he buried two fingers inside of her as well, right at the peak of her orgasm, and savored the sudden choked sound she made and how her entire body sagged into him.

"Perfect," he muttered against her skin, pressing a kiss to the back of each thigh. "Truly perfect."

"Elric," she whimpered, regaining her footing.

But he wasn't done with her. Not yet. So he straightened behind her, repositioning her hands so she was upright again. Holding on to her hip with one hand, he gripped himself with the other and met her gaze in the mirror.

"Look at yourself," he said, notching the head of his cock against her folds. "Watch how beautiful you are when you take me."

Her mouth dropped open and her eyes rolled back in her head as he sank into her, inch by warm, wet inch. He took his time indulging himself. He wanted to feel her this time. There was no rush, no hurry. He wanted this moment to be imprinted on their minds forever.

"Eyes on our reflection, Jessamine." He gathered her hair in his hand, tugging her head back so she was forced to look at the mirror. Those pretty dark eyes were so wide, so needy, as he drew out of her.

"Try harder," he said as her eyes drifted shut again. He wanted her to see them. To watch them. To see the absolute vision of their pleasure as he slammed back in.

They both groaned together, the guttural sounds so perfect in the still quiet of the room. Raw and unbound, he fucked her. Pounding against those pretty round globes and watching her blush spread over her entire body. She was breathing hard now, and so was he. The sway of her body, the way she took him so well, even the way she looked in the mirror and fought so hard to keep her eyes open. All of it captivated him.

"Give it to me," he rasped. "All of it, princess."

She clenched around him, so hard it made him see stars, and then he could feel her exploding around him. Every tiny grasp of her muscles, every twitch of her body that surrounded him.

Elric tumbled into pleasure after her, incapable of denying what her body wanted from him. He pulsed deep inside her, one fist holding her hair like reins and his other clutching her hip, perhaps a little too tight. By all the magic in this realm, she made him feel like he was so much more than just a god of the dead.

Breathing hard, he released her hair in favor of her throat as he gently drew her back to standing. Leaning her back against his chest, he took all of her weight with an arm around her waist.

"You did so well," he murmured against her shoulder. "So well."

"I don't even know my own name right now," she replied. The sound of her laughter was music to his ears, but it still wasn't quite enough.

Some dark part of him cried out for more. He needed excess from her, from this. He wasn't reassured that this was real between them. After all they had done today, after all *he* had done, he needed to know that she didn't look at him any differently. He had played the role of god perhaps a little too well, but to her, he never wanted to be that.

So he guided her to the bed, arranging her body comfortably with her head on a pillow and the blankets pulled away from her overheated skin. She gave him a sleepy smile as he coasted his hand along her ribs, but her sweet expression turned into a frown as he lowered himself between her legs.

"What are you doing?" she asked, those brows furrowed.

"I am a god, Jessamine. Do you really think I would be satisfied by that alone?" He knew the smile on his face was wolfish. "Relax, gravesinger. Let me take care of you."

Though her muscles were loose, he felt them tense again when he gave her another long, slow lick. Poor thing, he didn't intend to be finished with her for a few hours yet, at least. Even then, he wasn't sure he'd ever get enough.

8

The next morning, Jessamine rolled over and traced the outline of Elric's features with her gaze. He really was beautiful when he was in repose like this. Sunlight filtered through the tiny window in the cottage, dancing along his austere nose and the faint frown lines along his forehead. Even in sleep, he always looked a little troubled. Like he couldn't get away from the demons of his past.

She breathed out a long sigh of contentment. She'd never get used to waking up next to him. He was like a marble statue carved by an artist who knew what was deep inside her most private dreams. And he was hers. For now, at least. Jessamine knew it was foolish to believe she could keep a god forever.

Something in her heart skipped a beat every time she looked at him. And then there was the sex, of course. She couldn't think of anything better than that godly experience. Even now, she throbbed between her legs at the mere thought of his touch.

But she also had to respect that he wasn't just a god anymore. This body he was now in was very much human, or at least it seemed to be. He got hungry and tired. He needed rest less than she or Sybil did, of course, but he was sleeping so soundly now that it felt wrong to wake him.

She understood why people worshipped him and his siblings, though. If she'd seen him stride out of a forest toward her, she would have known what he was instantly. The aura that surrounded him was magnetic. She wanted to fall onto her knees before him. She wanted to worship the ground at his feet because it felt like that was what he deserved.

Or perhaps, what he demanded.

Slipping out of the bed, she tried to be as quiet as a mouse. There was a robe that looked almost like a dressing gown in her pack. She usually threw it on top of a shift if she was going out in public, but it would be good enough to sneak into the kitchen for a cup of morning tea. No one should be awake yet, anyway. This was an hour reserved for those trying to hide or those who couldn't sleep.

Jessamine supposed she was both of those people. Hiding who she was and why she was here. But also someone who couldn't find rest even after she'd long past hit exhaustion.

Perhaps it was because this wasn't how she had expected to live her life. She'd planned to be a queen, ruling a kingdom of people who loved her. A queen who still had her mother at her side, making it easy to run a kingdom. A queen who had a husband that loved her, supported her, and didn't try to kill her on their wedding day. Of course, none of that was going to happen for her now. Maybe it never would have.

Ducking out of the cottage, she padded her way toward the main house and the kitchen, which hopefully held some tea to wake her.

Her mind ran wild with all the things she had to accomplish here. Find Fortuna. Understand what connection her cousin had with Leon. Figure out why her cousin would betray her own family. The Pleasure District would make it easy enough for her to get around, but where Fortuna made her home, she had no idea.

She could already see this area of town had changed in the years since she'd last been here. The best she could do for herself was find a way forward. First, they would need to figure out disguises. Wandering around like grimy little cretins would certainly not do. Everyone in the Pleasure District had a certain style.

Perhaps they could steal clothing, like Sybil already had. There were plenty of vendors who could easily be distracted while Sybil or Elric took what they wanted. Maybe he even knew a spell to conjure the clothing she needed, although she had a feeling that wasn't Elric's kind of magic. Shadow illusions, yes, but those wouldn't be solid enough to fool anyone.

Opening the door, she stepped into the room full of birds and came up short as she saw Elissa Burnham sitting at her table with a regal-looking parrot perched on the back of the chair beside her. They both froze and looked at her, as though she had interrupted a rather important meeting.

"Sorry," she said slowly, moving to the back of the kitchen to pour herself a cup of the tea that was already steeping. "I didn't mean to interrupt. I didn't think anyone would be awake at this time of day."

"I didn't sleep," Elissa replied primly.

"Magic has a way of doing that to people."

"You've actually arrived just in time. I have some questions, if you'd be so kind as to answer them."

There was no question there at all, Jessamine mused. She chose a pretty teacup with blue butterflies painted on it and took her time pouring her tea. Even though she knew that it was important to answer the questions of this new witch, she also very much realized that she was the rightful queen of this kingdom. A fact that Elissa Burnham may have forgotten.

Settling herself opposite the other two, she took a sip of the scalding-hot tea before lifting her brow and inclining her head to indicate that Elissa could ask her question now.

"You said you were here for Fortuna Beaumont," the other witch started.

"Yes, we are."

"Do you have any idea how powerful that woman is?"

"I have some semblance of an idea." Jessamine sipped at her tea again. "I must admit, I have been away from court for quite some time. Dying tends to do that to a person. So I do not know what she has done or where she has been of late. That's why we're here. I remember her living in the Pleasure District, and I know for certain that business would not change so very quickly. The woman is particular about her money."

"That she is." Elissa shared a look with the parrot before clearing her throat. "She basically runs the entirety of the district now, but that is almost certainly because the king himself has gifted it to her. If anyone speaks ill of her, King Leon Bishop is certain to get involved."

So, she'd sunk her talons into him far more than Jessamine had expected. Although she supposed it made sense. If Fortuna wanted to ensure her position here never changed, she would need to make the king do more of the work for her.

"With her hand on the cock of the king, it's much easier to do whatever she wants, whenever she wants." Jessamine shook her head in disgust. "She always was remarkably ambitious."

"It's more than that. The rumor is that she's…" Elissa leaned forward as though the secret was too dangerous to say out loud. "A witch."

Jessamine leaned forward as well and whispered back, "*You* are a witch."

Elissa's face blanched, and she leaned back so quickly it appeared Jessamine had slapped her. "I am not… well, I *am*, but… Fortuna Beaumont is impressively powerful, and no one can stand against her."

The door closed quietly behind them, and Jessamine saw that Sybil had joined them. The dark witch snorted, her hair wild around her head and a shawl around her shoulders as she staggered toward the tea.

"If you think no one can stand against her, then you've never met Jessamine. The woman is ruthless."

"The Deathless One is ruthless," Jessamine corrected. "He's the one with all the ideas."

"You're the one who stood in the middle of a group of men, naked and covered in blood, and then cursed a man to be perceived by everyone else as a simpleton while knowing that he was once great." She poured herself a cup of tea, leaned against the counter, and then breathed in the scent of the black tea. "You could have just killed him and put him out of his misery. Instead, you wanted him to suffer for years to come. He had at least another ten years in him."

"More than that."

"He was infected."

Jessamine snapped her fingers. "Oh, that's right. Do you suppose if the infection continues to advance that he would remember who he once was, wandering the streets as an infected, but everyone would still see him as nothing more than a doddering fool?"

"It was a rather lazy spell."

"Well, I'll say." Jessamine shook her head. "I didn't think that one through. He'll infect a lot of people if they don't see him as such. Sounds rather dangerous to leave him in the Factory District."

"He'll only infect the other Iron Knuckles."

"That's all right, then."

Elissa's eyes pinged back and forth between the two of them. She clearly wasn't following the conversation in the slightest, but she was trying her best. "The two of you talk about dastardly things so easily."

Sybil looked at Jessamine, then Elissa, then back to Jessamine. "We're witches. Of course we do."

Well, it wasn't the best thing to say. Elissa was already a little skittish about the whole thing, and now here they were, talking about the horrors they'd inflicted and expecting that she would be fine with it.

A ring on Elissa's left hand rattled against her porcelain teacup as she lifted it to her lips. "It's just all very... terrifying."

"Witches don't live peaceful lives," Sybil said, her gaze narrowing on the other woman. "I could teach you, if you were interested in being taught, which I don't think you are. I think you lived in this comfortable bubble and were certain that if you called on a god, you had done all you could. Then the blame was no longer on your shoulders. You'd tried your best. And nothing would change or happen, so nothing was your responsibility. All the gods were dead, after all. What were the chances that one of them would answer you?"

Elissa's face went even more pale. "I want to be a witch. Just like my mother."

"Do you? Why are you so afraid of the magic, then?"

"I'm not." But then Elissa rubbed the new wound in the center of her chest. "It's just… not what I thought it would be."

"Surely you saw your mother's well of magic?" Sybil sipped her tea, then caught Jessamine's glance. With a quirk of her lips, she made it very clear that she was doing the same thing she had once done to Jessamine.

The ancient witch in the room did not look like the crone she was. And yet, Sybil was clearly the witch who would teach all the young women who came to them, even if that meant she had to do so with a little tough love.

"I saw it only a few times. She kept it hidden." Elissa's hand never moved from her own chest.

"Good. Keep yours hidden as well. It's unlikely that other people will see it, but if they do, they're far more likely to want to hurt you. And did you feel the power swell last night?"

"It felt like a wave," she whispered. The parrot stepped a little closer to her, reaching out with a wing and gently placing the tips of its feathers on Elissa's shoulder. "I could feel it cresting over my head, and I could either drown in it or I could allow it to sink into me."

Sybil nodded. "That's the connection you have with the Deathless One. He can give you power, and he can take it away. He doesn't even need to be in front of you to do it. We have a patron who gives more than he receives, and for that, you should be grateful. Few people are given the chance to explore their witchcraft, let alone those of us who were born for darker things."

Jessamine frowned and interrupted. "What power surge? I felt nothing."

Sybil lifted the teacup up to her mouth, her eyes glittering with laughter as she took a hefty sip. "That's because you were the reason for the power surge, my dear. Bravo, by the way. If I could feel it all the way in the other cabin, it must have been quite remarkable."

"Oh gods." She pressed the backs of her cool hands against her suddenly burning cheeks. "You've got to be kidding me."

The other two women burst into laughter, and soon enough, she joined them. Jessamine hadn't felt like she was among friends in a long time. But right now, they were just three women laughing about a sexual experience with a god. She wasn't even sure her friends in the castle *would* have laughed at such a thing.

She'd missed this sense of camaraderie. A family that had chosen to build itself was so much stronger together than they were apart. And yes, she didn't know Elissa all that well yet, but they were bound through their dedication to a god.

She shook her head, still laughing with the other two. "We all have our own way of worshipping, I suppose."

Lips pressed against the top of her head, just before a deep voice said, "And how talented you are at worshipping, *princess*."

The shocked expression on her face set the other two off into peals of laughter that filled the room. Jokingly, she glared at Elric as he joined them at the table. But even he had a soft expression on his face.

This felt like... home. Not the building or where they'd rested their heads, but in the friends that laughed with them and the people who felt like a warm hug just to be around.

She tucked her hair behind her ears and listened to the conversation that flowed easily among them now. They talked about simple things. Sybil needed to find new herbs, but she'd be happy to teach Elissa some herb magic. Elric told them both that he expected more sacrifices, and the two women laughed at his harsh tone as though they knew he was joking. More ribbing came about the magical spillage that had happened from their coupling.

It was light and easy until Elissa cleared her throat and stood. "If you're going to find Fortuna, then you need to look the part. You can't be walking around the Pleasure District like a trio of beggars who accidentally stumbled into the city. No one will talk to you."

"I think that's where you come in," Jessamine replied. "I had hoped you would cast some pity on a trio of beggars like ourselves."

"That is where you are wrong. I have very little money to my name. Unfortunately, this house is rather expensive to maintain, and a lifestyle in the Pleasure District certainly does not lend itself to wealth." A secretive smile twisted her mouth. "I do know someone who wouldn't notice if a few of her products are missing, though. She's a bit of a legend around here, but one who has been a thorn in my side for far too long."

"A thorn who won't recognize me?"

Elissa shrugged. "Who knows? I'm sure some people here still recall the princess of Inverholm, but maybe they don't."

She wasn't sure if this was a good idea or not. People could easily recognize her, even if Elissa's friend didn't know her. Frowning, she asked, "How well do you know this woman?"

"When I started my career here, I wasn't breeding birds. I wanted to be a fashion designer. My mother had skills in sewing, and I adored designing new dresses for both of us to wear. Unfortunately, another in the Pleasure District had different ideas. Fortuna Beaumont's mother, in fact. She made sure none of the ladies bought clothing from my mother until all the money just… dried up." Elissa crossed her arms over her chest. "No matter. I like breeding birds. Birds make sense where people don't. But this woman was the Beaumont woman's best friend, and I would still love an opportunity to rob this woman blind."

"So not so much of a friend, then."

"It's hard for me to call anyone what I really think of them. Friend, enemy. We're in the Pleasure District, Lady Jessamine. Those words are one and the same here."

It was a risk they would have to take. Jessamine glanced over at Elric and waited to see what he would say. The thoughtful expression on his face gave her pause.

But finally, he nodded. "We'll seek out your... friend tomorrow."

9

Jessamine only made it to dinner before Sybil cornered her. She was walking down the hall toward the exit of the main building when suddenly a dark hand grabbed her arm and yanked her into a closet.

She barely balanced the cup of thin broth in her hand. "Scalding-hot soup," she hissed as the door closed behind her and they were both sent careening into darkness.

"You're a witch."

"I thought burning was something witches worried about," she muttered.

Sybil lit a candle that cast shadows from beneath her face, sending her scowl into an even more dangerous-looking expression. "That's not funny."

"It's a little funny."

"It's not." Sybil gestured with the candle at her soup. "Put it down, then, we have work to do."

"What work? I'm going to eat this and go to bed. I think I've done enough work." Leaning forward, she blew out the candle in Sybil's hand and then reached for the door.

But the handle was locked, likely by magic, and the candle immediately burst back into flames. The orange pillar stretched nearly six inches high before it died back down to a reasonable size, reflecting Sybil's annoyance.

Sighing, Jessamine put the cup of soup down on a shelf. They were surrounded by cleaning supplies. Four brooms, buckets, glass containers filled with what she could only assume was birdseed considering all the animals Elissa had in this place. She really had hoped to get away with not having to do all this tonight, but apparently she didn't have much of a choice.

"Fine. What is it?"

"Elissa needs to be brought into the coven."

"She already has. Elric cracked her chest open and gave her all the magic, remember? We both watched that."

"Yes, but that doesn't mean she's part of the coven. Not yet, at least." Sybil handed the candle over to Jessamine. "We need to find out what kind of witch she is."

"So you're going to beat her over the head with a black book like you did me? I think the poor thing has gone through enough lately."

Another glare nearly leveled her. "You needed to be beaten over the head with a book. Elissa is delicate. She needs a lighter hand to prove that this is something she might want."

"Why didn't I get a lighter hand?"

She could answer that question for herself. But Sybil's expression was very obvious on its own.

Jessamine rolled her eyes. "Fine. Why am I involved, though? I'm not part of the coven."

"Oh, I apologize. I didn't realize the princess needed her beauty rest and didn't want to see the coven at work." Sybil crossed her arms over her chest.

"By all the gods dead and alive, you are the worst friend I've ever had," Jessamine muttered before grabbing the now-unlocked door and throwing it open. "Fine. What are we doing?"

"Lovely! I knew you'd be interested. Get Elissa and join me in the garden."

Sybil waltzed away, clearly pleased that she had gotten her way. The ragged ends of her skirts flared around a corner, and then she was gone.

Muttering under her breath about witches with personalities that were too big for their own right, Jessamine made her way to Elissa's room. A few knocks and the door swung open.

Elissa's eyes were ringed with red. The hollows around them were filled with shadows, and she looked like she hadn't slept in a week. Probably hadn't. The woman had gone through so much in the short amount of time since they'd burst into her home. Jessamine wasn't surprised in the slightest that she was exhausted.

"Would you come with me?" Jessamine asked.

"Why?"

"Sybil has something planned."

Elissa started to close the door. "I think I'd like to be alone tonight."

Well, that left her no choice. Jessamine caught her hand on the edge of the door and forced it to stay open or crush her fingers. "It's not something scary. I promise. We're just... finding out what kind of witch you're going to be, apparently."

"I still don't know if I even want to be a witch."

"And it's still too late for you to be second-guessing all of this." Jessamine smiled. "I know it's a lot. But a walk in the moonlight with a couple witches isn't going to kill you."

"It sounds like something that definitely will get me killed." But Elissa sighed, settling a silver wrap around her shoulders, and came out of her bedroom.

She was such a tiny little thing. The moonlight framed her lithe body beneath her pale nightgown as they both strolled toward the gardens in the back. The night seemed to come alive around them. Moonlight turned everything molten silver, with the trees' leaves edged in a shimmering glow. Fireflies had woken, each of them dancing around the petals of flowers that filled the air with the sweet scent of peonies. It really was lovely back here on the meandering paths through a flower garden that rivaled any Jessamine had seen in her life.

And there, in the center of this small garden, sat Sybil in a circle of candles. The elderly witch had spread her colorful skirts around her, and somehow those gave her an aura of wisdom. Each of the white pillars burned merrily, and the air was filled with magic. Jessamine could feel it dancing over her, like little bubbles of fizzling power popping all along her skin.

"Welcome, witches," Sybil said, her voice carrying through the garden with purpose. "We gather together to welcome a new witch into the coven, and to discover what power you might have."

Elissa looked at Jessamine, then back at the other witch. "Me?"

"You," Jessamine replied with a soft chuckle. She nudged her forward. "Step into the circle with Sybil."

As much as Jessamine wanted to join them, she knew she couldn't. Some part of her still could not fully *be* part of this coven. Someday, she would have to return to being a princess. She had other responsibilities and so much more to worry about. Joining the coven felt like a promise she wasn't all that certain she could keep. For now, she was a gravesinger, and that was enough.

So she stepped back, sitting on a small bench near the circle and leaning forward to brace her elbows on her knees.

Sybil extended her hands for Elissa to take, gently guiding the other woman onto the soft ground. They knelt together, a picture of two opposites. One pale woman with ghostly hair in the moonlight, the other all shadows and darkness.

"Do not be afraid," Sybil said. "There is nothing scary about finding your own power."

"It feels terrifying," Elissa replied. "I don't know who I am anymore. One moment, I was just a woman who bred birds, and now? Now what am I?"

"A witch, darling."

"Is that a good thing?"

"It is what you make it." Sybil's hands tightened on hers, drawing Elissa's fingers to open, palms up. "Being a witch is a wondrous thing. Do you remember the kind of magic your great-great-grandmother had?"

"She controlled bodies."

Well, that was ominous. Jessamine frowned and tried to decipher the expression that crossed Sybil's face. Was that a bad thing? They could certainly use someone that powerful in their coven, but also, what did that even mean?

Sybil revealed no emotion, however. "That is a rare gift. You fear it?"

"My family was known to do terrible things with that power. My mother was the first to go against that dark magic, and she died for it. I don't want to do what they did, but I don't want to die either." Elissa cleared her throat. "I'm not sure I'd be very good at any magic, though. Look at what I did to… to…"

Jessamine couldn't help herself. "My power has gotten out of control before as well. It's not the same, I suppose, because it isn't really my magic. I take it directly from Elric and turn it into something else. But I know what it feels like to have the intent to do one thing and then somehow end up doing it wrong."

A flashing memory of Benji choking to death in front of her turned her palms sweaty. She wiped them on the knees of her pants before leaning forward again. She met Elissa's startled gaze with a soft smile.

The young woman's throat bobbed in a harsh swallow. "I'm terrified that it will happen again."

"It happens. We learn and we move on. Living in our mistakes is like walking with ghosts. Why cling to them?"

"Walking with ghosts," Elissa muttered. "I suppose you're right. I feel like I've done that my entire life. My family line has always held on to that bottle of power with far too much reverence. It was the last bit of power we had left from your god, but we wouldn't use it even in the most dire of circumstances. My mother taught me the old spells, but she never even let me hold that vial of power. She told me I wasn't good enough to use that magic yet. I wasn't mature enough. And even after she'd passed, I couldn't make myself touch it. Not even to save Sarah."

"Familial ties run deep," Sybil said, shifting in front of her to draw the attention back to the circle. "But now is not about the women who came before you. It is about you, dear Elissa. Joining the coven with an open mind and also perhaps with the intent to learn what it is that you can do. By yourself. Not with anyone else watching you."

Jessamine watched the young witch draw her strength into herself. Perhaps it was the stillness of the garden and the magic that now soaked even the flower petals with drips of power. Or perhaps it was merely that she was ready for this. After all those years of carrying the expectations of her family tree, now she could finally do something with herself.

"Are you ready?" Sybil asked.

Elissa nodded.

"Breathe with, me then, witch. Together we draw the magic from your chest. It is a process, and you should not fear it. Fighting me will only hinder us."

Perhaps Elissa's face was a little paler than before, but she did nod. "I won't fight you."

"Good." Sybil turned her head to the side, and Jessamine heard her mutter, "Because it will really hurt if you do."

The two women drew slightly closer. Sybil tilted her head back to the moon and started to chant. The words were from a language long dead, impossible to understand, but beautiful all the same. They bubbled through the air, some of them sharp and jagged as knives, others soft and rounded as river stones. Jessamine could feel them cresting and breaking over her head, urging her forward.

Every bit of her wanted to walk into that circle. She wanted to step inside of it and feel her own magic, even though there was an aching hollow inside of her that screamed she had none. Not like the witches. Jessamine had not cracked herself open and taken in all that he was.

Voices all murmured in her mind at the same time. They all chanted out the same thing.

Deathless One.

Over and over again until the words reached a crescendo, and then it all… popped.

Gasping, she opened her eyes and stared into the center of the circle as a wind gust blew around them, suddenly there when there had been no wind at all. All the candles went out at the same time, leaving them all seated in silence as the coiled smoke wafted up where there had once been light.

Elissa let out a little whimper. She dropped Sybil's hands and then frantically tugged at her nightgown. She ripped at the fabric, tearing it right down the neck and revealing the darkened fissure that all the witches shared. But now there was more to the shadows in that crater between her ribs. They were moving like eels, stretching out into the darkness, and then, suddenly, Jessamine could feel it.

Magic.

It billowed through them, not like Sybil's magic of sharpness and softness. This was like silk. Like long tendrils of silk floating in the air, stretching upward. They all looked up as the stars seemed to fall among them, tiny pinpricks of light that peeled out of the very night sky and rained down like snow.

Jessamine held her breath as the beauty of the night sky itself captured her heart. She couldn't believe what they were seeing. Surely magic couldn't peel the very stars away from their home, and yet, she was seeing it happen.

Tears dripped down Elissa's cheeks as she reached her hands up and caught one of the stars in her hands. The light glowed through her fingers.

"What is this?" Elissa asked.

"Some call them cosmic witches," Sybil replied with a bright grin on her face. "You'll be able to read the future in the stars, if you wish. I knew some cosmic witches whose power was directly tied to the sky, however. The full moon will make you the most powerful, but you will feel bursts of power at other times as well. The new moon is when you should set intentions, the waxing moon for manifestation. Oh, I wish we were still in the old coven's home. There are books there that would help guide you better than I can."

But Elissa was barely listening. Instead, she was staring at the star in her hands in shock. More stars landed on her hair and shoulders, leaving her glittering in the moonlight.

"A cosmic witch," she whispered.

Jessamine slowly stood, making sure to get Sybil's quick nod of permission before entering the circle. And then she crouched in front of Elissa, grasping her hands in her own. "You are everything you ever hoped to be."

Elissa's eyes flicked up to her own. They were wide and full of shock, but there was something like belief there now as well. "Is this what it means to be in a coven?"

Jessamine tilted her head in question.

"To feel so... full."

Again, that hollow inside of her twisted. She didn't know if that's what it felt like. She'd only felt full like that when her mother was alive, and, she supposed, a bit when she realized how powerful the Deathless One would make her.

Sybil rushed forward at that, grabbing on to Elissa's hands and drawing her toward the house. "Come, bring your stars with you. I want to see what you can do with them."

They left Jessamine alone in the garden, still sitting in an empty circle with no more magic swirling around her. That hollow wanted to split, fracture, and ache even more. But now she was alone here, and again she wondered if she just wasn't doing enough.

"Nightmare?" The dark tones interrupted her thoughts.

"I should have known you would be here," she whispered.

He crouched beside her, his fingers finding the dirt and letting it trail through those long digits. "Do you regret it?"

She looked over into those dark eyes, so like her own, and she knew the question he was asking. She just didn't know how to answer. Not yet, at least.

"What would I become if I truly joined your coven?"

He sucked in a deep breath before rasping, "Endless."

"In power or in spirit?"

"Both. Neither. No one knows. No gravesinger has ever joined the coven. The rumor has always been that to do so is to join with me. Such closeness to a god has never been accomplished. I do not know if you would even survive it." He held his dirt-streaked hand out for her to take. "Come with me, nightmare. Such questions are not for late nights."

She took his hand, but that hollow feeling seemed to expand and grow into an ache that was hard to ignore.

10

He'd never understand witches. Elric stood outside the shop that was much more traditional than Elissa's birdcage. A classic square building with pretty white shutters and warm wooden walls, it was exactly what he'd expected the shop to look like. Even right down to the white fencing that was truly remarkable to look at. Completely white, enchanted to look like it was dusted with pearls. Beautiful, and not at all the kind of place from which his ladies should be stealing clothing.

Who was he to tell them what to do, though? Tonight Elric was just the muscle outside the door, with his eyes on the crowd that passed by. Apparently, he would not be helpful in this endeavor, likely because he was too much of a distraction himself. At least, that was what they told him.

He had a feeling both Jessamine and Sybil thought he would get overly bored with the whole deception and just start taking things. If someone tried to stop him, he was always happy to kill them. A human life was simply less valuable to him than the clothing that would get them one step closer to their goal.

And Jessamine's goal was his now. It was the only purpose he had while he floundered, trying to remember what it was to be a god again, and what he was supposed to be doing here.

Shaking his head, he tried to ignore those thoughts. They tended to make him spiral, and he had a job to do.

A woman strutted up to him wearing a tiny hat with a large blue plume on top. Her hair was so tightly coiled in ringlets they didn't look real, and that annoyed him. They looked like snakes next to her face. He barely even glanced at the matching blue gown that was sewn so tightly onto her body he wondered if she could get out without cutting it off.

"Well, you are certainly quite the vision." She looked him up and down in a hungry way that made him want to tear off his skin. "I haven't seen you in these parts before. Surely you aren't here for a gown?"

He looked back at the shop, then looked at her. "No entry at this time."

"Not even for little ol' me?" She pursed her lips, clearly trying to persuade him that he was attracted enough to let her in.

"Not even for you."

"I could make it worth your while." Her hand brushed his chest, fingers dancing along the lines of his muscles.

Immediately, dark memories flashed in front of his eyes.

Countless witches had done the same thing to him. Witches who had cocked their hips to the side and devoured him with their gaze. He was useful to them. He would be sacrificed to the few so the many could survive, but they had used him and they had twisted his mind just like this woman was trying to do.

Anger flared in his chest. It took everything he had in him not to snap. He could not be cajoled by a pretty face simply because she thought he was a weak man. He was a god, and for the life of him, all he wanted was to be left alone.

But then a small hand pressed against his lower back, and he felt himself ease like a cool wind had blown across his overheated face.

Jessamine leaned around him, a sharp smile on her face. "I'm sorry. Did you not hear him?"

"I heard him." The woman's expression tightened. "And who are you? His keeper?"

"In a way."

"You must be new to the Pleasure District, darling. We share all our good fortune here." The woman licked her fucking lips just like the witches used to. "And this one is very good fortune indeed."

Panic bloomed in his chest. He could feel his throat closing up and the guilt in his chest bubbling, because what if this woman was right? What if he really was only useful to satisfy the needs of others? This life was meant to be a new reckoning for him. A new coven, a new future, a new gravesinger who looked at him like he was more than just a tool.

But what if this was all a glimmer of nothing but fool's hope?

"Oh, I know my good fortune, but I do not share. Unless, of course, it is sharing in blood. I partake in the old ways, stranger. If you want him, you can try and take him from me." Along with Jessamine's words came the tug of magic from her side and the flare of desire that spread from his lower back straight to his cock. He almost arched into her touch, and perhaps did a bit because the stranger's eyes followed his movement before looking back at Jessamine.

"Interesting," the woman said—but she made no other protest before hurrying away.

He could hardly breathe after the magic Jessamine had siphoned off. She'd been ready to attack another woman for him, just because they'd made him uncomfortable.

Elric wasn't sure what to do. He was a god, after all. He should be able to protect himself, but knowing that she was so willing to do so for him at the merest hint of offense?

It made every hair on his body stand on end.

"You okay?" Jessamine asked, her eyes on his every move.

"Decidedly uncomfortable now, but yes. I am well."

Perhaps she could see how heated his cheeks were, or that his ears were aflame. Because a slow smile spread across Jessamine's lips, and she did her best not to roll those pretty eyes. "Deathless One, why don't you go wander? We're almost done here."

"How are you stealing the clothes?"

"Elissa is rather impressive. She has a bag from her mother that appears to be bottomless. Where the clothes are going, I have no idea. But we've been stuffing them in one by one while poor Sybil is torn apart by the harpy who owns the place. She's been forcing the shopkeeper to alter a dress while still on her form but keeps spelling the needles to prick her skin. There are at least fifteen blood spots, and they've gotten into four shouting matches already. Apparently, she's the most difficult client the woman has ever met." She huffed out a chuckle. "We'll be set for a while, I imagine."

"Good enough. What do you want me to do?"

"I want you to do what you want to do. You don't have to stand in front of this door and be subjected to… that." Her gaze was worried as it skated over his features, perhaps seeing how rattled he really was.

An escape sounded better than the alternative. So he decided to look over this Pleasure District a little more and headed down the small path to the street. Much of this place was unfamiliar to him, having changed dramatically in the 275 years since he'd last been here.

"Be safe," she breathed, but he would have heard her amid the screams of thousands. Elric knew her voice better than any other. His heart knew her every movement, her every tone, and every tiny bit of what made her… her.

Before he left, he took one last glance at the shop. Jessamine leaned out the door, keeping it slightly closed against her back. In comparison to the other women here, she stood out like a smudge of darkness, wearing a dusty black dress with an overlarge bodice that hung off her too-thin frame. The scar around her throat was bare for all to see, not to mention the others that they couldn't. All the marks of where she had almost died and where he simply hadn't let her.

How did he get so lucky as to find a woman like her? When there were countless who would have taken advantage of his weaknesses, she was the one to find him.

"Gravesinger," he said, his voice perhaps a little too loud. "I would worship at your altar if I had but a sacrifice worthy of you."

A pretty blush burned her cheeks. "Go on with yourself, Elric. Do what you must and then come home to me."

He sighed and disappeared into the crowd. It was easier to stay moving. No one suspected there was something odd about him when he didn't give them a chance to stare long enough. No one even attempted to talk with him as he made his way through the throngs of people. Sure, there were a few lingering looks from both men and women, but no one thought they could interrupt him.

And so Elric got lost in the crowds. He allowed himself to take a moment as he had many times when he was last alive. Whenever the witches allowed him outside of their coven home, or if he snuck out the way that he enjoyed, he always took a moment like this. Standing in the middle of a crowd with no one knowing who he was. He breathed in deeply and listened to all the conversations happening around him.

To his left, a man was buying a new dress for his mistress. He didn't want the woman only a few steps away to know, because she was his wife. In the back corner of the square, a little girl pointed out to her mother a window full of purebred cats. Their fluff looked so soft, and the little girl claimed she'd always wanted a kitten. But the mother sensed that there was something off about the cats, which there was. They were all spelled to look like cats, but really they were little spies who reported to the shopkeeper what people were looking to buy.

Elric turned away, listening to a group of women in the central square who had draped themselves beside a fountain. The statue in the middle was a beautiful nude woman pouring a pitcher of water into the pool below.

"Did you hear? Someone claimed the Deathless One is back," one said. Her flaxen hair was dangerously close to dipping into the water from where she lay, looking up at the clouds.

"Is he now?" replied a woman in a dark purple gown. She sat stiffly at the edge, likely because of the boning in her corset. "Do you think he could make us witches?"

"You shouldn't even joke about that. You know how the king feels about witchcraft."

"All the nobles hate witchcraft, but they always have. It doesn't mean we can't even talk about it." Purple Gown reached into the water and pulled out a gleaming coin. "Do you think if I made a wish to the Deathless One that he'd grant it?"

"We don't even know if he's really alive!"

"What if he is?"

"Then you making a wish to him is rather binding, and you don't want to bind yourself to a god. Who knows what he'll ask you to do in return?"

These were the musings of people who had lost their connection to the gods. A wish like that wasn't anything he could respond to, nor would he deign to do so. Wishes were the hopes and dreams of those who had nothing better to do. A sacrifice? Now that was a dedicated person who actually wanted his help. Not two women pretending at magic beside a pool of water.

As he turned to leave, he heard the one in the purple gown murmur something that made him pause. "If the gods are coming back, don't you think that's a good thing?"

"No. Not the Deathless One, at least. That right there is a villain, not a god."

"Or maybe he's come back to help all of us. Can you imagine? A coven of witches in this district? All the things they could do." A long, hopeful sigh trailed at the end of her words.

He could tell she was about to say words she couldn't take back. And some part of him whispered that this was his moment. All he had to do was encourage just one more word. So, with his power tingling at his fingers, he conjured all the shadows to him and spread them throughout the square. Her next words were amplified by magic that sparked and crackled around her. No one but a bonded witch would see his power, but ordinary mortals would yield to it nonetheless.

"I wish the Deathless One would give us proof that he's returned." She set the coin on her thumb and then flicked it into the fountain. It spun in the air, a glimmering silver piece that struck the water with a soft plop.

It appeared everyone had frozen, staring at the fountain with hopeful eyes or terrified gazes that feared what would come next.

He toyed with the thought of leaving them wondering. They should fear the gods, whether they were dead or not. He and his siblings had created a kingdom for them to live in and rules that should be followed, no matter what. He shouldn't need to prove himself.

And yet... some part of him wanted them to be afraid. Talking at a fountain about him and his coven could only bring about a darkness that none of them were prepared for.

With a flick of his fingers, shadows poured toward the fountain. They would be impossible to track to him, even if someone was looking right at him. He pulled shadows from nearby pots, plants, and even people. They weren't connected to him, but to everything else. No one was looking at him at all, because their eyes were on the fountain as if waiting for a miracle.

They had all forgotten that he was not his sister or his grandmother or any of the kindly gods.

A few people breathed a sigh of relief as nothing immediately happened in the fountain. No omniscient voice spoke to them through the stone figure and no wind swept throughout the courtyard. Some even chuckled as they all admitted they had thought, for a moment, that the gods were really returning.

"Wait!" the woman in the purple gown said, suddenly standing and almost falling as she stumbled away from the fountain. "It's not possible!"

He stood there, hidden in the crowd, as they all gasped and stared at the black tears that leaked out of the statue's eyes. And then it appeared as though dark blood began to pour out of the jug the statue held in its hand. Black as ink, with the faintest red hue. It filled the entire fountain with dark liquid that slowly spilled over the sides.

People screamed, rushing away from the water that poured out, threatening to overtake them. They couldn't run fast enough. And throughout all the chaos, he stood still and reveled in the madness that surrounded him.

He was still a god to be feared. He was still the Deathless One, the nightmare in the darkness. Though they feared him, they feared the loss of their lives more.

"He's returned!" someone screamed, their voice rising higher than all the others. "The Deathless One has returned!"

He certainly had. But he had a choice this time. No coven had summoned him; no witch tried to bend him to her will. He could be the god he once was, or he could become a god king who ruled this kingdom not just with a coven, but with a queen at his side.

The dark liquid paused, gathering back into itself and returning to the fountain. But it left a black smudge behind, words that, if anyone was brave enough to read, would reveal his message.

The woman in the purple gown was the first to approach, almost crouching as she braved the madness that had spilled out of the once-beautiful fountain.

"What does it say?" someone shouted.

"The king has returned for his queen," she read, her voice quivering.

"His queen?" another person asked.

He couldn't help himself. With another twist of his magic, shadows coiled around the statue. They gathered to create a dress that was eerily similar to the wedding gown Jessamine had been killed in. The crown he placed atop her head was the same Jessamine's mother had worn for years. He left the illusion for a few moments, until someone whispered, "Is that the Harmsworth crown?"

"But the Lady Jessamine is dead! The king threw her off the cliff's edge! What could it mean?"

Another person leaned to the side, muttering to their companion, "Didn't you hear something when you were in the Factory District last month? Rumblings about the princess being alive?"

"Yes, but that was right before the Iron Knuckles fell apart. They've been completely disbanded. Infection got all of them."

"But the Iron Knuckles were the ones containing the infection in that district. Didn't their leader work directly with the king?"

His work here was done. Elric let all of his shadows fall, and suddenly the square was sunny and bright once more, as though nothing had happened at all. More gasps echoed, some people even rubbing their eyes as though their sight was the problem.

Tucking his hands into his pockets, Elric whistled as he returned to the dress shop. Chaos needed to be sown in every district.

After all, it wouldn't do to let the king sleep well at night.

11

Nerves churned in her belly. Jessamine knew they were going to find Fortuna here. After all, the woman rarely left the Pleasure District. But she hadn't thought the mere anticipation of finding her cousin would be quite so terrifying.

They'd spent the last few days preparing for what to do and how to get to Fortuna. Elissa had some information on the woman, but not a lot. Which meant they'd needed to wander through the streets, asking people questions while avoiding bringing any sort of suspicion to themselves. Such was a task easier said than done.

Still, she'd found the address for Fortuna's house and eventually gotten too tired to wait. Elric felt the same, even if Sybil claimed the two of them were so impatient that they were likely to ruin the entire plan.

Night had fallen on the streets. As dark as it was, no one would see them. She wore all black, as did Elric. No one could even see her unless she lifted her face high enough to reveal her pale skin beneath the hood of her cloak. And even then, the moonlight turned her skin into such an unnatural color that perhaps someone would think they'd seen a ghost.

A soft chuckle escaped her at the thought as they rounded the last corner street they needed to traverse around.

"Care to share what is so entertaining?" Elric asked, his dark eyes constantly searching the streets for some unseen foe.

"I just had the thought that if someone saw me, they would think I was a ghost." Another giggle escaped her before she could catch it. "And wouldn't they be right?"

He cast her an annoyed glance. "You aren't a ghost."

"I'm dead, though."

"You have a body. Ghosts don't."

That stuck in her mind a little. He was right, and how odd it was to even think about that. "I suppose that is correct. What would that make me, then? A zombie?"

"Zombies don't have minds. They're more like your infected." Elric waited at the end of the street for her and then gestured with his arm for her to go ahead. "I would simply call you undead, princess."

"I don't think I like that term."

He caught her around the waist as she strode by him, tugging her against his chest so she had to plant her hands over his heart. She could feel it thundering against her palms as he leaned down and rasped in her ear, "Call yourself what you wish, gravesinger. Just know that the only thing you *have* to call yourself is mine."

She hummed low under her throat. "What a romantic you are for a man who made a gruesome spectacle in the middle of the town square."

"They needed to be reminded that I am here."

"You made a statue bleed."

"And I would do it again." He pressed a kiss to her throat before letting her go. "Come, we are close to your Fortuna's home."

The banter and joking was the only way she was keeping herself together. The closer she got to Fortuna, the less she wanted to be here. Jessamine knew this was the only way to get back to her throne, because Fortuna was the only person in Callum's memory who she knew could be useful, and yet...

"You hesitate," Elric said as they walked the meager few steps left.

"Fortuna and I have never had a good relationship. She was always the pretty cousin, but that didn't mean she had an easier life than I did. I was still the crown princess. She was always the woman who would never have the throne. It was difficult for her, to say the least."

"So you hesitate, why?"

"I don't want to make her life any harder than it already has been. We don't have very good memories of each other, but that doesn't mean I want to waste my time with revenge on someone who deserves it less than others."

"You are not the child you once were," Elric murmured quietly. "I thought you had learned that lesson after seeing Callum."

"I did," she replied. "I am a monster that none of them will recognize. For that, I am ever so grateful. But it will feel strange to see someone who once knew you and to know they no longer have any power over you."

"We're here," Elric said quietly.

They crouched on the opposite side of the street, tucked against the edge of a stone staircase that led up to an equally grand house. Fortuna's was the largest on the street, surrounded by a golden fence that was easily twice the height of a normal person. There were guards every ten feet or so, each of them in Leon's signature dark blue.

The house beyond was made entirely of white marble. It stood as a monolith of money, four stories tall, with pillars that made it look like a small castle. Glass windows revealed every single room to passersby, sparkling with so much light she could only imagine how much whale oil the house consumed. Even from here, she could see the riches inside. Gold-leafed walls, black-and-white marble floors, countless artifacts from artisans all around the word. Marble busts. Oil paintings. Gemstones in every bedroom that made it almost impossible to guess which was Fortuna's.

"She doesn't want anyone to know where she rests her head," Elric muttered, as though he had a similar thought to hers. "And the guards are certainly concerning."

Indeed they were. It suggested Leon had placed more value upon Fortuna's life than she'd originally guessed.

As they watched, the guards changed over. They did it in such a way that no one would ever be able to elude them. The guards were too vigilant, almost as though they knew someone was coming. Even as they changed over, they were back to back, both of them looking everywhere until the person being relieved could leave knowing that no one would sneak in on their watch.

"He's nervous," she whispered.

"Your king has heard about you," Elric said, his voice low and melodic. "I would say he's afraid there is a witch back from the dead."

"Whatever will he do when he hears I brought a god with me?"

They shared a look, but Jessamine knew this was the moment when everything changed. She'd always planned for Leon to know that she was alive. She wanted her almost-husband to be terrified as she crawled her way back to that throne. She wanted him to lie awake at night, haunted by the ghost of what he had done.

"You can't die," Elric murmured, his eyes on hers. "You know he can't kill you, because I will not let him."

"I cannot die, but I can still feel pain." The sensation of a knife sliding through her skin was a phantom memory that plagued her even now. Jessamine smoothed her hands down the shirt beneath her cloak.

Her fingers danced over the scar on her side where Callum's thugs had cut her up and left her for dead just because they found out she was a witch. Then she moved upward, feeling the mark on her ribs where a young man named Benji had thought to finish what his master had started. And finally, the last touch that always made her feel the worst pain.

She wrapped her hand around her own neck where her betrothed, who should have been vowing to protect her with his life, had slit her throat.

"I want my revenge," she whispered. "I want to know that everything he worked so hard to get, all that he desires, is ripped from his hands piece by bloody piece. I want to see him crawl and beg me for mercy."

"Where do you wish to start?"

"With what he loves." Her eyes moved to the stately home where Fortuna hid. And as if she had summoned the woman herself, Fortuna walked in front of one of the largest windows.

She was effortlessly beautiful in a way Jessamine never had been. But if they stood next to each other, one could see a family resemblance. Fortuna was lean and graceful, her skin moonlight-kissed and her lips a shade of dark red. Big, dark eyes made people want to protect her. The long waterfall of her dark hair never had a single strand out of place. She was stunning. Beyond beautiful.

But Jessamine could also see how steely Fortuna had become. The way she gestured to the servant who followed her suggested she'd gotten even meaner—which meant she would be a formidable foe who knew how to push all of Jessamine's buttons. In a way, Fortuna was more dangerous than Callum had ever been.

"I don't believe Leon can actually love anything," Jessamine said quietly, her voice pitched low so no one would overhear them. "But I do believe he covets that which is beautiful. He wants what he cannot have, which is why he wanted my kingdom in the first place."

"I still don't believe all of this is about a kingdom," Elric replied. "There is more going on here between these people than either you or I understand just yet. We need to know what they are doing, and whether they are going to continue doing it."

She didn't know if there was some grand plan that they needed to be terrified of. All she cared about was getting the usurper off her throne and making sure that her people were finally cared for in the way they deserved.

"Elric?" she asked.

"Yes, gravesinger?"

"There is only one way we're going to get the answers that we need. We need to get inside that house."

"You wish to walk into the belly of the beast?"

She grinned. "Is that going to be too difficult for you, Deathless One? I thought your magic was in shadows and souls?"

"It is."

"And yet tricking a few humans into allowing us to walk right in that front door is beyond you?"

She could see the heat flash in his eyes at her challenge. He liked her like this, when she was taking charge and ordering him around. She knew he wanted to press her up against the stone stairwell and kiss her breathless. Some part of her wanted that, too. He could distract her like no one else. But right now, neither of them could afford to be distracted when there was so much they still had to do.

"Jessamine," he said, his voice so low it was little more than a guttural growl. "Do not test me."

"I enjoy testing you."

"We cannot walk in the front door. That spider of a woman would know my power is in shadows. Considering Leon's guards are filling the city to the brim, I would suspect they are concerned with Callum's disappearance. They're not so stupid that they will ignore the rumors that I have returned, along with the rumors that you yourself are somehow still alive. I can get us to a window, but that is as far as I will risk. There are hardly any shadows in her home at all."

Ah. So that was why they were burning so many lights. She wasn't sure if that was a good or a bad thing.

"Did they know we were coming?" she whispered, looking back at the house.

"Didn't we already assume that? Leon must suspect you're alive, considering all the wall writing you did in the Factory District. With the death of Callum Quen, I can only assume he will put more protection around his own people. Clearly, Fortuna is the easy guess."

Humming low under her breath, she tried to think of a way around this. There had to be a window that would be useful, after all.

Snapping her fingers, she reached for Elric and shook him. "Nyx!"

"Bless you."

"No, Nyx. The familiar you gave me. She can find a way in. Surely there's an unlocked window or some kind of cellar we could sneak into. Then we just have to stay out of people's way."

"The windows, Jessamine? Anyone on the street could see us."

"We'll stay away from the windows, then. None of the guards are looking *at* the house, anyway! They're trying to keep people out, not assuming that we're already inside."

He shook her hands off him, sighing before nodding. "It's a start, I suppose. That familiar of yours is particularly good at squirreling herself into places she shouldn't be."

"Summon her for us."

"You summon it."

"You're the one who created her! Nyx is back at the cottage, hopefully staying away from all those birds. Please, Elric?"

She tried her best to bat her eyelashes like she'd seen Fortuna do so many times in her life. All that managed was to make Elric scowl at her. "Don't do that. I hate that expression."

"Would you prefer I argue with you until we're both blue in the face?"

"I'd prefer you to just stop speaking," he snarled, but his hands were already rising. Muttering a long spell under his breath, the shadows in the alcove at the edge of the stairwell gathered together.

The tiny form of a cat appeared, her arms sinking to the ground in a big stretch before she trotted over to Jessamine.

She really refused to grow. Still no larger than a kitten, Nyx sat primly on the stairwell and waited to be petted. Her ears had grown huge, with long tufts of fur poking out of them. Her bright green eyes blinked up at Jessamine before glaring at Elric.

"Hello, little one," she said, adding a few scratches at the back of her neck for good measure. "I know we've kept you locked up quite a bit, but we have a great need for you. Can you find us a way into that house?"

Nyx blinked at the glowing building, her pupils contracting before it seemed like the cat nodded and then trotted down the stairs. A few of the guards reacted, but they were no match for a cat who weaved through their legs and purred so loudly that Jessamine swore she could hear Nyx's rumble from where they were hiding.

"It's just a cat," one of the guard said. "Must be a stray."

"Haven't you seen the cats in that shop? Little spies, from what I've heard. Don't let it in."

But the first guard bent down and gave Nyx a good few pats as she wove through his legs again. "They wouldn't make a black cat for one of those. People think they're bad luck, you know. This is just a cat. Look at it! Scruffy and everything. Not a designer pet, this one."

She almost had half a mind to argue with the man, but Elric clapped his hand around her mouth and drew her against his chest. "Let the familiar work," he muttered in her ear.

She would, but she'd remember their faces. Scruffy cat. Nyx was better than both of them combined.

And then, with one more twitch of her tail, Nyx slipped between the bars of the fence and disappeared behind the house.

12

Elric watched her familiar disappear into the shadows of the house. Nyx had learned much in her short lifespan already, but familiars were always tricky little things. He'd created them more times than he could count, but they chose their own forms, their own witches, and even then, they were difficult to control.

Familiars required respect from their witches, and if they didn't get it, then they would find another. So the fact that Nyx was already willing to go to such lengths for Jessamine? It boded well for his little gravesinger.

They waited for a long while in the dark, neither of them saying a word. The guards changed shifts again. They seem to do that fairly regularly, almost at every hour. It seemed Leon wanted to make sure every single guard was always refreshed, and their eyes never missed a single detail. One of the guards even noticed a rat as it scurried across the street, and he was very quick to finish it before it could approach Fortuna's home.

But then, a little shadow passed underneath the gate and headed straight for them. The darkness of Nyx's form was little more than a blur, and not a single guard noticed as she darted across the street, over the stairs, and down onto the side where they hid.

"There you are," Jessamine breathed as she ran her hands over Nyx's sides. "What took you so long?"

There was a soft glare from her familiar before it reached out a paw and touched her cheek. Jessamine stilled, her eyes going glassy as magic passed between the two of them.

He'd only seen familiars do this on the rare occasion. The creatures were notoriously difficult to get to perform magic with their owners, being far more likely to hoard that power for themselves. Yet again, this familiar had surprised him.

Jessamine, returning to herself after communing with the little creature, said, "There appears to be a small servant's door hidden in the wall of ivy in the back. It's made to look like there's nothing behind the wall, but we should be able to get inside with no issues. The only problem is that there are guards on that side as well. They won't let us pass unless we look like one of the servants."

"Did Nyx see any servants? If so, I could steal their faces." It was a power he hadn't used in a while, but he would very much enjoy doing it again. There was a little pain involved, but did that matter in the grand scheme of things?

"No," she lamented before leaning away from Nyx's touch. "Go home to Sybil now, sweet one. I don't want you getting caught."

All the fur on Nyx's sides fluffed, and her tail doubled in size. Clearly, she was very unhappy with her owner for even suggesting such a thing. Familiars had their place, and that was with their witch.

Jessamine smiled and ran her hand down Nyx's head, flattening her ears against her skull. "This is too dangerous for a black cat. I'll make it home to you in no time, little one."

Though the familiar still wasn't happy with this option, the cat turned and disappeared back down the street. The cat would find its way home, without a doubt, but he had no idea what it would do when it found Sybil. Likely complain.

And perhaps vomit void dust into their shoes. It had taken him weeks to clean that curse out of them last time.

Sighing, he reached for Jessamine's hand and clasped it in his own. "Think of shadows, gravesinger."

"Why?"

"Because it is nighttime, and that is when I am most powerful. Think of shadows and how you are one. Together, we shall walk past these guards and they will never know that we were here."

"You can do that?" She looked him up and down, sizing up the god before her as though she questioned his power.

"Nightmare," he murmured, his voice pitched low and sultry. He stepped closer, reeling her into his chest. "Haven't you learned it's better to trust me?"

Her pupils enlarged, growing larger with desire as she used her magic. And then they were both in the throes of need as her power flowed through them. He tilted his head back, groaning quietly so they wouldn't be overheard. But every time she used magic, it was white-hot fire that flowed through his veins.

This magic was powerful, almost too powerful for him to comprehend. Witches weren't supposed to be able to use his magic like this. Or at least they never had before.

Not until her.

He breathed into the power, allowing it to flow from his fingertips and down into hers. The moment it entered her body, she changed it. Manipulated it. The magic became something far more than what he could do with it, because she knew how to use that power to her own advantage. No longer tied only to him, the magic became something else entirely.

"Shadows," she breathed. And then they became so.

He could feel his form disappearing. Soon enough, he could barely even see her. But he could feel the connection between their hands as they held on to each other. Elric could feel her heart beating through the tight grip with which she held on to him. And he could hear her soft exhalation of breath.

"Shall we?" she asked, though the words were strained.

Holding on to her, he maneuvered them out onto the streets. He wanted to make sure the spell worked first. If the guards got the impression of shadow figures walking toward them, he wasn't sure what the men would do. Likely shout and use those swords at their sides, or worse, use the rifles that were strapped to their backs.

Elric really didn't want to be picking shrapnel out of himself, or the little musket balls, which were painful even to a god. This new body wasn't as strong as the shadows he once was.

But none of the guards reacted to them in the slightest. The men just kept staring straight ahead, their eyes waiting for any movement to draw them. They could likely still hear them, though, so Elric couldn't praise Jessamine as he wished.

His gravesinger had come a long way from not being able to cast any spell. She deserved to know how good she had become. He was, unfortunately, only able to squeeze her hand.

She squeezed back as they rounded the house and then took the lead as they slipped through the servants' entrance and toward the wall of ivy that Nyx had shown her.

It was a complicated lock that required seven enchanted ivy leaves to be perfectly overlapped before there was the faintest crunching noise and the stone moved. He tensed, waiting for a guard to say something about a door moving on its own. But when he looked over his shoulder, the guard didn't look back.

Jessamine tugged him closer to her and whispered, "He probably thinks someone is leaving. Let's go before he realizes no one is here."

Elric took one look at the beaming blast of light that erupted from the small slot behind the ivy and sighed. He knew they had to do this, but he still hated it. The shadows were entirely banished by the light beyond, and though he was still a god, it would make him weaker.

At the very least, he had Jessamine by his side.

Together, they plunged into the light that burned the spell from their shoulders. He could almost feel the power slinking back underneath his skin like a beaten dog.

The room was so *bright*. Even worse than that, it was *light*. It appeared Fortuna was partial to white and gold; the walls were white with filigree gold dancing along the edges, and the floor was white with flecks of gold in the very stone beneath their feet. Gold framed the pictures on the wall, oil paintings of far-off places or boats for some strange reason. The furniture was white and looked decidedly uncomfortable to sit on. But he expected nothing less from a woman like this.

What an unwelcoming home. He grimaced as he looked at the room they stood in. "This place is ugly."

"What is within shows without," she murmured, her gaze moving down the hallway before she reached for his hand again. "Is there a spell that would let us know which room is hers?"

"Yes."

"Shall we cast it?"

He was reluctant to agree, if only because he secretly desired to look around this place. It was so different from anything he would have chosen. What kind of people would want to live here? The colors burned his eyes, and nothing was inviting. He'd choose a tomb over this place, and Elric knew most people would hate the thought of spiders, but he'd gleefully accept their company over those who willingly lingered here.

"Elric," she said with a soft laugh. "We need to get moving. Someone will see us."

"And if they do?"

"They'll sound an alarm and Fortuna will have to move houses because Leon will not know how someone got past his guard." She narrowed her eyes at him. "You can snoop later if you wish."

"I cannot snoop in this place. There are no shadows."

She stood in front of a light, and her shadow cast a long figure on the floor. "Anyone walking in this place would have a shadow. You can stitch yourself to it."

He sighed. "Fine, get this over with."

"What is the spell?"

Elric just cast the damn thing himself, sending out a thin tendril of his power to guide them. It flickered in the light often, requiring rethreading every time the lights flickered as whale oil dripped through a complicated piping system. Weaving the spell over and over again took precious time and power that he needed, but eventually, they entered a bedroom in the central part of the home.

"Why was no one in the halls?" he spat the moment they closed the door behind them.

"I don't know."

"We should have seen at least one servant. It makes little sense."

"No, I find there to be no sense here at all." Jessamine's brow wrinkled, but she turned to survey the room his spell had led them to. "Let's just find out what we can and then get out of this house."

It felt like a trick. There should have been guards inside as well as out. There should have been servants here to protect Fortuna. This felt like a trap.

But no one came out of the shadows. No blades parted through curtains, and no spells seared their flesh. This was just a bedroom. An ornate one, certainly, but a very quiet bedroom.

It was prettier than the hall. The entire ceiling was painted to look like a blush-colored sky with fluffy white clouds that a sunrise was just peeking through. The four-poster bed was bolted to the ceiling and the floor, with white marble pillars sanded smooth. The blankets were a lovely pale shade of blush on a bed so soft, it might have been the nicest he'd ever seen. A gold-edged vanity in the corner reflected the image of Jessamine and himself back at them—two dark stains in a house that had banished shadows.

Jessamine nudged the rug that was woven with strands of blush and gold. "This looks finer than a courtesan should have, don't you think?"

"I don't think she's just a courtesan any longer," he murmured, stepping into the room a little farther. "What are we looking for?"

"Clues. Notes. Anything that would give us an explanation for what Leon is planning, or how we can attack him without dying in the process."

She seemed so confident. He tried not to grin at the sound of her voice. Clues. Like she was a little detective who had been given an impossible plot to solve. What a strange creature this woman was. When he failed in hiding his smile, Jessamine glared at him.

"What?" she asked.

He leaned against one of the bedposts and watched her open the golden chest at the base of the bed. "Nothing."

"Would you look for something useful?"

"What do you consider useful?"

"I'll know it when I see it." She pawed through the fancy fabric contained inside the chest but then glared at him again as though that expression alone could light a fire beneath him.

He sighed and meandered throughout the room, taking in details as he went. This room was far too fine for a courtesan, that much was certain. He didn't know many women who sold their flesh who had gold-dusted rooms. This wasn't just gold foil, and it certainly wasn't just painted. Even the hairbrush on her vanity was made out of solid gold.

She'd been gifted these by someone with a significant amount of money. Like a king who found her valuable. Or perhaps, gifts to keep her mouth shut.

What did this woman know? He could only imagine it was secrets of the state that Leon Bishop did not want getting out into society. The more he looked, the more certain he became. The extravagance of the room didn't come from gifts that a man would give a woman he longed for. They weren't gifts that made him think Leon had any kindness in his heart for her in the slightest. Nothing here was personal, but they were valuable.

He reached down to open a pot of makeup on the vanity. Pristine, priceless blush. Crushed pearls that would make her skin glimmer. Rouge that he remembered from the old days in a pot made of gold with glittering rubies on the top.

"She knows something," he muttered.

"Like what?"

"Something Leon doesn't want her to tell anyone else."

So few people had items like this. Only the consorts of kings, at least. Opening a drawer, he noticed it was filled with letters signed with a royal-blue seal. But the moment he picked them up, they turned to ash.

Picking up another piece of paper that didn't disintegrate, he flashed it for Jessamine to look at. "And she's scared."

"Of what?"

She grabbed the piece of paper, her eyes flying over the words he'd already seen. Fortuna Beaumont was holding a ball for all the eligible and rich men in the Pleasure District. Even men beyond. On the top of the page were the words *Fortuna Beaumont is looking for a new suitor.*

"She's running," he murmured. The question was, from what?

13

Both of them left Fortuna's home far more uneasy than before they'd arrived and with a handful of the same flyers. She had thirty in her hands, which were on every surface of the house. Every bench, every side table, every room. It seemed impossible they'd walked in and walked out without anyone seeing them, almost as though it had been orchestrated to be that simple.

Jessamine had stewed in the discomfort throughout the walk home, mulling it over in her mind. Elric hadn't been all that interested in talking either, it seemed.

So much security outside. All those guards, and for what? She'd seen no one make a move toward the house. There hadn't even been anyone inside other than Fortuna, and they hadn't seen her when they were inside. Had she only made an appearance in front of the windows to tempt people inside?

But then why wouldn't there have been a trap? If Leon knew that Jessamine was here, and that she was coming for Fortuna, why didn't he attack then and there?

"I don't like it," she muttered as they paused in front of Elissa's home. "I don't feel like we're being followed. And yet, what other reason would he have to let us enter Fortuna's home?"

"If that wasn't the trap, then there is a more elaborate one we will need to evade soon." He shook his head, lingering in the shadows by the entrance. "I don't understand it myself."

"What was the point? Clearly they were tempting someone inside, and that Fortuna is looking for a new protector." She shook her head. "Or maybe Fortuna herself wished for us to know that. I have a hard time believing this was her plan and not Leon's."

"Do you think he's capable of planning something like this?"

"I think you were closer. It's more likely that Fortuna knows something he doesn't want to get out. Whether he is aware of that or not, or if he's gotten bored of her, it's hard to say." Jessamine put her hand on the door, readying herself to push it open. But she paused there, frozen. "I don't know what to do, Elric. I feel like anything I say will be wrong."

"You know what you're doing, nightmare. Just tell them what you would say if you were their queen." He leaned closer, his heat blanketing her spine as he murmured in her ear, "Because you are."

Squaring her shoulders, she strode into the house. Elissa and Sybil were waiting in the kitchen, along with the parrot who was apparently Elissa's former lover, and Nyx, who sat on the table staring at the parrot as though she wanted to take a bite out of it. Perhaps her familiar knew that there was magic in that bird... but then again, her familiar was a cat.

Frowning, she snatched Nyx off the table before they had to perform another resurrection. "Why does it seem like you've all been talking?"

"Because we have," Sybil replied.

"That sounds dangerous."

"Women talking tends to be dangerous." The sly smile on Sybil's face didn't seem all that dangerous, though. It seemed like her regular expression. "Did you find Fortuna?"

"We found Fortuna's home." Struggling to keep the wriggling cat in her arms still, she finally marched over to the back door and ushered Nyx out. "Go kill birds that didn't use to be people."

A faint squawk echoed from Elissa's lips. "No birds!"

Jessamine glanced at her over her shoulder and nodded, but then made eye contact with Nyx and whispered, "No pretty birds. Just pigeons."

Her familiar slunk off into the night, clearly not happy with this development. She sent a silent apology to the local bird population. But she couldn't worry about that blasted parrot while trying to explain to her makeshift coven that she wasn't sure where to go from here.

By the time she'd made it back to the table, she had a bit of a plan. But even then, it was really just her trying to figure out what her mother would have said in this situation. Of course, her mother wasn't likely to have consorted with witches in the first place.

"We found some semblance of Fortuna, I suppose. It was an unsettling evening." She sat down at the table, taking the offered teacup and bringing it to her lips. She allowed herself one swallow before sighing in displeasure. "It was all too easy. There were guards surrounding the house, all in Leon's colors, but they weren't there to protect anyone. We thought we saw Fortuna in the window, but then there was no one in the house. We walked right in easy enough and found a flyer on her vanity for a new ball she's having. It's as though she's trying to run from Leon, but none of it makes sense."

Even Sybil's brow furrowed in confusion. "That sounds like a trap."

"That's what we thought."

Elissa drummed her fingers on the table. "Fortuna is a smart woman. I wouldn't dismiss the idea that she was the one who made sure you were there, and let you find the flyer so easily. If she wanted to get a message to you, perhaps that would be the best way for her to do it without letting Leon know what was happening."

Jessamine shook her head. Shadows of the past played in her mind's eye. Fortuna used to make fun of her for being so much scrawnier, and how little Jessamine knew in comparison to the worldly courtesan who had started selling her flesh young. Fortuna had made money very early in her life, because even then she had ambition. But that ambition had gone beyond just being someone that men liked to buy.

"I don't think it's that," she murmured. "There is no lost love between Fortuna and me. I don't think she would reach out to me for help. And regardless, how would she even know we were here?"

Jessamine could hear the screech in her mind as she looked at Elissa. The woman went paler than normal, and her eyes looked down at the table. There was a halting moment of time as Jessamine realized that she wasn't safe here. She wasn't safe anywhere.

A crumbling castle that had been forgotten by time itself was the only place she could find someone to trust.

"You?" she whispered. "You told her we were here?"

Elric appeared behind Elissa, rage turning his features dark. Black shadows slithered out of his eyes, rolling underneath his skin as they spread until his eyes were ringed with darkness. "You'd best correct her," he growled, with a voice out of a nightmare. "Because if you don't, you've betrayed a god. I think you'll find I'm much more ruthless than a king's favored pet, Elissa."

The birdlike woman swallowed hard and kept her eyes on the table. "There are few in the Pleasure District who can escape her, Lady Jessamine. Fortuna runs this entire district with a heavy hand, and if I had said nothing, she would have destroyed my home. She'd have someone come in and ransack the whole place. It would be impossible for me to escape her."

Her heart shattered into a million pieces. It hurt to know that someone who she had blindly trusted was so willing to give her up. There should have been some kind of warning. They'd helped Elissa. They'd given her the power to become a witch on her own, so she didn't have to fear what Fortuna would do to her. All of these things were a blessing.

But then Jessamine remembered that they had terrified her as well. Elissa had been fine here without them. She'd thought that nothing could stand between her and the world, and that gods weren't real. They'd all died, and knowing that she was wrong in that aspect must have been more terrifying than losing her life. But there was something inside of her that remained faithful to Fortuna.

A terrible feeling burst to life, one she almost felt guilty for even feeling. But without a god at their side, she was not sure they would succeed in this. Fortuna had loyalty on her side. True, real loyalty that was far beyond what Jessamine had yet to inspire. If Elissa was so willing to betray them like this, when she'd thought they had built something together, had Fortuna already won? No. Not this time.

Fortuna might have her foot on the throats of those who followed her. She might inspire fear in their hearts and was certainly more dangerous at this moment, but *she was not a witch*.

Jessamine caught Elric's gaze behind Elissa, and froze. All of his magic had slid free from his shoulders. The shadows stretched from his shoulder blades and caught onto the rafters above him, onto the door, the windows, sticky ink forming the wings of a predator. He was a monster hovering behind a witch, ready to give her the retribution she deserved for betraying them.

But Jessamine still had hope that not all was lost. Because Elissa still wouldn't look at them. She kept her gaze far from any of their faces, and her body spoke of guilt as much as it spoke of fear.

Jessamine shook her head at the massive god behind Elissa, who would choose to end her life rather than save it. Elissa didn't need revenge right now. What she needed was a family to make her feel safe.

Standing, Jessamine walked over to a bundle of sticks that Elissa must use for some of the birdcages. There were many of them, each in different sizes and thicknesses and different kinds of wood. She picked them all up in her hands, slowly returning to the table. Elissa flinched, as though afraid she was going to whack her with the sharp ends.

Instead, Jessamine chose a thin branch and placed it in front of her. "Break it."

"What?" Elissa looked up at her.

"Break the stick, Elissa."

She looked between Jessamine and Sybil, her eyes wide and full of fear. Clearly, the young witch thought this was a setup. That as soon as she broke the stick, Sybil might launch at her. Or perhaps Jessamine would snap her fingers and the barely leashed god behind her would snap her neck.

Still, Elissa lifted her shaking hands and took hold of either end of the stick. With a soft movement, she broke the stick.

"Lovely." Jessamine took the two pieces of that stick and added two more. "Try breaking them now."

Elissa did, but it took her a little more effort to do so.

She handed her another stick to add to the bundle, this one black as night and thicker than the other four. "Now try again with this one."

Elissa added the stick to the rest, failed, and then looked up at her with confusion in her gaze. "Why am I doing this?"

"Because I need you to understand something. This is an important lesson, and I hope it will linger more than the others we have taught you. Try one more time."

Elissa tried again, even struggled with it on her knee underneath the table. But try as she might, Elissa could not break the bundle of sticks. Some of the ones on the outside creaked, but none of them broke.

Jessamine took the sticks back and took the original stick out of the bundle. "When you are a witch on your own, it's easy to feel breakable and overwhelmed. I certainly did. I looked at the world as the dangerous beast it was. A single witch is far too easy to break on its own." She lifted the other two. "A coven makes us harder to break. Still fragile, I'll give you that much. A coven is not indestructible."

Then Jessamine held up the stick that had never broken. The dark, thick stick that was infinitely stronger than the other three. She handed it to Elissa to hold, watching the other woman understand what she was about to say long before she said it.

"We are a coven of witches who will outlast the ending of time itself. The more witches in our coven, the stronger we will be. One becomes two." She smiled at Sybil. "And two becomes many. But we also have our god, who is unbreakable and unbendable. You were the one who sacrificed to him. You were the one who prayed to him, so you must have believed in some small way that he could save you."

Elissa's eyes welled with tears, her lower lip trembling. "Even if I believed it then, I still told her. I still stood by while you were all gathering clothing to hide in the crowds, and I still told her where you were and who you were."

She did. And that stung.

The truth hurt, but then again, it always did. The truth was harder to swallow when it was someone Jessamine wanted to trust. But that was life, and sometimes, people made mistakes.

"Did you tell her I was here because you are loyal to Fortuna?" And when Elissa shook her head violently, Jessamine lifted her hand so the other woman wouldn't talk. "I don't want to hear excuses. I want to know the truth. No matter what, if you are loyal to Fortuna, then I will leave this place with you safely behind. I have no interest in the blood play that the nobility so love. Your safety is a promise, Elissa. All I am asking for is the truth."

The last sentence vibrated with power that she hadn't called upon from Elric yet. Still, the Deathless One echoed in her voice, deepening it with magic that ripped honesty out of Elissa.

"I am afraid of her," Elissa replied. "I feel no loyalty to someone who inspires fear when she walks through the streets. I have no loyalty to anyone who runs this place. But I fear what she will do to me, and what she will do to those I love."

Elissa's gaze slanted to the parrot who still perched on the chair next to her. And Jessamine knew that though there was always a risk in manipulation, sometimes it was necessary.

"What was her name?" she asked.

"Sarah."

"Sarah is a beautiful name," Jessamine replied. "I hope you know I will always care for her. If your bravery ends in sadness, your family will always be safe with me. No matter how hard it is to provide them safety."

Elissa nodded, her eyes on her twisting fingers before she said, "Fortuna wanted to know when you were coming. There were rumors, you see. Rumors of a witch who killed Callum Quen. Then stories of a god reawakened. It all made them nervous."

"Who are they?"

"The nobility who betrayed you, and most of the people who run the Pleasure District. They all know each other, and they all know Leon Bishop. The kingdom prospers for them and them alone, but that is how it always works. Peasants break their backs to never see the fruits of their labor. Artists perform until their fingers bleed, but rarely are they paid. And the rich continue to play, on and on, until the world burns around them."

The haunting words played over and over in her mind. Because they were true. Because they hurt to hear. Because no one should believe that, and yet, what other belief was there?

Jessamine opened her mouth on an inhale and then blew it all on with a sigh. "If you are going to be part of this coven, you have to trust us to protect you."

"I don't know that you can."

It was Sybil who stood, her chair screeching across the floor as she reached for Elissa's hand. Dark and light, intertwined together as their fingers meshed like a woven tapestry. "We will bleed for you, Elissa. What more could you ask for? A coven is a family, and a family protects."

Elissa looked between the two of them as tears dripped down her cheeks.

Elric's hands came down on her shoulders, dark with claws that stretched from his fingertips. Yet they were gentle as he held on to her. And it was his deep voice that came and echoed what the witches had said.

"If you do not trust in your fellow witches, then trust in me." His fingers squeezed, and Jessamine could see the white marks he left with his tight grip. "There are no longer any gods left to save the few who would threaten you. But even in the days of old, when the gods still roamed this kingdom… *there were few they could save from me.*"

Elissa's eyes widened with every word, but Jessamine could also see her spine straighten. She finally nodded firmly. "I apologize for my mistake. I will not question the coven again."

"See that you don't," Jessamine replied before Sybil could beat her to it. "We do not forgive twice."

14

Elric sat up out of a deep sleep, gasping as a nightmare held him in its grip. He couldn't breathe fast enough to catch his breath. He was covered in sweat, slicked down his back and through his hair so thoroughly that he could feel droplets running down his spine in an icy trail. His heart thundered, and he wasn't even sure why.

"It was just a dream," he muttered, looking around the room to make sure that Jessamine wasn't with him.

She wasn't. She must have gotten up early to meet with the other witches. He knew they'd been talking with Elissa more, even though he had advised against it. The witch had betrayed them once already, and now she knew they wouldn't kill her for it. They should have beheaded her and set the head out in front of the home for everyone else to see.

Then no one would question what would happen if they betrayed Jessamine. No one would think for even a moment that they could test the might of the coven.

And of the Deathless One himself.

He swung his legs over the edge of the bed, trying hard not to think about the nightmare that had plagued him. It was another experience with a coven. He was certain of that. Just thinking the word made goose bumps rise on his arms. Witches could not be trusted. And he no longer trusted the one whose house they were staying in. No wonder the old memories plagued him.

He counted each breath, trying to force his lungs to slow down. This body was far more uncomfortable than he remembered it being. Or perhaps two hundred years alone in the dark had fractured his mind. He wasn't the same god he had once been.

Waving a hand and casting a quick spell to clean himself of the sweat and grime of the night, he dressed quickly before joining the others in the main house. He wasn't proud of how long it took for him to open the door after hearing the low mumble of words on the other side. He stood out there on the step, listening to the idle chatter within. The rise and fall of their voices should have calmed him, and yet, all it did was raise his hackles even more than they already were. He had to close his eyes and breathe again, counting to a hundred before he opened the door.

Immediately, his gaze found Jessamine. Her wild tangle of hair was tied atop her head, coiling curls poking out in all directions like she'd turned her hair into a bird's nest. Her cheeks were flushed with some emotion he couldn't guess at, and she was wildly flailing her hands in the air like she did when she was passionate about what she was speaking of.

He'd never seen her look more beautiful than she did right now. And something in his soul eased at the sight of her.

Because for all the witches that had harmed him, betrayed him, tried to make him hurt for the power he had that they didn't… there was one who only wished him peace.

"Oh, good, you're here," she said, her eyes finding his with a soft smile in them before she continued. "There's another witch."

Just like that, all the ease vanished. His gaze flicked to Sybil, to the traitor, and then back to Jessamine. "I felt no other join the coven."

"She has no coven," Elissa said, her voice pitched low and quiet as though she already knew he was angry with her. "She is known for her magic around these parts, though. An impressive spell caster, apparently, although I've never met her myself."

"Why are we investing our time in another witch?"

Jessamine seemed to hesitate before replying, "I don't know what Fortuna is up to. But I do know that we need more allies in this district before I feel comfortable walking into the lion's den. Elissa knows this woman well, and apparently she has connections we do not."

With a soft shifting of weight, Elissa stood. She looked like a rabbit caught in a wolf's maw when she glanced up to see his enraged features. "It's just... Agnes Jessup has lived in the Pleasure District her entire life. She's always been interested in magic, but more than that, she has her fingers in every person's life. She knows everyone, everything, and every step people take in the district. Not to mention she hates Fortuna. Agnes wants to control the Pleasure District, and used to in the old days. Before Fortuna, that is. If you want someone on our side who will be more helpful than a woman who breeds birds, then Agnes is easy to get. Bring her into the coven. Give her real magic. She will stop at nothing to gain more power."

Jessamine stepped closer to him and then placed her hand over his thundering heart. As though she knew the terror exploding in him. "The larger the coven, the stronger we all will be. I don't care about the Pleasure District. But Agnes is a woman who wishes for power that she's fought for her entire life. Give her whatever magic you can spare, and we will promise her this entire district if she helps us bring Fortuna down."

He didn't like it. He didn't trust it. But moreover, he thought it was a risky decision for any of these women to make. The more people who knew they were witches, the worse the outcome for all of them.

He'd seen it. He'd watched countless of his coven scream as they were tied to a stake while flames licked their heels. He'd been forced to stand there, watching their features melt and slide off their faces because he was unable to kill those who worshipped his own siblings. There were rules, even for gods, and he couldn't be the one to start a war between his family members.

Along the tail of that thought came a softness. An unraveling of who he had once been because there were no gods left.

Elric tucked a strand of her hair behind her ear, lingering on the soft seashell of flesh. "I will build you a coven that will destroy this entire kingdom, as I promised. But there are no more gods to save them if they harm you, nightmare. Make sure they know this."

His gaze slid toward Elissa, whose face had gone pale. He held it, hoping she could see that there would soon be a retribution for her as well. Elric was just biding his time with her.

But Jessamine was grinning. "Such a bloodthirsty god. I'm glad you've agreed, because we're leaving now."

"Now?"

"There's no time like the present. I'm certain if Fortuna was expecting us at her home, then she would expect us to regroup, knowing that they should have caught us in a trap. The last thing she would expect would be for me to wander the streets of the Pleasure District immediately afterward."

"You're taking a risk."

"Not really." She batted those eyelashes at him. "I'm pretending to be dumb."

This woman would be the death of him. And he was a deathless god.

Elric watched as the other women prepared themselves, and then they all left together. A dark witch with a bright yellow headscarf wrapped around her head. Another wearing a garish green dress and sporting a parrot on her shoulder. And lastly, his gravesinger. A haunting woman all in black velvet, with a slit up the side to show the knee-high boots that had seen more travel than most, her hair piled atop her head like a heathen.

Oh, people were going to stare, and he was certain that was Jessamine's point.

Elric walked behind them the entire journey to Agnes's home, and was surprised to see it was a rather utilitarian-looking building. There was little beauty here, only functionality. The home was built square, with sharp edges in sensible stone and a copper roof that gleamed in the sunlight. A black iron fence surrounded it, but there were no gardens on the other side. Just carefully laid stones that spiraled out from the home in swirling patterns.

Now this was a home that didn't offend his senses. He already liked this Agnes more than the others.

Jessamine waltzed up the front steps and knocked on the door as if she couldn't feel the spells woven into the stones around them. Whoever was inside that building already knew they were here. And they certainly had enough information on every single person who had stepped on a stone to give them pause.

The door opened quickly and a behemoth of a man stepped out. He had to exit sideways because his shoulders were so large, and when he straightened, he was easily a good foot and a half taller than all the women. He was taller than Elric—a fact that made Elric bristle.

"No solicitors." The big man crossed his arms over his chest and glared down at them.

"We're not solicitors. We'd like to speak with Agnes." Jessamine didn't back down. She glared right back at the big man, then crossed her arms over her chest, too. "I won't take no for an answer."

"She's not in."

"I have a feeling she is very much in and that she doesn't want to see us. Unfortunately for her, that is not an option."

To that, the big man did not reply. Instead, he just lifted his gaze over her head like she was no longer there, and remained silent.

A sharp tug of power nearly yanked Elric forward. Jessamine drew on their connection so hard, he knew whatever spell she was about to cast would likely turn the man to stone or blow him to smithereens. He just wasn't certain which she would choose. Rather than make a scene none of them could come back from, he lurched forward and placed himself between her and the big man.

"How much is it going to cost us to see the witch?" he asked, stumbling over the words before he could come up with a better plan.

"There is no witch in this house."

"There is a witch in that house, or if she isn't yet, she soon will be. Now, everyone has a price. What is yours?"

Elric could feel the aggression wafting off the man like he was neck-deep in a brawl rather than standing in front of a rather nice home. The faintest growl echoed from the bodyguard, and Elric decided then and there he didn't want to fight the man. This was a new body, and it was still in very good condition. The last thing he wanted to do was ruin it to get a witch he didn't even want.

He pretended to reach into his pocket, but really, he was letting his power slither out of his skin and roll down his wrist like beads of sweat. When the shadows had coalesced where he needed them, he lifted his hand and blew upon his palm.

Darkness scattered from his touch and covered the man's face. He flinched, lifting his fists to fight, but the surprise had made him inhale as well. It was more than enough for Elric's power to wriggle its way inside of him, and then the bodyguard's expression went slack. Jaw hanging, the man weaved back and forth a few times with his arms falling to his sides like an ape.

"You're going to let us inside now," Elric said. "And bring us to your mistress. Won't you?"

The man nodded, clearly incapable of speech. He bumped into the door before he twisted his body back inside. The man staggered as Elric followed him through the labyrinthine hallways.

This really was a lovely home. The interior walls were all paneled oak, very pretty and glimmering with wax. The floors were covered with deep burgundy carpets that his feet sank right into as they made their way through the halls. Heavy doors bracketed them on either side, interspersed with whale oil lamps and paintings of people who were likely important family members to those who owned the building.

Their escort, who was essentially brain dead, stopped in front of a door and limply gestured with one of his arms.

"This room?" Elric asked.

The man grunted.

"Good boy." Elric gestured for the women to head in before him. "If you wish to make her a part of this coven, I assume you'll need to speak with her first?"

Jessamine stared at him as the others entered the room, her gaze on him longer than he wanted.

"What?" he asked finally, before looking at the door again. "Aren't you supposed to be in there?"

"What did you do to him?"

"I just took his mind for a little while, that's all."

She planted her hands on her hips. "Where is his mind, then?"

He couldn't help the sharp-toothed grin that spread across his face. "The same place you and I met, nightmare. He's there alone for now, but if you wish for me to join him, I'm certain I could stand beside the door next to him while I vacate this form."

She shuddered. "No, I don't want you to do that."

Another voice interrupted them, this one snapping with anger and raspy, as though she'd spent years smoking. "Get in here, you two!"

Jessamine raised a brow and then entered the room. He already knew that the woman on the other side would be formidable, but he hadn't expected her to snap at them. Clearly, the spells on her stones outside didn't tell her all the details she wanted to know.

The room beyond was decorated very similar to the hallway. Warm wooden walls, plush deep-colored carpets, but this one had a fire in the hearth, multiple chairs positioned around a rather impressively large wooden coffee table, and an elderly woman seated in a plush rocking chair. Her white hair was a dandelion puff on top of her head, while her entire body was covered in handmade quilts, all in earth tones.

"You weren't expecting visitors," he said with a grin on his face.

"Clearly not, young man. What did you do to my bodyguard?"

"He'll be back under your power soon enough. He's just taking a small break from existence."

"I will not say a word to anyone here until he has been returned to me." An old, gnarled hand gripped the arm of her rocker, and even from where he stood he could see the age spots on it. "How dare you think you can enter my home in such a way! Do you know who I am?"

Elric blinked, and he was suddenly standing in front of her, even though he hadn't lifted a foot to move. He crouched and took her hand in his, knowing that his power had blackened his eyes. It took very little to peer into her mind, to soak in all the history of the woman before him. "You are Agnes Jessup. You have fought tooth and nail your entire life for a lick of power. You married a man who promised you the world, but all he did was beat you. You killed him in his sleep with a knife you'd hidden under your pillow. Another man came, and you had to kill that one, too. How many men have you killed? How many have broken at your feet and begged you for mercy?"

Her hand trembled in his. The fingers were curled with age, but he could still feel the strength in them. "Who are you?" she asked, her voice shaking.

Then his voice warped, filling with all the power of an ancient being who had an endless well of power inside of him. "I am who you have sought, Agnes. I am the bitter night and the ice-cold wind. I am the shadow who dogs your steps and the beast who writhes in the night."

"Deathless One," she gasped.

"You have clawed and fought for power your entire life, Agnes. When all you had to do was beg at my altar and I would have given you the world."

15

Jessamine held her breath, staring at the picture before her. A god on his knees before an old woman who would be a witch if there was only someone to gift her the power. She could feel energy crackling in the air, waiting for Agnes to say the words.

But the old woman had seen too much. She knew what promises were when they fell from male lips and how dangerous they were to believe. As he'd spoken, Jessamine had walked with Elric through the old woman's past. She had seen every single moment flickering behind her eyelids as the men Agnes had married died and so, too, had died her hopes and dreams.

Agnes looked at Jessamine then, and she suddenly knew the answer to a question that had plagued her for a long time. What was the role of a gravesinger? Was she only here to raise a god and then blend into the background?

Now, she knew. Elric didn't have the patience to convince someone on his own to join his coven. Witches had too much history in them. They knew the dangers that came with trusting anyone. She could feel it deep in her bones. The old history never died.

So she met Agnes's gaze and nodded. "It is time, old woman. You have fallen so far, but we are here to catch you."

"Fallen? I have not fallen at all."

Elissa gracefully sat in one of the chairs, arranging her skirts around herself just so. "Fortuna Beaumont runs the entire Pleasure District now. With the king at her side, she will not be displaced. You will die long before you claim this district as your own again."

It was fascinating watching Agnes's features change as soon as Elissa said that. She went from a scared old woman to a hardened warrior who had fought far too many people to ever suffer being spoken to like that.

"Watch your tongue, girl," Agnes snapped. "I have been in this district longer than anyone else. I know the rules of this place better than you *or* Fortuna. If she thinks she can take this part of the city over, then she'll have to pry it from my cold, dead hands."

"She might do just that," Elissa insisted, but she'd already started wringing her hands in her lap. "We're trying to help you."

"By barging into my home? By spelling my bodyguard? By..." Agnes seemed to trip over the next words that she might say because she looked back at Elric, who still had her hand in his grip.

And that was where it all changed, Jessamine could see. She'd been there before. There were so many things wrong with what Agnes had done in her life, but right now, there was a god holding her hand.

Anyone could feel his power. Elric was so magnetic to people who could become witches, though they were terrified of that sensation.

Sybil walked to Agnes's other side and reached for her free hand. Sybil didn't hide what her own hands looked like. They were gnarled and old as well. Ancient as time could let them get, and she grasped the old woman's fingers in her own as she sank onto her knees.

"You..." Agnes swallowed. "You look so young."

"I am."

"I can feel the wrinkles of your hands. You'll be hard-pressed to tell me that you are young."

"I am two hundred and seventeen years old," Sybil replied with a soft smile. "And I am young for a witch."

There it was. All laid out in the open for Agnes to know. They were witches, they were a coven who had come to collect her, and there was a god with them. But more than that, they were offering her immortality.

Agnes's lower lip quivered before she stiffened it. "Deathless One, please release my bodyguard."

"When we are gone."

"Now. He is my grandson, and I wish to speak with him before I make my choice."

Elric's nostrils flared, but then he nodded. Which surprised Jessamine, because usually he would have been much more hesitant to release someone who was so aggressive. But then again, he had the man's soul trapped. Perhaps he knew more about the grandson than even Agnes did.

A gasp echoed from outside the door, and then the man charged into the room. His face was red, his hands curled into fists like he was just waiting to put them through something.

"Easy," Elric warned with a quirked brow. "I can put you back there."

It was like watching a wall try to patch itself back up. The grandson pulled himself back together, bit by angry, vibrating bit, until he finally nodded and stiffly walked over to his grandmother. He stood behind her chair with his hands on the back of the rocker, holding it still as though his mere presence could keep her safe.

Only then did Agnes drop the mask of the frail old woman. She straightened, clearly far stronger than she had let on.

What a picture they were. An old woman, her hair white as snow, with the young man who was visibly her blood the more Jessamine looked at them.

"You offer me a great deal," Agnes finally said, her voice still warbling with age. "But the Pleasure District does not need a savior. Even I, although wishing to restore it to its former glory, am unnecessary for its survival. You offer me a coven of witches, but I have never wanted to bind myself to the weak. Give me something greater, and perhaps I will consider your offer."

Elric scoffed. "We are offering you the Pleasure District itself! What more do you want, you old bat?"

More wasn't necessarily the question, Jessamine mused. It appeared Agnes was of the old blood, just like the queen had been. Jessamine's mother would never make a deal with someone who was newly rich, or who had recently taken a throne from another. New blood hadn't worked through generations to get where they were, although such thinking had limited who she could work with. It wasn't that Agnes didn't recognize the power before her, but that she had no interest in it if there wasn't a connection as well.

Jessamine knew women like her. Agnes would make choices based on what other people would think of her. Would she align with a brand-new coven of witches who thought they deserved the attention of a god? No. She wouldn't. No one knew their names. To align herself with new blood was the kiss of social death.

Jessamine licked her lips, wondering if this was the right time to say anything. But at the very least, she knew they needed more connections. And if Elissa was right, this was the person they needed desperately to make a connection with.

"There was a time when the old blood mattered," Jessamine said quietly, and all eyes in the room turned to her. "My mother used to talk about the Pleasure District, not in hungry tones or with the idea that this was where she would disappear. The Pleasure District had a role in the kingdom. Political figures were brought here not to ply them with wine, drugs, and women, but to show them that Inverholm wasn't just a Factory District. It was filled with artists that rivaled the greats."

"Your mother is a wise woman."

"She was." Jessamine noted that Agnes caught the correction. Good. It was a detail she knew the old woman would remember. "I came here as a child. I don't know if I met you then, but I wouldn't be surprised if I had. A little dark-haired girl with bottomless eyes, that's what one of the men here said to me. He claimed he couldn't sell me, even if he put my price at the lowest he would take for a pound of flesh. My mother laughed and said it was good, because a girl like me would only sell her soul for the kingdom, not for a man."

Agnes's grandson shifted his grip on the chair, now clutching it like he needed the support. Agnes's eyes narrowed on Jessamine, her fingers curling a little harder around the arms of the chair. "This is a familiar story to me."

"Is it?"

"But it's not possible for you to be that little haunted girl."

"Why not?"

The breath caught in Agnes's throat, a little rattle that reminded everyone in the room just how old the woman was. "Because that little girl died."

Jessamine moved to sit on one of the sofas, crossing her legs and spreading her arms out across the back. Rather than look at the old woman, she let her head fall back, her scar revealed and her gaze tracing along the wooden knots on the ceiling. "She did."

"I saw her die. We all were watching the wedding down here. I saw the king in his dark colors and the princess with her wild, dark hair standing there. I saw him cut her throat and watched her body as it fell into the sea with a banner of blood marking her death. No one could survive that."

"I didn't say she survived it," Jessamine whispered. "I agreed that she died."

"No one cheats death."

The sound of footsteps approached, and Jessamine's view of the wood was obscured as Elric leaned over the back of the couch to loom over her. He braced his hands beside hers, staring down at her with those eyes that saw far too much. "Do you ever get tired of telling this story?"

"Sometimes."

"Do you want me to finish it?"

"If you'd like."

She watched his jaw tick, then his gaze ripped from hers to stare into Agnes's soul. "All the gods were dead. All of them except one, who was banished to a dark in-between realm until a gravesinger landed in his lap. And that god decided that death would not have her, because he wished to claim her for himself. Thus we are here, Agnes. We are here to give you an opportunity that you may never have again."

"Which is?"

He looked down at Jessamine again, as though he couldn't stand looking at anything other than her for too long. "Take back the Pleasure District. Help us find out what connection Fortuna Beaumont has to the king, and we will tie you not only to the most powerful coven this realm has ever seen, but to the queen who will take back her throne."

"If I don't?" Agnes's voice cracked.

Elric smiled, and it was the most terrifying expression she'd ever seen. "Trust me, Agnes. You don't want to know what I will do to all those who stand in her way."

There was a long silence, and then Agnes's shaking voice asked, "Haunted girl. What madness made you tie yourself to this brute?"

"I never wanted the pearls or the flowers that all the others brought. I didn't know what I wanted until I met the Deathless One, and then I realized... I wanted someone who would destroy the world for me." She lifted her head. Jessamine knew they looked a sight. Two dark figures, with equally messy hair and dangerous power at their fingertips. "I didn't want someone who would just promise it. I wanted someone who would do it."

"Why?"

"Because I was tired of having others constantly decide what my life would be. I wanted power, Agnes, just like you. So, do you want to be in this coven or not? Don't think I won't step on you if you get in my way. I will walk right over your cold body to get to my throne."

Even Sybil stared at her in surprise, but Jessamine was coming to realize it was the truth. She didn't want to play this game anymore. This game that the courts and nobility had made up wasn't healthy for anyone. She wanted her throne back, and no one was going to continue standing in her way.

She'd been nice.

Now, she had no more nice left in her.

Agnes stared for a few more moments before she chuckled. The old, raspy voice filled the room with mirth as she laughed until she couldn't breathe.

And when the old woman finally stopped laughing, running her finger underneath her eye to catch the tears, she said, "Now that is a woman I'll tie myself to. I told myself when I was very young that I would do whatever it took to get what I wanted out of life. I killed two husbands, and look at how far that's gotten me. If I'd decided to marry you, I might have been better off."

Jessamine arched a brow and nodded. "Might have been. It took death for me to learn how to be this ruthless, however."

"I have no interest in dying, not even if your man can raise me back." Agnes gestured with her hand, and her grandson helped her stand out of her rocker. It took a few moments, but together, they finally put her up on her feet so she could waddle in front of Jessamine. "You've won me over, girl. What does it take to be part of this coven?"

She didn't have the faintest idea, really. Elric was the one who decided who stayed and who was sent packing. Thankfully, the god answered for her.

"A sacrifice," Elric replied. "She might be the gravesinger, but it is still my coven."

"Ah, a sacrifice. Now, is that in the form of a pig?"

He nodded his head toward Elissa. "She sacrificed a cow."

"How gruesome."

Elissa nodded vehemently from where she sat. "It was not something I would repeat. The blood was *everywhere*. I had to throw the clothes away. Who knew there was so much blood in a cow?"

Well... Jessamine knew. She made a face when Sybil had to cover her mouth behind all of them. But at least she managed to not let out the giggle that was being contained behind that hand. If she had, then the entirety of the room might have broken out of this solemn spell.

Taking a deep breath, Jessamine glanced up at Elric. "Does it have to be an animal?"

"No. Sacrifices are the meaning behind whatever someone offers. Usually it is enough to give something up." He knew her too well at this point, though. Because his lips twisted in a slight smile before asking, "What do you have in mind, gravesinger?"

She shrugged. "Fortuna gave us an opportunity to see her. The ball is an actual event, I assume."

"Fortuna's ball has been months in the planning. How do you know about it?" Agnes asked.

"We peeked inside her bedroom and found the flyer. I have a feeling she wants me to be there." Jessamine tilted her head to the side, watching the old woman's features. "I think a sacrifice in the form of an invitation to that event might suffice."

"If she wants you there, then it's a trap." Agnes looked a little unsettled that Jessamine was even asking. "But I can prepare you the best I can for it. And I can get you an invitation if that's what it will take."

"Two invitations." Jessamine gestured to Elric behind her. "A gravesinger goes nowhere without her god, after all."

16

They stayed with Agnes for the night to avoid suspicion. Even the elderly woman made it very clear that they would not be leaving, and certainly not first thing in the morning. She still needed to figure out how to get them the invitations, not to mention that she didn't want anyone to talk. If people were coming to visit her, and if her grandson, of all people, had let them in, then they would not stay for barely an hour and then leave.

Decorum. All the flashing pageantry of what it was to be a noble. He'd forgotten what it was like to uphold standards.

There was so much gossip here, it seemed. The Pleasure District was certainly run like the city he remembered. Even in two hundred years, they might have changed what they sold, but the people were still the same.

Elric had been given his own room, and when he'd started toward Jessamine's, the old woman had been right there to beat him back with that cane of hers. "If anyone overhears I allowed an unwed couple to be in the same room overnight, I'll never hear the end of it. Get back, young man!"

He might have ignored her if she hadn't called him a young man.

When was the last time anyone had called him young? Perhaps one of his siblings back when they were alive. They'd all considered him to be younger than the rest of them, but he was still an ancient compared to everyone in this household.

So he'd listened to her request and returned to his bedroom full of priceless artifacts and its comfortable bed before he decided he was rather bored.

Elric didn't like being in a bed by himself. He'd been asleep for hundreds of years, put there by witches just like the coven that was being built. Too many dark memories tried to sink their claws into him, and he didn't have the patience for them. Instead, he wandered the halls of this sleeping household to see what secrets Agnes had hidden.

Peeking around a corner, he used some of his power to turn into shadows. At least no one would find him if they got up to get a glass of water. But as he passed by the room where all the women were sleeping, he discovered runes there that locked the door to men.

"Sneaky, sneaky," he muttered, shaking his head at Agnes's ingenuity. The woman wasn't a witch yet, but she certainly behaved like one.

He found the locking mechanism quickly enough. It was a spelled stone placed outside of the door. Bending, he picked it up and tossed it into the air, catching it lightly as the runes etched on the rock flashed with the movement.

A pretty spell. An easy one, too. But he could feel that it was old and long-lasting.

Curiosity burned in his chest. He wanted to know how Agnes, a noblewoman of all people, had access to magical objects. This woman had eyes on her the entirety of her life, and yet somehow had never been jailed for accessing such objects. He could feel the magic, and it was faintly familiar, as though he recognized the signature from a long time ago—and it was one that rang a bell of warning in the back of his mind. Perhaps it was time he ask Agnes herself, and understand where all the magic in her home came from.

Finding the old bat took time. She was far from the wing where she'd placed her visitors. Elric meandered through the darkened halls, seeking the only person who could give him answers. Unfortunately, he found himself far too distracted in the center of the home.

Halfway between the entrance and the back exit of this house, there was a hall of portraits. He stopped to look at them, admiring the craftsmanship in every paint stroke. But he froze when he saw a particular portrait that made him feel as though he had seen a ghost.

Olwyn had been high in the coven when he had last died. She looked as though someone had painted her soul into the canvas, every strand of her golden hair perfectly depicted. Her vivid blue eyes were just as beautiful as he remembered, as was the wicked grin on her face. The artist had painted her with her signature brown hawk behind her, the golden eyes of the animal the only indicator that it was her familiar.

She'd been ruthless in life. This was the first witch to suggest sacrificing him, but not just that, sacrificing all of them. She'd been willing to die in a blaze of glory to save the kingdom, even if it meant she wouldn't see the end result. A gravesinger of indescribable power, she was one of the best.

But all he could see was the knife she'd held in her hands. How she had slit the throat of her sisters, one by one. How'd he'd been forced to kneel there, chained to a stone altar while he begged and pleaded for them to see reason. The sickness could be fixed, if only they would take the time to find a new resolution. Instead, they were determined to sacrifice themselves. As though such self-mutilation would make history look upon them with kindness and not hatred.

He'd cried, watching them all die in front of him. Tears streaming down his cheeks while their blood reached for him, stretching across the floor in banners of pain. She'd been the last one standing with that bloody knife clutched in her hands and victory on her face.

"I am the last gravesinger," she had said as she approached him. "I sacrifice you so that all in this kingdom might be free of the gods. So that the land can right itself and this sickness will come to death with us. With *you*."

He still remembered the cold slide of steel across his throat and the wicked grin of victory on her face.

"I will join you soon, Deathless One," she'd said. "Soon, all of us will be bound for all eternity."

The ghosts of the past screamed in his mind. He could feel the gravesingers in their cage of his in-between realm as they rioted at the memory and the sight of their sister who had brought them to victory. The chains around their wrists rattled in his ears like the reckoning of a tide coming to sweep him away.

"Lost in memories?" another voice interrupted him, this one rattling with old age.

He startled, shadows coiling up his wrists and spreading out from his shoulders like massive wings before he snapped them back into his body. Agnes didn't deserve to speak with a man made of shadows, after all. He was a gentleman.

"How did you see me?"

She tapped the side of her head. "I grew up with witches, boy. They were the last of their kind, using up the magic their mothers gave them. I know how to see a hidden figure when there is one."

He hummed under his breath, turning his gaze once more to the portrait on the wall. He didn't have words to describe how that history still terrified him. How he knew that if he was asked to do it again, he would. All of his long life had been in sacrifice for them. There was no changing what he was made to be, even if he wished for that.

Elric barely heard her step closer to him. But he felt her hand on his arm as she tugged him to look at her.

Agnes's face bore the markings of time. Wrinkled and sun worn, she reached up with curled fingers to gently brush her knuckles across his cheek. There was the faint feeling of coolness before she drew her hands back down.

"Tears from a god," she murmured. "I'm sure there's some kind of spell or potion that would use these."

"Undoubtedly."

"What could bring you to such emotion seeing my ancestor?"

"You're Olwyn's granddaughter?"

"I told you I grew up with witches. But I do not know Olwyn. She died when my mother was a child, and I was born very late afterward." Agnes looked at the portrait, her brows furrowed as though she were seeing it for the first time. "My mother's stories painted her as ruthless and unkind. I know she was a hard woman."

"They all were."

"They had to be."

He shook his head. "The further I get from those memories, the more I wonder if they didn't have to be, but they chose to be."

He wasn't out here to have this conversation with an old woman, though. The past was in the past. There was no reason to dig it up.

"What do you want, Agnes?" he asked.

"I should be asking you that. You're the one wandering my halls in the middle of the night."

Elric held up the stone in his hand, the runes burning his palm. "Was this one of hers?"

"It was."

He let it drop to the floor with a thud that echoed through his entire body. He wanted nothing to do with the magic of such dangerous women. But then again, was it even their magic that he was so repulsed by? Or his own?

The old woman seemed to know all of this was going through his mind. But rather than pry even further and dig into the festering wound of his soul, she took his hand in hers and gave him two papers. "I sent my boy out to call in a favor. These are your invitations."

"That was rather easy for you."

"I told you, I have many connections in this place. But I do not believe you should enter as Lady Jessamine Harmsworth and her Deathless God. Trust me when I say this, Fortuna Beaumont is a worthy adversary. It's why she and I have battled for control over the Pleasure District for many years. The names on those invitations are for a couple who have lived here only a few years. They moved from another kingdom and are very new here, so few people have met them yet. They caused quite a stir when they first arrived. Foreign royals always are interesting. It's a shame they died just a few weeks ago. Use the names Farah and Martin Bloodworth when you enter, and introduce yourself as such to anyone who might ask questions."

Easy enough. Pocketing the invitations, he tilted his head to the side and watched as her eyes canted to the side. As though she was hesitant to make eye contact with him.

"Why are you wandering about the halls in the middle of the night with these invitations, Agnes?"

She swallowed hard, her throat working with the emotion. "My grandson thinks this is a fool's errand. He told me that I was selling my soul for a few years of power. I am old, Deathless One. I know that. My time here is coming to an end very soon, and I fear what that means for my soul."

He could tell her it meant very little. All souls went to the same place, and humans had never been able to dream up what death meant for them. He could tell her that someday her soul would wish to be reborn and that she would be given the opportunity to fix all the guilt that she carried with her into the afterlife. As unlikely as that was. A soul's history followed it into the next life and became an accumulation of all the mistakes that happened before, repeating a never-ending cycle that was so hard to break. But these were details no one wanted to hear. They weren't as comforting as humans wanted them to be.

"You have such fear in you for a witch," he murmured, eyeing her and seeing the toll it had taken on her body. "I thought you were smarter than that. You have seen Sybil, have you not?"

"I see a young woman who chose to take her power in her youth. I am old. No part of me wishes to stay this way forever, so I will take the power and live a natural life. That is my decision."

Something dark wriggled in his mind. A whisper that this was how he could punish the witches who had tormented him before. This was Olwyn's last bloodline. He could promise that she would have the power and let her die. Then he could see to it that her grandson fell in a tragic event, and Olwyn herself would die with him.

A scream echoed that only he could hear. The spirit trapped in his realm wished to claw her way out of the muck to ensure her bloodline continued. She raged in his mind, and that was enough torture for him.

Instead, he looked Agnes in the eye and said, "You do not have to remain old if you accept this power. Should you wish it, I would make you young again."

"Surely that's not possible."

"Dear one, you have such little faith in your god. Worship me. Sacrifice to me. Give me all that I desire from you, and I will not only make you immortal. I will give you back your youth."

He'd said the words countless times before. Cajoled witches into giving him more power with their sacrifices so that he could take from them. This was one of the rare times where he genuinely meant it.

Elric knew he could punish her instead. But what a shame it was to see a powerful line of witches wiped off this realm simply because one of them had harmed him. He was better than that, even if they weren't.

Ah, he hated growth. It was such a shame that he was no longer the bloodthirsty monster who had murdered witches for far less. Forgiveness was so much harder than just pretending they didn't exist. But he supposed he did feel a little better about it afterward.

With wide eyes, she nodded. "Then consider those invitations my sacrifice to you, great Deathless One. Hollow god whom I will fill with magic, grant me eternal life, and in return, I promise to serve you until the light fades from my eyes."

Ah, the ancient words filled him with purpose. Every witch seemed to know their meaning, and yet every single one of them had a new spin on how to bring the spell to life. He could feel the power from the invitations growing. Darkness spread throughout the hall, inky ropes clinging to the portraits and feeding into the magic he had stored in that other realm. He could feel it building in his chest even as he reached for the power that clung to him.

"With magic I take from you," he growled, his voice low and echoing, "I give it back tenfold. Join my coven, witch, and all your sacrifices will no longer be in vain."

Agnes parted her nightgown, and he reached for her chest. His hands slid beyond that wrinkled, sagging skin. Power flexed inside of him, and he cracked her open. Bit by creaking bit, he spread her ribs and left an empty fissure. For what was a witch if not just waiting to be filled by a god?

Shadows streamed down his hand. Writhing, ink-dark eels wriggled their way inside of her, and Agnes tilted her head back in a gasp. Her eyes opened wide with pain, but there was rapture in that gaze as well.

Though her hands remained wrinkled, curled, and scarred, the rest of her skin smoothed with the magic he fed into her. Age spots disappeared. Scars flattened into silver lines. What was an old face became young again, brimming with beauty and strength. White hair turned into strands of wheat-colored silk that slid halfway down her back. And when it was finally done, she was a stunning woman once more.

Agnes tied her nightgown back around her body, her hands shaking. "How do I look?"

"Young again," he replied, before touching his finger to her chin. Tilting her head up, he stared down into her eyes so she could feel the full weight of his godly powers. "If you betray me, Agnes, I will not be merciful. Jessamine is the only tether that helps me remain human, and if you betray her? I will take all this power back, and I will make you watch yourself age into dust before I let your soul be gathered by the keeper of the dead. Do I make myself clear?"

"Perfectly," she replied, but then a wry grin spread across her face. "She is lucky to have you, Deathless One. A man so feral for a woman will see she goes far in life."

"She is owed a throne." He released her chin and stepped back into the shadows. "But I am owed much more than that."

17

Seeing a young Agnes was more than a little startling. Everyone at the dining room table froze when she walked in. Clearly, it was her. She still had the same features and facial expression and voice, but she was now a stunning beauty. Even her grandson hadn't known what to say as he looked at the woman who had to be his grandmother. Jessamine had watched food fall out of the poor man's mouth before she'd caught her laugh with her hand. Sybil had been no better, and when the two of them looked at each other, it made their giggles all the worse.

But then she'd seen Elric's expression and all of it felt... strange. He was smiling at them, certainly. There was a grin on his face as he'd lifted his mug of coffee to his mouth, but there was something off about his eyes. As though he wasn't entirely there.

Jessamine followed him for the better part of a day after that before she realized what was wrong. And she was going to do something about it.

Elric wasn't himself. Not after adding Agnes to the coven and not after Elissa either. She'd only seen a few of his memories regarding witches, but she knew they weren't good. His own power had tried to sabotage him by forcing her to see some of his history, as though what he'd been through made him weak. And that wasn't something that was all that easy to get over.

Taking a deep breath to steady herself, she knocked on the door to his bedroom. It took a few knocks before she could hear him rustling about, and then the door opened. "Nightmare," he said, his voice pitched low as though he'd been sleeping. "What are you doing up?"

"I want you to come with me, if you don't mind."

"Where?"

"It's a surprise."

His gaze sharpened, his eyes narrowing on her. She knew she'd piqued his interest, now she just needed to get him to agree to do whatever she wanted. Which... really wasn't that hard with Elric, if she was being honest.

He leaned against the doorframe, crossing his arms over his chest and looking down at her. "You know I don't like surprises, nightmare."

"Well, I think you're going to like this one. It will be good to get out of the house."

"And here I was thinking Agnes had told us not to leave until she'd gotten all the details figured out. And aren't you supposed to have a fitting this evening with some fancy dressmaker to make you look like you fit in here?"

"I genuinely couldn't care less." Jessamine reached for his hand, tugging him out into the hallway. "Besides, no one tells us what we can and cannot do. You're a god. I'm your gravesinger. If we want to head out onto the streets, then we will."

He followed her with that bemused smile on his face, and she never let go of his hand. Together, they snuck out of the back and onto the street. It was late, and very few people were still about, but they stuck to the shadows just in case.

"Jessamine," he started.

"Not yet."

"Where are we going?"

"My favorite place in all of the Pleasure District. I was so excited when I found out it was still open, and I just had to bring you."

His hand squeezed hers, and he let out a huffing laugh. "If you wanted to bring me to a brothel, you only had to ask."

"Elric."

This time he did laugh, and the sound bubbled out of him with such mirth that it spread to her as well. At least he could still laugh. At least he still found some hilarity in all that they had done, even if he was nervous about giving people more power as well. She had given him that, and for now it would be enough.

Finally, they slipped from the streets to a massive building stretching high above all the others, surrounded by white columns. It was a monolithic beast compared to the other buildings around them, overpowering everything in size and stature.

"What is this place?" he asked, staring around them in awe before following her as she headed up the stairs.

"You'll see."

"Jessamine." His tone was cajoling now.

"You really don't like surprises, do you?" She was slightly out of breath from running up the stairs, but turned her back to the door to give him one last look. Bright red flushed his cheeks where he showed only the slightest state of exertion. His lips were parted with surprise, but his eyes still watched her, just staring at her as though she was the wildest thing he'd ever seen in his life.

"I hate them," he said, bracing his arm on the door above her head and leaning into her. "But I have found that I very much enjoy your delight, gravesinger."

"Good."

Jessamine shoved the door open and sent all the prayers she could think of that the temple would be empty. It was, after all, quite late. Very few people brought offerings to the gods at all, and this place was mostly used as a museum rather than an actual temple these days. She was lucky enough that it was empty, although there were still a few incense bowls burning with sacrifices.

The temple was exactly as she remembered it. Eight-foot-tall carvings of all the gods lined the entire room. A wall of them, all twenty that had once existed. Each one had a massive space around it, with individual mosaics on the floor that were hand laid with tiny chips of gems. Every single god had one, each with their own sacrifices from people who visited them.

The first was, of course, the God King. He was massive and tall, wearing his armor like in every depiction of him that she'd ever seen. But in this carving, he had laid his sword at his feet, and instead stood with his arms crossed over that barrel chest. He was lit by braziers that hung from the ceiling. They filled the room with a strange flickering ambiance that made it feel as though one needed to be quiet when entering this space.

Jessamine breathed in the scent of incense and felt the warmth crawling up her arms. The temple had always felt peaceful to her with its silent halls, like the building was holding its breath.

"Is this where you came to worship?" Elric asked, his footsteps echoing as he started down the line of statues.

"My mother worshipped more than I ever did. She was the one who had the proclivities toward the gods. I…" She paused when he looked back at her with a bemused expression. "I never found the right god to worship."

"Interesting." He arched a brow before meandering again. He clasped his hands behind his back, pausing to look at every single statue.

Jessamine let him take his time. Part of her wondered how long it had been since he'd seen a depiction of his siblings while they were still alive. After all, the other statues were usually destroyed when a god died. Even the witches had removed part of the statues and filled the remains with flowers or moss.

But these statues were pristine. They were exactly how the gods had looked when they were alive, if the artists were to be believed.

"Who did your mother worship?" he asked.

"The Wizened Crone." She paused in front of the old woman's statue. She was a bent-backed lady with a cane who stared down at everyone with a disappointed expression on her face.

"Ah, the mother of wisdom. It is no surprise the queen worshipped her. Her followers always thought themselves better than even the scholars of my sister the Inquisitive One, because their knowledge was boundless and unending." He snorted. "She only let them gather information about the things she didn't care if they knew. She kept her secrets for only the most loyal."

"All the gods seemed to have their favorites."

"All of us did." Then his expression turned sly. "Do you know where my statue is?"

Of course she did. It was the first thing that she had looked for when she entered all those years ago. The Deathless One had always intrigued her, or perhaps scared her. A god for only witches, very select in who was even allowed to worship him.

"I remember there were many who refused to even walk by your statue," she said, striding past him down the long rows. "They had to move it, you know. You were in the middle for a very long time, but then they placed you all the way down here because people were afraid to speak in front of your visage."

"You know how I love flattery."

"I thought you'd like that." The smile on her face felt permanent as she walked over to his statue.

It was obviously much larger than he was, but his features were very similar. The artist had done a good job capturing his smirk. They'd carved him with his hand outstretched, as though he was waiting for someone to take it and allow him to draw them into the darkness. He had longer hair then, though. The statue's hair was tied behind his neck, a few locks falling around his features, just enough to barely hide the eyes that had been carefully chiseled to place obsidian chips in them.

"Here you are," she said, staring up at the statue. "Do you know how many women I heard walk by this statue and claim that you were the most handsome god here?"

"I'm sure my brothers rolled in their graves every single time it happened." He leaned closer to her, his breath fanning across her neck. "Take my hand."

"Elric. It's just a statue."

"Then it shouldn't mean anything to take its hand."

But that childish part of her that was terrified of the statue trembled. Yet, it was him. The statue was only an extension of the god she trusted, and she had no reason to fear it. Still, her fingers shook as she reached up toward the outstretched hand.

"Why do you want me to do this?" she asked, her palm hovering over the cold stone.

"Trust me." His words seemed to echo around her. The brazier above the statue flickered with power, as though the shadows were already threatening to drown the flame out. What light should ever exist when he was here?

Her palm came down on the icy stone. For a moment, nothing happened, but then she could feel the stone take life. Fingers curled around hers, and the statue straightened. It pulled her toward the hard visage of the man she adored and spun her around.

Gasping, she found her back pressed against the statue with its arm firmly locked around her chest. She couldn't move. Not if she wanted to. Her arms were pinned at her sides, and she was forced to look down at where the living Elric stood with his hands in his pockets. He looked up at her with hungry eyes, and she knew he was about to desecrate this temple.

"What are you doing?" she asked, her voice breathless.

"I just like seeing you pinned." He stepped up the small podium at the base of the statue, putting her at eye level with him. "Now what am I going to do with this nightmare I've found in my temple?"

"Elric?" she breathed.

She had no idea what he was going to do with her now that he'd quite literally used himself to hold her in place. But her heart fluttered with excitement and her breath was ragged as she watched his eyes trail over her entire body.

"Delicious," he murmured, before sinking to his knees before her.

How sacrilegious it was to see him kneel like that, worshipping at his own altar as though he had forgotten he was the god. Elric shoved aside a few burning bowls of incense and a bundle of crumpled flowers a pitying soul had left a few days ago. They tumbled onto the ground, the metal bowls clanging and rolling for what felt like forever, until silence descended upon them.

"There is no greater worship of a god than giving him your body." He reached for her ankle, drawing her skirts up slowly to reveal first one long leg, then the other.

She could feel his breath against her inner thighs. The panting puffs of air let her know he was just as affected by this as her. She gripped the stone arm wrapped around her chest, breathing out slowly as he lifted one of her legs and braced it on his shoulder.

"Elric—"

"If you are going to say anything, it should be to grace this temple with the cries of your pleasure, Jessamine. Anything else I will punish you for."

She pitched her voice low as he pressed a kiss just to the left of where she wanted him most. "Won't the other gods be able to hear? Even if they are dead?"

He looked up at her from beneath her skirts, their gazes meeting with passion and heat. "I want them to hear, nightmare."

And then he devoured her.

With lips, teeth, and tongue, he sank into her body without mercy. She might have held on for a while, drowning in the pleasure without having a single cry drop from her lips. But he didn't give her the chance. From his hands gripping her thigh wrapped around his neck, to the plunging tongue that sank into her body, she could hardly stand.

His stone figure kept her upright, though. And when she tilted her head back, she stared up into the stone face and knew there was no other god she would ever worship.

He sank his fingers inside of her, curling them just so, and she saw stars behind her eyes that only a god could have birthed. No temple had ever been desecrated so thoroughly, and yet she found prayers still dripping from her lips.

Prayers for more.

Invocations of need.

Moans that fell from her lips like hymns.

Supplication in the form of spread thighs and whimpered desire as the sounds of their pleasure filled the temple. Wet, slick sounds that were just as sacrilegious as they were the purest form of worship.

His stone statue shifted again, and she barely would have noticed if she didn't hear him grind out, "Open your mouth, nightmare."

She did, tilting her head back without question before fingers slipped between her lips. Cold, stone fingers that slowly felt warm as she sucked on them, and he groaned with her at the sensation.

She tightened, every muscle in her tensing as an orgasm rippled through her in wave after wave of excruciating pleasure that had her babbling out his name. And then he rose, standing from between her thighs as she shuddered in the endless pleasure that still ran throughout her entire body.

His face was wet with her desires. The statue shifted, freeing her mouth from its grip so Elric could grab her by the hair and pull her in for a searing kiss. She could taste herself on his lips, and the hunger that still ran throughout his entire body.

"Perfection," he growled against her mouth. "Absolute perfection. Now, you will give me more."

18

Elric stood behind the coven as they surveyed Elissa's home. Obviously, a coven stuck together. Witches were stronger when they were capable of sharing magic and knowledge easily without having to sneak under the cover of night. It was a difficult thing to do when they were hiding from so many eyes.

But now they had a lady in their mix. A woman who was used to much more than what she had been given, and at the twisted expression on Agnes's face, he didn't think she was going to stay in this birdhouse.

Her grandson even looked a little… distraught.

Elric leaned over to mutter to the man, "I never caught your name."

"Hugo."

"Hugo," he repeated with a nod, before looking at the expressions on the women's faces.

Sybil was far too gleeful, and he could already tell she'd make all of this worse, given the chance. Of course, Elissa just wanted to go home. She looked at the others with far too much confusion, because she didn't understand why the others weren't as excited as she was. Jessamine just looked apathetic, while Agnes looked as though she had just stepped in horse shit.

"Hugo," he said with a sigh. "I don't think we'll be staying here very long."

"I don't think we'll be staying here at all."

He didn't suppose they would, not with Agnes looking like that.

"This simply won't do!" Agnes said.

"My home is very safe. The only people who ever come here are the ones looking for a bird." Elissa twisted her hands together and gestured toward it. "I have very few clients these days. The new king doesn't fancy birds, so it's unlikely that anyone will be coming to see me for a while yet. Bird buying has a season, you know."

Jessamine crossed her arms over her chest. "Didn't you think we were a client when we first came here only a week ago?"

The witch went pale. "Well, that was a rare lapse in judgment."

Elric had never been more entertained. The other witches lit into Elissa like sharks scenting blood in the water. All of a sudden, they wanted to know everything about the house. What spells protected it? Her mother had been the one to build it, but how good of a witch had the old bat been? Far more questions than Elissa knew how to answer. Of that much, he was certain.

He watched it all with a bemused smile on his face before shaking his head and looking at Hugo. "I don't suppose you know of a home that would be discreet for all of them?"

"There aren't many abandoned buildings in the Pleasure District. A few, yes, but not many. And they're all old."

"That doesn't matter to me. I'm a god, Hugo. I can conjure whatever I want." Elric flexed his hands, savoring the new power from the two witches who had joined his coven.

The stronger the coven, the stronger he was. As a god, he had control over shadows and the realm of the dead. He could conjure spirits to do his bidding, and he could stop a soul from ending up in the realm beyond. But with a coven? Especially a strong one? Ah, he had many more skills than that.

"Where is one of these homes you speak of?"

"One is at the corner of First and Seventh." Hugo shrugged. "Lots of people walk past that house often, but it's the largest one."

"We don't need large. There's only six of us." But there might be more soon. With the way Jessamine was building her coven, he wouldn't be surprised if there were six more in less than a week. Pinching the bridge of his nose, he shook his head. "We'll need more than that, though."

"There is another house. Still large and fairly falling apart. No one goes near it, but that's at the very end of Rose Street." Hugo shrugged. "If you're powerful enough to turn that into a home? No one ever looks twice at it. Said to be real haunted."

"Haunted, you say?" He snorted. "That's the place we should be, then. No one will go into the building, and I have a soft spot for wandering spirits."

"Whatever you say, mate." Hugo looked at the witches and then back at him. "You know where Rose Street is?"

"I think that's fairly easy to find."

"I'll manage the ladies until then."

Elric watched as Hugo approached his grandmother and laid a hand on her back. With a few words, he cajoled the old woman into Elissa's home, even though they all knew she wasn't going to like it any more from the inside. It would start an argument that would last a few hours, though, and that was all Elric needed to get their new home set up.

"Rose Street," he muttered.

He strode away before any of them noticed he'd left. The streets were filled with people, so if Jessamine came stomping after him, she would lose him eventually.

In the meantime, it let him feel out his powers so he could get an idea of what he could do.

The new sacrifices had done more than he'd expected. Elric was used to an entire coven being required to get his power back to godly levels. But these women had been heartfelt in their need, and their magic ran through his veins with more strength than he'd expected. If the haunted home was in shambles, he was quite certain he could fix it.

Rose Street didn't take very long to find. And as he strode down the sidewalk, seeing the stream of people ebb into little more than a trickle, he felt the tug in his stomach that was

Jessamine. She wanted him to come back, likely because the argument was getting out of control. But he had never lived with his coven. They were always the ones to figure out their own arguments.

Besides, she'd always said she was going to be their queen. She would need to live up to that legacy soon enough.

Finally he was at the end of Rose Street, staring at the building Hugo had remarked would be perfect. From the outside, he had to agree. The wooden exterior had likely once been vibrant and waxy, but time had aged it. The wood grayed and pieces were tearing off from all ends that he could see. Nearly every window was broken, although not many were still on the house. The rest were boarded up. But it had lovely turrets on either side, and a shape that looked like it was out of a horror novel. The grounds were hardly cared for, little more than yellowed dead grass surrounded by a wrought iron fence that tilted forward slightly after the ground had shifted during their long winters.

As he stared, he heard the distinct sound of a wail. The haunting sound echoed, perhaps just the wind, or perhaps more than that. All the hairs on his arms rose as another cry whipped through the home, and he swore he saw a figure standing in one of those shattered windows.

"We couldn't have asked for a better house," he murmured before striding toward the building.

He felt his power already boiling. The shadows inside of him wanted to stretch. It was almost like a living being inside of him that he'd consumed from only two sacrifices. Such power for such little things, and yet, he couldn't stop himself from using it.

The door screeched as he yanked it off its hinges, and already the shadows were pouring from his form. They dripped from his hands like ink, covering the worn floor with holes throughout. With every step he took, the holes were fixed. The wood gleamed with new life and the faded, peeling wallpaper regained its vibrant floral pattern. Its swirling labyrinth of deep colors led him through the halls.

It was a large home with easily fifteen bedrooms, more if he gave some thought to where he would put them. A large kitchen that his magic soon cleaned entirely until it looked more like a working kitchen. Already he could imagine Sybil in the corner, hanging bundles of herbs from the exposed beams.

There was a comfortable library, and a room that might have once been an attached greenhouse for Elissa to keep all her birds in. And still more that his magic found, healing every single nook and cranny until the inside of the house was finally befitting a coven.

He heard the softest moan from overhead, from the attic, where his magic had not yet reached. He pulled the shadows back, making sure they didn't invade the home of that ghost.

"I won't change everything," he called out, certain that the ghost was listening to him. "There is much we will use this home for, though."

A cold gust of wind trailed down his spine, as though someone had tried to grab on to him and then realized he was not someone they could simply grab.

"I am a god." Elric narrowed his eyes, following the path of a small silver orb of light that moved just out of reach. "You will not banish me from this home, nor will you banish the coven of witches who will join me. If you stay out of our way, I will not usher you into the realm of the dead that you have been so adamantly avoiding. Do we have a deal?"

Again, a hesitation from the spirit before it rushed up the stairs and back into the attic. He'd leave it alone up there. The spirit had been here much longer than him, after all.

Turning, he surveyed the work he had done. Everything was nearly perfect. If anyone walked into this dark home with the warm wooden floors and deep-colored wallpaper, they would know it was a home for witches.

One final touch. He allowed his shadows to stretch into the basement and raise up an altar where his witches could all worship. An altar covered in runes of power. His shadows transformed the stone into black obsidian that gleamed in the meager light. And because he was their benevolent god, he also added indentations in the floor where they would kneel before it for their sacrifices, just so that they would be more comfortable instead of kneeling on sharp stones.

"There," he muttered before he tugged hard on his connection with Jessamine.

It was no longer a thread of darkness between them, but a rope that he could see with his mind's eye if he looked hard enough. Thick as his wrist, it connected them no matter how far away he was.

And then Elric waited. Because he knew his gravesinger well. Jessamine had never been able to deny him when he called for her.

In a mere half hour, he met the four witches and Hugo at the end of the dirt path leading into the house. Jessamine had her arms crossed over her chest, and those pretty dark eyes were flashing with curiosity.

"What have you done, Deathless One?" she asked.

He gestured toward the entire coven and then bowed long and low. "My coven could not stay in such a small home. Elissa's home is too well-known, and besides, there are certain places that are more safe than hiding in plain sight."

"This looks like a crumbling hovel."

"I assure you, I have prepared everything inside for you, my gravesinger. You deserve the world, and I am only here to lay it at your feet."

He could hear the sharp intake of breath from Agnes, and knew that he had won points with those words. Perhaps she didn't know their connection yet, but Agnes would soon see that he was more tied to his gravesinger than he had ever been to any other witch.

Jessamine was everything to him. His reason for being started and ended with her.

Shaking her head with a wry grin, Jessamine strolled past him and hooked her fingers in the front of his shirt, practically dragging him to the front door as she advanced up the steps.

"Come on, Nyx, let's see what decorating skills a god has."

Her black cat suddenly appeared, twining around his legs and almost tripping him before the familiar slipped into the house ahead of them. He could almost hear the excitement as Nyx let out a meow that sounded like a battle cry and thundered up the steps to the attic.

"A creature that small shouldn't be able to make so much noise," he muttered.

"A cat is a cat."

"It's a familiar."

"A familiar that is a cat," she corrected before releasing his shirt.

Elric smoothed it down as they both walked into the house, and he anxiously studied her features to see if she liked what he had done. At the smile on her face, it appeared he'd done well.

"Look at you," she said quietly, turning in a circle and then stepping into the first room. "First you build a coven, and then you build us a home."

He caught Sybil's gaze as the dark witch walked into the house with them. And for once, all he saw in her gaze was approval.

"It's long past time that I respected the coven who worships me," he murmured, before tugging Jessamine into his arms. "Now, no one will be able to touch us."

19

Jessamine had forgotten what it felt like to have a home. In all that they had done, all that she had suffered, the memories of having a safe place to rest her head had simply filtered out of her mind. She'd been so confident that she'd never forget her past, but somehow... she had. In one moment, she was sure she hadn't changed that much, and then she was reminded in an instant that she had.

Safety in these walls meant she could fully relax. She didn't have to sleep with one ear listening or try to pay attention to the meaning of the stillness of silence. Her sleep here was more restful than she had felt in ages. Her head had hit the pillow, and she hadn't even remembered falling asleep. She just woke up again feeling more like herself.

The room Elric had created for the two of them was far cozier and less spooky than the rest of the house. The wallpaper was a lovely maroon color with bits of gold flecks sprinkled throughout, and the ceiling was wallpapered with the same pattern. She stared up at it, trying to trace imagined shapes as Elric woke.

His warm arm snaked around her waist, tugging her a little closer to him as he rested his head on her shoulder. "You're awake too early, nightmare."

"I'm always awake before you."

"And I don't know how you do it," he murmured, snuggling a little harder against her side. "The morning is not meant for being awake like this. The morning is for lazing about in your bed until someone tells you it's time to get up."

"Spoken like a veritable god who has been worshipped his entire life." She tilted her head to look at him, grinning as he cracked only one eye open to glare at her.

"Were you not a princess in another life?" he muttered. "You must have lazed about in bed far more than I did."

"Elric, I promise you, there wasn't a day in my life that I lazed about. Besides, there's a lot to do today."

"Why?"

"We're preparing for the dinner party tonight, remember? The one where we're supposed to trap Fortuna and get more information on how to stop Leon from completely taking over my kingdom until all hope is lost?"

He blew out a long breath that stirred her hair. "Oh, that's what you're all worried about. We'll be fine. Go back to sleep."

That was... not helpful. Besides, she really needed to get out of bed if she wanted to prepare herself.

Untangling their limbs, she pecked him on the forehead before leaving him strewn out on her bed, his arm halfway off the mattress and a pillow over his head. The man really couldn't be more dramatic if he tried, but she'd learned a long time ago that the Deathless One was not a morning person.

Padding down the halls of her new home, Jessamine let herself soak in all that had changed. They could remain here after dealing with Fortuna. Agnes would take over anyway, which meant the coven itself would run the Pleasure District. Let Leon bring all the foreign dignitaries here and see how much they liked her kingdom when they were met with witchcraft. Perhaps then Leon would realize that she would not give up without a fight.

Of course, she wasn't all that certain he knew she was still alive. Rumors weren't facts. A king like him wouldn't take rumors from peasants seriously; he'd need to see for himself that she was the one behind all this.

"Your Highness?" The raspy voice stopped her in her tracks.

"Agnes?" She turned with a soft smile on her face for the once-elderly woman. "What are you doing up this early?"

"I rarely sleep. Even before the Deathless One gave me these powers, I was not one to spend my precious time on dreams."

"You look well." Agnes had been a beauty in her day, and now looked almost identical to the women Jessamine had seen painted on her walls.

Long blond hair, strong features, and a powerful build that suggested if she wanted to, Agnes could have been stronger than the average man. And yet she held herself with the grace and confidence befitting a woman of her station. Even her gowns suggested that. Silk, velvet, hand-stitched golden threads on the edges… Jessamine would have looked twice at those gowns in the parties at the palace, and there were an infinite number of rich people at those parties.

"If you wouldn't mind coming with me?" Agnes asked.

Jessamine didn't think she had a choice. She followed the old witch all the way to her room, noting that Elric had done an impressive job with this one as well. It reminded her of old money, of castle rooms that had been in the same style for ages and yet were still far more functional than any of the new ones. Rosewood warmed half of the walls, and the other half was painted a lovely deep violet. Hand-painted stars decorated the ceiling, and all the furniture was made of the same kind of wood as the walls, creating a harmonious impression.

The thick carpets on the floor certainly helped as well. Jessamine couldn't even hear their footsteps as they made their way across the room, and Agnes pointed for her to sit on the small chaise lounge at the foot of the bed.

"You are going into Fortuna's domain," Agnes started, her face wrinkled with worry. "I fear that none of you know who she is now. From what Sybil has told me, you knew Fortuna when you were children, yes?"

"She is my cousin. We grew up together when she visited the castle with her parents, but obviously they were nowhere near as well-off as we were. My mother was the queen, and Fortuna's mother was my mother's cousin. Disgraced from the royal family for marrying one of the tavern owners in the Pleasure District after she'd fallen in love with him." Jessamine curled her fingers in her lap. "I always thought it was a romantic story, but I know Fortuna felt differently."

"I'm sure she felt as though her mother had blighted her chances at gaining a throne herself. So she made herself one." Agnes tsked before walking over to the wardrobe. "I took the liberty of ordering your outfits for tonight. It's very important that you look as though you fit in."

"I doubt fashion has changed so much in the six months since I've been dead."

Agnes gave her an unimpressed look. "My dear, you underestimate Fortuna already. The moment there were rumors the princess wasn't dead, Fortuna began her plan to make sure that you would be found out quickly and without hesitation."

"What does that even mean?"

"She changed what we consider to be beautiful. All the gowns have changed. All the accessories are different. Anyone who doesn't know what is now considered fashionable becomes the laughingstock of any room she is in. She ensured you would be spotted out by all of those who saw you, and even in a crowd, you would stand out." Agnes arched her brow. "Or did you think you were blending in?"

She had thought they were doing a fine job of it, but clearly she'd been wrong. Wrinkling her nose, she looked down at her bedclothes before looking back at Agnes. "Then what has changed?"

"Getting you ready for this party is going to be an all-day ordeal, my darling. But we're all ready for the fight that this will be."

"Fight?" Jessamine shook her head. "We?"

At that, the door opened, and Sybil and Elissa walked in with their arms laden. Tools, implements, makeup, hair appliances, everything that she hadn't seen in months were suddenly carted into the room. Elissa shot her a bright grin before leaving once more, and Sybil stuck her tongue out at Jessamine.

"Why didn't I realize you were going to be so much work?" Sybil asked as she started back toward the door, too.

"Where are you going?"

"There are more boxes."

Jessamine's jaw fell open, and then she looked to Agnes for confirmation. "More boxes?"

"I told you. This will be an all-day event, and don't think that you are going to get out of this. Elric is a man. All he has to do is wear a dark suit and exude confidence and control, which he already does. You, on the other hand, have to be the flower that hangs on his arm. You must be the beauty that all who see him envy. And if you are not? You will expose the both of you. Now. First things first." Agnes grabbed Jessamine by the arm and carted her over to the window. "We're going to fix that hair."

"My hair?" Jessamine touched the dark locks, wondering what was so wrong with it.

It had changed after her death, of course. There weren't a lot of brushes when one was living in an abandoned home, and even then, it wasn't easy for her to take the time to get the tangles out. She did what she could with her hands, and she'd thought she'd done a fine job of it.

"This looks like a bird's nest on the best of days, and on the worst…" Agnes winced. "When you walked into my home, I was certain we were handing out charity to someone who had never been inside a house before, my dear."

Well, that certainly put it into perspective.

Jessamine remained where she was while Agnes rummaged through the boxes that Sybil and Elissa were carting in. She returned with handfuls of brushes, two of which she handed to Sybil and Elissa, and all three women hovered behind her.

"This isn't going to be pleasant, I fear," Agnes said, brandishing the brush like it was a sword. "But it must be done."

Jessamine tried her best not to complain, but she had a lot of hair. They started at the ends, which were nearly to her waist now and continued upward. Every single snarl, tangle, and knot fought them. It was like her hair had taken on a life of its own, and it wanted to be the most difficult beast any of them had ever dealt with.

She wasn't sure how long it took, but by the time they were done, Agnes was complaining about the state of her wrists.

"Elissa, dear," Agnes said dramatically as she sat down on the edge of the bed. "You're perfectly capable of curling it, I imagine?"

Oh, lovely. They brought out an implement that Sybil warmed with a spell, and off they went again. The room was soon filled with the scent of burning hair, and still they would not slow down. Once all of her locks had been appropriately curled, Agnes set out to complete her makeup.

"You have a lovely bone structure," she claimed, tilting Jessamine's face back and forth. "But we'll have to hide all that we can. Look at the scars on you, my girl. No one in the nobility would ever dare publicly bare their scars like you do."

"It's not like I have a choice."

"Perfection is what we're going for," Agnes said. "And one cannot be perfect with a mark across your throat like someone murdered you."

Jessamine ground her teeth together. "Someone did."

Agnes ignored that as she began to apply Jessamine's makeup. Heavy rouge made her lips look like they were dripping blood. Blush, fake freckles, and ringed kohl around her eyes made the darkness in them seem even more dark. She was shocked to look at herself in the mirror when Agnes finally finished.

"You weren't kidding when you said things have changed." She leaned forward and touched her fingers to her face, trying to see herself in the reflection of the mirror. "This is... This doesn't even look like me! Just a few months ago, everyone was trying to look as natural as possible. And now this?"

"Most of us aren't happy with it." Agnes tilted her head to the side, surveying Jessamine in the mirror as though she noticed something was still off. "I suppose it is pretty on you. I hadn't expected you to look quite so different, my dear."

Neither had she. But with all her dark hair piled on top of her head in complicated coils and the makeup on her face, Jessamine wasn't even sure she would recognize herself.

"Now, the last piece is the gown." Agnes walked over to the wardrobe and yanked it open. "I spoke with a dear friend of mine who was certain this would look absolutely lovely on you. I told her you were rather waiflike. I think she heard wight-like, but that's also appropriate given your... bone structure."

The black dress was made out of the finest silk. It swayed as Agnes brought it out, the gown rustling on the ground as it moved. It was long and would cling to her like a second skin. The top was little more than a braided pattern and would show significantly more skin than she ever thought she would.

Jessamine stripped down and stepped into the skirt portion. The other women immediately twined the braids around her torso, making sure the braids were laying over the most important bits. But really, only her nipples were covered, and everything else was still rather revealing.

Her arms, shoulders, and back were nearly bare. Her stomach was only mildly covered by the complicated braids. But then Agnes brought out an additional piece of twisted silver from the wardrobe.

"Now, this is the part that will make sure no one questions you in the slightest." She held it up, and Jessamine held her breath in shock.

It was a metal rib cage. Worn with tarnished edges, the silver had turned black at the curves of each rib. It opened along the sternum, sealing itself around her in a hug far tighter than any corset she'd ever worn in her life.

When she looked at her reflection now, all she could see was a woman half in life and half in death. A skeletal creature who looked both terrifying and beautiful.

"Oh," she whispered. "How lovely."

"It goes perfectly with the mask." Agnes walked up behind her and settled the mask on top of her face. It looked like a skull, but with intricate carvings all around it. Butterflies, birds, tiny lizards, everything that was life itself crawling all over the skull that stopped just below her nose.

The other three witches seemed to hold their breath as she looked at their final work, and then Jessamine slowly smiled. The bloodred lips were a garish streak across her face as she whispered, "What a haunting visage."

"And what a perfect last sight for Fortuna," Agnes replied.

20

Elric yanked at the neck of his ridiculous outfit as they strode down the street with all the other partygoers. There wasn't anyone who would recognize him, so his mask covered only part of his face, but that didn't make it any more comfortable. Just like the rest of this stupid costume.

The witches had made it very clear that he was to pay attention to his surroundings and not deviate from their instructions. He would endanger all of them if he did. That meant he had to wear the clothing they had picked out for him, and no, he couldn't conjure his own. Someone would ask "Lord Bloodworth" where he'd purchased his outfit, and he'd have no good answer.

But why this suit? It was starched so heavily that it barely moved when he did. The creases down the legs were so sharp, he was certain they would cut someone if he got too close. The black silk shirt underneath the velvet jacket made him a little too warm, and the vest in between, embroidered to look like a rib cage, was just silly.

Still, it was quite nice to walk down the street freely with Jessamine. And she looked beautiful.

He glanced down at her again, willing himself not to get hard the moment she looked back. Those dark eyes bored right into him, and all he wanted was to strip her out of that silk and watch it pool at her feet.

He wanted to worship her like this. Worship her like he had against his own shrine. Every moment with her made him more and more obsessed, and sometimes he feared what that meant for him. For her.

For their kingdom.

Sighing, he turned his attention back to the crowd around them lest he walk into the party with a hard-on that he couldn't explain.

"So, this is the place?" he mused, as though they hadn't ever been inside this building before. Too many prying strangers could be listening to their conversation.

"They say Fortuna's home is the finest in all the Pleasure District," she said, leaning against his arm and trying to flutter her eyelashes but failing spectacularly. "Do you think someday you'll build me a home like this?"

"Anything you want, darling." Elric raised her hand to his lips. He could hear the couple next to them sigh in happiness at their love, but he could see by the glance they shared that their reaction was fake. Later, they would speak of the sickly romantic couple who had been so cloying to stand next to in line.

There were so many people here. Far more than he had anticipated, and quite a few who didn't look like they were even from Inverholm. Leaning down, he pretended to kiss Jessamine's shoulder while he murmured questions against her skin.

"Does it look like the man beside us isn't from here?"

She glanced that way, tilting her neck so he had more access to it. "He's from a neighboring kingdom. Not Leon's."

"What's he doing here?"

"Fortuna's net is wide." She cast her eyes at another couple, the movement so small he might not have caught it if he wasn't so attuned to her. "They're also from another kingdom. Although I'm not sure if they're together or siblings."

He looked at the way the man's hand hovered at the base of the woman's spine. "I think siblings."

"Interesting choice, then. I'm not sure why they would be here when Fortuna made it very clear she was looking for a husband."

He shrugged, then stood up straight again. All of this still felt like a trap, and he couldn't figure out why. Clearly, Fortuna's party had attracted all the greatest people in this kingdom and beyond. But why on earth had she allowed both of them to enter her home undisturbed?

Gut churning, he moved forward with everyone else. There were guards out front as they had seen before, again wearing Leon's colors. A statement of Fortuna's favor with the king, no doubt. One that they should not ignore.

As they approached the guards, Elric could feel himself stiffening. Perhaps this was the moment Fortuna would make her move. Perhaps someone would approach them, because certainly everyone could tell that he and Jessamine were different. They were far more than any of these people could ever dream of being.

A guard placed a hand on his chest as Elric started to walk past him. He looked down at the guard coolly, hoping the hatred in his gaze would sear his face into the man's memory for years to come. "Yes?" he growled.

"Name and..." The guard cleared his throat, looking down at the paper in his hand. "And where you are from? Sir?"

The faintest movement beside him suggested that Jessamine had covered her mouth. If she started laughing, then he would do the same and everything would fall right apart. His woman needed to get herself together.

"Lord Martin from Castlery," he replied, sighing as though it was the worst thing anyone had ever asked him. "By the gods, man. Pull yourself together and look for the name."

The guard didn't rise to Elric's bait, but the exaggerated way he looked at the paperwork, running his finger down the list, was clearly to make it seem as though he was doing far more than he actually was.

"I'm sorry, I don't see your name on the list—"

Jessamine leaned across him and gently tapped her finger against the paper. "Here. Lady Farah and Lord Martin."

Elric didn't have even a moment to bemoan that his name had been *second* on the list before the guard straightened and nodded. Really, what was Agnes thinking? "Yes, yes, of course. I see now. You may enter."

They strode past as though they hadn't a care in the world, even if Elric was already fuming. He wanted to let all of his shadows fly so that no one in this place would ever question them again. He wanted to show them what angering a god looked like, and if they weren't capable of seeing that, then he would prove to them—

Jessamine's hand slid beneath his vest, close enough to his skin that he could feel the heat of her palm against him. "He was just doing his job, Martin."

He hated that she had to call him anything other than his name. Few people knew what his name even was, so to have her calling him something else? He would lose his mind by the end of tonight.

"I dislike this," he muttered, walking into the gardens with her. "This is all far too dangerous."

"We're rubbing elbows with so many people who know what happened," she whispered. "I recognize many faces from the castle in here. This isn't just about Fortuna anymore."

"From the castle?" He racked his mind, trying to remember what he had seen in her memories. Nothing of note that he remembered, although perhaps there was more he hadn't seen. Elric called upon the shards of her soul that he'd kept to peer into. What he found there surprised him. "I thought they all died?"

"All those I saw that day did, but it seems as though quite a few survived. I had assumed after my death that Leon killed the rest of them."

They both stepped to the side as a couple walked past them, both the man and the woman dripping in so many jewels that Elric wondered how they could walk. The show of wealth was tacky, in his opinion, but that was what Fortuna liked and thus, that was what the Pleasure District liked.

Elric had seen the few people who tried to deviate from that style while he walked the streets. They were ridiculed, shunned for their difference. It was like someone walking into the town square naked. Fortuna's control over this place seemed infinite.

Jessamine tugged him just off the garden path, toward a cluster of roses that were so pungent he felt a headache splinter at his temple.

"Listen to me," she whispered. "I want to talk with some of them and see what they're thinking about, knowing that the princess might be back."

"Why would we do that?"

"I just have a feeling."

He groaned. "Your *feelings* get me in trouble. I thought we weren't going to start anything tonight."

"And here I was thinking you enjoyed me getting you in trouble." She grabbed his hand and tugged him back onto the path.

"I do," he growled. "I just prefer to be the one starting it. It's entirely unfair that you told me to be on my best behavior tonight, while you don't have to be."

Two young men startled at his words, looking them over with clear suspicion. One of them had a bright mop of chestnut hair that he'd carefully curled into unnatural spirals, and the other was wearing the most gods-awful puke-colored doublet dotted with rubies.

Elric grinned at them. "She can't keep her hands off me, but the moment I want to put my hands on her, suddenly I'm the problem. You know how it goes, boys."

The two of them eased their suspicious stares, but Jessamine slapped him hard on the chest.

Worth it.

Together, they strode through the crowd and *mingled*. He hated being around any of these people, let alone having to talk to them. He was certain they were all part of the problem, and now that he knew many of these people had stood by when Jessamine was killed, he itched to return the favor.

She dragged him toward a knot of people standing around a bar made out of fine golden filigree, looking as though it were held together by sugar rather than sturdy metal.

"Darling Martin, would you get me a drink?" Jessamine batted her lashes at him.

"Ah, Farah. Anything for you, dearest." He ground the words out through his teeth, and he wasn't certain they were very believable.

She seamlessly fit in with these people, though. Even as he watched, she meandered through the crowd, reintroducing herself as someone she wasn't, the story they'd memorized note-perfect. And they believed her. They adored the Lady Farah, who had only recently married the rake Martin. No one had ever been able to get the man to settle down. Wasn't she so pleased she was the first and only who had managed to do so?

"Whiskey," he told the man at the bar.

"Sir, there are themed drinks for this function. If you would like me to tell you about them—"

He silenced the bartender with a glare. "Whiskey."

"Right. Very good, sir."

In moments, he had a glass of whiskey in his hand as he turned his back on the bartender and watched Jessamine shine. For all she had bemoaned the fact that she wasn't the same person she once was, she was the same stunning woman who had captured his attention in her memories. The guests were all eating out of her hand in moments.

A crowd had gathered around her, laughing at what she said. Soon enough, she was *the* person at the party. Everyone wanted to be around her. They all wanted her to look at them, to listen to their gossip, for her to laugh and tell them they had the best story she'd heard all night. It likely took her half an hour at best.

Why were they all still out here in the gardens? Wasn't this supposed to be a ball?

Looking down at the glass in his hand, he was disappointed to see that it was empty. "Another whiskey," he said, only to pause when a firm hand touched his.

Frowning, he looked at the man who stood tall and broad beside him. This wasn't a man like the others here. He wore a suit of navy blue, but it wasn't quite as pressed as the others. The buttons gleamed with gold, but he could see the bottom one had a few pieces of that gold paint flaking off. His hair wasn't perfectly in place either; there was one piece that wasn't slicked back like the rest, right at the top of his head like a cowlick that wouldn't settle.

"Do I know you?" Elric growled.

"Can you please get him the gin and tonic?" the man said to the bartender. "It is the special of the night for the gentlemen, after all."

Elric frowned. "I already ordered what I want."

"Trust me on this. You want the gin and tonic."

He did not, in fact, want the gin and tonic. But he did want alcohol, so he took what the bartender offered and wondered idly if the drink was poisoned. He stared down into the clear liquid, then looked back at the man standing beside him. "If you poisoned this, I'm afraid you'll be disappointed."

"I'm sure a man such as you has encountered much poison in his life. Whatever tincture I picked to kill you would certainly fail."

Elric could only frown. "Now, what would make you say that?"

The man nodded toward Jessamine. "Any man who has claim to a woman like her knows better than to assume another won't try to take what's his."

His hand clenched around the glass. "Is that a threat?"

"Merely an observation. After the loss of the princess, I think all of us are watching our women a little more closely." But there was something in the man's gaze, a tightness as he looked at Jessamine and then back at Elric. "Most of us have heard the rumors, you know. That the princess isn't dead. Have you?"

"I heard she fell off a cliff after getting her throat cut. That she plummeted into the ocean, which, from that height, would have shattered every bone in her body." Elric knew better than most. He'd knitted every single one of those bones back together. He drained the gin and tonic before setting the glass on the bar top. "Now, if you'll excuse me, it sounds as though this place might be a little too dangerous to leave my wife alone in."

"I think anyplace might be too dangerous for that." The man leaned a little closer, so that no one would overhear their words. "The walls have ears in this place, and so does everyone within them. Keep her safe."

And then he walked away, slipping through the crowd, which gave him odd looks, sensing he was out of place.

Frowning, Elric walked back to Jessamine's side and tugged her against him.

"Oh," she said with a small chirp that was entirely unlike her. "You're back! I was just talking with Lord Henry here about his time in the castle. Such a sad thing to lose so many nobles at once."

He hummed low under his breath, bending down so it looked like he was nuzzling her neck. "Not everyone here is what they seem."

"I've already discovered that," she whispered in his ear. "Who was just talking to you?"

"I have no idea." He dragged his lips up her throat to her ear. "But he knew who you were, princess. And he knew I am a god. So keep yourself alert."

And he would do the same. Just because he'd promised to behave himself didn't mean that he would if someone dared to touch Jessamine.

21

Everyone here was a snake. She'd made that assumption the moment she started talking to the nobles who were going about their lives as though they hadn't watched their queen and princess murdered in front of them. Six months was all it had taken. They hadn't even mourned her mother for an entire year.

But she plastered a fake smile on her face and pretended it didn't bother her in the slightest. After all, she wasn't the Lady Jessamine who had died in front of them. She was Lady Farah, a foreign dignitary who lived very close to this kingdom and who had just married a rake. One of the many women here who they likely hoped would slip off with them for a quick fuck in a closet.

She was just about to ask the man in front of her if he'd heard the rumors about the princess not being dead, when there was a loud bang at the front of the house. A few people jumped. One woman even spilled half of her cocktail before she caught the glass. All the nobles turned to see a man standing atop the white marble steps leading toward gilded double doors, wearing a fine suit of ivory white.

"Esteemed ladies and gentlemen! It is my pleasure to welcome you to the home of Fortuna Beaumont! A truly unique experience awaits you beyond. You shall be plied with the finest of foods, the rarest of wines, and the most unusual beauties this kingdom can offer you! Please, enter and enjoy."

And, damn it, the nobles all filtered out of the garden. She wasn't going to get a word in edgewise while they were all walking, which meant she was forced to stride behind them and enter the home.

Sighing, she looked over her shoulder at Elric, who was so close she could feel the heat of his body. "Shall we?"

"I've always been intrigued to see how the legendary Fortuna Beaumont lives." A few people beside him made noises of agreement, although they all gave him a side-eye when he added, "Some say it rivals the beauty of the royal castle itself… but surely that would be impossible."

This man. He was so beyond what she had ever dreamt of having in her life, and yet here he was. Right in front of her. Or behind her, as it were.

Biting her lip, she walked with the others up the stairs. She stayed in the back of the line, though. No need to rush into a house they had already seen, after all.

From the outside, she could see that Fortuna's servants had decorated with even more gold, if such a thing was possible. It looked like it was pouring down from the ceilings in great swaths of drapery, and every single item of food on a plate that moved past the window had gold on top of it as well. Desserts that looked like little pillows. Delicate crackers with what looked like duck liver pâté. Even the small ribs on bones had gold dust on top.

"Everyone's going to be shitting gold when they leave this place," Elric murmured in her ear.

She tried her best not to giggle, but that one got her. With a startled laugh, she leaned back into him when everyone turned to stare. Thankfully, he just wrapped an arm around her waist and flashed them all a grin.

"She's always been a lightweight," he said with a chuckle. "I'll keep a watch on her, don't you worry."

And just like that, they were dismissed.

Finally, they were entering Fortuna's home. The massive entrance hall glowed with so much light it looked like the sun itself had been captured. The black-and-white-checkered floors gleamed like mirrors, and every room had been opened. The guests wandered to and fro, exploring whatever room where they wished to see the various entertainments.

"It's just you and I," she murmured, glancing around to see that almost everyone had left the hall. Remaining was just them, the servants, and a podium with a guest book that everyone else seemed to have signed.

"So it is." He narrowed his gaze on her. "Are you about to make a foolish decision?"

"No." But the grin on her face said otherwise.

She felt him lean over her shoulder to watch as she signed the guest book.

Dead Girl and the Reckoning.

"Jessamine," he snarled.

"*Farah*," she replied, closing the guest book with a sharp thud. "No one will look until we're all gone, anyway."

"Unless a servant gets curious." He took her hand and put it on his elbow, drawing her away from the podium.

"If a servant looks, they will say nothing. I highly doubt any of them have the slightest loyalty to Fortuna." She tossed her head before remembering most of her hair was coiled in a precarious updo. "She wasn't kind to servants as a child, and I highly doubt that has changed since."

Shaking his head, Elric drew her into the nearest room. Inside, it appeared to be a hookah den. Smoke coiled to the ceiling and billowed like clouds against the ceiling. She had yet to see such pristine white smoke in her life, but then again, she hadn't been in a hookah den before either.

Smokers, mostly men, filled the room, all of them puffing on hoses leading to metal contraptions that bubbled with liquids. A few daring women enjoyed pipes of their own, but they were few and far between.

"See anyone you recognize?" Elric murmured in her ear. Together, they watched the crowd to see if anyone reacted to their presence. "Because the man in the garden made a very precise suggestion that he knew who you were."

If Elric believed him, then it was true. And that meant there was more than one person who knew, for no one in the Pleasure District kept secrets. But she had no clue who that stranger could be.

"No one," she replied, before sneezing. Loudly.

A few people looked over at them with annoyed expressions, and she took that as their cue to leave. Elric cleared his throat, nodded to the other men, and then nearly dragged her out of the room.

"What?" she asked.

"You can't sneeze in a room full of smokers."

"Why not?"

"It's rude."

She supposed it might be. After all, everyone was in that room because they enjoyed smoking. She did not.

They moved into the next room, one she hoped wouldn't aggravate her lungs. Thankfully, this one was for food. The table in the center was piled so high with delicacies that they were quite literally toppling onto the floor.

Jessamine watched a young woman burst into delighted laughter as her partner lifted an oyster from the table and "dropped" it onto her bosom. He licked the oyster off her skin without hesitation. Juices dripped between her ample breasts, and Jessamine had to look away before the man chased those droplets into hidden shadows.

"Is that a whole roasted pig?" she asked to distract herself. "On top of a bed of… salmon?"

"That is what it looks like."

What a waste. The salmon was crushed under the weight of the massive beast on top of it, and no one was eating the fish that had soaked up all the fat from the pork above it. Lady Fortuna might have money, but it was clear once more that she lacked taste.

"Oh, there's someone I recognize." She grabbed Elric's arm and practically dragged him over to an elderly, rotund gentleman. His whiskers were curled into sharp points on either side of his mouth, and his eyes were rather sunken into his skull for such a large man.

This man had once been important in the castle, Jessamine recalled. As her mother's grand advisor for all things financial in the kingdom, he was one of the few with access to the treasury. She hadn't liked him then, and she certainly didn't like him now. But he had loose lips when he was drunk, and she was hoping that he was drunk at this point.

"Follow my lead," she said, walking up to the other side of the advisor before loudly proclaiming, "I want a piece! I'm just so nervous to grab it."

Elric reached for one of the ribs before he paused, apparently realizing this was her plan. Dramatically yanking his arm back as though he was disgusted, he sank into the role of rake. "Well, don't look at me, darling. I'm not grabbing one for you. There are servants for that."

The portly old man beside her was quick to jump in and be the hero. "Allow me."

His thick fingers sank into the skin of the roasted pig, which crackled under his touch. Those fingers sank into the flesh, rooted around with squelching noises, and then he pulled out a hunk of meat attached to a rib. He looked like he was just going to hand it to Jessamine before he thought better of it and set it on a plate that he handed to her. His greasy fingermarks remained, but it was significantly better than the alternative.

It took everything in her not to let her face twist in disgust. She could see the imprint of each finger on the fine porcelain, shiny in the candlelight.

"Thank you," she tried to simper, but she could hear the shudder in her voice.

Jessamine took the plate and tried her best to look like she could eat it. She really tried. But all she could think about was that he'd taken the meat with his bare hands, and she'd just been watching him lick the same fingers clean. If she put any of that meat in her mouth, she'd spew all over this fancy floor and then people would know she didn't belong here.

"Allow me," Elric said, leaning over her to take the plate with a warm chuckle. "She's so picky about her food. Poor dear couldn't have any of this pig without a little sauce on it. Such a delicate flower."

And then he walked away, leaving her standing with a grinning man who should have recognized her, considering he had been in her life since she was a child. "I appreciate a woman with an appetite."

A shiver trailed down her spine at the slimy words. "Ah," she said, a little breathless with distaste. "Lovely. You're an advisor at the castle, aren't you?"

"I am."

"How fortuitous it is that you're still with us. I heard the past queen's end was rather grisly and that most people in attendance at that wedding were slaughtered."

He frowned, those whiskers twitching. "I didn't say I attended the wedding."

Shit.

"I simply assumed a man such as yourself must have gone," she replied, pressing a hand against her chest. "Or did they slight you? My dear lord, there is simply no part of me that could believe they would treat you so unjustly!"

Elric returned with the plate, handing it over to her with a rib that looked suspiciously different from the one the man had given her. She took the plate as he interjected. "Someone treated you unjustly? Shall I duel them for you?"

They were leaning too far into this ridiculous ploy they had going on, Jessamine thought. Still, she simpered, tittered, and then flattened her hand on Elric's chest. "He is a good duelist, you know. But *were* you at the royal wedding?"

"I wasn't," the portly man replied, but she could already see him stiffening. "And I have no need for another man to duel for me. Ridiculous suggestion, that."

She'd lost him. The advisor was already turning a little red, and she had a feeling that if they stayed here for much longer, one of them was going to get yelled at.

"Why don't we take this food into the next room," she said to Elric, still trying very hard to laugh and sound positive when all she wanted was to shriek.

She'd been so close! He knew something. They all did. She could feel it.

They trailed into the next room, which appeared to be where everyone would go if they wanted to drink. Feminine servers flitted through the room in tiny gold outfits that were little more than chandelier chains dangling from their shoulders and hips. Each one had tiny diamonds encrusted all along it, and they swayed with their movements. They all held massive serving trays with drinks in every color, shape, and size.

"I could use one of these," Elric said, snagging a glass before handing one to her as well.

"No," she muttered, narrowing her gaze on the crowd. "I don't want it."

She handed off the plate to a servant because she didn't want to keep thinking about that old man's grubby hands. There wasn't anyone familiar in this room either, so they moved to the next.

This one was a pleasure room. There were courtesans, both women and men, in various states of undress, even some completely nude reclining on the sofas. It was the most crowded room, full with people of all ages wandering around the models. Apparently, this room wasn't for sex, but it was for looking and touching. She watched as an older woman walked right up to a nude man and ran her hands down his rather chiseled stomach. She looked away before she could see where those hands were heading.

"See anyone here?"

"No," she murmured, but then a flash of blond hair caught her attention.

A grating laugh filled the room. Or maybe it was just that she would recognize that laugh anywhere. It was the same laugh she'd heard when she got her first bruise from his grip on her arm, and the same laugh after he'd given her a matching one on her ribs. It was the laugh that haunted her dreams, and the same one she'd heard in her ear before she was tossed off a cliff.

And then he turned. That handsome face didn't look in her direction, but she'd know it anywhere. The perfectly coiffed blond hair. The blue eyes that were just a shade too light for warmth. The easy grin on his face that he used to get his way. All he ever had to do was smile and people fell at his feet to do his bidding.

"Farah?" Elric asked, his voice pitched low. Then he stepped closer to her and lowered his voice even further. "Jessamine, what's wrong?"

She swallowed hard, trying to get her mouth to open so she could voice her fears. All she could croak was, "Leon."

Just saying his name made the entire world tilt. She wanted to run. She wanted to hide. She wanted to turn around and never come back because this was the man who had killed her. He'd killed her mother right in front of her, and laughed as it happened.

All she could see were ropes of rubies around her mother's neck that bled into wounds that could not heal. She felt the pain around her own throat, the sensation of her skin parting as she felt the sword slash through her. The wind whistled in her ears as she fell countless stories to the sea, knowing it was going to hurt even worse when she struck the waves.

"I think I might pass out," she whispered, before the world started going dark at the edges of her vision.

22

It took Elric a few seconds to catch up as Jessamine pressed back against his chest, her eyes wider than he'd ever seen them before. He followed her gaze to see the man standing in a crowd of people. Leon looked exactly as Elric remembered seeing him in her memories. Handsome. Calm. Confident. He had the entire kingdom in the palm of his hand.

No one would dare stand against a king like that. They all bowed before him, fawning over this man on a stolen throne who had no right to all the respect they threw at him.

Elric wanted to murder the man right now. He wanted to let all of his power seep out of his body and send his shadows racing across the room. He'd enjoy watching them tunnel into Leon's eyes, popping the orbs with a satisfying squelch.

But no, that wasn't what he wanted. Elric had used his powers so many times to kill people that such a death no longer felt personal, and it was personal with this idiot. He would walk right up to the king and wrap his hand around the man's throat. He'd use his power to make sure none of the guards could get to them, that much he would allow. But Elric wanted to sink his own thumbs into the man's eyes and watch as the blood poured out of his skull while he writhed beneath Elric's grasp.

"I think I might pass out," Jessamine whispered, and his attention snapped back to her.

All of his care. All of his worry. None of it meant anything without her. In that moment, Elric realized that her reclaiming the throne had become important to him. Not because he owed her or because he... felt strongly for her, but because he believed that she deserved that throne more than the idiot over there did.

"Do you want me to kill him?" he murmured in her ear, holding on to her elbows as he steered her away from the crowd that was gathering.

"No." She paused, and then added, "Yes. I don't know. I can't think straight. I'm seeing black and white spots, Elric."

"Just keep pretending you're fine. Lean on me more, nightmare."

He kept his hand at her waist so it appeared that she was walking in a lover's embrace, not because she couldn't stand on her own. It killed something inside of him not to set her against a wall and then rush back in to destroy the man who had harmed her. He'd never wanted to hear someone scream in pain more than he did in this moment. But he had someone else to look after.

Jessamine's breaths were coming in little pants. Even though she was trying her best to keep her face from showing her distress, he could see through her paper-thin skin how fast her heart beat. Her heart thundered against the back of his hand where it was pressed to her ribs, and he could practically feel the panic rolling off her body. Her jaw was clenched so hard he feared she would crack her teeth.

But worse than all of that was the fear in those dark eyes. The way she looked at him to help, even though both of them knew there was nothing they could do in this moment.

Leon was here, and there was nothing either of them could do about it. They'd walked into a trap, he was certain of it, and their opponents had wanted Jessamine to see that Leon was unfazed by her return. And it killed him that he couldn't help her more than simply removing her from the situation.

Growling low under his breath, he couldn't help but send a small wriggling shadow to cause problems. It sank into the skin of one of the performers, a man so well-endowed that Elric wondered if the gods themselves had blessed him. That performer immediately started bothering Leon. First by hitting on him, and then later he would just follow Leon to remind the king that even though he might have a throne, he would never have as impressive a weapon as that performer.

A satisfied snarl twisting his face, Elric ushered Jessamine to a more private space. A guard stood in front of a hallway, farther away from the party and certainly easier for them to hide in.

"No admittance," the man said, bored with his job and having said those same words far too many times. "Go back to the party."

Elric blew in his face. But his breath was a thick black sickly smoke. The man inhaled it before he knew what he was doing, and by then Elric was already in his head.

The bored expression changed to one of stupor as the man shifted to the side and let them pass.

"You saw nothing," Elric hissed.

"No one has come this way," the man repeated.

And then Elric moved the two of them toward a room he had seen the first time they'd snuck in here. A room that was private, cozy, and somewhere that Jessamine could catch her breath.

The furniture here was plush, with such depth that Jessamine sank into the cushions as he set her down on the bright yellow couch. It was far too light in here, still. There were so many sconces that the entire room made his eyes burn. With a harsh crackle of a spell, he sent out his shadows to take care of those flames. One by one, they blinked out of existence until there were only three still flickering. It enveloped the room in a sense of privacy that they had yet to find in this place.

His magic created a dark bubble that only contained the two of them. He sank to his knees before her and lifted her shaking hands to his lips. "Nightmare," he murmured against her skin. "You are safe with me."

"I know," she whispered.

"Are you sure you know?"

Jessamine only managed a stilted nod in response, a surefire sign that she was not, in fact, certain.

"Do you know what I wanted to do to him?" he asked, his voice low and murmuring in the stillness. "If you had given me even the smallest permission, I would have sunk my claws underneath his skin. I would force his soul to remain in his body so that he had to feel every bit of me skinning him alive. I would peel his flesh from his body, bit by bit. I would make him watch as I removed every single one of his organs, leaving his heart for last, which I would place in between his jaws so that he could taste his own death as I finally allowed him to move into the next realm. And then I would keep him there, in that realm of darkness you have seen, and I would do it all over again. Over and over until you said he had been punished enough."

Those shaking hands stilled in his. "You would do that for me?"

"All you have to do is ask," he breathed, before pressing a kiss to her knuckles again. "I'm on my knees begging you to ask, Jessamine."

Her fingers curved in his grip, coming up to set against his jaw, where she held on to him like he was the last stone in a stormy sea. "I want to take my throne the right way. I don't want to release you upon this realm like another plague, because no one will ever trust me again. If I am the queen who wields a god, then this kingdom isn't mine by choice, but by force. I will not become *him*."

Clapping from the doorway startled them both. Elric whipped around, his hands already poised to spill shadows on the floor and attack whoever dared look upon them.

But it was a woman in the doorway. A shapely figure outlined by a wave of light.

Dark hair flowed in a waterfall to her waist. Her clothing clung to her skin like it was soaking wet, and still it moved in a soft hush as she strode into the room and closed the door behind her. Her hair swayed, the bells on her wrists jingling just barely enough to entice those who might be listening.

She was a creature made for pleasure. A dangerous, wild thing who had only one thought on her mind. Power.

Fortuna Beaumont turned to them with a sinister smile on her lips and venom on her tongue. "What an interesting way to gain back a kingdom, Jessamine. But you always did want to feel valued, even when you weren't."

This little bitch. She was alone with them now, and Elric could kill her so fast that no one in the room would know what had happened. He could catch her spirit in the other realm. Perhaps she would be more inclined to answer their questions there.

But Jessamine put her hand on his shoulder, and he stilled all those murderous thoughts. He was here to serve his queen, after all, and if she wanted him to stop talking, then he very well would.

"Fortuna," Jessamine said, her voice pitched low in case anyone else was listening to them. "You have to know this is a terrible idea."

"What's a terrible idea?"

"Everything that you're doing. Working with Leon? He killed my mother. He killed *me*."

Fortuna shrugged. "He's killed a lot of people, Jessamine. And you and your mother were both very much standing in my way. I had no reason to save either of you when he brought up that plan."

Jessamine's fingers clenched on Elric's shoulder. "You knew he was going to kill us?"

"He tells me everything." Fortuna headed to one of the other plush seats and perched herself on the arm. "I knew he was going to kill you, yes. I knew he was going to overthrow the entire kingdom, and I knew I had tied myself to the man who would be king."

Elric couldn't prevent the growl that echoed in his throat. "Not for very long."

The woman looked at him, her dark eyes so similar to Jessamine's that they were eerie to stare into. "Down, boy. Your handler is clearly telling you to let the women talk."

"You speak to a god." He couldn't quite believe this woman was so daring with her responses, but then again, he had seen the choices she'd made in her life. She thought she was untouchable.

Fortuna sighed. "Yes, yes. Jessamine has caught herself a god while I have caught a king. I'm curious what your plan even was, Jessa. You thought you would raise a god from the dead and somehow control him? You do realize the Deathless One is uncontrollable? Soon enough, he's going to get too far off that leash you've been keeping him on, and then all of a sudden you'll realize that he always bites the hand that feeds him."

He could feel Jessamine shaking behind him. Her fingernails sank into his shoulder, but he needed the pain to ground him.

He hated these people. They thought so little of him, of her, of all the people he had protected his entire life. Fortuna was a prime example of why he'd chosen to become a god, even though it had been violent in the process. People like her deserved to be punished. People who thought money measured their worth. People who confused justice with power.

He had taught such people centuries ago that strength came from magic, and those who were considered the weakest were the quickest to draw blood.

Fortuna watched the two of them, her eyes missing nothing. She blew out a long sigh and shook her head. "The two of you think this is going to work, don't you? You think that it'll take so little effort to overthrow him and then... what? What are you planning to do with the kingdom you take back? Jessamine, you are so underqualified to run a kingdom. You didn't know half of the things your mother did, and even before you died you didn't want to."

"It is *my* throne. I survived death itself so I could take it back, and you will not be the one who stops me." Jessamine stood, her dress coiling around her body and the ribs expanding with her breath. "You are just a stepping stone, Fortuna. The fact that you have aligned yourself with Leon Bishop is a sad one, but it changes nothing."

"Doesn't it? Because he has all of my tools at his disposal. I knew the moment you came into my district where you were, what you were doing, and where you were going. Even if I hadn't, your little bird breeder couldn't wait to tell me everything." Fortuna looked down at her nails, fanning her hand out before smiling down at the gold tips. "You never were as good as me, Jessa. It only takes a few needling jabs and you're quaking. Just look at you! What queen shakes when she's afraid?"

"Someone who cares," his gravesinger spat. "Someone who knows that there is more than just pride that affects what we are doing here. The people in this kingdom need someone to save them."

"And that person is going to be you? With what? A god who hasn't been alive for centuries and three witches who are so far beyond cooked they have no idea they're even in the pot? Your plan is so full of holes."

Jessamine shook her head and took a step so she was beside Elric. He stood with her, looming over both women with barely leashed tension.

But he could see his Jessamine was no longer afraid. She looked at the other woman with contempt and something bitter twisting her mouth. "And to think, for a few moments, I wondered if you were reaching out to me for help. If you let me come into this house and see this party because you wanted me to get you out from under his thumb."

Elric stared at Fortuna, willing there to be some emotion other than disgust on her features, but there was nothing. Fortuna just looked disappointed.

So, they had been wrong about this viper. She was someone's pet snake, one who would bite before it accepted any help.

"You always wanted to see the good in people," Fortuna said, standing as well. "But you never understood that some people just aren't good, Jessa. Sometimes, they're here to gather as much power as they can and explode into the stars. You always stood in my way."

"Because what you wanted was wrong."

"Maybe to a weak mind like yours. But if you want to know what Leon is up to, you'll have to follow me." Fortuna reached into her pocket and snapped a fan open, gently casting the breeze over her face before shrugging. "I don't think you'll be able to find me in the crowd, and certainly not without your god. But if you have the guts to face me alone, then maybe I'll tell you what Leon is up to. What do you think? A little race? Just like old times."

And with that, she turned and bolted.

Elric only had a moment to crinkle his nose in confusion before Jessamine darted after the other woman.

"Jessamine!" he shouted, forgetting that they were trying to hide. But when he followed her, the two women were already whipping around the corner of the hall and nearly out of his sight.

23

Jessamine sprinted after her childhood tormentor, knowing this was a trap. But there were too many loose ends. Someone already knew who she was, and he'd talked with Elric. Fortuna had known who and where she was although Jessamine was wearing a mask that should have concealed her. None of it made sense.

There were no spells that revealed her true nature. No people who could even suggest that they knew Jessamine was here.

Had Elissa said something again? She doubted it. Jessamine reached for a corner of the wall, allowing her weight to propel her forward around a tight corner as she raced past a crowd of people and back into the party. Her mask was already twisted askew, and her breathing was far too ragged for anyone to ignore. But she didn't care.

Fortuna was here. And she would be damned if she'd let a bully beat her so easily.

She could hear Elric's cursing behind her. Clearly the god was not in favor of her disappearing into the crowd without him, but Jessamine needed to know this information. For herself. For the memory of her mother.

For all the people she'd let fall underneath his thumb.

She could see in the expressions of the crowd that they didn't care who led this kingdom. They would support whoever put money in their pockets and power in their palms. They fed upon this kingdom like vampires, leeching blood out of every limb until it had turned into an empty husk.

But Inverholm was her home, and she wouldn't let them continue this any longer. And the first step in regaining the beauty she remembered was interrogating the viper that slithered away from her.

"Come on, Jessamine," a voice whispered in her ear. A voice that sounded like Fortuna's but surely couldn't be. *"You used to be faster. You were better at chasing me when you were a child. Remember?"*

Of course she remembered. But Jessamine had only chased Fortuna when the other girl had stolen something from her. A favorite hairpin. A cuddly kitten who had disappeared only moments afterward. A sweet that her mother had brought from another kingdom specifically so her daughter could taste it.

Nothing good ever came from Fortuna getting her hands on something. All Jessamine knew was that if she didn't catch up to Fortuna now, she would lose everything.

A glimpse of Fortuna appeared in the powdered crowd, a dark splotch in the sea of gemstone colors. There was the darkness of her hair whipping around a corner. And there, a door opened and closed, but Fortuna was nowhere in sight. Surely she'd slipped inside.

Jessamine shoved through the crowd and yanked the door open before launching herself through it. She didn't think of the danger, nor did she worry about what might be waiting for her. She could already feel magic brewing in her fingertips, just like it did when Elric was touching her, but this time, it was so much more. It was born of rage—and it was *hers*.

The interior of the room was pitch black, but she walked through it confidently. Until there was the sharp sound of a match striking, and then light bloomed in the distance. She found herself in a gallery, with portraits hung all the way down the corridor. Paintings of Fortuna's family stared down at her with the same expression they always had—dismal disappointment. She was the ugly duckling, the one who didn't quite fit in.

And now she was even worse than before.

Suddenly, one of the portraits moved. A woman wearing a wig taller than she was wide lifted her hand to her mouth as though shocked at the sight of Jessamine. The man in the portrait next to her sneered and lifted his hand to his face as well, as though he'd smelled something disgusting. Then there were the murmurs.

She could hear them *talking* as though they had the ability to do so. They whispered in the darkness, turning toward each other so that Jessamine could barely hear what they were saying.

"Is that the girl?"

"Somehow she's gotten even worse than I remembered."

"Do you see that scar around her neck? Now what do you think gave her that?"

A man with a carefully coiled mustache looked right at her and said, "I heard she died. Serves her right for what her family did to ours."

Lies.

All of them were lies.

Jessamine wanted to press her hands to her ears and scream at them all to stay quiet, but she had to forge forward, forcing her body to move through the hall even as those hands reached out through the paintings for her. She could feel their bony fingers grabbing at her dress, holding on to the metal rib cage and trying to drag her toward them. The sharp edges of their nails tore at the silken fabric, and still she fought.

No one would stop her. Not ancestors. Not the people she was supposed to impress. And certainly not the faint memory of those who had been part of the problem in the first place.

"Begone, spirits," she hissed, feeling a slither of darkness coating her skin with power. She reached for the metal rib cage and dragged her finger underneath a sharp seam. A bead of blood welled on her finger, dropping onto the floor, where it sizzled as it hit. "Or I will send your souls into the darkness where I will keep it. I am the Deathless One's gravesinger. I command the afterlife, and if I wish to torment you, I will."

They leaned away from her, hissing out curses and spitting angry words as though that would scare her off. She reached the end of the hallway, grabbing the doorknob and wrenching it open. With one last look back toward the remnants of what once was, she plunged into the next room, knowing that there was more Fortuna would make her endure.

And she was right. The moment she crossed the threshold, a sticky substance covered her eyes, and she could see nothing but red.

Jessamine swiped at her face, her fingers slipping in something thick and wet that covered her skin. Cursing, she struggled against it, yanking and pulling what felt like handfuls of slick meat that she tossed onto the floor until she could see again. This room was coated in blood. Or at least, that was what the spell wanted her to see.

Whose magic was this? Surely not Fortuna's. Her cousin had never been inclined toward magic, and certainly wasn't a witch. Elric would have known if she was worshipping him, or if he'd given her magic. Perhaps it was old. A leftover horror from a time long ago.

Stringy sinews covered the floor and walls. They were red, glistening, like an open wound that she had walked into. If she looked closely, she could see those sinews pulsing. Threaded together, they moved with a heartbeat that thundered in her ear.

Her own heartbeat.

She took one step into the room and felt her feet sink into the tendons as a stabbing pain in her chest made her gasp. It was an illusion made to convince her that she was walking through her own heart. That any movement would damage something inside her chest she couldn't fix.

Another step. Another sharp jab that had her freezing and placing a hand over her heart like she could will the organ to still. But there was nothing she could do. The spell was thorough and strong. And it had been woven into the fabric of the floor by a particularly talented witch.

But Jessamine was more than a witch. She was a gravesinger with a connection to a god, and she knew that connection was more powerful than anyone who had come before. She could use him, and more than that, she could use his knowledge.

Her voice was thin and reedy as she whispered, "I call upon the Deathless One. The god who gives us power. I do not recognize the spell I face, but you, in your infinite knowledge, will."

Immediately she felt it, a swell of dark power that rose throughout her entire body, as though he was there by her side. She knew he hadn't entered the room, still caught up in the crowd outside. But he was here with her now, even if he couldn't touch her.

"An intricate spell indeed," he muttered in her mind, and she could feel the pain lifting as though he had shouldered her burden. "But you are stronger than this, nightmare. You aren't thinking with your head; you're thinking with the pain in your chest."

"It's a little hard to ignore," she hissed as she took another step forward and felt an unusual thud in her chest that made every hair on her body rise. Her heartbeat paused. Suddenly stilling, as though it wouldn't continue, until there was another, harder thud. "How do I fix it?"

"You already know where the spell is coming from, do you not? Woven into the fabric of this room, those are your thoughts, Jessamine."

"Speak straight with me, Elric. I'm having a hard time concentrating."

Had she fallen to her knees? She certainly didn't feel upright, and she was much closer to that pulsing, blood-slicked sight that moved right in front of her gaze now. It was so close she could touch it. If she wanted to, she could put her hands on those sinews and tear through them. End it all. Let all of this pain disappear.

"What is fabric in a room like this, Jessamine?"

The words seemed garbled in her mind, but some part of her screamed that she had to listen and... Rugs. Rugs were fabric. And if she was on her knees, then there was something rather simple she could do.

"I have never been good at basic spells," she muttered, feeling around with her hands even though it made her chest spasm. All she needed was one... one...

There. The faintest sensation of fur against her fingertips. With a gasp, she rattled off words that were drilled into her head by both a god and her witch teacher, hoping to reveal the true nature of whatever hid beneath her hands. But it didn't work. She was horrid at simplicity and, even if she was stronger now, it didn't work. Spells never listened to her.

Instead, she simply whispered, "Burn." It wasn't a spell she'd been taught, but she knew words made a spell happen. There was ritual, reason, meaning behind every single spell. There were candles to light and bowls to offer sacrifice. But those rules had never gotten her anywhere.

Jessamine dug deep inside of herself, pushing for that connection to magic that she'd found through Elric. She begged. "Burn, please," she whispered.

And then she felt it. The writhing beast inside of her seemed to ease. It unraveled like there had been a tangle inside of her, knotted by expectations and rules and requirements and chains that she had wrapped around herself.

That unraveling released something that had desperately been wanting to get out. Her fingertips heated, and then she could feel the searing ache of fire on her hands. It spread out from her fingertips and as it did, it burned away the vision of organ meat and pulsing blood. Like a piece of paper she had lit from the middle, the room revealed itself as she burned the rug where the magic had been woven.

Every moment she gritted her teeth and endured. Her fingertips burned with it, sizzling as she smelled the scent of her own cooking flesh. But then it was done, and the fires were extinguished.

It wasn't much of a room. It wasn't even that big. If she had known it would take only a few more steps, she might have mustered the courage to keep walking.

Gasping, she stood on shaking legs and cast her eyes around the nearly bare room. The rug burned at her feet, and that was almost all that was in here. A few portraits were covered with faded sheets. Bare boards lined the floor, worn from years of people who had walked over them and never once sanded or refinished. A small chest in the corner had seen better days and looked like someone had taken an axe to it.

But on the far side of the room was a balcony overlooking the back garden. A balcony where Fortuna stood with a cigar in her hand and smoke coiling around her. She didn't look back at Jessamine. Instead, she just stood there, gazing out over the gardens like the room wasn't burning behind her.

"I caught you," Jessamine rasped, her voice still aching with the pain that was a dull echo behind her ribs. "Now you are going to tell me his plan, Fortuna."

Fortuna lifted the cigar to her lips, and then blew smoke rings out toward the stars that laid out above them. With a long sigh, she turned so Jessamine could see her profile. The moonlight played across her satin-smooth hair. "You burned down my pretty spell. You never did have any tact."

"What is he planning?" she asked again, joining the other woman on the balcony. The air was so much better out here. No cloying perfumes to distract her, nor the murmur of people to cloud her mind.

Just the silence of the stars and the sweet smell of roses wafting up from Fortuna's beautiful garden. And beyond that, the glow of the Pleasure District. Even from here she could see men and women on the streets, drunk and laughing. The faint trill of distant music coiled into the air, along with smoke from the cigar dens.

"This is the city you're fighting so hard for?" Fortuna asked, waving a hand at the scenery. "It's full of crooks and robbers.

People who only think about themselves at the best of times. No one here gives a shit whether you live or die."

"I know that."

"Then why are you fighting so hard to take it back? Let Leon have it. Let the gutter trash live with all the other gutter trash. Get on a ship, Jessamine. Go somewhere beautiful with that new god of yours and learn how to take a kingdom there. Perhaps that would be more worthwhile for you to fight for."

"This is my home." She leaned against the railing of the balcony, staring out at the speckles of light that continued far past the Pleasure District. All the way to the very edge of her kingdom, where the moonlight played on the sea. "I will fight for it until the very last of my breaths. And you are the first to know what Leon is going to do with this place. So excuse me if I cannot let it go. I will kill you if I have to."

"I know you think you will. But you're only angry at me because you're losing, Jessa." Fortuna took another drag off her cigar, the smoke pouring out of her lips and nose. "You're going to lose. This place will be his dumping ground, and in case you were unaware, it's going to get a lot worse."

"How?" If Jessamine had to play this game, then she would. She would ask all the questions that Fortuna wanted her to ask.

But Fortuna shook her head and sighed. "I just need a little of your blood and you'll see."

"My blood?"

There was a dagger in Fortuna's hand. She didn't know when it had shown up or if Fortuna had been hiding it in her skirts this whole time. It flashed in the moonlight, and Jessamine didn't even think to dodge it. She just stood there, allowing Fortuna to swipe that blade across her cheek even as the blood welled and the pain slowly registered.

"Why?" she asked. "You are no witch."

"I think you've forgotten that there aren't only witches, Jessamine. Even without a god, magic always wants to be used." Fortuna rubbed the line of blood from her cheek. "And now you're going to realize why you're so dangerous. Not because you're connected to a god or because you have a coven that follows you. But because you are a royal, and royal blood has so many uses."

24

The damned woman had escaped him again. Jessamine had a way of disappearing into a crowd that he would never understand, considering he was a god directly connected to her, and he should have been able to follow her anywhere. But then someone had grabbed his arm, asking him a question like he was the man he was pretending to be. He'd shaken them off, only to be waylaid yet again.

But this time it was the man who had warned him off in the garden, the young man who now had wild eyes and looked very much like he'd seen a ghost.

"What?" Elric snarled.

"We have to leave."

"Leave? Do you think I would even entertain leaving without my lady on my arm?" Elric wanted to punch a hole in a wall. At least then, maybe it would feel like he was doing something.

But the young man shook his head frantically, his hair flopping in all directions. "Listen to me. I know what they're doing. I know there is a risk that you cannot take. We have to go."

"There is no risk too great for her," he muttered, looking through the crowd, hoping to catch a glimpse of raven hair. "If you wish to run, young man, you should."

"We can't stay here! Someone needs to survive—"

Elric reached out and snagged the young man by the lapel. Dragging him so close he could see the young man's pupils dilate with fear, he hissed, "Who are you? And how do you know so much about all this?"

Hands wrapped around his own, but the man wasn't struggling. Not in the slightest. He was just holding on to Elric for dear life. Fear ran throughout his entire form, but he was clutching Elric not with fear *of* him, but fear *for* him. "I will gladly tell you everything you wish to know if we leave this place!"

"Then you should leave. I have a house at the end of Rose Street."

"The haunted one?"

"Yes. Meet us there when you can, And if you touch anything that is my property, I will flay your skin from your form and make you eat it piece by piece. Do you understand me?"

He hadn't thought the young man could get any paler, but there it was. The last bit of blood rushed out of his features and away from his lips, leaving him rather corpse-like in appearance.

But then the young man ran from the room, pushing and shoving people out of his way as though there were hounds nipping at his heels. A murmur rose through the crowd. Obviously people were getting uncomfortable with so much activity. Elric couldn't blame them. This was supposed to be a party full of people reveling in their own power, yet there had now been instances of four people *running*.

He would have found it all amusing if he didn't feel the tingle of magic running through the room. He hadn't felt even an ounce of it before now. Jessamine was whispering a request through him, and he knew that something terrible was about to happen.

He helped her with a protection spell but felt the magic still building around him, like a lightning storm was brewing where he least expected it. The power actually lifted the hairs on his arms, and he hadn't been around a spell like that in a very long time.

Strange. Even stranger that no one around him seemed to react to it. Most people were milling about the main area of the home with the black-and-white-checkered floor. They lingered by the stairs, clearly expecting Fortuna or someone else to appear at the top of them. And yet, Elric still had the sensation that something terrible was about to happen. Something he couldn't control.

This magic wasn't his, but it was familiar. There was but one god who had given their people the ability to cast spells like this. The Crone and her priestesses had magic born from the heart. It was, essentially, magic created from emotion. The greater the emotion, loss, rage, fear, the better the spell. He hesitated to use his magic to prod at it, because he wasn't sure what it would do in response.

Could a priestess of the Crone have survived this long? He doubted it. The Crone wasn't able to control life or death. Her priestesses died far more often than his witches, in fact, because they were usually too pious to sell their souls to him.

But why was there priestess magic in this room?

Hissing out a long breath, he tried to move through the crowd unseen, but another older gentleman grabbed his arm. "Martin! I haven't seen you in years."

"Always good to see you, old chap," he muttered, slapping a hand a little too hard on the man's shoulder and trying to disentangle himself.

"Do you still have that... playroom?" Something disgusting twinkled in the old man's eyes. "I would love to come up to your hunting cabin and experience it for myself again. I did very much enjoy my time there with you."

"I'm sure you did." Elric wanted to put his fist through this man's chest and yank out his still-beating heart. "But unfortunately, I sold the cabin."

"Whyever would you do that?"

"Too many dirty old men soiled it." With a snarl, he ripped himself free from the old man's grasp and moved through the crowd again.

There it was. A boiling, crackling sensation that only got worse the more he focused on it, like a bubble of magic building around them. Something was about to happen. He knew it. And then… it burst.

An icy tingle ran down his spine, like water dripping from the nape of his neck all the way down to the backs of his knees. Then the first person groaned. It was a woman next to him, her bright red corset making it hard for her to bend at the waist where she was clutching her stomach. She moaned again, her voice carrying over the sudden silence in the room as everyone seemed to hold their breath.

"What's wrong, sweetheart?" the man beside her asked, placing his hand on her back.

She opened her mouth to reply, but instead vomited blood. It poured out of her mouth in a fountain of bright color and splashed on the tile beneath her. The blood spread too quickly, like it was thinner than normal blood should be.

Everyone stared at the red liquid splashed across the pristine black-and-white-checkered floor. No one moved. Not even a cough.

"Was it something she ate?" someone muttered, their words carrying a little too loudly in the room. But then another guest gasped and clutched at their stomach, flailing for support, but no one wanted this person to touch them. The entire crowd lunged away from the two people who were now vomiting on the floor.

"What is going on?" Elric murmured, sidestepping a pool of blood as he tried to move toward the stairs.

A guard there held out his hand to stop him, his eyes wild with fear. But there were veins in that man's eyes that were far too visible. Red striations that looked like they were writhing in the whites. And suddenly, the guard hissed out a breath. Those eyes roved, but they were suddenly staring past Elric.

"Who turned out the lights?" the guard snarled.

"No one." Elric moved out of the man's way as he lifted his arms and wildly waved them in front of him.

"What do you mean, man? I cannot see!"

"You're blind." Elric watched as a few more people in the crowd shrieked and started clawing at their eyes. One woman did it so hard that her nails left bloody strips as she tore at her own face. Panic had started to set in. Soon enough, people were running for the doors.

But the doors were closed. Locked from the outside.

All of these people, the greatest and most powerful in Inverholm and the kingdoms beyond, were trapped. No one was going to let them out, and no one was going to help them. Not while they were sick.

And that's what they were, he realized. They were infected. One by one, their skin mottled. Pustules bloomed on their flesh as they scratched at their arms and cried out for help.

He stood there by the stairs, watching with shock as they all ran for the doors. They plastered themselves against the wood, rattling it so hard he was surprised it didn't burst from its frame. They were shrieking now, too, begging gods who weren't listening for mercy.

"Open these doors!"

"Please, someone help us!"

"This is a mistake! I wasn't supposed to *be* here!"

Over and over, they cried out. One of the men shouted in a tone that was different from the others, and Elric feared he was being crushed against the door, but there was no room for mercy here.

An old woman slipped in the blood on the floor, falling onto her back and crying out in pain. But no one reached out to help her, not even to pull her upright. It was complete and utter pandemonium, and there was nothing anyone could do to stop it. Not even a god.

Eventually, a few other people realized that as well. They were mostly older, wiser. People who had seen their life flash before their eyes a few times now, and knew this time they wouldn't cheat death.

They backed away from the door, and that's when he realized how much this kingdom still needed the gods. Because in the hour of their need, many of them dropped to their knees, and they *prayed*.

What a horror it was to watch. His siblings were dead and gone. They hadn't been in this realm for centuries, and the only god left was him. But still, these people believed. They begged and pleaded to gods who could no longer hear them, and likely wouldn't have helped even if they were still alive. They promised all the good deeds they would do and all the lives they would save. The sacrifices they would make. The children they would teach to worship the gods as well.

So many offerings to gods who no longer existed.

Someone touched his leg, and he looked down to see a young woman there. Her eyes were bloodshot and wider than they should have been. A small trickle of blood trailed down her chin, and when she smiled up at him, her teeth were coated red. But still, the little redhead tried to be pretty as she met his gaze.

"You aren't like us, are you?" she asked, her voice thin and reedy.

He bent down, easing onto his knees before her as he looked her over. "No, I am not."

"Are we dying?"

"I don't know. I have never seen a person become infected before." He tilted his head to the side, watching as a blister formed on her cheek, marring her pretty face even further. "What does it feel like?"

"Not quite like death at all," she whispered. "Like I can feel myself leaking out of my ears and I don't know how to plug the hole."

"How tragic."

"Indeed." She took a deep breath, or at least tried to do so. Something wet stuck in her lungs when she did, and a wheeze rattled in her chest. "Are you a god?"

"I was once."

"Can one become something other than a god?"

He pondered the question, knowing that she deserved an answer in death at the very least. "I became a god, so I suppose there is a way for me to unbecome one as well."

"Do you know how to do that?"

Elric shook his head. "No, little one. I do not know how to shed the chains of godhood any more than you could escape the web of mortality."

"Oh." Her eyes turned glassy, and he watched their vivid blue be overtaken by cloudy gray, as if there was nothing left for her to see but a shadow of the world she clung to. "Do you want to become something else?"

"Once upon a time, I would have said yes. I had days when I wanted to be human more than anything else in this world. I wanted to live as you do. I wanted to see the world as you did. Feel pain, suffer, love, and endure." He reached out for her, dragging her body across the floor so she could lean her head against his side. "But now I would not give it up for anything. This power is what keeps the people I care about alive."

"Could you keep me alive?" She'd tilted her head against his shoulder, but he knew she couldn't see him anymore. "I would do anything if you kept me alive."

He could. He could gift her life and keep her as a pet. There was a time in his life when he would have. But when he looked at this woman all he could see was Jessamine, and how lacking she was in comparison to his queen.

So instead of casting any spell, he merely stroked his hand through the woman's hair and held her face against his shoulder. "No, my dear. I'm so sorry to say that I cannot keep you alive."

"Cannot or will not?"

"Both."

"All right," she sighed, and he could hear the rattle even further. It was deeper in her chest now, more prevalent than before. "What god are you?"

"What do you mean?"

"Who are you? Who do I say led me to death when I am in the other realm?"

He smiled and pressed a kiss to her forehead. "The Deathless One is with you, child. My shadows will guide you through the next realm toward a happier place."

And then she died. So easily. There was no battle, like Jessamine, who always fought tooth and nail against losing her life. This woman was here, and in a blink, she wasn't. Until her body suddenly inhaled again. She gasped, but it wasn't her in there. He didn't feel her soul at all. Not in the realm where he had promised her guidance, and certainly not in this room.

Elric stood with her, watching as the girl rose to her feet. Her hands were claws at her side, her body twisted in a strange manner that wasn't human at all. Her head cocked to the side, her mouth working as black ooze started leaking from her lips.

She made a horrible grinding sound and then shuffled forward. There were only a few people left alive in the room, he observed, all slowly turning into these shambling creatures.

Not a single one of them had a soul. And not a single one of them had passed through the in-between realm where he was supposed to feel them.

"Jessamine," he growled, before turning and taking the stairs two at a time. He would find his gravesinger, and then they would discover what Leon Bishop was really doing.

Because the king was no longer here.

25

Blood hovered before her eyes, dripping from the wound on her face and floating back into the room she had vacated. How? She had no idea. Jessamine watched in both shock and awe as the blood drifted in tiny droplets, dancing in front of her eyes before levitating into the next room. It hovered there in the air, joined by other particles of her blood until they created a circle in the room.

"There," Fortuna said, striding past her and into the room beyond. "That wasn't so hard, was it?"

Her mind was screaming, shouting that she had to move. That if she didn't, something terrible was going to happen. But Jessamine was frozen. Stunned to silence. Shock turning every muscle in her body to stone. Fortuna shouldn't have any power, not like this. She wasn't a witch. She wasn't connected to any god or goddess, because they were all dead. And yet, this blood magic felt familiar.

Not because it had the same taste or sensation of Elric's magic, but because it was *magic*. There was a crackling energy in the air that Jessamine was unused to. This energy filled the room with electricity, not shadows. This wasn't death magic, but it was equally dangerous.

"How?" she finally croaked.

"What? This magic? How am I casting a spell and somehow affecting you?" Fortuna chuckled, shaking her head as she meandered around the circle of blood and started fiddling with something in the back of the room. "Did you really believe you were the only person with a connection to a god?"

"The gods are dead, Fortuna."

"Yes, they are. But there are still ways to use them. After all, Leon is a very smart man, and he comes from a very connected line of people who know the difference between fable and truth." She lifted a small chalice in the air, exhaling smoke from her nostrils as she approached the circle of blood. "*Fable* says that the gods are dead. *Fable* believes that we needed them to be alive for magic in the first place. The belief was always that you would get power if you sacrificed to a god. But what power would you get if you sacrificed a god himself?"

Jessamine knew exactly what kind of power they would get. Elric had done that for ages, and he had made witches the most powerful creatures in this realm. He had been the one to show what true power was, but none of his siblings had been so willing to offer their lives. That was why he was the god of the dead. None of his siblings could die, and they feared what would happen if they did.

But then Fortuna reached into the chalice and drew out... a piece of flesh.

Leathery and ancient, it wasn't a piece that had been recently removed. It looked like a bit of back skin, but Jessamine couldn't guess where it had actually come from. She could hear the paperlike sound as Fortuna lifted it into the air. She caught a glimpse of more scraps of skin in that chalice. Thin. Leathery. Ancient.

"What is that?" she asked, her voice shaking as Fortuna lifted the skin and let it go. Like a bird in flight, it drifted to the center of the circle that had been made with her own blood.

"This is all that remains of the Crone," Fortuna said, her voice vacant of emotion. "The Crone herself allowed her priestesses to preserve her body. She knew all the gods were going to die, and she wanted to make sure there was a small sect of us who could still use her power."

So the Crone was still dead. That was good. But... there were pieces of her?

"You're using her actual body in spells?" Why did that make her want to vomit? She knew the price of working with powerful magic like this. But...

Jessamine shook herself free from the paralysis that had caught her in its web. She pressed her hands to her mouth to hold the bile in, fearful of what Fortuna would do with that bodily fluid as well.

"Yes, the Crone was always very useful. But we're running out of her, so the power can only be used in dire circumstances." Fortuna's mouth split into a grin that looked far more evil than any other expression she'd worn. "Taking over a kingdom counts as dire circumstances, wouldn't you agree? Soon, a priestess will walk beside the ruler of two kingdoms, and together we will take far more than that."

Jessamine watched as her blood slowly converged on the skin. The ring grew smaller and smaller until it was all absorbed by that dried, mummified piece of a fallen god. And then... The skin pulsed and power surged out of it, forming a ghostly image of the ancient goddess. She could see that the Crone had once been a kind-looking woman with skin honeyed by the sun. And yet, her power was bloodred, flowing out of the skin and speckling itself on the floor until it seeped between the floorboards and disappeared below.

Jessamine could feel it tugging at her stomach. It was a terrible feeling. An awful, ice-cold surge that trickled down her spine and turned her breath to frost. She gasped at the feeling, watching Fortuna's eyes as her cousin crowed with glee.

"You were once a useful enemy," Fortuna said, her words tinged with laughter. "But now? Now you're going to shamble through the streets, just another forgotten woman who has no one left to remember them."

The infected? Was Fortuna telling her *this* was where the infection started?

A rough jab of magic thrust itself against her belly like a sword had been jammed between her ribs. Coughing, she bent over at the waist, hugging her arms around herself as she tried to stop the feeling. There was a fist in her guts, twisting them this way and that as it tried to wriggle inside her body. But the new magic inside of her fought back. Elric's black power merged with her own, both of those powers reacting like a fever burning through her entire form.

She heard the faint sound of movement, and turned to see Fortuna crouched low to the floor, staring at her with her fists pressed against the ground, watching every reaction Jessamine had to this spell. Jessamine could feel it breathing, writhing, trying to shove its way into her body when it had no right to do so.

"You're feeling sick right now, aren't you?" Fortuna asked. A fervency lit her gaze, turning those pretty dark eyes into swirling orbs of madness. "You want to vomit. But if you vomit, it's only going to crawl its way deeper inside you. If you don't vomit—and some people don't—you're going to claw out your own eyes. You won't be able to see soon enough, anyway. The death is the easiest part. Then I will take all that makes you *you*, and I will use it however I please. Your body can wander your home, though. At least you'll have that."

What was she prattling on about? Because Jessamine *did* want to claw at her eyes. They were suddenly so itchy that she wanted to scream with the sudden ache of them, but she wouldn't give Fortuna the satisfaction. Instead, she ground her teeth and stared her cousin down.

"You're so stubborn. But I can see how bloodshot your eyes are, Jessamine. Soon enough, they'll cloud over, and you'll fall to it just like everyone else."

Then it all clicked into place. She'd seen enough of the infected to know that their eyes were constantly weeping and blood trickled out of their mouths, dark as merlot. Just like the color of the spell seeping through the floor.

"The plague?" she whispered, feeling like she might fall onto her hands and knees soon. "*You* started the plague?"

"The Crone saw that there was a kingdom we could take. We had to clear it out, though, remove all the inhabitants without alerting the other gods. After all, we knew she was going to die, and we needed to figure out how to live without her. A mummified body only lasts so long, and so much power would be required for our plan. The kingdom was ours, and we are a patient bunch. Why wouldn't we just…" Fortuna shook her head. "So silly of me to prattle on like this. It's rude to talk about plans while you're dying."

"I'm not dying," Jessamine hissed, but then fell to her hands and knees. She couldn't quite prop herself up. One side could only balance on her forearm, and the other arm refused to work at all.

Fortuna crawled closer until her breath fanned the back of Jessamine's neck, lording over her in the way her cousin always believed she should. "Of course you're not, dear. You're already dead. What a pity."

The chalice was in her hand again. When had she picked it up? Jessamine swore she'd set it on the ground, but now Fortuna was reaching in to pick out another bit of dried-up skin.

"I know that these are supposed to be conserved, but we're so close. I suppose using one more to hurry this up won't make anyone too angry. Open up, Jessa."

What?

Jessamine tried to struggle, but her body was already so heavy. There was very little she could do to stop Fortuna from prying her mouth open and placing that bit of skin on her tongue.

A burst of salt hit her immediately. It was like a coating of dust filled her mouth, so salty that it dried up all the saliva on her tongue. The magic of the Crone writhed on her tongue, and she could feel it sinking bitter barbs into her lips as it tried to force its way deeper inside of her.

Fortuna watched with that mad gaze, clearly waiting for the moment when it would all burst free. But it didn't. Instead, black shadows poured out of her body. The magic she had taken from the Deathless One leaked out of her eyes and streamed from her nostrils like blood. It gathered around her mouth, prying her jaws open even as the Crone's magic fought to keep them closed. Her jaw muscles screamed, but then she rolled onto her side and spat out the withered bit of flesh.

The wad of spit and skin splatted on the floor at Fortuna's feet, but Jessamine didn't have very long to celebrate the small win.

"Huh," Fortuna said, taking a step back from her. "So that's what he did. It seems you don't have a soul after all."

"A soul?" Jessamine wheezed, planting her palms on the floor and readying herself to get up. "What do you mean, I don't have a soul?"

"Souls are the strongest fodder for magic, and we are going to create the most powerful spell this world has ever seen." Fortuna said the words like she wasn't really paying attention to them. Instead, she was watching Jessamine until a little bubble of a chuckle escaped her lips.

"Fortuna," she snarled, shoving herself upright and forcing herself onto her knees.

"He took your soul, little cousin. He took all the bits and pieces of what made you *you*, and he hid them away to keep you safe. How tragic. You're just the shell of a person with no soul—and he never told you." Fortuna tilted her head to the side, backing toward the door. "No wonder you don't feel like yourself, because you *aren't* yourself. No soul. No life. No kingdom. You're a sewn-together doll that he brought back from the dead to puppet around. Poor little princess. You have no idea how much he has taken from you."

Then she opened the door and walked out.

Jessamine let out a guttural shriek that echoed through the room. Her anger pulsed with a tinge of madness that made her wonder what she would do if she could just summon her strength. Bits and pieces of the Crone's magic still tore at her, but Jessamine refused to let Fortuna go.

Not when she still had so many questions. What was Leon planning? What was the spell that tasted like ash on her tongue? What had Elric done to her?

She crawled toward the door, moving through the remnants of Fortuna's spell and slipping in her own blood. Her hands grew slick with it as she smeared the liquid all over the floor, but she would get to that door. She pulled herself up on the doorjamb and staggered out into the portrait gallery. Her legs were liquid, her strength waning, but fury alone kept her going.

"Burn," she muttered under her breath. The shadows that had always resisted her command now slithered at her sides like snakes made of ink. They surged ahead of her and soon enough, she could hear the portraits screaming.

"Burn until they are nothing more than dust," she spat out.

She didn't care if they were remnants of the family's souls. They all deserved to die for bringing into this world a woman who could curse a kingdom into ruin. Fortuna would pay for what she had done, if Jessamine could just *run*.

But she couldn't. Her body refused, and even as she fell to her hands and knees and crawled her way underneath the smoke, one thought stayed with her the entire time.

She didn't have a soul.

What did that mean for her? Was she feeling things less because she lacked such an important part of what made her human? No, she was certain she could still feel because this anger rolling through her entire body was all-consuming. She wanted more than revenge. She wanted Fortuna to suffer for centuries on end. Jessamine wanted that woman's head as a sacrifice, and then she wanted to bring her back and kill her again.

Power flexed between her fingers and writhed in shadows that ached for her to use them. They waited for an order that would end the lives of anyone who stood in the way of the vengeful goddess she'd become.

Maybe that was what came of missing a soul. Maybe she was a monster now, and these emotions weren't even hers.

Even now, as she slumped against a wall and tried to hold herself up, ash raining down on her head from the burning portraits, she wondered if these feelings were his. Had he made her an empty vessel for his own rage and resentment?

Because she'd never felt as empty as she did now.

26

The second story of the home contained more guards. More people who were slumped against walls and choking on their own blood. Elric didn't stop to help them, but something in his chest burned with the knowledge that he'd been tricked. This whole house had been a trap.

They never should have come here, and he was the one who had led them inside. When he got his hands on Fortuna, he would make her suffer worse than any of his other victims.

"Jessamine!" he shouted, trying to get his bearings in this massive home. He could feel that she was still in the building, but he couldn't sense where she was. He had to find her. That was all he needed to do. He needed to get her out of here. Then they would regroup with the rest of the coven and figure out what the fuck had gone so wrong.

As he passed another guard, he had the distinct horror of feeling the man's soul go in the wrong direction. It was leaving the house, yes, but it wasn't disappearing into the next realm. Something—or someone—was taking the souls of the people here.

But he'd never heard of a spell that could do that, not even one of his own. And again, all the hairs on his arms stood up as he was brushed by magic that was eerily familiar. He could taste it on his tongue, and... ah, yes, he had it now. He could hear the Crone's voice in his head.

Oh, Elric. You are the youngest of us. Surely you don't think you know everything?

It was like she was right here with him. Like that wrinkly old woman had crawled her way out of a grave just to torment him some more. She'd always thought she knew more than the rest of them. And sure, she was one of the oldest of his siblings. But he had learned a long time ago that age did not equal wisdom, no matter how much she wanted to believe that.

"Get out of my head, you shriveled old bat," he growled.

Even though he knew she wasn't really here, some essence of her still remained. A bit of the creature who had terrified him in his youth and then tormented him as he grew older. She was still the Crone, after all, and even a bit of her magic was dangerous.

He could hear her laughter, that grating, awful noise that had always set his teeth grinding until there was a flicker of pain in his jaw. Then it all clicked into place; his mind always had worked faster when she was laughing at him.

"A magical malady," he muttered, just as he had when he'd first seen the infected.

One of the guards slowly stood, leveraging his body upright and staggering toward Elric. He only had to shove the man aside for it to stumble, for this wasn't a person anymore. There was nothing inside of that body at all.

"Someone is taking your souls and using them for power," he said, more to himself than to the man. "But the question is, what are they doing with all that power?"

It was a question that would have bothered him for long moments if he hadn't smelled something burning. Running down the hallway now, he skidded around a corner and saw the smoke billowing from underneath one of the many closed doors.

"Jessamine?" he shouted, running to the door and throwing it open.

And there she was. Slumped against the wall, staring at the floor with her head lolling to the side. It was a room full of burning paintings, and he could only just glimpse the portraits screaming in pain. She had protected herself. She'd cast magic like nothing he'd seen her use before, and all without touching him.

"There you are, nightmare," he breathed, falling onto his knees beside her. He cupped her shoulders, holding on to her for dear life, just to remind himself that she was alive. "Jessamine, look at me."

Please don't let her be gone, he thought. He knew, realistically, it couldn't. The spell was using up people's souls and taking them somewhere. And Elric had her soul safely tucked away.

But then she looked up at him, and he knew something was very wrong. Those bloodshot dark eyes were filled with sorrow and fear. And something tinged with anger, although that flashed only briefly.

"Were you going to tell me?" she asked.

He was lost. "I don't... What are you talking about, Jessamine?"

"Were you going to tell me that you had taken my soul?"

All the air was ripped from his lungs. He didn't know how to speak, let alone what to say. She wasn't supposed to find out. She wasn't supposed to know what he had done.

The choice he had made was entirely selfish, even if it had saved her now. Keeping her soul wasn't right. He shouldn't have taken it from her in the first place, and he certainly should have told her that he'd done so. He was a monster. He was the terrible creature who had stolen from her without consent, and he knew what that felt like. But he hadn't said anything because he had known that once this conversation happened, she would hate him for it.

"No," he answered truthfully. "I don't think I would have told you."

"That's what I thought." She braced her hand against the wall, shaking him off when he tried to help her stand. "I suppose I should not have expected more from a god who doesn't understand what it means to have a soul."

He didn't, but the words still stung. "Jessamine, let me help you."

"I can do it myself."

She could, but it would make him feel better to know that at least she would accept his help. It would feel better to do something other than stand here with his arms at his sides, watching the woman he loved tremble where she stood.

He couldn't breathe. Because he loved her. He'd never really said it to himself, just that he loved parts of her. Pieces that had always captivated him, and he'd told himself that he loved those parts. Only now, he had the epiphany that he loved her. All of her. Every piece, every struggling bit, every dark edge that was sharper than a blade. He loved her.

And she was walking away from him.

He wanted to scream it at her. To shout at any person who would listen that he was not as broken as he feared, because his heart beat for her and no one else. But he had made the mistake of stealing from her, and a soul was precious.

He could fix this. He had to. Because without her, there was no life any longer. It was just gray madness without the taste of her on his tongue and the scent of her in his lungs.

"Nightmare," he said, and hope bloomed when she turned to look at him. "I did it for you."

Those haunted eyes seemed empty. "I know you did, Elric."

"Did I break us?"

"I don't know."

She turned away from him and started down the hall. But he had hope now. Hope that he clung to desperately as he followed her toward the stairwell. Because now that he had her, now that he realized how deeply he felt, he couldn't let her go.

Jessamine staggered through the halls, turning the correct way to go to the main stairwell and then pausing at the top of it. He joined her, and together they looked down at the crowd of infected who milled around where there had been all the rich and famous only moments before.

Her expression was lax and her words far too emotionless when she said, "So they're all dead, then."

"I don't know if we could call them dead, but…" A flashing memory of the woman dying against his shoulder burned through him. "But I think they are gone. Yes."

"Like me."

"You aren't dead, Jessamine."

"You've called me 'dead girl.' So many other people have as well." Those haunted eyes caught his gaze and refused to let go. "I *am* dead, Elric. My soul left my body for who knows how long as I drowned in that ocean. I am dead, and nothing can change that."

"I gave you life!" he fiercely replied. "I gave you all that you lost and more. You are no more dead than I am, nightmare."

She looked him up and down and then whispered words that seared him to his very bone. "Are you sure you aren't dead, too, Elric?"

The question staggered him. All of his siblings were dead, that much he knew. His family was dead. Perhaps he *had* been dead as well. Maybe this rotting corpse of a form was one he conjured until it was too hard to hold on to it any longer. There were too many doubts roving through his mind, but he cleared his throat and asked, "What makes a person alive?"

She stared at him blankly.

"Is it the soul in their body?" He took a step closer to her. "Is it the heart that beats in their chest? Or is it the hopes and dreams that draw them through life as they change the lives of others? What is life to you?"

"I don't know. How can any mortal know the answer to that question?"

"Shall I answer it for you? Shall I tell you what life is?"

Her eyes were wide, and he could see her heartbeat thundering in the vein at her throat. He caught her hand, placing it carefully against his heart, which beat just as fast as hers. "*This* is life, Jessamine. You and I, standing here, fighting for what we believe in. That is life. You cannot doubt it simply because it frightens you to no longer have a soul."

And yet, he wouldn't let her go. Even if she wanted to die, he knew he wouldn't let her soul go to the afterlife. He would keep her here, no matter how much she begged, for he couldn't imagine his existence without her.

Jessamine didn't react, just turned her head to watch the infected people move toward the windows. From up here, he could see one of the neighbor's servants walking a dog in the street. She had frozen in place, staring at the house full of infected with his jaw hanging open. All the infected people were moving toward the life they could see, and the person who would feed them.

"They don't have souls either," she whispered. "Why am I not like them?"

He squeezed her hand against his chest. "Because I kept it safe for you. I have kept it safe from the moment we made our first deal. The moment I knew you were my gravesinger, I took your soul, and I placed it where no one would ever find it but me."

He couldn't tell her he had shattered the whole thing. He could piece it back together, although it would take a long time. But he'd needed to see every part of her. He'd wanted, in that moment, to gain control over everything she desired.

And now, he used it when he was lonely. When he was alone, he took the pieces of her that would explain her behavior, or sometimes he just watched her memories because they made him smile.

She'd lived so much happiness, and living in those moments made him feel closer to her. Even if it was wrong to do so. Even if it was a betrayal.

The door to the portrait gallery crashed to the floor, the loud bang echoing throughout the house, and some of the infected turned toward the sound—finally noticing Elric and Jessamine standing above them. Three turned to shamble toward them, like they didn't remember how to use their legs properly.

"We should go," Jessamine whispered.

"I need to know that you are all right. That *we* are all right."

"This isn't the time. I don't want to fight any of them when I know how…"

She didn't finish the sentence, but he knew what she was going to say. Jessamine feared killing them when she knew technically she was as soulless as they were.

"Nightmare," he murmured, tugging her toward him even as she fought against him. "You are *not* them."

"No, I have the help of a god who made sure I still looked somewhat passible."

"You know that's not what I have done."

She freed herself from his grip, ripping away from him with an angry cry that caught the attention of quite a few others. "No! No, that's exactly what you have done. What would I look like if you hadn't healed all my wounds? Would they have healed themselves?"

She jerked her head back, pointing at her throat before gesturing to her other scars, silvery and writhing with his magic. All the pieces of her that he had put together after every attempt on her life.

"Don't do this," he muttered.

"No, I want to know! I'm dead, aren't I? So would these injuries have healed themselves or knit back together? Or would I be oozing blood for the rest of my days, just like the creatures down there? If it weren't for your magic keeping my soul in my body, would I be wandering in search of something that I will never find? Would I be losing pieces of myself just like them?"

He didn't have an answer for her because he didn't know. Elric had brought very few people back from the dead. That power was the difference between him and his siblings. Elric always made certain that his people remained who they were when he brought them back from the dead—because he didn't know what would happen if he didn't keep watch over their souls. Clearly, the infected people in this kingdom proved he'd been right to be wary of the undead.

"I don't know," he murmured, holding out his hands as though she might take them. "I don't know, Jessamine. But you are yourself now, that I can promise. I changed nothing about who you were. The only thing that is different is that I hold your soul safe. It kept you alive then and now."

"Am I supposed to thank you for stealing my soul? For lying to me?" She shook her head, turning her back to all the groaning infected and heading back the way they'd come. "There should be a servants' exit here. Come with me."

"Jessamine, we are not finished with this conversation."

"No, we aren't," she snapped. "But I don't want to die again with all those others. It's too symbolic, don't you think? They won't stop moving until they're ash, and I will just have to suffer with them."

If she wanted to be dramatic, fine. He stalked behind her, throwing up bits of magic every time one of the lumbering guards came near her. They made their way out to the gardens, but Jessamine turned and slapped her palm onto the door they'd just left, muttered out a curse, then turned to him. Grabbing his hand, she startled him as she rattled off a locking spell that would keep all the infected inside the house, even if a door was opened or a window shattered.

"What are you doing?" he asked.

She paused the spell for only a moment. "I'm keeping them contained."

"But they're important to the kingdom, are they not? And not just to yours. People need to know that they're dead."

She didn't listen to him, though. She cupped her hands together and breathed into them. Unlike his own magic, she did not create black smoke, but a glowing mist that pooled in the palms. Flicking her fingers toward the house, tiny droplets of glowing gold floated toward the building. Beyond the door, he heard the roaring sound of a flame bursting to life. Then more groans. The closest thing an infected could manage to a scream.

Fire reflected in her gaze as she replied, "I'm doing them a favor, Elric. I'm killing them, because no one else can."

27

Elric loved her when she was bloodthirsty. He loved her when she walked away from him with her head held high with anger, her nose so far in the air he didn't know how she saw where she was going. His heart beat only for her when she was brave, when she was kind, and when she regarded the world as hers to take. He just loved her, a confession he repeated over and over in his head.

Elric followed her through the streets, making sure that no one even looked at her twice, no matter how many times she bumped into someone or shoved them. There were a lot of things going through his nightmare's head. And she had every right to be frustrated with him right now.

He had taken something very dear to her. Not that he would ever understand the depth of losing such a thing. He wasn't human anymore. He didn't have a soul to take or steal. But then his mind got tangled up with the thought of her on a throne, and he remembered how she had conjured her own in that realm in between and turned his dark world into one of bright colors, and he couldn't stop himself from thinking about what came after that.

The taste of her. The little sounds she made when she threw her head back in rapture. She captivated him with every tiny movement when she was in the throes of passion.

Maybe that would get her out of this funk. He took a few steps closer to her, and then immediately dropped back again as she glared at him over her shoulder with a gaze that said if he even touched her, she would cut him to ribbons with those sharp claws of hers. There was pain and retribution in those eyes.

Perhaps not, then.

If she wanted him to follow her, then he would. They made it all the way back to their home at the end of Rose Street, with a wind that howled through the broken windows in the front and the suggestion of a figure standing in one of the second-floor rooms. This haunted home was so perfect for them, and yet, she didn't even pause as she stomped inside.

Sybil had already thrown open the door, clearly waiting for them to return. Her brows furrowed at Jessamine's angry expression.

"Did it not go well?"

"Could not have gone worse," Jessamine spat before she took the tempest of her emotions down the hall toward her bedroom. The slamming sound of her door echoed.

Sighing, he pinched the bridge of his nose. "It was a trap," he explained. "Fortuna infected every single person at the party. Apparently, they're using the souls of the infected for a much larger spell."

Sybil blinked up at him. "Ah. So it really *couldn't* have gone worse."

"She found out I stole her soul when she first made a deal with me, and that I still have it in the other realm."

"Oh." The word was long and drawn out. "I stand corrected. It could get much, much worse."

"Women are complicated."

"I think you know exactly what you did and why she's angry, but allow me to remind you just in case. You stole her soul without letting her know, and apparently you then just… kept it? A soul is a deeply personal thing. It's our connection to the land of the living and our ticket to the land of the dead. It's what makes us who we are." Sybil's hand clenched on the door. "I should slam this in your face and tell you to sleep on the street for the night."

"We both know I'd just walk in anyway."

"We do."

And still, her hand clenched harder around the door before she stepped out of his way. Even he could see the disappointment in her expression. Her forehead wrinkled with the knowledge that he had taken something so dear from someone Sybil valued, and he knew she had a right to be angry with him, too. He knew that there was so much wrong with what he had done, but he'd done it already. Elric might be a god, but even he couldn't go back in time and stop his former self.

But there were plenty of people losing their souls in this kingdom, and if someone was stealing the souls of the infected, that was a much larger problem than he or Jessamine had imagined. Souls were costly to claim, and only used for world-altering spells.

"I'm going to fix this," he said as he walked by her. "I don't know how, but I'm going to fix it."

"You can try."

Unfortunately, Sybil proved to be right. Every time he tried to speak with Jessamine, every time he tried to make things better, she brushed him off. She had no interested in talking to him. For an entire week, he tried his best to convince her to at least give him a chance to talk, but she denied him every time.

And he was going mad with it.

Elric used the time to plan. He would not be defeated by the revelation that he had her soul. It didn't mean he'd done something wrong. He'd kept her safe by keeping her soul.

Look at what would have happened if he hadn't! Leon and his cronies of religious fanatics would have stolen her soul for some spell that they still did not understand. She would have been lost to them all. Even his magic had its limitations.

But she didn't see it like that. Jessamine just kept closing the door in his face, ignoring that he was in the room, and only responding when someone else talked.

Finally, he couldn't take it anymore. He stalked into their room, the door banging against the wall and shaking the entire space as he stood there, chest heaving with anger.

She was already dressed for the evening in a long black wrap tied at her delicate waist. She was still rail thin, a skeletal creature, and yet he had never seen anything more beautiful. He was starved just for the sight of her. Starved for an ounce of her attention and for the barest hint that she wouldn't be like this forever.

That he hadn't lost her. That this was fixable. Because all he wanted was to fix it.

She sighed and turned her back to him.

"How long will you punish me?" he asked. "How long do you expect me to endure this?"

Still no response.

Panic set in. His heart thundered in his chest, an uncomfortable feeling that somehow made his anxiety even worse. He couldn't live like this. Not with her denying him even the sight of her gaze. He had to know that she was all right. That they were going to be all right.

And he didn't know why he cared if these mortals were okay. He had tried. He continued to try, and nothing had helped.

Elric sat on the edge of the bed and looked down at his hands. "If I show you the greatest secret of the gods, will you forgive me?"

He had always known her curiosity was the one thing he could play off of. She would not be able to deny herself the knowing of what he was going to give her. Surely she would talk to him now.

But she only turned her head just slightly in his direction and asked, "How?"

"It is a memory. Much like the ones you have walked through with me before."

"I thought your memories were jumbled and hard to find."

"They were." Elric closed his hands into fists. "But they are returning, the longer we are together. If you wish to walk through them, to see what my family was like and who I was before the death of all the gods, I am willing to share those memories with you."

Jessamine turned to look at him. The dark wrap twisted around her body, graceful and so pretty it made him want to trace those lines with his fingers. "This will not make me forgive you."

He hoped that it would, though. Instead of telling her that, he breathed out into his hands. A black smoke exhaled from his lungs, the memory dripping from his lips almost like ink. It gathered in his palms, thick with all the emotions that were there.

Holding his cupped hands out to her, he waited until she walked a bit closer. "This one you will have to drink," he said. "But I warn you, the memories of gods are often cruel." Memories he would rather have forgotten.

She did not reply. Instead, she leaned down and sipped from the memory. The black ink stained her lips, and he tumbled into the past with her.

Elric closed his eyes, preparing himself for what he was about to see. He breathed in calm, exhaled fear, and when he next opened them, he was in the most holy place this realm had ever seen.

Years and years ago, the greatest temple had actually been their home. It was more opulent than anyone had a right to live in. They stood in the great hall, where his brothers and sisters had chosen to make this place look even more otherworldly. The floor was molten gold, but they had encrusted it with every gemstone known to man. Rubies, emeralds, pearls, all glistened underneath their feet. Great swaths of crimson silk hung from the ceiling in billowing waves that shivered with every breath of the gods. The room was lined on all sides with thrones, each tailored to the god or goddess who sat on it.

He looked to his right, where the Crone herself sat. The old woman was wrinkled and wizened, her visage a choice he'd never fully understood. Her throne was made out of twisted, aged oak, specks of moss clinging to the knots of the wood. And at her feet, three priestesses lounged in sheer dresses.

Next to her sat the Many-Faced Mother. Her throne was austere and minimal, a gold throne similar to what a human king would have sat in. Her dark hair was pulled back from her face, so tight that it made her appear even younger than she was. Sometimes she was young, sometimes old, sometimes matronly, but she always wore the same severe expression. An expression that could not compete with the royal-blue pleated fabric that covered her form.

To his left, his sister's throne. The Huntress had made it entirely out of antlers from every mythical beast she murdered. She lounged upon it, barely dressed in a leather skirt, with one long leg hooked through an antler that made up one of the arms.

On and on the gods went. Twenty of them in total, a family who stretched their powers wide.

And him. Elric. Standing there staring down the long lines at the very last man who was at the head of all thrones.

"Who is that?" Jessamine asked, her voice breaking through the nerves that churned in his belly.

"The Warrior King himself," Elric muttered.

The fatherly figure to all of them sat on a throne made entirely of skulls. Each one of them were kings who had denied him fealty, warriors who had not bested him in battle. Snakes slithered through the eye holes of the skulls, twisted through the labyrinth that contained them. And the Warrior King himself was fully in armor, even the helm, which had protected him for ages. He clutched a spear in one hand and a sword in the other. Always ready for a battle.

The door behind them opened, and Elric felt the first blast of pain. Because now she was going to see his greatest failure.

They both turned to see *him* walk through the front door. Elric when he was young and brash and thought too highly of himself. He had longer hair and a nose that was far more hawkish, and he'd chosen a visage that made him taller. More muscular. But it was still him. Still all dark magic and shadows and madness through and through.

"Is that you?" Jessamine asked as she watched this younger version of himself strut through the hall to a throne made of shadows.

"It is," Elric said.

The memory burst into movement once more. The Crone leaned forward, her fingers toying through the hair of one of her priestesses. "There must be a prophecy announced. There are too many humans deciding not to worship."

"We will send a plague," came a voice from far down the hall. Elric didn't need to look to know it was the Blighted One. He was always covered in boils and oozing sickness.

"Who would worship that?" Jessamine hissed.

"He takes illness away and onto himself," Elric replied. "Or at least, that is what people believed. He did not. But the gods' powers are all a lie in some sense."

His siblings continued to argue while the younger version of him merely lounged on his throne until finally, he heard himself make the stupidest declaration that he could have. "Why don't we decide not to punish the humans for not worshipping us, and instead, give them a reason to actually worship?"

Sudden silence.

Everyone stared at him, and even he cringed to watch his younger self. How could he have been so foolish? To think that he could convince them to actually *be* gods? They didn't want that.

"Why are they all staring at you?" Jessamine asked. She walked down the memory without fear to stand beside who he had once been. He admired that. Because even now, trailing after her, he was terrified of their eyes on him.

Clearing his throat, he paused the memory. "Because they did not want to be gods. They wanted blind loyalty and the barest of effort to give any of these people just a hint of magic. Humans were beneath them, even though we were all... once human."

"I thought you were something else?"

"In a sense. Not all humans could survive what we did to become what we were." He flicked his hand in the air, allowing the memory to continue. "Power-hungry gods and goddesses are unlikely to share that power."

The Warrior King rose from his throne, his gauntleted hands curling around the staff. "Deathless One," his eldest brother murmured. "Stand before me."

Even now, he remembered feeling so confident. He watched himself saunter up to stand before the Warrior King, before all the other gods, to give the most powerful of them all a mocking bow.

"You wish us to be gods?" the Warrior King said.

"The humans have not seen true godly power in a long time," Elric murmured in unison with himself. "All we do is punish them. Perhaps we should gift them all with something to remind them why they worship us in the first place."

Jessamine looked back at him. "It's not a bad suggestion."

"It was not," Elric agreed. "But they did not care to rule like that. The gods here, the ones you see surrounding you? All of them wanted to hoard their power, and they certainly didn't want their worshippers to have it. They would give people only an ounce of attention and expect them to fall onto their knees and thank them for it."

And here it was. The worst part of the memory.

The Warrior King himself strode down the hall to stand in front of Elric. Then he reached out his hand, placed it on the side of Elric's neck like he was going to be kind and thank him for his thoughts. Instead, that hand then grabbed on to his throat with a pressure that immediately made Elric's face red.

Jessamine hissed out a breath as the Warrior King spoke.

"You stupid boy. They are beneath us. You want to give them more? Like your little witches who run around and cause problems for the rest of us? Is that what you want? You spoil the gifts that you were given, handing them over to unworthy creatures who should be groveling at your feet. We are too powerful to ever give them what they want. Do you hear me?"

And still, Elric argued for them. "They deserve more than to grovel."

"They deserve to tremble at my feet and thank me when I spit on them," the Warrior King snarled. His eyes glowed red beneath that helmet. "We fought for this power. We earned it. They never would have survived the spell that gave us this. Never forget, Deathless One, that you were created by desperate women while the rest of us were worshipped from the beginning. We were born from the desires and dreams of thousands."

With the barest of movements, the Warrior King snapped Elric's neck.

Jessamine cried out. She even lunged forward, the brave and stupid woman that she was. She tried to grab for him, but the memory fell through her hands as he lay there on the floor, his neck at an odd angle while he gasped for breath. He watched himself claw at his throat, his hands turning into darkened claws that rent tears through his flesh as he tried and failed to stop himself from dying.

The Warrior King tilted his head back and breathed in the scent of fear that permeated the room. "Ah." The old god drew out the sound of pleasure. "I do so love killing him."

He strode back to his throne as Elric's younger self stopped moving entirely. He just... died. Right there on the floor in front of them. Without even a whisper of a fight.

Jessamine fell onto her hands and knees beside the memory of him, shock stilling her tongue until she finally stammered. "Why? Why would you let them do this to you?"

He knelt on the other side of his body, tilting his head as he looked down at himself. "Because that was who I was. The Deathless One. They killed me hundreds of times, Jessamine. But I always came back."

She seemed to struggle with something, some inner argument, until she finally blurted out, "Why would you show me any of this? What is this secret of the gods that you want me to know?"

"That we did not care for humans," he replied, staring down at his own body. "And that I fear my destiny is to become them."

28

Jessamine stared down at the dead version of Elric and held her breath with him. Why would he want her to see how horrible the gods were?

She twisted her shaking hands in the wrap that failed to keep her warm. "What?"

"Humanity viewed the gods as wonderful creatures who came down to help everyone. Not a single god here, not even me, really looked at humans as though they were worth helping. You were all tools. A means to an end. Even those who worshipped without question, and some who still worship my family even though there are many who shun them, those people would do anything for gods who did not care for them."

He wasn't looking at her, though. It was like he was saying the words to himself. To the broken man on the floor whose own family continued to talk while he died in front of them, frozen as he was.

And then the younger version of Elric gasped. His neck gave a sick crack, twisting back into place as his back arched and his eyes flew open. She recognized the pain there. The fear. The sudden realization that he wasn't dead at all and the thunderous ache in his heart that said he had to run for no reason at all.

She remembered it. Because it was the same way she had felt when he'd raised her from the dead.

"But why?"

"Because they were shit gods," he muttered, but then shook himself. "No, not just that. Because I wanted you to know that fighting for the gods has always been a fool's errand. If anyone should know that, it was you. Losing them was the best thing that could have happened to humanity. It's just... a lot of people don't realize that yet."

She frowned. "And that's why you don't want people to worship you? Is that why you're so hesitant to grow the coven?"

She watched the words stick in his mouth. For a moment, he seemed terrified by his own thoughts until he finally relented. "No one deserves to be a god, Jessamine. Not even me."

The memory faded around them, slowly but surely. And she looked at all the gods one more time. Who else would have the chance to see them like this? All of them still alive, still looking at the world with a shrewd gaze for what it could give them. Every single one of them made her uncomfortable, though. Each one of them was wrong in some way. Twisted and corrupted so much that it bled through their very pores.

Her bedroom came back into view. Elric still sat on her bed, staring down at his now-empty hands. She hated seeing him like this. Because she knew that there was still a part of him that was good.

But she was still so mad at him. So angry that he hadn't told her how he'd stolen her very soul. Who *did* that? What kind of a person could do that to the person they loved?

"Thank you for sharing that with me," she finally said, but then pointed to the door. "Now you can get out."

A shaky, long breath expelled from his lungs. "If that's what you want." But then he paused at the door, looking back at her. "Do you miss us at all?"

"Desperately," she replied. "But I am so angry at you that I cannot even think through the anger."

He nodded once, twice, and then left.

Life without him was boring. She went to bed, she talked with the other witches, she learned what she could, all while feeling like she was in a fog. The worst part was that she did miss him. Terribly. She wanted nothing more than to be at his side, knowing what he was thinking about, what he was going through. She wanted to talk to him about every step she was thinking of taking, and it frustrated her to no end to realize that she didn't want to make big decisions without his approval.

Because she adored him. Because she genuinely believed that he had good opinions and he was, regularly, her voice of reason.

Even standing in the garden didn't help. She liked to be outside to think. It helped her mind to still and her heart to relax a little. But now being outside didn't change anything whatsoever.

She tilted her head back, trying to breathe through the worries that plagued her. Fortuna was part of something so much more than any of them could have guessed. Leon had some magic spell up his sleeve that would trick the entire world into doing... what? All they'd uncovered thus far were more questions and more fears that she just couldn't understand.

Fortuna knew more than she was letting on. When they were children, Fortuna had always been the ambitious one. Power had been all her cousin wanted, but now it seemed like she hungered for more than that. She wanted to be the queen, whom everyone feared. Leon was the easiest way to get there.

But there wasn't a way to stop her. Not yet, at least.

Jessamine hated evenings like this. Everything felt too tight—her shirt, her pants, even her skin wrapped her in an inadequate prison.

"I feel like I'm missing something," she muttered.

"I know a way to clear your mind." The silken-smooth voice made every part of her shiver.

And therein lay another problem. Every time Elric walked by her, she felt like her entire body was on fire. She wanted him. She hadn't had nearly enough of him. This deathless god lived inside of her head without her ever giving him permission to be there.

"Whatever you're thinking, I'm still mad at you."

But that voice trickled from over her shoulder, dripping down between her breasts in tantalizing need. "You can still be angry at me and let me do what I want to do with you."

That hunger in her grew ever more. She hated how weak she was. She hated that he was even here.

Elric circled her, and the moonlight played across the revealed muscles of his chest. He was shirtless and glorious. All that smooth muscle laid out for her to see was far too tempting. He knew it, too. He knew what he was doing to her as he paraded in front of her and then lifted an arm over his head as though he was stretching.

"Elric. I haven't decided how to feel about what you did."

"You don't have to decide. But why punish both of us? At least you could get something out of it." He reached for her, those hands too hesitant when she knew how he could grab her.

Then he did. He had his hands on her waist, slowly pushed her backward, step by step. "Why punish yourself? You know what you want. I know what you want. Use me, gravesinger. I'm begging you to."

She let him push her until her back hit a wall. A cool breeze brushed along her suddenly overheated skin as Elric braced himself on his forearm just above her head. Trapped against his body, all she could think about was the way he smelled so warm and how needy she suddenly was.

Pressing her thighs together, she tried her best to stay grounded. "I don't see you begging."

"Is that what you need?" He quirked a brow. "I will take whatever you give me, gravesinger. If you think I am above begging because I am a god, you would be sorely mistaken. If you want to use me, then use me. It's better than your silence."

She was a weak, stupid woman. Because she put her hand on his shoulder and gently pushed down.

He didn't hesitate. This unending god filled with power sank to his knees. He placed his palms on his thighs, looking up at her with complete and utter joy on his face.

"Beg me," she said, her voice ragged with some emotion she could not name. Anger? Yes. Frustration? Certainly. But also something more.

For a moment, his eyes widened. But then she saw something shift in him. Some part of her deathless god who needed to pay a penance for what he had done with her. To her.

His hands glided up her thighs, fingers trailing along her skin even as he shifted closer. "You are the only goddess I will ever worship," he murmured. "Please. Let me touch you."

"You're already touching me."

"Let me taste you."

She tilted her head to the side. "Maybe. Beg me more."

"I have been unable to sleep without you by my side. The mere thought of you lying in our bed, without me, is torture. I wish nothing more than to pleasure you, nightmare. I do not even require pleasure of my own. Just let me make you feel better." He leaned forward, pressing an open-mouthed kiss just above her hip. "If you want to use me, then I will grovel at your feet for an ounce of your attention."

The words were eerily similar to what he said the other gods had done to humans. Eerily similar to the Warrior King's words himself.

This man. He always managed to get under her skin.

She fisted a handful of his hair, making him look at her. "I have my own needs, Deathless One. You are lucky that you satisfy those needs."

Those wide eyes still stared up at her. "What does that mean?"

She tugged on his hair, making him slide his way up her body until their mouths were just a breath apart. "It means, I think you're right. I don't have to like you right now to fuck you. Because you are ever so good at fucking."

Their mouths crashed together. She wasn't sure if she was the first one to move forward, or if it was him. It didn't matter as he groaned into her mouth and surged forward. Elric smashed his hips into hers, shoving her against the wall infinitely more firmly as all of a sudden he consumed her.

His lips tasted like desperation. His movements were frantic as his hands grabbed her waist, one sliding up her ribs and the other down to palm her ass.

She could feel the hard bar of him pressed against her belly, but also she knew that this was his chance to show her what he wanted. What he needed.

It was also her chance to show him that she would not be controlled.

Breathing hard, she nipped hard at his lips. "I hate that you thought you could do this to me."

"I know," he murmured, pulling away from kissing her to press those kisses to her neck instead. His hand came up, palming her breast and flicking his thumb over her nipple in the way he knew she liked.

He played her body so easily. All he had to do was touch her and she was on fire. She hated that.

Elric slid his knee up hard, pressing the muscles of his thigh where she ached the most. She could feel how wet she already was; even worse, somehow he managed to press his knee right against her clit. Sparks of pleasure danced behind her eyes as she squeezed them shut.

All of this was made even worse because she didn't hate what he did to her. She just hated that she had no choice in the matter. That she'd been wanting this, needing this, and it wasn't just about the sex.

Because his hands made her feel wanted. The breathy sounds he made against her neck made her proud of what she could do to him. And the closeness when his fingers danced along the edge of her waistband? It made her feel like the goddess he swore he worshipped, after all.

Again, he groaned against her neck before giving up on her pants and moving his hand underneath her shirt. He cupped her breast beneath it, that same groan again echoing in his throat.

Like a starving man, he begged her with every needy noise. This wasn't a side of him she'd seen before.

Gripping his hair, she urged his head down so he caught the tip of her breast in his mouth. The way he immediately swirled his tongue around her nipple, scraping her with his teeth. His other hand encouraged her leg to wrap around his hips.

He rocked against her. Every nerve ending in her body fired white hot as his cock ground against her through their clothing. She wanted him so badly, and she hated that this entire interaction was cursed by what he had done. Because she wanted his dirty words in her ear. She wanted to feel every bit of him thrusting inside of her.

But, she supposed, he had said he wanted her to use him. If this was his way of making amends, even if it wasn't entirely going to work, then she would do it.

Because perhaps this was her way to make amends as well. Jessamine hated how she'd hurt him by distancing herself. He was right, after all. She was punishing both of them.

Grabbing his hair again, she yanked him back to her lips. "This changes nothing."

"Not a single thing."

"I'm still mad at you." She wrestled with his belt, tearing it off like the long tail of a whip and throwing it into the garden behind him.

"I would expect nothing less." He grabbed onto her pants and yanked them down, hard. They tangled around her thighs for a moment before he managed to get them off and let them pool at her feet. "You hate me now."

Growling, she kissed him hard enough to taste blood. "I could never hate you, Elric. That's the problem. I want to hate you for what you did, but you are still breathing and so I cannot hate you. Because the only thing that would make me actually hate you is losing you."

He appeared shocked for a moment, but she barely let him think about the words before she grabbed his cock. Then he wasn't thinking about anything other than her fingers wrapped around the base of him, choking all the thoughts out of his mind.

He grabbed onto her waist again, tossing her up the wall and steadying her with his body.

With a single thrust, he was in her. She threw her head back, her eyes caught on the stars as she was stretched nearly beyond her limits. Even Elric froze, their breath held as they both paused.

She shouldn't look at him. This wasn't about connection. This was about using him to feel better about herself and to distract herself from... everything.

But her gaze still moved. She looked at him, at his face framed by starlight and the silhouettes of unkept roses behind him, and all she could think was how handsome he was. How much her heart hurt when he was around because some part of her was terrified about what it would mean if she stayed here with him. Losing herself to a god? Was she mad?

He'd shown her all those memories to make it very clear that he was terrified he would become like them. That someday he would lose every ounce of his humanity and his respect for the people who worshipped him.

Elric shook as he leaned down and pressed his lips to hers. Not a biting, angry kiss like all the others. No, this one was soft. An apology whispered through the soft glide of his tongue against her bottom lip.

"I am so sorry I cling to you, nightmare," he whispered. "It's just that you make me feel like I actually exist."

She sucked in a ragged breath. This was too much. She couldn't do this. Not with him. Not right now.

So she shifted her hips, arching so that she drew back and then slammed back down against him. This she knew. Pleasure and pain mixed together as they tangled around each other.

He hissed out a breath and his hands clutched at her hips. Together, they spun into madness. With every thrust, she forgot what she was angry about. With every slap of his skin against hers, she could tell herself that her heart wasn't breaking because of all the things she had to decide were right or wrong.

His fingers bruised her skin. She reached for his hair again, tugging on it far too hard as she forced him to do what she wanted, what would feel good for her and not him. Because this wasn't about him.

And yet it was. Because with every hissed breath, every gasp, every aching cry that slipped out even though she didn't mean for it to do so, she found her heart starting to forgive him.

Pleasure fractured. She could feel herself spinning out of control, growing more and more tense.

"I can feel you," he hissed, his teeth bared in an animalistic snarl. "Come for me, nightmare. Let me feel you unravel."

At his order, she did. Splintering apart with a moan even as he joined her. Spilling inside of her in a wet gush that she could feel already dripping down her thighs.

He let her legs go. One after the other.

They stood there, panting for a few moments. He stared at the wall behind her shoulder. She stared over his shoulder at the roses.

Then, he swallowed audibly and nodded. "Sleep well, nightmare."

She watched him walk away with her eyes burning. Tongue tucked into her cheek, she told herself not to call him back. He couldn't just *do* that. He couldn't just fuck her and then leave because he felt bad for what he had done.

But she supposed, in a way, she felt bad, too. This fractured version of them didn't feel right.

29

Her words haunted him for days after that. Days after he had found oblivion within her body, but also embarrassed himself to no end. Had he really repeated the Warrior King's own words to her? He was just as bad as his siblings after all.

Those were the thoughts that haunted him as he walked down the hall to her room. But he was the Deathless God. He had been created to rule these people, and he would be damned if a single mortal woman made him fail for the first time in his life.

Yet still he paused in front of her door, searching the wooden surface for answers that were not there. How *did* he fix this? How did he mend what he had broken a year ago?

Blowing out a breath, he decided the best thing he could do was just to make it happen. So he opened the door without knocking and just… strode in.

Jessamine was seated at the vanity, unraveling the long coil of her hair. "I don't want to see you right now."

"Well, I think we need to talk about this."

"I'm saying I don't want to talk about it."

"If we don't talk about it, then we're both just going to get angrier at each other. We have to work through this. Together."

She picked up a brush, and it looked like she was holding a weapon in her hand. "I think it would be smart of you to stop talking."

Was that a threat? She shouldn't try to fight him. It only made him more excited about the entire situation. "Jessamine—"

"Elric. I'm telling you right now that I am very angry with you. I don't like what you did, and I don't want to talk about it until I've had some time to think. Once I can do that, then I will ask you to have this conversation."

"How long is that going to take?"

"I do not know."

"Then that doesn't work for me. I need to know that we are all right. I need to know that we are not broken."

"I don't have an answer for that right now! I deserve the space to think—"

He felt something in him explode. "Space? Jessamine Harmsworth, the last thing I want from you is space! I want to inhale the very air you breathe. I would live inside of your skin if I could. I want you more than anything I have ever wanted."

Her fingers curled even harder around the brush. "Then you shouldn't have taken my soul and then lied about it, you stubborn moron!"

"You want to fight? Is that what you want? Fine, then. We can do that, too."

He only had a second to see her exasperated expression as he approached her before he slapped a hand on her shoulder and dragged her consciousness into his realm of darkness. Neither of them had been back here since he'd acquired a physical body, and it hadn't changed.

The shadows reached for them, inky hands grabbing on to their ankles until he kicked them away. And like always, he could feel his emotions leach away from him. This place wasn't where he could feel anything important. Gods could not feel like humans, or they would make poor choices. Gods were not allowed the luxury of making decisions with their hearts.

She wrenched away from his hand on her shoulder, already spitting mad. "You can't keep doing whatever you want, Elric! I did not want to come here!"

"You needed to come here."

"I am so tired of you telling me what I should or should not do. I am not your puppet!"

"I never said you were."

"And yet here we are, in the realm I did not want to go to because you decided we need to have a conversation I do not want to have!" Jessamine ran her fingers through her hair, tearing at the dark strands he so adored.

"Everything I do, I do for you."

"No, you don't, Elric. I cannot tell you how many times you have done something for yourself and pretended that it was for me. Where is my soul? Is it here? You said it was in this realm, so if you brought me here, then surely you are going to give back *what is mine*."

He couldn't, though. Especially now that he knew Leon Bishop was stealing people's souls to use for some dark spell. He couldn't risk her.

But if this was what had stuck in her head, then fine. He waved a hand, and the shattered pieces of her soul appeared beside him. They were a small, neat stack with the mirror memories facing up. And with a thunderous voice, he shouted back, "You want to see it? Then fine, Jessamine, here it is. What else do you want me to tell you? Do you need me to admit that I looked through every single one of your memories?"

"You bastard."

Elric picked up the one on the top and turned the small palm-sized piece to face her. "Do you need to hear me tell you that in my darkest moments, in the moments when I was the most alone, that I looked at my favorites? That I stared down at the images of your tiny face as Callum taught you it was safe to love dogs again? That I rode with you on horseback as you barreled through your teen years like a storm cloud on the horizon? Do you wish me to tell you how many times I looked at Leon Bishop's face? How many times I wanted to bury my fist in his chest so that you would not suffer the pain he caused you ever again?"

Her expression twisted, though he thought this time it was discomfort rather than anger. "No, I don't want you to tell me any of that! They aren't your memories."

"Because I have no such memories," he shouted. "Because I was created as a god, manipulated by magic, and then given to witches for their pleasure and their pleasure alone. But with your soul here, I wasn't so alone anymore. I wasn't stuck with my guilt or my regret. Instead, when I was forced to return here without your guiding light, I could still seek solace in the silver moonbeams of your memories. I could still be with you, even when I was not."

Something in him felt like it had cracked open. He couldn't stop saying the words, even though they laid him bare in front of her.

"I couldn't be with you, because I wasn't gifted a body. Do you know how hard it is to see other people living their lives and knowing that you will never experience that? Do you know how hard it is to see someone like *you*, someone I so deeply wanted and desired, and to know that I could not touch you?"

He brought the shard to her, handing it over even as he grabbed the back of her neck with the other. Her fingers curled around it, the shards slicing through her flesh, and vivid red stained his black-and-white world. She stared up at him with those big, dark eyes that saw far too much, and he could feel himself breaking.

Elric's voice lowered into almost a whisper. "It was torture knowing you were so close and yet so far. I drowned in your memories so that I did not have to suffer as mine started to return, my nightmare. You were a balm for my wounded soul, and I will not apologize for that."

"You should apologize for taking it without my permission. You should apologize for not telling me that you even had it." But her words were a little softer, her lips less pressed together in a white line. "I cannot just forgive you every time you make some grave mistake, Elric. You are a god, I know that. I know there are things that I will never understand. But I need to know I can trust you."

"Why could you not?"

"Because you *took my soul*!" she shouted. Her words echoed in the dark place around them, like tens of voices were repeating her words. The other gravesingers, furious at him for what he had done.

"I took your soul as payment for your life," he whispered, his thumb pressing down a little too hard on her neck.

He could lie. He could tell her that she had given it to him and just didn't remember. He could tell her a hundred other lies that would last throughout her lifetime, however long he wanted her to live.

Instead, Elric sank to his knees before her. He kept his eyes on hers, knowing that she watched his every single movement. And while on his knees, he conjured a wicked blade.

It manifested in his hand, black metal glinting in the dim light. The handle fit his grasp perfectly, and it was not a pretty thing. Such a beast required no adornments. Plain, but efficient and wickedly sharp.

"Take it," he said, holding it by the blade.

Jessamine wrapped her long fingers around the hilt.

"Nightmare, I have stolen your soul from you, and I know that means much. I know you suffer now with the knowledge that you lack a soul, and for that, I will never be able to apologize enough. Your suffering was at my hands. It is an act even I cannot forgive."

"Elric, what is this—?"

"Take my heart," he interrupted when she would have gone on a rant of her own. "Take my heart, nightmare, because you already own it."

Her eyes widened. He could see the shock in those depths, but also knew without a doubt that she didn't believe him. "This is far too dramatic, Elric. Get up off your knees."

"Did you hear me?" he asked, his voice low and meaningful. "I have your soul, Jessamine Harmsworth. Now I wish for you to have my heart. A trade, if you will. Because I have no intent of returning your soul to you in such a dangerous time."

There was a small pause. A moment where her lips parted and showed the lovely pink tip of her tongue before she shook her head. "This is insane."

"I will keep my heart here, along with your soul. Safe. It will be yours, though. Should you die under my watch or choose to go to the afterlife, I will send it with you." He wrapped his hand around hers and drew the tip of the knife to his breast. "Take it, Jessamine. It's been yours far longer than either of us has realized."

She pressed the tip forward, sinking it into the pale skin of his chest, and he tilted his head back in ecstasy. If there was such a thing as exquisite pain, this was it. The parting of flesh. The sensation of white-hot heat and the warmth dripping down the planes of his chest as she continued pushing the blade forward. It sank through his skin, moving forward, searching, slicing, *aching*.

Then he reached to help her, grabbing either end of the narrow wound, sliding his fingers into his own flesh and pulling. His ribs cracked, more blood poured out, but in this place it wasn't death that leaked out of him, but magic. The raw, visceral parts of who he was. Magic that spilled out and pooled at her feet, coiling up her legs in a caress, because even that part of his godhood loved her.

Because she was stunning, standing above him with a knife as so many witches had done before. But this one he had begged. This one he had pleaded to do what she had done, and when he had made enough of a gap between his ribs, she reached inside and pulled out his black still-beating heart.

She held it up between the two of them, and he felt the feral grin on his face. "You, my darling, deserve every bleeding bit of it. I am your god, but I worship at your feet. I promised the shards of your soul that I would keep it safe in return for a throne of bloody bones, and I will uphold that promise. But along the way, somehow, this heart became yours."

"This is too much," she whispered, but her fingers curled around his heart a little harder.

"It is not enough. But your name was the prayer that dripped from my lips on the evenings when I felt like my own world had shattered around me. You are the most divine creature I have ever met, Jessamine Harmsworth. A life without you lacks all reason for living."

And with that, he saw her resolve bend, and then slowly break.

"Elric," she sighed. A stream of blood welled between her fingers and then dropped into the darkness between them. "You make it so hard to stay angry with you."

30

Jessamine left Elric's heart with her soul in that realm where only the Deathless One could go. And even though she was still angry at him, there was a certain amount of pleasure that came with knowing her man would get down onto his knees and let her carve out his heart when he made a mistake.

Holding that still-beating organ showed her just how much power she had over him.

Elric hadn't been joking when he said she had his heart. She'd held it in the palm of her hand and watched as he looked up at her with rapture in those eyes and she... believed him.

She believed he wanted her soul to keep him company. That he was an empty, aching man who had been so lonely he'd thought peering into memories would make him less so.

They came back to the realm of the living, and she opened her eyes to stare at their reflection in the mirror. She knew she would forgive him for all this. He knew how wrong it was and that of all people, she had never anticipated that he would betray her.

It hadn't been the right thing to do, but he had done it for the right reasons, and he was a god. He had done it because he'd been so lonely that he wasn't thinking straight. And perhaps a bit because he did not understand that it would hurt her.

She knew what it was to feel lonely, even while surrounded by crowds of people.

Breathing out, she looked at their reflection and wondered what had brought them here. This time, he left his hands on her shoulders, his gaze meeting hers as they both surveyed themselves in the mirror. A pale young woman seated with a brush in her hand, and the dark shape of a god looming behind her. He was too tall, his fingers too broad, the scars on them catching the delicate silk of her dress. But somehow, she'd never seen a more handsome sight.

He swallowed hard as he noticed his scars had caught on her dress, his hands still lingering where she had previously not let him touch. "Jessamine?" he asked, his voice a little uncertain, as though he wasn't sure if he was allowed to speak.

"Yes?"

"We should get you out of this dress."

The underlying question was there. Did she want him to touch her? Did she want to allow him that gift? Because now that he had bared his soul to her, she knew that it was a gift. Every time she let him linger in her body, find solace in the moonlight of her form, as he had claimed, it was a balm to the aching wounds that ran centuries deep.

She stood, still watching him in the mirror as they both backed up. Like they were dancing, their bodies were so harmonious with each other that she knew how and when he was going to move without ever looking at the step he was about to take.

"We need to talk about one more thing," she murmured, even as his hands slid away from her shoulders and down the wings of her shoulder blades.

"What do you want to know, gravesinger?"

His talented fingers made quick work of the knot at the waist of her robe. Soon enough, the ties of her wrap loosened, and she just barely caught it before it slid off her.

"The creatures that we left there, the ones I burned. They were infected. Does that mean all the infected have had their souls taken?"

"We've already gone over this, Jessamine. A magical malady like that would suggest that none of them have souls. Not a single one. The mindless nature of their being is to spread that strange curse through touch, and that makes more sense now. It's a curse that grows on its own without someone continually conjuring it. A rather impressive creation, even if I do hate that it was likely influenced by the Crone."

"You don't ever call her your sister," she mused as his fingers toyed with the ends of the robe ties. "Why is that?"

"She came into this life an old woman, and it's rather hard to imagine her as a sister when my only memories of her are as an old wrinkled bat." He paused, the backs of his fingers pressing against her belly. "But you know very little of my family dynamics, I'm now realizing."

"I know very little about you as a person, Elric."

"There isn't much to know. I was alive, and then I died. Repeat for centuries on end. You know, I used to pray to the gods as well. My siblings could hear any prayer, even those uttered by another god. I prayed the first time I was sacrificed, carved into pieces to make it a glorious sacrifice that would give the witches the most power. None of them offered to save me, and not a single one offered comfort." His face twisted with disgust. "My family was not a kind one."

The front of her robe parted, and she held on to it with her arm as she looked at him in the mirror. "No, I don't suppose it was."

"The gods are difficult on their own, but they had expectations that no one could ever live up to. I was the youngest, you see. And they all had their own opinions on what made a god good. The more they told me, the less I believed. But it does not surprise me that of all the gods to linger, it would be the Crone. She had the closest to my kind of power, death and life as pieces in her chess game. If she wished, she could give them power over the dead, knowledge of the spirit realm, and even raise up servants from bodies that souls had long since fled. The priestesses were basically witches, if one looked at them from the outside."

"Is that what I should expect to fight against? Priestesses?"

He looked... troubled. Elric didn't reply immediately. Instead, he reached out and took the robe from her hands. He drew it down her form, allowing the darkness to pool at her feet and his eyes to heat with hunger. She could see how much he wanted to touch her. How much he wanted to draw her hands away from her breasts so that he could look his fill.

But he didn't touch her. At least, not like he wanted to. Instead, his warm palm landed on her waist and he gently turned her toward the bed. "Sit, nightmare. Let me brush your hair before you sleep."

"I'll admit, this isn't what I thought we'd be doing."

He shook his head at her, retrieving the brush from the vanity while she sat on the middle of the bed and turned her back to him. With her legs curled under her, she was far more comfortable than sitting at the vanity.

And then his voice was right in her ear, deep and guttural with emotion. "I have to earn the right to touch you again, my nightmare."

A shiver trailed down her spine, but then he was brushing her hair with infinite care. She'd already taken the pins out, so it was easy for him to slide the brush through her long locks. He took his time, being careful with every knot that he came across. The silence between them was no longer heavy, though. Instead, it was the comfortable silence of two people who knew each other's souls.

Even if it still stung to think that he had hers. Still, on the end of that thought was the reassurance that she now owned his heart.

It took a long while before he sighed. "I think we may be dealing with priestesses."

"Why does it sound like that upsets you?"

"Because it does." The brush smoothed through her hair so gently, at odds with the violence in his voice. "I always considered them misguided. Witches understand that magic has a price. They have always known that they must sacrifice to gain power, even if the sacrifice is something very dear to them. Magic is not something to take lightly because it takes from you. Priestesses believe that magic is their right. Their magic was given to them by a goddess because they are better than anyone else."

"That does sound dangerous. Not because they are more powerful than us, which I do not believe them to be. But because they think they have a right to what they are no longer able to access."

"Precisely. And my fear is that there are more of them. If they are using pieces of the Crone's body, then they should almost be out. Which will only lead to them becoming desperate to get more power."

She let those thoughts roll around in her mind until she could figure out what was bothering her most about it. "If Leon promised them more power…"

"Then they will do anything to get it. I fear he believes there is a way to bring back the gods. I could not hazard a guess as to why, unless he believes that he can control them once he brings them back from the dead." He replaced the brush, his calloused hands smoothing down her bare arms before he got off the bed.

She could feel the ache in him, because it was the same as the one in her. They were different now. She had no fear they wouldn't mend this, because she'd already forgiven him. But it was an odd, gnawing sort of hunger as she watched him walk away from her.

Elric set everything right on her vanity, the brush at a perfect angle, and all the perfumes settled where they would be easy for her to reach in the morning. And then he braced himself on the wood, his head hanging as he stared at the gnarled circles of wooden knots.

He was the picture of defeat. A man who had nearly lost everything and who must have believed that he would never get it back.

A knife twisted in her heart, because even though she was dreadfully angry at him, that didn't change how she felt. She feared nothing could change how she felt about him.

"Deathless One," she said, her voice a low murmur. "Come put me to bed."

He moved only his head, looking at her with those dark soulless eyes. "You try my patience, gravesinger. If I put you to bed, I will not stop there. And as you said yourself, I need to earn your trust."

"What I meant was that if anyone was going to punish you, it would be me. I do not give you permission to punish yourself."

He turned with a gleam in his eye. But still, he did not come to bed. Instead, he leaned against the vanity and crossed his arms over his chest. "You're making it hard for me to atone for my grave error."

Jessamine rearranged herself. Draping her body over the pillows, she leaned back on her elbows. It put her entire form on display for his gaze to rove over, and she knew how beautiful she looked to him. Because now she'd seen the covetous way he clung to her soul and her past. Her entire future was his, anyway. He just didn't know how badly she wanted to give it to him.

"Good. I want it to be hard for you." But her eyes danced down his body to the bar of his cock, which already pressed against his pants. He always looked so handsome in black, and she'd been wanting to tear his clothes off him since the moment she'd put her eyes on him.

He, apparently, had different ideas. "Jessamine. I am making up for what I did. I will not fall under this spell of yours."

"You should fall under it. You've been a very bad god, and I am offering a way for you to make up for it."

She quirked her brow at him, willing the god in her room to bend to what she wanted. Needed. There was a fissure between the two of them, and she wanted to fill it with burning passion and arduous panting in her ear until they both forgot that they'd been arguing only moments before.

"Jessamine."

"Come here, Deathless One. I will not beg. But I will make you beg, if that is what you wish."

She could see the muscles of his arms and chest bunching with need. He seemed to swell, every bit of him, from his shoulders to his cock, all of it suddenly larger than it had been before. His eyes turned into black holes, obsidian darkness staring back at her like a predator from the shadows.

He swallowed hard, his eyes never leaving her, before giving a sharp, stilted nod.

She tilted her head to the side. "You want to beg?"

Another nod. This one accompanied by bared, flashing teeth and a tongue that ran over his lips.

Leaning farther back into the pillows, she slowly spread her legs. Felt the weight of his gaze travel up her long, pale limbs. "Then you may beg to touch me. But only if you really want to."

He bit his lower lip, those teeth pressing down so hard she was afraid he'd draw blood. "Oh, I definitely do."

"How badly?"

"There are no words to describe how much I need you." He prowled toward the end of the bed, an unleashed beast who only barely had control over his own reins. But she knew all she had to do was say a single word and he would freeze.

He put one knee on the bed, then a hand, bracing himself to crawl over her, until she lifted a single foot and planted it on the muscular cap of his shoulder.

"Stop," she said.

He froze.

"In your shadow realm, you said I have your heart." His gaze flicked up to hers, and she could see the worry in them.

This was a ragged-edged wound. One that was still bleeding, while all his previous torment had healed in some way or fashion. But his feelings for her still affected him. They still made him ache.

"Say it again," she said.

"You have more than my heart," he said, his fist curled so tightly on the sheets that his knuckles were white. "You have every bit of me. Every piece of my heart is yours, every beat of the organ is in your name. You own my body, my heart, and my power."

She took a deep breath, her nostrils flaring. She'd made him show all his cards. It was only right that she do the same. "I love you. But those words are not strong enough for the connection we have. Love is fragile. Love can be broken. We are bound, you and I. Soul, heart, mind, body, power. All of it. Bound together and woven in a web of pain and ruin. We will destroy all that stands in our way and piece it back together in our own image. This is more than love. It is an obsession, and perhaps a poison that I will never escape. Nor do I ever wish to rid my veins of it."

He broke free from his frozen state to run his tongue from her ankle against his shoulder up to her knee. He was shaking as he said, "I am begging you, gravesinger."

"What do you want, Deathless One?"

"You," he gasped against her skin, pressing his open mouth to the sensitive skin at her knee. "I've always fucking wanted you."

A flare of triumph burned in her chest, and she opened her legs further. "Then have me, god of my soul. Consume me with your darkness and purge your guilt inside of me."

31

Elric left their bedroom, gently closing the door behind him so she wouldn't wake. After the horrible things that had happened in front of her, and the night they'd had, she deserved a long rest this morning.

He had no idea what to do. He had to believe the priestesses had carved their own path, because it was impossible to believe the Crone would have ordered such madness. His siblings had known from the first flicker of his power that Elric would outlast them all. He couldn't die, after all.

Of course, there was always the chance that the ancient goddess had a plan that went far above the heads of any other god or goddess. Perhaps this was a last-minute ploy to use her own body to remain relevant for the longest time possible. Perhaps she'd resented the end of her reign and grown desperate to forestall it. He hadn't been there when all the gods disappeared, which meant he wasn't entirely sure how it had happened. He just knew the moment they'd all died.

Felt all of their lights dimming, one by one.

Blinking, he came back into his body as though he'd been sleepwalking. The kitchen was already in movement. Sybil had started early, it seemed, considering the scent of scones filled the air and tea was already on the stove. He caught the kettle just before it shrieked with steam.

"Sybil," he scolded. "Let everyone sleep in."

"I think you and I need to have a talk. Excuse me if I'm waking you a little earlier than you are used to." She turned, her dark hair piled on top of her head and sticking out in all directions. There were deep hollows under her eyes, as though she hadn't slept at all. "They're using souls?"

"Yes."

"For a spell that is likely far beyond what any of us could ever guess?"

He poured himself a cup of hot water and plunked a tea bag into it. As the red stain of tea spread in the water, he nodded. "That is what it seems."

"That's not good," she breathed. "Would have been helpful to know sooner than now. You were too distracted with Jessamine to tell us, clearly."

"You're right. It is not good." Did he want sugar and cream this morning? After all that he'd been through, he decided that he did. A sweet treat first thing in the morning might wake him up. Of all people, he needed a sharp mind.

So he got his cup ready and sat down at the kitchen table, waiting for Sybil to join him. She was angrily clanking around back there, likely trying to cook something else that would calm her nerves, but there was no such recipe.

Only the two of them understood how horrible this was. Even though Sybil had been young in the days when the witches had given up their lives, she knew what it meant that souls were now in play.

Finally, she sat down in front of him with her own cup of tea, still drinking out of a chipped mug. He mused how she always found the broken one, no matter where she was, when she finally spoke.

"I think the coven needs to be stronger."

"It does."

"And you sent a man back here."

The swift change in the subject reminded him that he had, indeed, done that. A young man who had been more than a little curious during their time at Fortuna's home. "He was at the party. He knew who Jessamine was, even with the mask, and he warned us to leave before the spell was unleashed. He knows something."

"Of course he knows something. Did you not even ask who he was?"

"He didn't answer." He sipped the tea, then scowled down into the mug when he found it was still too hot to drink.

"He's a Bishop."

"I don't need any religious men here."

"He's *Leon* Bishop's brother, Elric."

The world seemed to stop spinning as he looked at Sybil, feeling his gaze heat with the massive amount of hatred that burned inside him. "Excuse me?"

"He is Leon Bishop's brother. He is here because he said he saw you and Jessamine at the party, and he knew something that could be told only to the Deathless One himself." She quirked her brow at him, clearly waiting for an explanation that he did not have. "So I tell you again, Elric. This coven needs to grow, and it needs to become significantly stronger than it is. You want Jessamine on a throne? She's going to need a lot more than just a single god on her side."

Yes, he was seeing that now. She would need every ounce of power he had to get there, and all of this was unraveling at a terrifying pace.

"Why are you looking at me like that?" he asked, narrowing his gaze on her.

Sybil had leaned forward against the table, her hands braced on the edges and a wild expression on her face. Her eyes were too wide, her jaw jumping as she ground her teeth. There was something going on in her head and he didn't like it.

"The covens of old were powerful because they had a leader," she said. "Groups are powerful, but better when there is someone at the helm. You know this. I know this."

"What are you getting at?"

"I think we should ask her."

It took him a moment to follow her train of thought, but then he groaned. "You are not going to ask her what I think you're going to ask her. Sybil, it is too much! She already wants to become a queen, and if she does, she will have an entire kingdom to run."

"Yes, with a god at her beck and call. She is no normal queen. We both know that, so why not ask her?"

"Because it puts her in even more danger. Because it exposes her to the underbelly of our world, and I had hoped to save her from all that. I do not wish for her to know what it truly means to be a witch."

"I have to ask. You cannot protect her from who she is. She's a gravesinger, Elric."

The door creaked open behind them, and Jessamine walked in. Her hair was mussed and tangled, not just from sleep, but from his fingers running through the locks all night. She was clearly beyond exhausted. She stood there glaring at the two of them before stumbling over to the teapot on the now-cooling stove.

"Ask me what?" she finally said, turning toward them.

Elric groaned. "I really don't think it's a good idea."

She frowned to silence him before turning her attention to Sybil. "Ask."

"Every coven has a high witch. A leader who tells us what to do, and who wields the coven like a blade." Ignoring Elric's growl, Sybil continued. "I wish for you to take up that mantle."

"If anyone should lead the coven, it is you."

There was a long, drawn-out silence after Jessamine said that. Elric could read the thoughts running through Sybil's mind so easily. It was a dangerous position to offer any witch. A head witch in a coven told the others how to think and what to do with their magic. If the wrong person got into that position, then the coven became a powerful weapon easily aimed at the wrong target.

It was beyond unthinkable for Jessamine to deny the position. And yet, here she was, willingly passing it over to a witch who had wielded very little power in her life.

Sybil swallowed hard, her throat bobbing up and down as she thought about the offer. Her voice was low and raspy as she replied. "I... I cannot take that offer. Jessamine, you are the gravesinger who is directly connected with the Deathless One. You are the one who raised him from the dead. We are all here because of you."

"And someday I might not be here." Jessamine lifted her teacup to her mouth, blowing on the steam while looking at the two of them over the rim of her cup. "Isn't that what you were suggesting, Elric? I'm going to be queen. There will be a hundred things to do, thousands of people to satisfy, and simply not enough time."

Sybil stood, letting out a scoff as she gestured at Elric. "You cannot listen to him, Jessamine. The future is entirely unwritten. If you wish to be a witch queen and rule this kingdom with an entire coven at your disposal, you can do that. Just because he is old doesn't mean he knows what to do with our lives."

"I take offense to that," he replied dryly.

The kitchen witch glared at him. "I hope you do."

"What would you suggest, then?" Jessamine asked, interrupting before they started bickering like children again. "Is your suggestion that I become the first witch queen this kingdom has seen?"

"*Yes!*" Sybil practically shouted. "You are more than capable of doing both. I have seen how you are with the people of this kingdom. It comes naturally for you to talk with them, to ease their minds. At first, I thought this meant it would make you a good queen. But then I saw you with Elissa, with Agnes, even with Agnes's son. I have seen the way you speak with people like us, and I have seen the ease with which they look at you. Even with witches, you make them feel seen."

Jessamine sipped the boiling-hot tea in her cup and barely reacted. Elric tried his own but recoiled the moment it touched his lips. How was she drinking that?

"Sybil," Jessamine finally said. "There is no reason that you cannot be that person. I listen. I learn from what they say and

I allow them to speak their mind. The mark of a good leader is simply being willing to hear what other people have to say without bias."

"You have the training from the greatest queen this kingdom has ever seen," Sybil murmured. "It would take me years to learn that. Years during which I might run a coven into the ground and destroy all that we have built. I've watched it happen. You asked me once what I wanted. And what did I tell you?"

"A quiet cottage, and a family by the sea," Jessamine murmured.

"Do you really think I can do that if I'm the head witch of a coven? You're asking me to give up my dreams."

Elric straightened in his chair. Both the women looked at him, but he had eyes only for Sybil. "You never told me you wanted a quiet life."

Her features darkened with a blush. "You never asked what I wanted."

He supposed she was right. He had never asked her what she wanted because he'd never really thought a witch could want anything other than power. She was more classically a witch than any of the others in this coven, and he had just assumed…

"I'm sorry," he mumbled. "I didn't realize you wanted anything different."

She stiffened, but nodded in response. Perhaps it made her uncomfortable to know that a god could apologize, but it made him uncomfortable to realize that a god could be wrong.

After all these years with witches, they still surprised him—and he supposed that was part of their beauty. They were capable of great darkness and horrible magic, but they were also capable of understanding and kindness that, in the end, always persuaded him to sacrifice himself for them.

Jessamine looked between the two of them, her eyes missing nothing. "You two know witchcraft and covens far more than I do. What would you suggest?"

When Sybil looked at him to answer, Elric took a slow, deep breath and replied, "I don't think any of us knows covens anymore. It has been a long time since this kingdom has seen the true power of witches. And I believe that means it's all changed. What we did two hundred years ago may be the wrong thing to do now."

Sybil nodded. "I agree. I think following in the footsteps of our predecessors is the wrong choice. They were known for cruelty and overlooking so many, even those of our kind who were simply less powerful. Perhaps we do not need to do the same."

A sharp knock on the door drew his attention, and he glanced over to see both Agnes and Elissa standing in the doorway. The two women wore soft expressions on their faces, a strange thing indeed for a hard woman like Agnes.

She strode into the room like she owned the house, her grandson trailing after her and pulling the chair out before she sat down at the table with them. Elissa sat down on her right.

The once-old woman sharply said, "I agree."

"You agree with what?" he asked dryly.

"I agree. We don't have to follow in the footsteps of those who came before us. I believe the covens were not run well. Giving more power to the most powerful person is simply foolish." She laced her fingers together and placed them on top of the table. "I will gladly take over the position if I am asked to."

Jessamine snorted. "I wouldn't give you any more power than rule over the Pleasure District. You are too hungry for it."

A quiet giggle filled the room. Then Elissa froze when she realized they were all looking at her. "Well, I'm not going to do it. The last thing I'm equipped to do is talk to large groups of people without having someone else beside me."

Agnes sighed. "Then perhaps we should ask Hugo to do it? After all, if wanting the role is bad, why wouldn't the coven agree to be run by a man who has no magic?"

Her grandson seemed to take offense. He took two healthy steps away from his grandmother's chair and crossed his arms over his beefy chest. "If we're doing that, why don't we ask the man chained up in the basement?"

Jessamine slammed her cup onto the countertop, cracking the handle clean off.

Everyone's eyes turned to the gravesinger, whose face was mottled red with anger. Jessamine took a deep, steady breath before hissing, "There's a man chained in the basement?"

"Yes, ma'am," Hugo replied. "He's been there a few weeks."

"*Why* is there a man chained in the basement?"

Elric answered before anyone else got their nose bitten off. "He was from the party. The one who recognized you and then found me before the curse spread and told me to get out. I believe he knows more than he's letting on."

"Why didn't I hear about this the first moment I came home?"

"We were rather busy, darling."

Sybil sighed. "A man in the basement or not, there is plenty for us to talk about here first. Let the man rot. Nothing he can say is more important than this."

Agnes seemed to agree, because she immediately said, "Hugo will handle that business in the basement. For now, we must make this choice."

Her face turned even more red with the memories that were rather blatant on her features. Everyone started talking over each other then, arguing about who should run the coven. Everything from insistence that Jessamine should do it, to perhaps they should seek out more coven members and perhaps one of them would be the right fit.

Finally, they all fell silent as Jessamine shouted, "Enough!"

The silence was deafening.

Jessamine leaned against the table, braced on both arms while looking down at the wood as she spoke. "I wish for no one to be higher than any other. I am your sister, just as you are mine, and no one witch is more powerful than the others. Together we are stronger. We will not make the same mistakes as the women who came before us. We share our magic, our knowledge, and we fight for all witches."

She looked up, and even Elric felt all the hairs on his arms rise. This was a queen who stood before them. A queen who knew what she wanted and did not fear taking it.

"There is no one ruler of this coven. We are a band of women who rule together or burn together. If you do not wish for this, you should leave this coven now. I give you your freedom. But if you are willing to fight with me, then this is how we must move forward."

It was Sybil who made the first step, as always. "Rule together or burn together," she said. "It has a nice ring to it."

"It does," Agnes agreed.

"I like it," Elissa added, lifting Sybil's teacup to her lips.

And thus Elric watched a new age of witches born right in front of him. A bloom of pride unfurled, along with the hope that perhaps it would really be different this time.

At least, until Jessamine looked at him and said, "Now about the man in our basement?"

32

Jessamine didn't want more power. That was the reality of it. When she became queen—and she knew that was a when, not an if—she didn't want to be responsible for even more. There was too much at risk here, and too much that she could take.

It was tempting, though. So tempting to look them all in the eye and tell them she would take care of them. She would make the decisions, lift the burden from their shoulders, and if anything happened, it was no longer their fault. They would be absolved of all responsibilities if she took over the coven. But she could not.

For too long, Jessamine had been the one who looked the others in the eye and told them she was right, even if she feared she was wrong. She'd held that burden along with all the others that plagued her. She couldn't do that anymore.

Elric saw right through her. He could see the worries in her gaze, the fears she hid from everyone else. He was the reason she'd said no. Because if anyone knew the depths of her soul, it was him. Everything was already a little too much for her. She'd lost her life to Leon, then her soul to a god, been forced to kill the man she looked at as a father figure, and now? Now she was planning to ruin the life of her own cousin like it was an afterthought.

Jessamine wasn't sure she liked who she was becoming. It was far too easy to believe she should kill Fortuna and get it over with, far too easy to want to hurt her childhood tormentor. But was such an action the just choice? Would her mother be proud of her for making it?

She took a deep breath and watched them all settle into idle chatter. The witches in the room all started talking about how many more witches they would like to add into the fold. Both Agnes and Elissa had candidates they thought would be important to bring in. Women who were trustworthy and who hated how the Pleasure District was being run.

"Don't forget the Factory District," Jessamine mused, making eye contact with Sybil. "It's already in turmoil. If we can find someone with enough power to take over there, we can make sure we have our fingers in that place as well."

Sybil nodded. "I know just the person. A wife of a politician there, a man who is younger than most. He's quite persuadable, and easy for her to control. If there's anyone who could rise after the Iron Knuckles dissolve into chaos, it's him."

"Get a message out."

She nodded and then turned to the others who were still talking about those in the Pleasure District they would need to convince. It didn't escape Jessamine's notice that Elric's hands were twitching underneath the table. Just a few shudders that he likely didn't even recognize were happening.

She knew him well. Some part of him was excited to feel the sacrifices that would soon flow in his direction. But there would always be a fear inside of him because he was dealing with witches. They were glutting him. Fattening him up with magic, and soon enough, someone would want to take that power from him. She just had to be strong enough to stop them.

Hugo meandered over to her, his big arms crossed over his chest as though he was trying to take up the least amount of space possible. Like he was sneaking over to her so his grandmother wouldn't notice him.

She took another sip of her tea, watching him over the rim of the cup until he leaned against the cabinets with her, watching the other witches. It took him a while to start talking. But when he did, her entire body stiffened.

"The man in the basement wants to talk to you," Hugo said.

"I heard he knew who I was."

"He's been asking about you this morning. It's the only thing he'll say. He doesn't want to talk to anyone but Lady Jessamine Harmsworth." A shadow flickered in front of his dark eyes. "I don't like it that he knows so much, and I don't think you should trust him."

"No, I don't doubt that I should keep my guard up around him. Do we know who he is yet?"

Hugo shook his head.

That wasn't a lot of information to go on, but Jessamine loved a mystery. Glancing over at Elric, she made eye contact with him and then pointedly looked at the door. With a small nod, he stood as well, and together they strode out of the room.

Hugo didn't come with them, Jessamine noticed, but she hadn't expected him to. He was never far from his grandmother's side, even now that she was younger. If nothing else, he was loyal beyond reason.

"Where are we going?" Elric asked, his voice a little too bright.

"You know where we're going."

"I'll admit, I'm curious to understand how he even found us. He didn't say, and when I asked, he practically ran from me," Elric mused as they approached the basement door. He held it open for her in a mockery of chivalry, his arm outstretched for her to step into the darkness.

She waltzed in front of him without a hint of fear in her step. And that… was odd.

"You know," she said as she placed her hand against the wall for balance, "I used to be scared of the dark."

"Is that so?"

"When I was little, I had to have a candle going all night. If it went out, I would run to relight it in a panic, my hands shaking and my heart racing like something would come out of the shadows and get me if that candle wasn't flickering in the room." She could feel an echo of the memory, her heart kicking up beneath her ribs, the familiar claws of fear tangling around her mind and coiling through her body.

Her feet hit the basement floor, and Elric's warm arm wrapped around her waist. He tugged her back against him, flush to the heat of his chest and the hard planes of muscle she now knew so well.

"What changed?" he growled into her ear, his muscles bunching beneath her fingers.

"You."

That growl turned into something far more possessive. He tightened his grip on her, dragging her deeper into his embrace before murmuring in her ear, "If anything happens, turn your head."

"Why?"

"Because I don't want you to see the pieces of him that will be left after anyone tries to touch you in front of me. I will suffer fools if you wish, but the moment they try to harm you, Jessamine, I make no promises." He pressed a kiss to the side of her neck, trying to make what he just said a little less monstrous. "There will not be much left of him, but I would appreciate it if you did not see what I can really do."

She swallowed hard, then nodded. Because even though it was wrong, even though she should have feared him as he said that, she just wanted to turn him around, press him against the wall, and have her way with him again.

Jessamine had spent her entire life with people who were willing to take care of her. There had been countless guards who would have laid down their lives for the royal family in a moment. But no one had been willing to be a monster for her. No one had been willing to be so… evil.

"Understood."

"Good girl."

He released her onto wobbly legs and chuckled as she made her way to the rooms in the back of the basement. She could only barely see the doors, the candlelight down here was so weak. But she'd seen the rooms when she'd first taken the tour. Very simplistic, with little more than a cot, an end table, and a bare light that hung above their heads.

"Did we really need a prison down here?" she muttered.

"Yes," he replied before walking ahead of her and opening the door. He looked inside with a disapproving glance before nodding at her. "We clearly did."

She strode inside and was shocked to see the young man chained to the wall in there. The brilliance of his golden hair, the rather greasy complexion that she'd never seen so slick with sweat. The wild look in his handsome eyes. All of it was so familiar to her, though slightly different at the same time.

"Jessamine!" the young man gasped.

She knew him. She recognized that face, his hair, the sharp beak of his nose. "Unchain him," Jessamine said, her voice shaking.

"Jessamine," Elric started.

"Now."

She waited as Elric moved forward and did just that. And then stepped forward as the young man rushed to her without any fear of the god who stiffened at her side. He gathered her up in his arms, ignoring the immediate tension that rose in the room, and said, "You're all right."

She remained frozen even as he hugged her. Her cheek was pressed against a very real shoulder, but her mind was wandering so far that it was impossible to even think straight. It wasn't possible that this was... he couldn't be...

"Alexander?" she asked, her voice raspy with sudden confusion. "Is it really you?"

"It's me." He leaned back just slightly with her still in his arms. "You are well? He didn't... When I heard you were still alive, I didn't think it was possible. I saw you fall. I *saw* you fall into the sea, but then everyone was talking and I heard you were here and I couldn't... The spell they are using, Jessamine. It's so terrible. You could have been caught in it."

Stunned, she barely had time to even open her mouth before another voice interrupted them.

Elric's tones were dark, laced with violence as he quietly said, "It would be wise of you to take your hands off her, boy, if you want to keep them attached to your body."

She looked behind her to see that his shadows had spread out like giant wings. They were burned into the very walls by the single light over their head, pulsing with power and magic as he leaned against the now-closed door. He had one foot up on the wood, his arms crossed over his chest and his head tilted just slightly down. But those eyes... Those dark slashes were filled with more malice than she'd ever seen.

And he was looking at the points where Alexander touched her. He didn't stop staring at the man's hands until Alexander took a few stumbling steps back.

"M-my apologies," he stammered, distraught. "It's just... I didn't think she was actually alive, you see. I saw her at the party, but some part of me still assumed it was all a lie. She was masked, I was mistaken that I'd seen her, and that she was still dead. I'd convinced myself that was the truth. Can you blame me? It's a miracle."

"It's not a miracle. It's the touch of a god." Elric didn't move. It was hard to even see his lips moving, yet alone the breath in his lungs. All of it made him appear otherworldly, like a statue speaking rather than a flesh-and-blood man. "*My* touch, mortal. Do not try to erase it."

Was this... jealousy?

Was Elric jealous that Alexander had hugged her? There was a vibration of violence around him she'd never felt before, a sensation that if she even took a step in the wrong direction, he'd kill the young man without thinking. Alexander's death would be on her hands, just like so many others.

So she didn't step toward the young man. Instead, she took a large step back, toward the enraged god. "Alexander, I believe you've met Elric."

"Elric?" Alexander looked between the two of them, suspicion in every line on his face. "I thought your name was Martin?"

"Oh." She exhaled. "You don't know who he is."

"I don't know where I am, Jessa. He told me to come to Rose Street, but this house is known to be haunted. There shouldn't be people here at all, and now I know that you were actually here, that you were actually alive, and I…" He ran his fingers through his hair and shrugged. "I can't stand by him anymore. Not when he's killing innocent people and his own *wife*."

She didn't give Elric a chance to reply. Jessamine could feel her face curl into a snarl as she spat at him, "It took you *months* to be angry at him for killing me. Let's not lie. If I were actually dead, you would still be at his side."

Alexander's face paled. "You don't know what he's capable of, Jessa. I know you think he's a fool. I did, too. But there's something different about him lately. Something that's set all of us on edge. I don't know what is changing, but it's going to be bad. You saw what they did to everyone at that party. You saw what influence *she* has had on him."

"Fortuna? That's the woman you speak of?"

"Yes. That bitch sank her claws into my brother, and suddenly he's spouting religion. He's sending sacrifices to dead gods and bringing bodies into the house with us. Our father's house is dripping with blood and corpses." Alexander pressed the back of his hand to his mouth and started pacing. "I don't know what his plan is or what he's going to do, but I heard the rumors that you had survived coming from the Factory District, and something in me snapped. I knew I could not stay with him any longer."

"Alexander."

"There is so much going on that I had no idea about. I buried my head in the sand for too long. I was all too pleased to accept that my place was by his side because I was important to him. But he's been asking for stranger and stranger things, Jessa. Just two days ago, he asked me for blood. *My* blood. He wanted me to drain it into a cup, and when I told him no, there was a moment when I thought he might make me."

She took a step closer to him, ignoring Elric's warning growl. "Alexander, I need you to listen to me."

"I don't know what he has up his sleeve, but it's not good. Killing another royal family is evil. It's bone deep in him now, Jessamine, and I don't think there's any way to save him. He's my brother. I'm supposed to do whatever it takes to keep him and our family line safe. But I..." He looked at her with ghosts in his eyes. "I think he's too far gone."

"Are you finally listening to me?"

He nodded.

"Look at me, Alexander. And then look at the man behind me. You don't recognize him, but you should. You prayed to him in secret back then, hoping for someone, anyone, to hear you. I remember catching you in the chapel and how embarrassed you were. Have you forgotten, Alexander Bishop?"

She watched his eyes flicker over her. Really looking for the first time since they'd walked into the room. His eyes lingered on the silver scar at her throat, then shifted to her wild hair, like a crown of shadows itself, and the aura of magic that she knew followed her now. And then he looked at Elric. Really looked.

She knew what he was seeing. A dark figure cloaked in shadows, not a figment of illusion or happenstance, but because those shadows *were* him. Shadows that moved through and with him, creating a figure that was so much more than just darkness. He was the stuff legends were made of.

Alexander took one step back, shaking his head in disbelief. "No. That's not possible."

The shadows around Elric's mouth split, revealing a sinister smile. "If you worshipped at my feet, boy, you should have known I wouldn't stay gone for very long."

Again, Alexander shook his head. He continued backing away until he hit the cot and sank down onto it. "But..." He looked away from Elric and then to her. "But that means you're a witch..."

Jessamine squared her shoulders, perfect posture giving her a little more confidence than she felt at this moment. "Oh, I'm so much more than that, Alexander."

"And you're..." He lifted a shaking hand to point at Elric.

"I am the god-born rancor that will cleanse this kingdom. I am the claws in the shadows at night, and the drifting bitter wind. I am the Deathless One, and your prayers have been answered." Elric moved then, so quickly mere mortals couldn't track him, and suddenly he stood in front of her, blocking Alexander from her sight.

She soon saw why. Elric's power spread around him, his wings so wide and dripping with ink. Pulses of magic seared through them like little lightning strikes in a starless night sky. No beauty, only harsh, ragged edges and thunderous magic.

"Alexander Bishop, you will atone for your brother's transgressions. You will stay here, and while I will not make you suffer in his place, you will provide us with all the details you know about the man we call Leon Bishop and the demon he is becoming."

She heard Alexander swallow. And then, as she peered beneath Elric's arm, she saw the young man fall to his knees before the sight of his god.

"I will serve you in whatever way you wish," he vowed. "My lord and liege."

33

Elric preferred detailed plans, long hours of haunting the steps of those he hunted, and foolproof execution. But the anger that coursed through his veins urged him to rush into Fortuna's home again and pop skulls until the entire home was flooded with blood. The entire kingdom would speak of his attack for years to come, and he would relish in their fear. Yet, he understood that there was a decorum to taking over a kingdom.

He just hated every second of it.

Every person in the house sat in the great room, all of them on cushioned chairs and sofas that he had needed to conjure more of before tonight. There were also three new faces, women who'd arrived so recently, he had not even taken the time to learn their names.

Agnes, Elissa, and Sybil had each brought one witch, women who were born with potential but lacking in magic because no god had given them that ability. His coven had taught them how to sacrifice, and in turn he had gifted the newcomers with a taste of power.

He didn't care what their names were. He didn't even look at their faces. All he knew was that the coven needed to be more powerful, and so he helped. He consumed their sacrifices and gifted them with token magic in return. A hedge witch, a spirit witch, even one who appeared to be just raw power, with no inclination toward a specific magic. All three women were now strong.

But the first of the coven were always strong. Those who joined later would be weaker than this first group of initiates, as his magic had to be shared among more and more witches. It was what inevitably drove them to sacrifice him, in the end. He didn't tell them that, though. He just sat there on the couch with Jessamine beside him, his arm outstretched behind her in a show of what little ownership he could claim. She was, after all, his.

None of the other witches were, and he wanted them all to know that.

Shaking hands stayed on their laps. Elissa kept opening her mouth, then closing it. She clearly wanted to say something, but none of them wanted to be the first to speak. Even Hugo lingered behind his grandmother with a troubled expression on his face.

Finally, Elric couldn't take it anymore. "We all know what we're doing?"

Agnes's head snapped up, looking at him in surprise. "Of course we know what we're doing."

"Then why don't we all review our jobs one last time?"

The silence that stretched out among them was bittersweet. This was the last time they would all be together before the moment when they changed the world. And it seemed that they were all thinking the same thing this morning.

Agnes reached for Elissa's hand. "Elissa and I will go with the newest witches to the central square. Together, we will conjure a spell to make it obvious that the coven has returned. No matter who tries to stop us, we will practice witchcraft in public. Real, meaningful witchcraft that will strike horror into the souls of those who see us. We will not stop until we see you again. Then you will join us, after proving that the Deathless One is who he says he is."

He bared his teeth in a grin that was anything but happy. "For a price."

"You've already promised me the Pleasure District, yes, but I will take more power before you and Jessamine move toward her stolen castle. Elissa would like her lover to be turned back into a human." A disgruntled look marred her usually severe face. "You still claim that is impossible, so you have offered to give her the ability to speak as a person would."

He nodded, then looked at Sybil.

His dark witch, the first of his coven and the only remaining legacy of the old days, smiled at him. "I will go with Jessamine to where we believe Lady Fortuna is now hiding. Together, we will get from her the information that we need."

And then he looked at Alexander, the young man who had been shaking so badly when they released him from the prison that he looked like he might throw up. The pallor of his skin had yet to change. After all, he was as shocked by his role in all this as Elric.

"I will be going with you," Alexander murmured, his voice low and reverent. "Together, we are the distraction."

"Indeed we are."

He glanced down at Jessamine, who had curled her hands into fists on her thighs. She was shaking, too, although he had a feeling it was from anger rather than fear.

"Are you sure this is the right time?" she murmured, looking up at him through those dark lashes. "You have never wanted people to know you have returned."

He pressed a kiss to the top of her head. "Yes, my nightmare. It is time that everyone knows the gods have returned."

"Gods?" she replied with a soft laugh. "Only one is here."

"Ah, but I was lonely, and so I created myself a goddess to worship." He tucked a finger underneath her chin and tilted her head up for his kiss. Elric lingered on the plush softness of her lips. He didn't care if everyone watched them. Let them see. Let them watch as a god treated his queen the way she should always have been treated.

When he finally drew away, her lips were dark red, deeper than blood, and her eyes had a slightly glazed look in them.

"Listen for the words," he said quietly. "You will hear them all bend a knee to the Deathless One who has returned. Then you will return to me, nightmare. My gravesinger. My soul."

"Be safe," she whispered.

And together, at the same time, they said, "I love you."

The words were whispered like they wouldn't ever see each other again. But how silly it was for him to fear that, because he knew he would. Death itself could not take Jessamine from him, no matter how many times it tried.

Pressing his lips to hers one more time in a fierce, hard kiss, he stood. He looked at everyone in the room again, imprinting their faces to his memory, even the new witches.

And then he bowed to them all. Low and deep, his hand tucked against the small of his back as he gave them all the greatest honor a god could bestow. "My coven," he said, his voice deep as he straightened. "All your life you have been told you are weak, because the wild feminine in you seeks chaos. That order and reason are denied by your nature and that you should fear what lives inside you. But now you are witches. You should not fear yourself; it is they who should fear you. You need no longer fear the darkness, for a god has made it your home. Rage, and do not fear your own anger. Tear it all down!"

Alexander stood, and together, they left the room of women, who were already brimming with so much magic he could taste it in the air. They were going to make quite the scene.

"That was... inspiring," Alexander said as they walked out into the sun.

"Don't talk."

"Sorry, I just... I don't know how to act around a god."

Elric turned his gaze to the sky and took a long, deep breath. "Listen to me, boy. You have a very simple job. Just tell people who I am. I will make sure that they believe you. We will do a lap of the Pleasure District, causing as much chaos as possible, and then we will join the witches, where we will make a final display that will ensure everyone in this kingdom knows I have returned."

"I know you explained it, but..." Alexander had to hurry to catch up to him. "But why are we doing this again?"

Elric paused, stopping in the middle of the street and staring down at Alexander. Gods did not need to explain themselves to anyone, least of all a trembling worshipper like this princeling. Licking his lips, he looked around them before he just... stopped. He didn't want to hide anymore, and he didn't care if people overheard him.

"To give her time. Because if everyone in this district is looking at me, then no one is looking at her."

With a determined nod, Alexander removed the tie around his neck and loosened his shirt. He rolled his sleeves up strong forearms and then took a deep, steadying breath. "Right, then. Where are we going?"

"I thought we'd start in the temple."

"Do you want me to sacrifice to you?"

It wasn't what he had planned, but... "That would work. I can emerge from my own sculpture. Should startle many people."

"It's a good time of the morning to go. Quite a few people visit the temple. It is a spectacle on its own, but also, there will be many visitors there this time of day. Considering no one seems to know what happened at Fortuna's home yet, there are also quite a few visitors from other areas of the realm who have never seen this place before."

It was good enough. They didn't talk until they strode into the temple, and Elric was surprised to feel magic here. Someone had been making sacrifices in this place. Even though the gods were dead, they still clung to the hope that if they prayed, someone would answer. Few dared pray directly to him, however.

Alexander strode right to the statue, and Elric let himself fade into the shadow realm. He watched as other people looked askance at Alexander lighting incense at the Deathless One's feet. A few people even muttered that surely he didn't know who he was sacrificing to—until Alexander set the burning incense down at his feet and stared up at the statue that Elric and Jessamine had desecrated only a few days before.

"Deathless One," he called out, a tinge of desperation in his tone. "Our kingdom is falling to pieces. We give our fealty to a man who murdered his wife, our queen, on the very day of their wedding. My soul is shattered with sadness for the infected who die in our streets with no one caring that they are ill. We are broken. And there is no other god to save us."

An elderly man chuckled. "The gods are long gone, boy. No one's listening. You might as well be talking to stone."

Elric merged his body with the statue and prepared to put on a show. All the candles flickered as though a gust of wind had blown through the temple, but the air was still. Then a deep groan rumbled through the room, a rasping growl that echoed in the silence.

He strode out of his statue and crouched on the dais before Alexander. Darkness clung to him in strings, like some primordial ooze birthing him out of his own statue, strings of it dripping onto the floor in wet, echoing plops. Slowly, he looked up to meet Alexander's gaze.

Someone gasped.

Another screamed.

Then all fell silent again as they stared at the god who had just appeared before them. A god who rose before Alexander and cupped his chin in his hand. He made the young man look at him, so that they both knew this moment was very, very real.

"You've done well," he said, his voice amplified by magic and power. "This kingdom is full of those who have forgotten who I am."

He let his gaze linger on all the sacrifices left at the altars of his siblings. And the hatred he felt in that moment was very real. He hated that all of these people had seen value in his siblings yet constantly overlooked him.

He was a god, one more powerful than any of his siblings, but they had never seen him as worthy of their attention. Instead, all these mortals had looked at him as a visage of evil. Shadows begot madness, and therefore, he was evil. Surely there wasn't anything good in a creature who served a coven of witches, who fed the creatures they had long feared.

All that anger stretched out of his skin. He could feel it growing in waves of darkness that spread out from his throat like a cape, joining the wings that slowly emerged from the statue behind him and grew wider as he stood to his great height.

"Perhaps I need to remind you all why I am called the Deathless One."

Then he felt it. The thrum of sacrifice pulsing through the connection to his coven. He could feel that blackness stretching throughout the kingdom, seeping into his skin and bloating him with even more power.

He lifted his arms above his head and released his shadows to snuff out the lights. One by one. And then he filled the statues of his siblings with dark magic. They all stepped down from their pillars, the crunching of stone echoing in the room. Screams joined the sound of stone on stone. And soon enough, he strode out of the building with the ghosts of his siblings walking behind him. Or at the very least, the stony visages of the gods who once were.

A crowd had gathered in front of the temple. Their gazes turned to him as he spread his wings wide at last. It had been such a long time since he'd allowed his magic to really stretch around him, to be the glorious god who had once terrified this kingdom.

"Where is my coven?" he snarled, the words cast out like a net around the people who stood and stared at him.

The stone gods around him turned as one and began to walk through the Pleasure District. He followed them, pausing only when someone fired a shot at him. It was a brave young guard wearing a navy suit with sparkling gold buttons.

Elric reached into his own chest, where the shot should have hit his heart, and pulled the crushed bullet out. Black blood seeped through his fingers, but when the bullet clinked onto the ground, the man was already lifting the musket again.

"Don't," he said, pointing at the man with a clawed hand.

The guard started to squeeze the trigger, and Elric unleashed all the rage he'd been harboring for ages.

Shadows crawled free from his body. They scurried like rats up the man's legs, biting into him with teeth and claws that shouldn't exist on mere wisps of darkness. So many innocent souls watched in horror as they crawled into the man. Biting, gnashing, gnawing through his skin until they were visible lumps beneath his pale flesh, racing up his torso and arms, coming out of his throat in a wet gush of blood that sprayed onto the person standing next to him. The woman froze in shocked silence for a moment before releasing a bloodcurdling scream.

Good. Let her scream. They should all be terrified of what he could do and what he would continue doing if they failed to worship him as he deserved.

Anger still seethed underneath his skin. Some of these people had continued to worship his siblings, believing his siblings were more worthy. Even after centuries, it was still a bitter ache in his soul. He *was* worth their adoration. Far more than his brothers or sisters, because he was the only one who had ever fought for mortals.

As he strode through the streets, he allowed his shadows to disappear into the skin of anyone who tried to attack him. Witnesses cried out that a monster was in their midst and that he would be the death of them all. The end had come, and the god of death had returned.

These people hadn't seen real magic in centuries. Now he was going to show them all just how powerful he was.

The town square was filled with people barely held back by the bubble of magic that surrounded his witches. Five of them, all seated cross-legged on the ground with their arms around each other. They swayed back and forth, chanting in a black tongue that had cast more curses than spells in its time. The runes etched into the ground around them were starting to wear thin from all the weapons that cracked against their magical shield.

With a flick of his fingers, he strengthened each of those runes, searing them into the ground so that no manner of cleaning would ever remove them.

Agnes looked up, and then Elissa. Both of their faces were streaked with dirt, and he could see Hugo looming behind them. It had likely taken every bit of self-control for him not to push people away from the circle, but the man had managed, knowing how important it was to demonstrate the strength of the coven's magic. And for that, he would be rewarded just like all the others.

Elric looked up at the sky. Fluffy clouds surrounded a sun that merrily beat down on a scene straight out of a nightmare.

"My coven!" he shouted, and everyone who had been trying to get to the witches froze.

They turned to see a god with dark wings silhouetted by the sun itself. And then he let his wings spread ever wider, the grin on his face one of pure euphoria as he drew every ounce of bitterness from himself and let his magic fly free. "Let us bring night to this cursed kingdom, and plunge it into unending darkness until the very world repents."

Their chanting grew louder, filling the town square with an eerie song of witchcraft and madness as his shadows boiled above them to blot out the sun.

34

Sneaking through the streets felt wrong when she knew all the others were risking their lives. But finding Fortuna had taken time. Now, they knew where she was hiding out and they knew how to get to her. This back alley had seen better days. Water slicked the cobblestone streets, and it was the only area of the Pleasure District that didn't sparkle even in the moonlight. But what a place to hide.

As they rounded the last corner, Jessamine felt the surge of power at the same time Sybil did. It was the first moment she'd felt connected to the coven. Usually, she relied on Sybil to know what was happening when it came to their powers, but right now, it was almost like she was the same as the others.

But anyone who knew what witchcraft felt like could tell what was happening in the Pleasure District. It raked down her body, sending claws down her spine that felt so good and so unnatural at the same time. She could feel the ends of her hair lifting, and had a sensation that she wasn't alone.

Finally, she could feel it. There were so many other women just like her, and their calls and chants filled her entire being with reason. The family she had so hoped to find, and they were right here with her. A coven.

Sybil motioned to her, and together they lifted the hoods of their cloaks and slunk down the street. People were already whispering about the madness they had seen at the temple and beyond.

Gods had come back to life. Hysteria had descended upon the Pleasure District.

And then the world went dark.

Jessamine tilted her head up at the last second, risking being seen just so she could watch Elric's powers float around her. The darkness that existed in him alone had expanded and blotted out the very sun. She couldn't see anything at all. Just an undulating blanket of power that moved like waves of ink, not water. Then it seemed to peel off of itself, still dark but raining down featherlight motes of...

She caught one on her fingers and rubbed it between her thumb and pointer. "Ash," she whispered, showing it to Sybil. "It's raining ashes."

Sybil grabbed her hand, staring down at the darkness smudged there. "What does it mean? What message is he trying to send?"

"What better way to show the entire world that he's returned?"

They both shuddered before rushing forward again. After all, things were clearly in movement, and she had no intention of waiting to see what would happen next. She needed to keep going.

Alexander had told them that Fortuna had a safe house. Jessamine wasn't entirely sure if she could trust Leon's brother, but he seemed suitably shaken by the events of the party. Even if this was a trap, she was prepared to walk into it. After all that had happened, all that she lost, she would not fail herself again.

Fortuna had seen Jessamine at her weakest. She had trapped her when Jessamine had been stuck in her own mind. A part of her still wanted Fortuna to be the cousin she had known, the same person that Jessamine had always hoped she would become. And that sentimentality had cost her.

This time, she would not make the same mistake.

"Here it is," Sybil murmured, pausing in front of a quaint cottage that seemed far too meager for Fortuna, even as a hiding place. It was small, with stone walls and a fence that was well kept, with flowers all around it.

"This looks like a fairy house," Jessamine muttered. She placed her hand on the front gate, pausing only when Sybil touched her arm.

Jessamine quirked a brow, looking at the other witch, who should have been rushing just like her.

"Don't make any rash decisions in there," Sybil muttered.

"I don't plan to."

"You've made a habit of doing so, Jessamine. I want you to know that I will be there with you, but neither of us can underestimate her. She is a dangerous woman, a viper waiting for us to come to her in her den. You get lost in your own mind and memories sometimes, dear one."

Jessamine nodded shakily. "I'm not here to save anyone or to linger in the memories I have of *dear* Fortuna. What I once felt for her was lost the moment she killed all those people in her home. There is no saving a woman like her."

"Then what are you planning to do?"

Jessamine could feel the costs of her past churning inside her. All the people who she still felt guilt over losing. Benji and the terror he'd felt as she yanked his memories out of him. Callum, the man who had once been like a father to her and who had betrayed her for fear of what he would become.

Fortuna would be another name added to that list. Yet another person who had once been important to Jessamine. But now, she would have to suffer.

Licking her lips, she replied, "I'm going to do the same thing I did to all those who stood in my way before. Callum's punishment is a mere flicker compared to what I intend to do to this woman who took so much from so many."

Sybil's hand landed on top of hers on the gate, and she squeezed Jessamine's fingers. Together, they stared at each other. Two women who had gone through too much in their lives. And this was their moment to take down a part of what had made it so hard.

"Together," Sybil said. "For all the witches who came before us."

"And all the witches who will come after."

They pushed the gate open and strode toward the front door. Jessamine could see there was a moment where Sybil started to go around the back, but Jessamine wasn't going to play that game. Instead, she spread her fingers and called upon the magic that was finally listening to her.

Elric's shadows always seemed to cling to her. But now they crept out from underneath the bushes, rolled over the edge of the roofline, and dropped down at her feet. Even Nyx appeared from her shadow, prowling out of the darkness and arching her back beside Jessamine as she stared at the door.

"It is time, my darlings," she whispered. "Find her!"

They slithered away, sinking underneath the door and through the cracks around the windows. Anywhere they could get into the house, they did. The only one who remained at her side was Nyx, who snarled and hissed as she stared at the door. One by one, all the lights in the house blinked out.

"What spell is that?" Sybil asked, her brows furrowed in confusion.

"It's not a spell. It's just... magic."

The other witch looked at her then with a sharp expression, her eyes narrowed in suspicion. And perhaps Jessamine should have felt the same way. She didn't know why she was able to do this now, but since the party at Fortuna's, her magic bent to her will almost intuitively. All she could figure was that she was closer to Elric than she had ever been before.

And with that closeness, something inside of her had awakened.

She opened the front door, and Nyx slipped through her legs to disappear inside. A glimmering dark thread connected the two of them, linking her with her familiar, making it simple to follow the little cat through the house.

Nyx was the first to find the wards that Fortuna had thrown up with the last sliver of the Crone she still had. The throbbing red magic permeated the house, but it was weak. Far weaker than it should have been.

Jessamine reached for Sybil's hand, and together, they whispered a spell. The words were ugly and dark, but they severed through the Crone's magic with ease. There wasn't much left of it, after all.

She could hear the faint sounds of Fortuna moving about. Her cousin wasn't being quiet, which suggested she believed her wards would hold. So Jessamine slipped into the single bedroom and sat down in one of the twin chairs before a fireplace. Sybil remained by the door, ready to close it behind Fortuna once she decided to join them.

It was a nice room. The cottage had likely once been owned by someone with excellent taste. The chair was deep and comfortable. The bed was cushioned nicely and decorated with a hand-sewn quilt that looked ready for grandchildren to bounce on top of it. There were even paintings on the wall, clearly done by a novice artist but depicting flowers from the garden they'd just walked through.

The door opened, and Fortuna walked through with a candle in her hand. "He couldn't have put me up in a nicer place?" she muttered. "Of course not. Why would a king spend any money at all on the woman who got him his throne? Damnable man."

Jessamine felt Nyx crawl into her lap. The tiny cat sprawled over both of her thighs, her eyes reflecting the candlelight back at Fortuna.

Fortuna shrieked and backed toward the door only to realize that Sybil had locked it behind her. Without a word, Jessamine urged Elric's shadows in this room to dim the light. The only thing illuminated by the candles was her dark figure sitting in the chair before Fortuna, deciding just what terrors she was going to face.

Her cousin went pale as snow. "Feeling better, I see."

"Did you think that would be the last time you saw me?"

"I suspected it wouldn't be. After all, it is very difficult to kill a thing without a soul."

Jessamine gestured toward the other armchair. "Have a seat, Fortuna. We need to have a nice long chat."

"I think I'll be taking my leave. You can't keep me here." But then she froze at the sight of Sybil's grinning face in the darkness.

Jessamine rarely had thought of her friend as a witch. Sybil, in the beginning, had seemed more like a creature from the sea. A siren with black-pearl skin and wild-woman hair, who had seen more of the world than Jessamine could ever dream. But in this moment, with the shadows clinging to her form and her eyes narrowed in sharpened hate, she could see the witch inside Sybil.

She might call herself a kitchen witch, but there were still knives in a kitchen, and Sybil knew how to use them better than anyone.

"Sit," Sybil said, her voice low and filled with anger. "You dealt with a god last time, but forgive the poor dear, because he is still a man, and men are such flawed creatures. Now you deal with two witches, and we will be much harder to escape."

"You forget I still have the blessing of my goddess on my side," Fortuna hissed.

Jessamine breathed out a sigh. "I see no goddess here. You have the skin of a creature who was more powerful than you could ever hope to be, yes. That gives you some magic. But even the priestesses of old knew to fear the witches."

"You have no power over me! Get out of this house, Jessamine, or I will banish you from it!"

Jessamine lifted a hand, feeling the shadows coil through her fingers like she held a snake in her grip. "No," she murmured. "I don't think you will."

With the flick of a wrist, she let the shadows fly free and savored the sense of power that came with it. Coiling around her cousin, Elric's shadow-snakes swiftly bound Fortuna's arms behind her and dropped the woman into the chair. Jessamine noted a heady sensation and a ringing in her ears—this level of power was addicting and amazing and terrifying all at the same time. If she wanted to, she could really hurt someone.

And that gave her pause. She took a moment, allowing her eyes to roll back in her head as she reveled in the sensation before returning her gaze to Fortuna's.

"I think you have forgotten what witches are," she said quietly. "You think I am weak because I am not like you. You thought I was weak as a child because I saw use in those you did not. Your judgment of other people is your greatest weakness, Fortuna, and my greatest strength is that I see beyond what you do."

"We are both just women seeking power."

"I am nothing like you," Jessamine replied. She let the words seep from her tongue and sink into her skin, where she knew they needed to be. She said the words to heal herself and all the past that still clung to her like sticky glue. "And I cannot express how happy it makes me to know that I will *never* be like you."

Silence rang between them, a thousand words said all in an instant. She could see the fear in Fortuna's expression, and the thoughts glinting past that sharpened mind. Fortuna would try to spin a tale now. She would try to appeal to Jessamine's softer side, hoping to crack open some fissure of kindness that would let her go.

"I don't want to let you go," Jessamine said, her voice a little harder than before. "I don't want to be kind to you right now. In case you missed it, I have been kind to you since the moment I stepped foot in this district. I sought you out, hoping that you were doing all of this without realizing who you had attached yourself to. I thought you were worth saving, Fortuna."

"I am. I have to be. Because there is never anyone beyond saving—that's what you used to say. You were always the better of the two of us. You saw so much more with that kind heart of yours. I was wrong, Jessa. I was so wrong, and I have given a dangerous, powerful man too much information. I am sorry for it."

But those words dripped from a poisoned, desperate tongue.

Sybil leaned against the door, her arms crossed over her chest and her dark eyes narrowed. "Lies."

"It's not a lie, witch," Fortuna snapped. "I do feel guilty."

"You couldn't feel guilt if you tried. *You* were the one who set the spell and cost all those people their lives and souls. *You* invited them. *You* provided your home. *You* are the reason they are now dead." Like a raven, Sybil cocked her head to the side. "Would you go back and change anything you did? Or do you, even now, still think you made the right choice?"

And there it was. The flicker of defiance in Fortuna's gaze.

Jessamine sighed, then said in a bored voice, "You have one last chance. Tell me what he's doing, Fortuna, or I will rip the memories out of you."

"You can't do that."

"I can. I already have from others. Benji, your little accomplice. Callum, the man who guided you." She leaned forward, her hand on Nyx's back. She wanted Fortuna to look into her eyes and see madness in her own gaze as well. "And I will do it again."

But Fortuna had never been easily frightened. Her cousin straightened her back on the bed, primly crossed her legs, and looked very much like she wasn't tied up with shadows in her own safe house. "I will tell you nothing until I am unbound."

A small prick of sadness broke through Jessamine's hard shell. "I wish it didn't have to be like this, Fortuna. I remember when we were young. I remember looking up to you so much, even though you were so cruel to me."

"And I remember you as a snot-nosed brat who wouldn't leave me alone."

Right, then. She had done all she could.

Jessamine stood, shadows roving over her shoulders and around her neck. She stood in front of Fortuna without even a prick of sadness now. "Do you see this scar around my neck?"

"It's hard to miss."

"This is where he killed me, Fortuna. My questions will start there. Because I want to know how long you have been planning this with him, and just how deep the poison goes. Do you understand me?"

"My silence is unchanging," Fortuna spat.

Jessamine lifted her hand, guiding the shadows toward Fortuna's face. They sank into her mouth, splitting open her jaw until it nearly cracked off her skull. She could see the shadows writhing and wriggling into Fortuna's mouth, disappearing down her throat as they sought out the memories Jessamine needed to see.

"You will tell me everything," Jessamine replied quietly. "And I will make it painful."

35

Fortuna coughed, and black smoke erupted from her mouth, pouring more and more out until it filled the room up to everyone's knees. Jessamine leaned forward and wafted it toward her with a hand, inhaling the smoke and ignoring the whimpers that soon filled the room. Even Sybil seemed a little uncomfortable with what was occurring in front of her, but there was no room for pity in this moment. She needed to know what happened, and she needed to see it directly through Fortuna's eyes so that she knew what dangers were coming.

There was a time for kindness, and there was a time for brutality.

She dove into Fortuna's mind and disappeared into the memories. There were a lot of them to paw through, but her magic had already found what she wanted. She felt like Elric was there with her, as though her god was guiding her through the mess of this woman's head.

Just like when Elric had taken her eyes so that she could see, she found herself stepping into a frozen memory that Fortuna had fought hard to hide.

Fortuna and Leon were cozied up on a bed together, white gauzy curtains frozen in a moment of billowing movement. Fortuna leaned against his chest, her hands playing with the hair there as she looked up at him adoringly. But Leon?

Leon was looking right at Jessamine. As though he knew she would someday stand right there, seeing all the darkness of his soul laid bare. He stared at her with those bright blue eyes that she had once thought so handsome, and Jessamine knew immediately where they were.

They were in the castle.

This was the day that he had proposed to her. The same day he had gotten down on his knees before her mother's throne and vowed to give Jessamine all the years of his life. He'd declared he would be the best husband for her and no one would ever take her from his side. She remembered seeing her mother's jaw clench, but then she had agreed.

They'd all agreed to fall into bed with this snake, it appeared. Because he hadn't actually wanted Jessamine as his bride. Instead, he had Fortuna in his bed mere hours before he had proposed to another woman.

No wonder Fortuna had wanted to hide this memory. This was the moment petty jealousy had festered into violent hatred. Jessamine had the throne, she had power, and she had stability. Fortuna had wanted all of that, and at this moment, she'd also wanted Jessamine's soon-to-be husband.

Jessamine approached the bed, narrowing her gaze on the couple and trying to keep her anger in check. "Proceed," she said, as though Elric were here to shift the memory. But instead of him, it was the magic that throbbed in her veins, just as angry as she was.

The couple before her started moving like time hadn't stopped.

"What do you mean, you want this kingdom? You have your own," Fortuna asked, her fingers petting through his chest hair as the curtains twisted before their image, obscuring Leon's expression for a moment.

"I want everything, dear Fortuna. Don't you? Don't you want the entire world to bend at your feet and worship the ground you walk upon?"

Fortuna's face twisted slightly, as though she was confused by the statement. "I suppose. But I've always thought that the right man would give it to me."

He surged upright, rolling her over so he could loom above her pretty features. "I want the world. And I will give it to you if you help me."

"What do you want me to do?"

Jessamine stepped closer because he had leaned down to whisper in Fortuna's ear, no doubt to prevent anyone in the castle from overhearing him. But Jessamine heard him, just as clearly as Fortuna had in the moment.

"I'm going to kill the entire royal family, and then I'm going to take this kingdom for my own. No loose ends. And I will make you its queen."

The hunger in Fortuna's gaze was familiar, the expression of a woman who recognized her moment to strike. If she wanted everything, and she did, then this was the time she needed to stand up and be brave enough to claim it.

What Fortuna hadn't known was that Leon offered her a kingdom of the dead. He'd infected its citizens, spread all that pain and fear and hatred. This wouldn't be a kingdom at all once he was done with it.

Fortuna pressed her lips to his cheek and replied, "I want it all. All that you can give me."

The movements under the covers were enough. Disgusted, Jessamine waved her hand in the air and said, "More. Show me something else."

The magic twisted through her fingers, coiling along her arms as it advanced time. Now she recognized her wedding, but from an angle she never would have seen from the altar. Fortuna stood beside Callum, who had his arms crossed over his broad chest. They were both inside the castle, on a balcony overlooking the ceremony.

"Are you sure about this?" he grumbled, his voice lower than she remembered. Raspy, like he'd been drinking heavily the night before and the whiskey had burned his throat.

"Of course I'm sure. Aren't you sure that you want to cure yourself? I'm the one who found the book for you, and I'm the one who made sure that page stayed the way it was." Fortuna turned toward him with a delicately arched brow. "Or are you suddenly feeling bad for the queen you thought you loved?"

"Don't."

"I'm just saying. Sometimes you have to pick yourself first, Callum. If you want to stay alive, this is the only choice you have. It's okay. We all know that you're a good man, regardless of what you're choosing to do now."

But as Fortuna strode away from him, leaning over the edge of the balcony for a better view, Jessamine noticed the twisted expression on Callum's face.

He hadn't wanted to help Leon. But he had been so afraid. That fear was clear as day on his face, and she paused the memory.

Walking up to him, she touched her fingers to his jaw. "You were the best of them," Jessamine whispered.

She felt the memory twisting, warping, and there was something very wrong with the sensation. Memories weren't supposed to change, and yet, Fortuna's did. The woman's image behind her turned to look right at Jessamine.

"Even the best of them fall," Fortuna said, her lips warping over the words like it was a struggle to say them. "Even you."

Jessamine frowned. Was she... changing the memory? Had Fortuna somehow followed her into her own memories and was now manipulating them? That wouldn't do. If Fortuna could change this moment right now, what could she do to memories that she wanted to stay hidden?

"Priestess magic?" she asked, turning away from Callum and facing Fortuna now. "Or just a natural-born talent of yours?"

"The Crone provided her followers with more knowledge than witches could ever hope to acquire."

"Fortuna, I'm going to tear apart your memories one by one. This can be painless, or I can make you writhe in pain while you bleed from your eyes. Please, let me do this without killing you."

A drop of blood beaded in the corner of Fortuna's mouth. Jessamine could only assume the red smudge reflected what was already happening in the real world, that Fortuna was struggling so hard against Elric's dark magic that the shadows were tearing into her flesh.

"You will get no information out of me," Fortuna said, her words slightly garbled through the pain. "I will tell you nothing."

Jessamine didn't respond. She just lifted her hands and let the magic coil between them again. "Show me the truth."

The power seemed to dance with glee between her fingers. It wanted her to see these betrayals, to know that this was the right choice, that she shouldn't feel guilty for this woman who had betrayed her time and again.

As she skipped through the memories, she noticed a few moments when the magic slowed down, showing her all of Fortuna's little cruelties. The times Fortuna had teased her for her hair. When she'd stolen sweets. All the little attacks that had made Jessamine feel unworthy of the love that other people had shown her.

And then the memories slowed down, turning instead to the evening after her death. She could see still her own blood on the lapel of the jacket that Leon wore as he strode into the same bedroom where the couple had lain together. Fortuna stood near the balcony, those gauzy white curtains fluttering in front of her lovely dark form.

"Is it done?" Fortuna asked.

"All the infected have been removed from the castle grounds, yes. You are free to wander again with whomever you wish to keep here. Although I wouldn't suggest remaining in the castle until we're certain the other nobles won't get any ideas." He caught her up in his arms, bending her backward for a bruising kiss. "Are you ready for me to tell you everything?"

"I've been ready for a while, you tease! You somehow convinced me to overthrow the remnants of my entire family for you, and I still don't know why." Fortuna backed toward the bed, falling on it while displaying her body for him. "Your grand plan is already in motion, my king."

He put a knee between her legs, pinning her to the bed. "And you will not just be my queen. You will be my high priestess, my—"

The memory warped again. Freezing in place as Fortuna appeared to split in half. Another face stretched beneath the one in her memory, a face that pulled free from her skin and then suddenly seemed to control her entire body. Strings of power roped around her, stretching out like elastic before snapping in two. Her power was limited. Whatever spell she'd used in a last effort to control everything was already unraveling.

"No!" Fortuna screamed, wrestling herself free from the memory and splitting from her body. She peeled out of herself and charged toward Jessamine.

But priestesses were weak compared to witches, and Jessamine was so much stronger than the average witch. She stepped aside from the charging image of Fortuna. A single gesture, and tendrils of darkness shot from her hands like ropes. They twisted around her cousin, coiling around her body and pinning her arms to her sides, just like she had in the real world, holding her in place.

A searing light illuminated from Fortuna's hands and burned through the dark ropes, which fell to the floor at her feet. Strange—Jessamine hadn't thought that was possible here. She chewed on the inside of her lip, but then crossed her arms and frowned at her cousin.

"That wasn't very nice," Jessamine scolded.

Fortuna was breathing hard, her shoulders rising and falling in rage. "Get out of my head."

"Or what?"

"Or I will scratch your eyes out. I will do whatever it takes to keep him safe."

"Why?"

Fortuna seemed to freeze for a moment. Her expression fell into surprise before she stammered, "Why what?"

"Why are you trying to protect a man like him? He left bruises on me, Fortuna, and I wasn't even sleeping with him. I can only imagine the marks he left on you. He promised you a kingdom and a castle, and you're still here in the Pleasure District. Still a toy for them to wind up and watch dance until they are bored with you, and then what?" Jessamine rolled her eyes and turned her back to the fading image of Fortuna. "You are just a shadow of the woman I thought you would become."

"How dare you." Fortuna raced forward, her fingers trying to catch Jessamine by the hair. But she fell right through Jessamine, falling onto her hands and knees like a supplicant at her feet.

Jessamine crouched so they were at eye level. "I'm not really here, Fortuna. I'm out there. Living, breathing, calm as a sea on a breezeless night. But you? You *are* here. And anything I do to you in your own head? I do in the real world, too."

It took such little effort to grab her cousin by the hair. She was stronger in this realm of memories, stronger than she had any right to be as she tossed Fortuna's spirit into the corner. Her cousin slid across the floor and hit the wall. Her form slumped, her head lolling with the impact.

"Stay there," Jessamine said, before moving the memory forward yet again.

Now Leon crawled up Fortuna's body, pressing kisses to her neck as he made her way to her lips. "I promised you a kingdom, but I want more than that."

"Is that so? What more is there than being a king of two kingdoms? Three?" Fortuna let out a bubbling laugh. "Do you want all the kingdoms at your beck and call?"

"In a way."

The crumpled version of Fortuna against the wall stirred, then shrieked, "Stop it! Shut up, shut up, shut up!"

Jessamine threw her hand back without looking as shadows swarmed to seal her cousin's mouth.

Leon's voice seemed to echo in the room as he said, "I found a way to bring the gods back."

It struck her right in the belly. So he really was going to do it. He wanted them to be indebted to him, or some other mad explanation for why he had killed her and everyone else who had any meaning to these kingdoms.

Fortuna's memory giggled. "Bring the gods back? That's so silly! Why would we want the gods back when *we* could be the most powerful people in the kingdoms?"

There was an edge of fear in her words. Like in the moment, even Fortuna had heard how insane Leon sounded.

He reared up, sitting on top of her, looking every inch the king he thought he was. "Of course not. I'm going to become the vessel for a god. And you, my dear, will be the vessel for another. I don't want them to rule this kingdom again. I want to make their power my own. I know how to bind them, how to make them bend. And then I will become a god, just as they once were."

"Oh," Jessamine breathed, feeling all the blood drain from her face and her body grow faint. "No."

She dropped the spell at the same time shock made her stumble back from Fortuna. Back in the human realm, she felt Sybil's hands slip underneath her shoulders as she staggered away from her cousin.

Fortuna slumped on the bed, spitting blood from her mouth where her jaw hung unnaturally loose. But she still reached up and held it to her face so she could hiss, "You're already too late."

"We're not."

"You are," Fortuna snarled.

The shadows had done a number on her face. Her jaw was barely attached, and there were scratches across her eyes, down her cheeks, where she had clawed at her own features to rip the darkness away. Her beauty had been shattered, bit by bit. There was no healing what had happened, not when the shadows themselves had started to stitch her together, leaving horrific scars and dark lines of magic as grim reminders of their power.

Those deep furrows slowly became ragged wounds that quickly filled with wriggling maggots. Her hollow eyes were blackened holes. And that jaw... that waggling, loose jaw kept her mouth constantly open.

No matter how many sacrifices she made to her goddess, Fortuna's beauty was no more.

"I'm so tired of your lies," Jessamine said. "I'm so tired of all the things that mind of yours has done. I took Callum's mind, you know. Everyone believes him to be a doddering old fool now. They know what he once was, but all they see is a child locked in the body of a man."

She could have been kind. She could be benevolent. But when had Fortuna ever been benevolent toward her?

Jessamine lifted her hand and twisted her fingers, pinching the shadows and then sending them to her cousin again. They writhed over Fortuna's body, and the woman shrieked as they tunneled back into her mouth. She couldn't even close her jaw to prevent it from happening.

A splash of blood speared the air before her cousin, and then a small bit of meat splattered onto the floor.

Fortuna's tongue.

"Let's go," Jessamine whispered, holding on to Sybil's hands.

"You want to leave her alive?" Sybil asked.

"Leon is vain. He won't want a consort who cannot stand by him as a trophy wife. And everyone else? They'll look at her with pity... and then they'll forget her entirely." She leaned on Sybil until the doorway, pausing to look back at Fortuna one last time.

She saw the moment Fortuna caught her own reflection. The scream of horror was ragged and raw before her cousin turned to her and shouted. Jessamine could understand Fortuna's words, even missing her tongue. "Kill me! Kill me!"

She shook her head. "I used up all my mercy for you long ago, cousin. Do it yourself if you seek death."

And then she walked out of the house, Sybil supporting her, as she contemplated just how horrific the future could and would be.

36

Something was wrong. Elric couldn't explain the sensation, only that his stomach twisted and his blood boiled. The sacrifices to him were public and very hard to forget. The amount of blood that coated the town square had shocked even him. But he was bloated now, flush with power even as he stood with his coven to provide the protection they so desperately needed.

It wouldn't be smart to stay here much longer. There were more men with muskets. More regular citizens who had emerged from their homes with swords and knives and pickaxes, anything they could fight with. His time was running out.

Even Agnes had looked over her shoulder at him, deep hollows under her eyes. Casting spells like this wasn't easy on anyone's body, even worse for those who were unused to it. Jessamine needed to hurry.

But then Hugo shifted at the edge of the shield Elric had summoned, and the entire crowd turned to look down a street that was cast in dark shadows. He could feel her there. His Jessamine. His nightmare walked toward him, shuffling her feet as though she had aged a hundred years in the time since he'd seen her.

And something loosened in his chest. He hadn't been afraid she would die, not really. But there was always the fear that he would miss her in the realm beyond. That she would slip through his fingers and move through death when he wasn't ready for her to do so. He hated the thought of her in that darkness alone, or worse, banished to wander the realms without a soul for the rest of her life.

Because he couldn't help himself, because she deserved to be honored, he allowed his shadows to part above her. There was no sunlight streaming in through the hole he made above her head. Time had passed faster than he'd thought. Instead, moonlight illuminated his gravesinger, who straightened the moment she realized people could see her.

Sybil released her hold on Jessamine's waist, allowing her to walk on her own. Elric watched with pride as the princess pieced herself back together. Like armor, she forced her spine pin straight, clenched her hands at her sides, then released them in graceful, delicate lines. Only then, ever so slowly, did Jessamine pull back her hood.

The moonlight played over her pale features, highlighting the stunning beauty of her dark hair and the sharp peaks of her cheekbones. But it was the wound at her throat that glowed with power. A silver scar sealed by magic, a scar that marked her as someone they all knew.

One person in the crowd whispered her name with the reverence she deserved. "Lady Jessamine?"

Then another. "Is that the princess?"

"Surely not. She died!"

"There were rumors, though. Rumors that she was back."

And then they all looked at him. Some of them were piecing it together. He could see the moment they realized Princess Jessamine Harmsworth had found herself a god.

She walked up to him with her shoulders held straight and strong. Not an inch of her looked like she had just been in battle, but there was a shadow in her eyes and a weight on her shoulders that hadn't been there before. It turned his stomach to see her like this. To know that there was something desperately wrong. Worse than ever before.

And still, she kept her eyes on him. She didn't even look at the crowd with torches and weapons who could so easily attack her. Because she didn't have to.

Her history preceded her. They all knew who she was, and they had loved her when she was alive. Yet some of them now feared her, because they knew she was dead.

"A ghost?" someone whispered to his left.

"No, surely she wouldn't wander her kingdom as one of the undead, unless…"

A young woman watched him through the shadow shield he had created. Not Jessamine, but him. He could feel the hollow in her, just waiting to be filled with magic like all trueborn witches were.

Then the woman's lips quirked in a half smile. "The Deathless One returned when someone prayed to him, saying this kingdom was broken. Perhaps he is here to fix things."

"Fix things? The Deathless One destroys everything and anything in his path!" a man shouted, holding his gun over his head. "There are witches in our town square! Are we all going to stand by and allow that to happen?"

But then the crowd quieted because Jessamine had reached them. She walked through the beating heart of the crowd, the danger that had threatened her coven. Moonlight followed her, and she looked more ethereal and otherworldly than she ever had before. Even Elric's breath caught in his throat as he watched her gliding through her subjects.

And then she reached for the man who had spoken. His face paled, his hand clenching around the gun still held above his head. But she didn't want to hurt him. Elric could feel it as though she had whispered reassurance to everyone who held their breath.

Instead, she just cupped his jaw. Shadows crawled out from her hands, sinking into his skin, and suddenly, she spoke in that soft voice that had captivated him from the very first moment he'd met her.

"I am not here to hurt anyone," she breathed. "I am here to take back what was stolen from me."

The man gulped. "Stolen?"

She released him, her fingers lingering on his face until the very last moment, and the man leaned into her touch like he wanted those cold fingers against his cheeks for just a few moments more.

Jessamine turned to the crowd, her eyes meeting each and every one of them. "My life was taken from me. My throat was slit on the day of my wedding, and my mother was killed before me. I made the choice to put myself in that danger—for you. I would have married a man who left bruises on my body, believing that he could protect this kingdom. I would have sacrificed anything to keep you all safe. It was *what he promised me.*"

The last words were almost shouted, guttural and aching with her pain. He could feel it. Everyone in the square could feel it.

"I put my faith in a man who murdered me. I put my kingdom in the hands of a monster who would rip out your beating hearts to place himself on a higher pedestal. With one hand, he releases the infected into our realm, while with the other he reaches down to help you, but only to lord his offer over you all. His offer of help is a reminder that he believes you are beneath him."

Elric let the shield around his witches drop, and his coven's spell fell silent, but its echo remained. It was the haunting cry of women who had years of pain deep within their bodies. They had been betrayed, too. The shield turned to ash, leaving a black ring burned into the very stones of the town square alongside the runes etched by delicate hands.

The young woman who had smiled at him stepped into the circle he had created, joining the women who had so much raw magic and yet were shunned and feared. Then another woman did the same. A third.

Jessamine raised her voice higher. "I am Lady Jessamine Harmsworth, rightful heir to the throne of Inverholm. My death was only the beginning. As my soul fled my body, I heard a voice in the darkness, and it promised vengeance. It promised me that I could reclaim my kingdom if I was willing to fight for it, and I tell you now, I have never stopped fighting for any of you. You are my people. This is the soil upon which my mother's blood was spilled, both in bringing me life and in her own death. This is the land I will fight for until my last breath and beyond."

The crowd fell silent, entranced by the words of their princess. Elric watched as Jessamine spun her words in a web around them. "I make no false promises, nor do I exaggerate. I tell you now, in the spirit of honesty, that I am dead."

A few people recoiled as she said the last words, but Elric could feel in his bones that she had made the right choice. Jessamine was no longer the queen they knew. She was not the princess who had won their hearts.

She was the walking dead. A nightmare who would give them everything if they begged for mercy at her feet.

Then she turned, stepping into the dark circle to stand among the women who had risked their lives for her. She trailed her fingers along their linked arms until Agnes and Elissa broke apart so she could stand in the center of their circle.

"Two hundred years ago, we feared witches... but witches have always borne the brunt of this kingdom's fear. I am here to tell you that witches have returned. And my coven is the one that is going to save you." Her jaw ticked, teeth grinding as she stared everyone down.

Elric had never been more proud. Even as the crowd began to shout accusations, Jessamine stood strong in the growing circle of women who looked up at her like a goddess.

"Witches caused all this!"

"Witchcraft is evil!"

"We won't stand by your kind here!"

She took it all. Allowed their angry and heated words to flow over her. All that darkness, that real, true evil, poured over her and slid off like she didn't even hear it.

Elric walked behind her, his wings spreading wide, providing her with all the reassurance she might need. And as he laid a hand on her shoulder, everyone stilled. They watched the god among them with fearful eyes and a mistrust that came from ancient times.

"My coven is all that stands between you and the end of all things," he said, using his magic so his words boomed throughout the town square. "Your princess, my gravesinger, summoned me from the dead, and all who stand in my way will bend a knee. I am your god, the only god who lives. And I will make this world quake in fear if I must."

The ground rumbled under their feet, a small hint at what he might do to them all. Not that he could. His brothers were far more connected to the earth. But Elric could make them all believe the world was shattering.

Jessamine placed her hand on his, gaining his attention with the smallest movement. When he looked down at her, she was staring at the young woman who had smiled at him. The first to step into the circle.

He could have summoned the women closer, but it was Jessamine who spoke. And he used his power to amplify what she had to say, because all in this crowd needed to listen.

"It is my greatest fear that women will forever pay for the fear of men," she murmured. "For we are haunted and vicious beasts they could never understand. They will never know the amount of abuse it takes to be so soft. They will never understand that to tame a wild creature, she must first be broken, and it takes us years to find that wildness again. We are divine victims and wrathful fury, and both forms are worthy of worship. There is a goddess in all of us, and she cries out to be seen."

The young woman grinned again, this time with a feral smile that reflected all those years where she should have been more powerful. She walked over to Agnes, and the witches beside her lifted their arms, tucking the newcomer in among them. Then another woman did the same. More and more women made their way forward from the crowd, until there were dozens of women all seated in a circle around Jessamine and the Deathless One. Women who had been forgotten by so many people. And women who had found their sisters at last.

Elric breathed out a long sigh before touching the closest one with the tip of his shadow wing. She wore a rapturous expression he had seen many times before, one he knew was dangerous and yet called to something deep inside him at the same time.

It was an expression that asked him to save them. But it was also an expression that whispered she would do whatever it took to keep the power he gave her, and to grow even stronger.

He had created, yet again, a coven with teeth and claws. And there would forever be the fear deep in his chest that he could not protect himself from their hunger.

At the sound of the crowd's growing fury, he decided that it was time to leave. With a nod to Alexander and Hugo, who both disappeared into the teeming mass of angry people, he spread his dark wings wide and bent to cover the witches around him. He held them close to his heart with a whispered promise in the air.

The Deathless One would keep them safe. He had centuries ago, and he would do so again. They were his. His women, his witches, his coven. There was no one in this world who would do more for them, or protect them better than he did, no matter the cost to himself.

With a quiet spell, the words guttural and deep, he whisked them away.

As the shadows fell from the sky and the moon and stars reappeared, all that remained was a dark circle where the witches had been. They had disappeared into the night, leaving anger and madness in their wake as they reappeared in the home he had built for them. A haunted house of nightmares and spirits who lived in the attic. But it was their home. It was magic, deep in the floorboards, and they could feel it.

He untangled himself from them, panic already setting in. He did not know these women or what they were capable of. He just knew they would want pieces of who he was and what he could give them. Power and magic and control, which they had never had in their lives.

But then a hand touched his chest, a familiar, warm palm with long fingers that stroked his skin. Calm tendrils spread from her touch, as she was the only woman who had ever been able to tame him.

"Thank you," Jessamine whispered, but her words felt like a shout. "Thank you for saving us all."

He didn't know how to speak. He couldn't. Because everyone was looking at him now, all of them with those eyes that were so needy and hopeful. He inclined his head toward all of them, a slight nod in the hopes that they wouldn't ask for more.

Jessamine turned to them all. "We have rooms here, and you may join us. I don't know if there's enough for all of you, but tomorrow night we will welcome you into the coven. If you change your mind, that's all right, too. We're not going to make any of you stay."

They all walked away, talking among themselves. The excited chatter of witches was something he had forgotten, but… there was deep pleasure in hearing the excitement around magic again. Spells and curses and ingredients that were needed to do both. All of it was wondrous to hear.

But then his stomach twisted as Jessamine's dark, haunted eyes turned toward him. "We need to talk," she whispered. "Something terrible has happened."

37

Being home settled Jessamine's nerves. It helped her to know that after all of this, madness hadn't sunk its claws into her. It had been long past time to let her people know, without any level of uncertainty, that she was alive. Danger would now follow them wherever they went, of course. The rumor of her survival was not the same as a crowd of people actually seeing her. She risked Leon's backlash once he discovered she was, in fact, within his grasp.

Now he knew for certain.

So Leon Bishop was well aware that she was back, and that there was a tidal wave coming toward him. That was why he'd been at the party. He'd wanted her to see him, to know that he wasn't afraid of what she had brought back with her from death.

Walking down the hall to their room, she suddenly gasped as she realized why the party had been filled with so many important people. "Souls with meaning," she whispered.

"What?" Elric asked, but then his face drew down into a troubled expression. "Shit."

"Come on, I don't want anyone to overhear this."

It took them only a few minutes to get to their room, but then they were alone. Elric cast a spell that lined the rooms with shadows. She could see them writhing on the ceiling, spreading around them until they could speak in perfect privacy. No witch could hear them.

"Tell me," he demanded in that way of his that always sent shivers down her spine.

He looked angry. Furious, even, and she realized that she hadn't seen him look like that since Callum's men had killed her in the alley. He was usually so calm and composed, even in the face of grave danger. But right now he was vibrating with anger.

At her questioning look, he tried to put himself back together. Jessamine watched him shove the anger deep into the depths of who he was, using perhaps a hint of his power to make his expression serene once more. But there was the faintest metallic scent in the air, like someone was already bleeding.

"If she touched you," he muttered, his voice low. "If *anyone* touched you, Jessamine, then tell me who they are. Allow me to peel the skin from their flesh, to feed them nightmares until they go mad. It would be my greatest honor to torture anyone who dared to harm you."

So he'd been worried.

Poor man.

She stepped forward, her hands on his chest so that he could feel she was still here. "Elric, nothing happened. Nothing... well, everything happened, but I am unharmed."

His hand snaked around the back of her neck, tugging her close so he could rest his forehead on hers. He took a deep breath, drinking her in until he nodded. "What has scared you so badly?"

She told him what happened as they had approached the house, and how she had used his own magic to rip out Fortuna's memories. She told him that Leon had been in bed with Fortuna and had the distinct pleasure of watching him tense again. But when she spoke of the last piece, it became hard to say the words.

Finally, she just blurted, "Fortuna said that Leon knew a spell that would bring the gods back. Not just bring them back, but channel a god into him. His body would be a prison for one of them, and their magic. He was going to put a god in her, too. That's how he plans to take over not only his kingdom and my own, but all the known world."

Elric froze in her grip, his muscles so tense it was as if he had turned to stone. He pulled away from her slightly, his face expressionless as he took one shaky step, then another, before he landed on the bed with a low moan.

"What?" she asked. "That's not possible, is it?"

"I…" Elric dropped his head into his hands. Bowed over like that, he appeared to be a man who had lost everything.

She sank down onto the small bench seat before her vanity. "It's bad, then."

Her words weren't a question. She could see it in the arching of his shoulders and the way he'd stopped breathing.

She didn't know how long he was lost in his own memories, but eventually he straightened and blew out a long breath. She'd never seen his face so pale or the furrows around his eyes so deep.

"The gods did not walk into this realm fully formed, Jessamine. I know the legends suggest that we were omnipotent our entire lives, but that is not true. I kept my original name. Elric Hellebore. That is who I was before…"

He paused, and her heart twisted in her chest.

"Before?"

"I was just a man." He looked down at his hands, spreading his fingers wide as though his palms held some secret. "I don't remember much of who I was. It makes it hard to… remember. When you take the powers on. But every god is more a figment of creation than a physical being. The power is immense, but it is impossible to contain without having a form. I don't know who the first god was. I don't think my siblings remember either.

"All I know is that when I was created, I woke up without a single thought in my head. No memories of who I was. I only pieced together some bits of who I used to be because of the people I encountered and how they reacted to me. Did I have a family? A wife? I have no idea. One moment I was dead, and the next, I woke with more power than I knew what to do with.

"It was infinite. All the darkness and shadows that spread through my body like veins. I could see everything and nothing at the same time. It's very natural for gods to react with confusion or rage when they ascend. And then I had the choice of what I wanted to be and who I wanted to serve me. But I was very young. There were many gods already, and when my sister made me, there weren't a lot of realms left."

Jessamine gasped. "Which sister?"

"The Crone. She created me, although we do not call it giving birth. That was…" He blew out a long breath and curled his fingers into fists. "That was never part of becoming a god. So when you say he wants to channel a god, that is not what he's doing. He's going to take the power that was once here, a power that should have disappeared with my siblings, and he's going to put it in his body so that he becomes a god himself."

There were no words. Only silence that stood like a veil between them and the world who did not know that the gods were awakening. That a man who had killed so many people was only going to give himself yet more power…

"Oh," she whispered. The word shook with fear. "So he's…"

"He's going to make himself a god, yes. And if I had to guess, he is going to seize the strongest power that he can—the Warrior King himself. It is an end to all things if he succeeds."

But that would mean the entire kingdom was lost. That would mean that no matter how hard they fought, no matter what they did, they would fail. Because that was a power that they couldn't fight against unless… Hesitantly, she asked, "Are you more powerful than—"

"No," he interrupted. "No, I never was."

"What if we sacrifice—"

"No, Jessamine." He lifted a shaking hand to his hair and ran his fingers through it. "No, there is no way to make me more powerful than my brother was. The Warrior King was the best of us, and for good reason. We were all just replicas of his greatness, striving to be just as powerful. I certainly did."

Well, that made everything even worse, she supposed. She'd been thinking it was terrible that he was going to use a god, because someone like Leon shouldn't be able to channel a creature like that. But to know that he was going to *be* the god?

She couldn't breathe. She couldn't get the air into her lungs fast enough, and everything felt like it was crumbling, until she didn't know how to continue forward.

Tears welled in her eyes, tears that stung because she didn't see how they were going to fix this. And so she looked at him, watching to see her powerful, capable god who knew how to fix everything, and she waited for him to reassure her. For him to tell her that everything was going to be all right.

But he just looked back at her. Those bleak, dark eyes didn't see a way forward any better than she did. They stared at each other like they'd already lost, and she simply could not suffer through that.

"Elric?" she asked, her voice very quiet.

"Yes, nightmare?"

"Is there anything we can do?"

"Not that I can think of right now."

"But we're still going to fight?" Jessamine chewed on her bottom lip, watching him to see if he'd given up.

She wouldn't blame him if he did. He was a god, just like Leon wanted to be. And if Leon succeeded, then they were the same creature. She couldn't imagine it was easy being the only god alive. Maybe he would welcome a family of his own kind.

The thoughts festered within her and she had to say something before they exploded out of her.

"If you want..." She paused, the words sticking in her throat before she continued. "If you want to align yourself with him, to ensure that you are no longer the only god that serves this world, then I will not be angry with you."

At his incredulous look, she blew out a little laugh.

"Fine, I will be furious. But I will understand. This must be a very lonely existence for you, and I can't imagine it was ever your choice to be the only one left. If you want to side with him, to help bring about another age of gods, there is nothing I can do to stop you. I won't even…" She took another deep breath. "I won't even try to stop you, Elric. This can all end now, if you wish it. You always said you wanted to tear the world down."

It would break her heart to stop fighting. It would fairly kill her to know that she would never get her mother's throne back or that her people would continue to suffer. But if this was the only way to save more lives than lose them…

Elric sank to his knees before her. He braced his hands on her thighs, spreading her legs so he could move even closer to her. "My love," he whispered, and those words made her entire being ache. "I would never abandon you."

He laid his head in her lap, wrapping his arms behind her waist and holding her tightly against him. Jessamine folded. She laid her arms on top of him and rested her torso on the god who had given her so much, the god who would continue to fight until the very last of his breath, just because she wished him to.

She just didn't know if it was the right choice. What if she got all of these people killed? She'd never wanted that. Death was permanent for them, and while it wasn't for her… maybe it should have been. Maybe they deserved more than a soulless creature who only saw a single way into making this world better.

"Stop those thoughts," he muttered against her skin, his lips pressing against her thigh. "You are the queen they both deserve and need, Jessamine."

"I don't feel that way."

"And that is precisely why you should be the one on that throne. You will not deny them the life they need, because you will always seek to satisfy their needs before your own." He leaned up then, framing her face with one hand. "Where is my nightmare? Where is the woman who will fight tooth and nail to get what she wants? The woman who would destroy an entire kingdom just to know that it wasn't in the wrong hands?"

"She is frightened."

"Of what?"

"Of a god stronger than both of us. Of a kingdom that will be lost if I make a mistake." Her hand shook as she placed it over his on her cheek. "What if we fail, Elric?"

"What if we win?" He drew her forward for a kiss that seared through her. "What if you are the queen that you always believed you could be? What if you take this kingdom into a new age where there is magic in the streets? Where you could walk through the Pleasure District and spell-cast letters flying through the air. Or talking creatures in shops. Perhaps you would see the world as a different place, and if you succeeded in doing so, then Jessamine, you would be the greatest queen this realm has ever seen. Can you deny yourself and your people that future?"

Of course not. Of course she would fight until her last day to know that her people were happy and safe and taken care of. But today she would be weak. Today she would fear for what the future might become. Tomorrow, she would wake and she would fight, just as she had for all these months.

She'd come back from the dead for them. And if she had to die again, then she would. Time and time again.

She leaned forward, pressing her lips to his in a kiss that was blinding. "Make me forget," she whispered against his mouth. "Make me forget that there is a god we have to fight and a kingdom to save. Make me forget everything but the man I love, Elric."

He groaned into her mouth. "You don't know what it does to me that you see me as a man. Jessamine, my heart soars when you speak with me."

She knew the feeling. Because just the touch of his hand on hers, just the movement of his lips, the way he breathed into her like he didn't exist without her, it did something deep inside her as well.

As he lifted her from the vanity, gracefully standing with her in his arms as though she weighed nothing, she found herself disappearing into this man who laid her out on the bed like she was a banquet and he'd been starving for ages. He was everything to her, too. Fighting with him at her side was a little easier than without.

Jessamine arched into him, and she let all the thoughts in her head trickle away. They would fight. They would win.

Because there was no other choice.

38

Elric slipped out of their bed, making sure not to disturb her. They'd spent hours exploring each other's bodies, and she was exhausted. A deep, primal pride bloomed in his chest as he saw her lying there, spread out underneath the covers like she couldn't move even if the world was ending.

He'd put in the work to get her that way, but she deserved it. Jessamine had been too in her head, and he needed her to be that wild woman who had begged him to give her another chance, even if that meant she had to destroy her own kingdom to do it. And look at her so far, holding true to her word. After everything that they'd done, this kingdom was more in turmoil than it ever had been before.

He pulled on a loose pair of pants and threw a robe over his shoulders before leaving the room. She needed sleep, but he needed to talk with the others. There was much more coming for them, and they could not be unprepared.

A gravesinger could only do so much to lead her coven, after all. Jessamine hadn't wanted to be the person who runs it, but he'd only ever let covens think they controlled everything themselves. He was the god who gave them power. In the end, it was what he wanted, not what they wanted.

He'd already summoned the witches he needed. Sybil, Agnes, and Elissa waited for him in the kitchen, all of them bleary-eyed and far more tired than he'd expected them to be.

"Did you get no sleep?" he asked, taking the glass of whiskey that Sybil offered him.

"We've been settling the others in. They've had a lot of questions, considering they were leading their normal lives until yesterday, when a god awoke and took them from their homes." Sybil grinned. "They were good questions, mostly. I think they will be good additions to our family."

Of course she thought that, though. Sybil had always wanted more people in the coven. She missed being part of something bigger than herself. A coven moved as one, and it was more than just a family. It was a unit of women connected by trauma and pain. It wasn't how their lives should have gone, and yet, they were born into it. Centuries of pain all culminating in one witch.

They all looked at him with hope in their eyes, and he hated to destroy that hope in one fell swoop. But he had to.

"Leon Bishop has discovered how to awaken a god." He shook his head. "No, it's more than that. He's discovered how to become a god himself. That's why he took all the souls of those people at the party Fortuna put together. Souls that had meaning. Souls that were connected to many other souls and therefore had more weight, in a sacrifice greater than anyone could ever dream of."

He'd expected the sudden silence. What he hadn't expected was for it to be broken with a snort of magnificent proportions from Sybil. She hid her face in her cup, her eyes wide with the knowledge that it wasn't the appropriate response, but also aware that she couldn't stop.

"What are you laughing at?" he groaned.

"Well, it's just… It feels like we've gone back in time. I remember the coven complaining about your siblings. That they were all so hard to pin down, that they were ridiculously undisciplined and that, for the most part, you all squabbled like children."

He had no argument for it. That was how they had treated each other. So he shrugged and sipped at his whiskey.

"I can't imagine there's going to be much squabbling between you and the man who killed the love of your life.

There will be no arguments when the two of you just want each other dead." Sybil snorted again. "Who'd have thought that I'd get all my powers back and suddenly be thrust into a war of the gods?"

Agnes snorted then, too, yet another unladylike sound from a woman who knew what it meant to be ladylike. "I didn't think I would be the third generation of witches only to end my life fighting for a god that none of us liked. No offense."

"None taken," he muttered.

And then Elissa straightened her spine and gave him a sharp nod. "Well, I suppose there's a first for everything. If we have to fight a god, then I will very much enjoy doing so. I have spent my entire life believing I wasn't very capable. And look at me now, perfectly capable of anything that I want to do, and with more power than I ever had before. I believe we can beat him."

"We can't." Elric needed them all to understand this. "If we fight him, then there is no coming home. We must make sure he doesn't complete the spell. I don't know where he is, only that he was here in the Pleasure District very recently. It seems we know very little about Leon Bishop."

There was a faint knock on the door, and he stiffened. He had brought the three of them here in the dead of night to make sure that no one overheard them. This was a conversation for the coven and the coven alone.

But a familiar bright head filled the doorway, with a shadow of a big man standing behind him. "I might be able to help," Alexander said. "I know my brother well, and... I don't want him to become a god, if I'm being honest."

"Of course you don't."

"He's not a good man."

"No, he is not." Elric curled his fingers a little too tightly around the glass in his hand. "If you're willing to help us, I will make sure you are rewarded, Alexander."

"I don't need a reward. Just don't let him become a god." He walked into the room with Hugo on his heels. "Some people deserve power, but he's the last person I would ever choose to worship. He thinks everyone should, though. And that makes him a lot more dangerous than the nobles give him credit for. I'm here to fight him with all of you."

Hugo nodded, walking over to his grandmother and standing between her and Elissa. He crossed his arms over his chest. "I have no interest in another god in this realm. No offense."

"I'm starting to take offense to all of you saying that," Elric muttered.

Sybil reached over and touched his arm. Her grip was soft but firm, forcing him to look at her and really hear what she was saying. "You don't have to fight alone, Deathless One. That is what we're all saying. Neither you nor Jessamine are alone anymore, and we are all here for you. Together, we'll beat him."

For the first time, he had a little hope that it might be possible. Even if it was going to be a battle greater than any of them had ever seen. Even if some people died. They might actually win.

"Then you all have a lot of work ahead of you. I expect my coven to be stronger every single day. They need to memorize the spells. They need to learn how to protect themselves and others."

"We know," Sybil replied with a soft smile. "I will make sure they are ready when you call, Deathless One."

He wasn't sure how to respond to that. His heart felt strange in his chest. And it was odd to realize that he could trust these people when he hadn't trusted anyone in a very long time.

With a low rumble, he handed her the whiskey back. "All right, then. I'll go make sure she's still sleeping."

"Good night, Deathless One," Agnes called out. "Take care of her."

"Always." He would always take care of her, no matter what came their way.

Elric strode down the dark halls alone, and the musing in his mind of what a family felt like was hard to shake. The covens saw him as a means to an end. He was just a man who would eventually be sacrificed, so why would they waste their time and effort on getting to know him? He'd never had anyone who wanted him around, just for himself.

But these people, they felt like friends. Like he could talk to them about nearly anything and they would listen. It was a novelty. A strange new world that he'd woken in, and he thought, perhaps, he liked it.

Elric walked by one of the doors that was left ajar for the new witches and heard giggles coming from within. That squeezing in his chest only grew stronger. They were *happy* here.

He paused in front of it, listening for the conversation and the hope that he knew they were feeling.

"A witch!" one of them whispered a little too loudly. Her voice was filled with excitement. "I always knew I was stronger than my sister. But I didn't know that I was a witch!"

"And did you see the god? I'd serve him any day."

"So handsome!"

His cheeks burned. He hadn't expected this. Perhaps he should give them space to gossip. He didn't need to know that they found him attractive. Women found this form appealing, so it made him easier to trust.

But just as he moved, he heard something else.

"Did you know in the old days they used to sacrifice him?" A different voice, calm and quiet. "They took his body, and they bit into it with knives and teeth and claws. They tore him apart, and then he gave them all the magic he had gathered from all the sacrifices they made. Magic all expelled at the same time. An infinite amount of power, all poured into the witches who sacrificed *him*."

"How's he still here, then?"

"They bring him back. That's what Jessamine is for. She'll bring him back for us time and time again, and all we have to do is glut him with sacrifices and then we get to take everything he has gathered."

Giggles erupted from within the room. "Do you think we'll be sacrificing him soon?"

"I imagine so. The entire kingdom knows she's back. She'll want more power to protect herself and us."

"Oh! I'll hold a knife, then. I can't imagine a god can even feel pain."

He staggered away from the door, trying to remain quiet so they wouldn't know he had overheard them, but bile rose into his throat. It was happening again. They already saw him as a tool. Soon it would be time, and he would have to say goodbye. They would dig into him with sharp knives… and he would let them.

He always let them.

Elric didn't know how he found his way back to his room with Jessamine, but he braced himself on the doorframe before entering. His breathing was ragged, his vision blurry. All he could think was that soon enough, he would endure pain and torture.

For her. Always for her. Because if this was what it took for Jessamine to get everything she wanted, then he would sacrifice himself a hundred times.

Taking a deep breath, he forced himself to pull it together. All the fear and anxiety and aching heartbreak of disappointment, he shoved into the darkest part of himself. And then he opened the door to worship her again.

For as long as he could.

Acknowledgments

No book is created without an army (or should I say coven?) of people behind the story. Rachel, my agent, you are the best person I've met in this authorship journey! Your resilience, kindness, and patience in handling every single one of my far too many emails, phone calls, and the like, have always been an inspiration.

Abby, thank you for giving me and this entire series a chance. You've taught me so much about my writing and all the wonderful things it can bring. You saw my bloody, disgusting, wriggling story and you made it so wonderful alongside me. I cannot thank you enough for giving me such a blessing as this new adventure.

To the team at Gallery, thank you for being so wonderful. I have published many times on my own, but having a crew of people who are all so talented and thoughtful behind me is a rare and wonderful thing.

And finally, to my family. Mom, Dad, I told you I'd be in bookstores someday. And to the love of my life, thank you for being all that you are. A shadow daddy doesn't hold a candle to you.